THE BONDMASTER BREED

PRIME BREEDING MATERIAL!

'Five fine virgins, what!' Carlton waved
Brett to step around in front of him. 'Step
ou' yuh shifts!' he shouted to the girls.

Sulkily, the five wenches removed their
osnaburg dresses and stood naked in front
of Carlton. He licked his lips. Melia was
staring with dark eyes that challenged him.

'Come!' Brett said, squatting on his
haunches as the girl walked over to stand
in front of him. He placed his hands on
either side of her hips the way he had seen
Carlton do it. 'She is wide-hipped, sir!' he
said.

'Aye, boy, so she is. Fine conny on her,
what!'

'Yes, sir.'

'Pass her here, boy.' Carlton held out his
hands for Melia to step up to him. 'Watch
us, boy.'

With deliberation, Carlton squeezed
Melia's young breasts. They were firm to
the touch. He ran his fingers swiftly
around the nipples, noting Melia's instant
reaction. He slid his hands down . . .

Also by Richard Tresillian in Sphere Books:
THE BONDMASTER
BLOOD OF THE BONDMASTER
FLEUR

The Bondmaster Breed
Being Book Three of the Bondmaster Saga
RICHARD TRESILLIAN

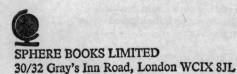

SPHERE BOOKS LIMITED
30/32 Gray's Inn Road, London WCIX 8JL

First published in Great Britain by Arlington Books
(Publishers) Ltd 1979
Copyright © Wordsman B.V. 1979
First published by Sphere Books Ltd 1980
Reprinted 1981, 1982

TRADE MARK

Printed in Great Britain by
Collins, Glasgow

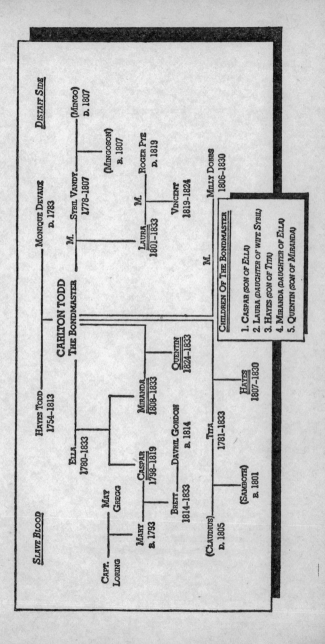

SLAVE BLOOD

CAPT. LORING — MAY GREGG

MARY B. 1793 — CASPAR 1798-1819

BRETT 1814-1833 — DAVIEL GORDON B. 1814

(CLAUDIUS) D. 1805

(SAMBOTH) B. 1801

TITA 1781-1833

HAYES 1807-1830

HAYES TODD 1754-1813

ELLA 1780-1833

MIRANDA 1808-1833

QUENTIN 1824-1833

CARLTON TODD
THE BONDMASTER

M.

MILLY DOBBS 1806-1830

MONIQUE DEVAUX D. 1783

DISTAFF SIDE

(MINGO) D. 1807

(MINGOSON) B. 1807

STBIL VANDY 1778-1807

M.

LAURA 1801-1833

M.

ROGER PYE D. 1819

VINCENT 1819-1824

CHILDREN OF THE BONDMASTER

1. CASPAR (SON OF ELLA)
2. LAURA (DAUGHTER OF WIFE SYBIL)
3. HAYES (SON OF TITA)
4. MIRANDA (DAUGHTER OF ELLA)
5. QUENTIN (SON OF MIRANDA)

"Roxborough Estate in the Layou Valley was the most productive of Dominica's sugar plantations until it declined at the end of the eighteenth century when the Todd family started the first slave warren in the British West Indian islands.

"The Bondmaster, Mr. Carlton Todd, is reputed to have made a considerable fortune by his selective breeding of enslaved Africans for sale to the plantation owners of neighbouring islands.

"A Roxborough slave became renowned throughout the West Indies as the elite of that subjugated race, and it is said that many of today's native citizens of prominence have descended from the line begun by the Bondmaster of Roxborough."

From: *A History of the British West Indian Islands* by Sir Verne W. Bisset, Bart. Published by Shankland & Box, London & Cambridge, 1913.

THE BONDMASTER BREED

PROLOGUE

A Wedding

1824

Chapter 1

Milly Dobbs smiled pleasantly at the young Negro walking backward out of the hotel room. Seeing the smile, the slave paused in the doorway and, with his eyes fixed on Milly's face, bowed deeply from his waist. Raising himself up he reached for the door and closed himself out of the room. Alone in the corridor, the slave's face creased into a bright grin and he rubbed his crotch enthusiastically with his massive hand.

Milly sighed.

She looked around the hotel room at the three trunks which the slave had carried up for her from the hotel lobby. They contained her entire possessions, dresses and materials she had bought while she was in England. There was nothing else. Her mother had died leaving only a whisper of advice to Milly to return to Dominica and marry well.

Milly unlaced her bonnet and sat down with relief on the thick mattress of the four-poster bed. She tossed the bonnet carelessly onto the couch and glanced around the room. It was adequately furnished: rugs on the polished floorboards, shutters in the window overlooking the hotel's minuscular courtyard, a dresser for her clothes, the couch, and the bed. Milly wondered if she should unpack the contents of her trunks. She had no idea how long she would have to stay in the hotel—that would depend on when her brother could find suitable lodgings. Or when she found a husband.

Dyce, Milly's brother, had met her when the ship she had sailed in from Bristol anchored in the Roseau roadstead. A canoe had deposited Milly and her baggage on shore, and Dyce engaged three Negroes to carry her trunks to the hotel.

It had been two years since Milly had seen Dyce. He had not changed in that time, she was sure. But she had.

"Welcome home, Milly!" Dyce had told her cheerfully, gripping her arms. "What a beauty you have become!"

"You say that after such a dreadful voyage. I declare I must look a fright!"

"You poor flower," chuckled Dyce, steering her through the potholes and cart tracks of the mud street. The slaves trotted in front of them carrying the trunks.

"I'll wager you will soon have this town in an uproar. When the word spreads, every bachelor and lecherous officer in the island will be launching a campaign to snare you. There is such a shortage of white women here, Milly, you shall have your pick of the finest, richest men in Dominica."

"That was Mother's dying command, Dyce." Milly lifted her dress above her ankles to avoid the puddle at the hotel entrance. She followed her brother up the stone steps, clutching his arm at the door. "I'm frightened, Dyce."

"Nonsense!" Her brother's voice was gruff. "You'll enjoy it. And remember, Mother left us nothing here, not even a slave. Our future, yours and mine, depends on you." Dyce pushed open the door into the hotel and stood aside to let his sister enter.

Milly sensed the stir caused by her entrance. A hush of speculation descended on the merchants and soldiers in the saloon, broken by arrogant voices baying to each other about who this newcomer might be. Milly closed her ears to the callous appraisals of her figure and the raucous comments about Dyce.

Her brother scowled. "Those self-important white exploiters!" he exclaimed. "They bleed us dry, Milly, but now it's our turn. They'll come grovelling at your feet within hours."

Milly looked at Dyce in amazement at the bitterness in his voice. Then she recalled her mother's warning that Dyce was a rogue in the same mold as her father, who had been killed in a foolish duel when she was five. Up to that moment, Milly had not dreamed that Dyce intended to use her to settle his private scores with the island's upper crust.

"Dyce," she stated firmly. "Mother wished me to marry well. I will choose my own husband when I am ready."

"Hah!" Dyce guided her across the room to the portly white man who was eyeing them disdainfully from the center of the saloon. "You must be ready soon so that you can get out of this expensive place. Mr. Gold"—he smirked at the hotel owner—"I present my sister, Millicent."

"Room ten, Dyce. No male visitors in your chamber, ma'am. Payment in advance, if you please."

Dyce protested, but he knew it was useless. In a small town like Roseau, every one knew Dyce Dobbs. Credit was something no one would extend to him as long as he had neither land, slaves, nor employment.

Milly was determined not to be judged by her brother's reputation. She smiled her prettiest. "Of course, Mr. Gold. It is so reassuring to know that you have an establishment where a lady will not be disturbed." She took some coins from her purse and pressed them into the hotel owner's hand.

"If you would be so good as to count these coins and to give me a receipt for the number of nights they represent, Mr. Gold, I would be most grateful. And perhaps," she added, her smile belying the ridicule in her voice, "you would ask a trustworthy nigger, if you have one, to carry my trunks to my chamber."

Milly lay back on her bed and smiled to herself at the thought of Mr. Gold's expression of disbelief.

Dyce had left her sharply, striding over to join the men at the bar. Alone, Milly had followed the Negro up to her room.

The Negro, despite his fawning manner, had an air of independence which appealed to Milly. She was surprised by her feeling. When she left Dominica she had been a shy sixteen-year-old, terrified of every black she saw. Her mother had warned her repeatedly of the treachery of blacks and also of the carnal lusts of whites. Not having seen a slave for over two years because she'd been in England, Milly found she was intrigued by the Negro.

When Milly had lived in the island, her mother chaperoned her zealously. Milly's mother saw Milly's maidenhead as her sole asset to be bartered for a good marriage: her only opportunity to change her status in society. She shielded her daughter rigorously. In England, where the threats to a girl's virginity were fewer than in the colonies, Milly's mother censored her every move, even from her sickbed.

With her mother dead, Milly had no alternative but to return to the island where she was born. She was still a virgin but, Milly mused, quite unaware of the grinning slave manipulating himself outside her closed door, that status would soon be changed.

Milly pulled herself off the bed and walked over to the mirror-glass on the dresser. She was sure she looked a fright after the voyage. How difficult it was to sleep on a vessel that rolled every second of the night. And quite impossible to make more than a pre-

15

tense at personal toilet. Not that Milly had felt obliged to impress any of her fellow passengers—quite the contrary. There were two gentlemen of color, brown men of political pretensions returning from a circuit of the home counties, and a spluttering cleric with an ambition to save the souls of Dominica's Negroes. As if Negroes had souls! thought Milly, gazing at herself in the glass.

She sighed, wondering how she should commence her pursuit of a husband. "Of course," she told herself as she stared at her brown eyes smoldering under the crescents of her finely arched eyebrows, "only the purest-blooded and wealthiest of white men will be worth considering."

She would enlist her brother's help, she decided, in drawing up a record of the eligible planters, merchants, and other bachelors on the island. There was nothing to be gained from wasting her time on men who might look presentable but had no fortune. She hoped that the odious innkeeper, Mr. Gold, would not be one of the candidates.

"Fie!" she exclaimed aloud, brushing at her copper-colored hair with her hand. "Who am I to put partiality ahead of expedience?" She gazed at the young face staring back at her from the mirror. With a delicately white finger, she traced a line from the curve of her eyebrow, down her cheek pinkened by the sea voyage, and under her small, dainty chin. She rested her chin on the finger, marveling at the straightness of her nose and at the symmetry of her lips.

"Milly!" she uttered, smiling happily. "You shall have the most handsome, richest, and most gallant man on this island. You shall have a carriage, a boudoir, jewels, clothes, and a score of niggers to attend to your whims!"

Her sensitive nose flared as a breeze wafted through the jalousies. She frowned with distress. "Milly, my dear," she said scornfully, "none of these shall be yours if you do not wash away the odors of shipboard life!"

Milly rose from her chair in front of the dresser and looked around the room. There was a cord hanging from the ceiling by the door. She walked over to it and pulled. A bell jangled outside her room. She wondered who would hear it and pulled the cord vigorously a second time.

She was surprised by the prompt knocking on her door. "Yes?" she called, her hand still clutching the cord.

The door opened. The Negro stood there, his lips parted in a broad, almost an expectant, grin. "Yas, ma'am?" he leered.

Milly studied the boy closely. She had no idea of his age. His golden-colored shirt with its full sleeves only hinted at the muscles Milly suspected were hidden underneath. His black breeches clung to his thighs like a second skin, accentuating a formidable bulge which caused Milly to avert her eyes in consternation. She felt herself blushing.

"I want to take a bath!" she snapped, hoping to hide her confusion.

"Very well, ma'am." The slave answered her calmly. "I shall tell the chambermaid to bring water and towels. Is there anything else, ma'am?"

Milly looked at him sharply, wondering if his servile tone concealed the real meaning of his question.

"No!" she replied haughtily. "Just the bath. Make haste, please."

The slave backed out of the room with a flourish, leaving Milly to prepare herself. Thirty minutes later there was a knock at the door and the Negro entered carrying a metal bathtub which he set down in the center of the room. He was followed by two black wenches, both bearing pails full of boiling water. The

17

Negro smiled at Milly and backed out of the room, returning quickly with two pails of cold water.

He stood in the center of the room staring down at Milly.

"What's your name?" Milly demanded, certain the slave was trying to intimidate her.

"Cuffy, ma'am." He bowed his head.

"Well, Cuffy, you may go now."

"Yo' don' wan' de maids to pour de water fuh yo', ma'am?"

Milly stared at the Negro's eyes. They were dark and almond-shaped. His eyelashes flickered as though suggesting something.

"Of course. Yes." Milly pointed at the smaller wench. "You may stay. Now, out of this chamber, both of you," she said to Cuffy and the second girl. "I am so weary after my voyage, I must bathe immediately." Milly turned her back on the Negro to avoid having to challenge the impudence she detected in his gaze.

She walked over to the door and carefully turned the large key in the lock when the two had left. "What's your name, girl?" she asked the wench who had begun to pour water into the tub.

"Hannah, ma'am," the girl answered huskily.

She was a pretty wench, not more than fourteen. Her black face was fairer than Cuffy's. Milly wondered if she had some white blood in her. She moved easily, filling the tub carefully before testing the water with her finger.

"Yo' does like de water hot, ma'am?"

"Warm enough to soak in, Hannah." Milly stepped out of her gown, laying it on the bed. She shook her petticoat down to the floor and glanced at Hannah. The girl put down the pail she was holding and quickly picked up the petticoat. She smiled sweetly at Milly.

18

"You are a pretty wench," said Milly, attracted to the girl. She felt sufficiently relaxed in the slave's presence to shed all her clothes. She stepped over to the tub.

"Good gracious, Hannah, what are you doing?" Milly glanced at the girl in surprise. The slave slipped out of her shift and stood naked beside the tub.

"Ah does take off mah shift, ma'am, so as not to wet it when ah does sponge yo', ma'am."

Milly was intrigued. She stepped quickly into the tub, sinking her bottom down and pulling her knees up close to her chin so that the water could lap as much of her body as possible. For the first time since leaving England she felt completely relaxed.

Hannah took the soap in her hand and began to rub Milly with it, forming a sparkling lather. Water splashed over the edge of the tub.

"Yo' see, ma'am," murmured Hannah, "if ah does not be naked, too, ah does wet."

"Yes," breathed Milly, letting her head loll back onto the edge of the tub and closing her eyes. Hannah's hands smoothed the lather gently across her breasts, stirring a delicious feeling of ecstasy.

"That's nice!" Milly marveled at the slave's practiced touch.

"Ah does know how to bathe a lady, ma'am, so she does feel real nice."

"Oh, yes, Hannah!" Milly thrilled to the girl's touch, her nipples stiffening as the slave's fingers fondled her. Milly tightened her stomach as Hannah's hands crept lower, soaping her with a circular motion which set her whole body tingling.

Milly groaned softly. The girl's soapy fingers slipped into her. Milly squirmed at the slave's touch but made no effort to stop her. It was so nice.

Hannah splashed Milly's breasts with water to wash away the lather. She bent her head low as her lips

19

pouted close to Milly's nipple. Suddenly, she sucked the hard flesh into her mouth, working her fingers between Milly's loins.

A tremor soared through Milly and she gasped, feeling herself flowing with an exquisite agony into the bath water. She put her hands out to clasp the naked black girl, pulling her down into the tub on top of her.

"Did yo' enjoy yuh bath, ma'am?" Cuffy was standing outside the room with a foolish grin on his face when Milly opened the door for Hannah to leave.

"Of course, Cuffy." Milly's voice mocked the Negro's own. She had never felt more radiant after Hannah had dried her, helped her to dress, and brushed her hair. Milly needed no rouge on her cheeks to add color to her white complexion. She was glowing.

"You may clean up my chamber, boy." She smiled demurely at Cuffy.

"Yes, ma'am."

"And Cuffy. This wench, Hannah. She is to sleep here tonight as my chaperone."

"Mr. Gold don't like no niggers to sleep in the chambers, ma'am," Cuffy coughed. "Not even me."

"Nonsense, Cuffy. Please arrange it for me, will you?" Milly reached up and patted the slave on his cheek. "There's a good boy," she pouted at him provocatively before gliding down the corridor, her gown rustling over the polished floorboards.

Cuffy cupped his breeches to hold down the reaction Milly's casual touch had stirred in him. Hannah brushed away his hand and laughed in his face as she squeezed him viciously.

"De mistress does be a virgin, boy. Yo' ain' de one to taste her!"

Cuffy groaned, his eyes following Milly as she descended the stairs into the crowded saloon below.

Chapter 2

Walking down the curving staircase, Milly noticed a boy who could not have been more than ten years old watching her in amazement. His mouth was gaping open as though he had seen a divine vision.

The boy was sitting on a bench in a corner of the crowded saloon. Milly remembered that it was the custom for slaves to await their masters in such a manner, but she could not believe that the boy was a slave. He had white features topped with hair which was a mass of black ringlets. His eyes, a bold and piercing yellow, attracted Milly.

She lost his gaze as the curve in the staircase brought her round to overlook the densest part of the crowd of revelers in the room. She paused, gripping the banister rail for support. The bawling and braying coming from the men was worse than the noise of a pack of wild dogs. Guffaws of masculine laughter and feminine shrieks gave the bar the air of a common casino instead of a hotel saloon.

Milly faltered momentarily until she remembered Dyce's assurance that the cream of the island's society was to be found here. Her eyes located her brother through the smoky haze hanging over the drinkers. He stood with a group of young blades whose dress and mannerisms suggested that they were as knavish as he was. She continued down the stairs into the throng, aware of the little boy's eyes still staring at her.

A break occurred in the noise of the crowd as she stepped into the saloon. Appreciative murmurings gave way to outright demands.

"Hey, *ma'mselle*, let me escort you!"

"Honey, you looking for me?"

"Come, join us!"

Milly ignored the chorus, sailing forward haughtily as the clusters of drinkers parted for her to pass. Dyce pushed his way to her side.

"Milly, I had no idea!" His rugged face was creased in a smile of pride. "And to think you are my sister!"

Milly smiled appreciatively, knowing this time his compliment was sincere. She laid her hand on his arm. "Dyce, I am not a young girl any more," she whispered huskily into his ear.

"Eh! Eh! Dyce, you want to keep this sister all for yourself!" a young blade in the group shouted. "Share her with your partners, damn you!" Roars of laughter greeted the remark.

"I'll present you out of respect for our friendship" —Dyce glared at his cronies forming a circle around him—"but I'm telling all of you now, there are none of you here who need to trouble your heads with designs on my sister. She is to be married, and not to one of you impecunious popinjays!"

The raucous laughter filled the air, causing the more serious drinkers to turn in their direction. The Speaker of the Legislature, sitting in a corner with his colleagues, frowned his disapproval. The old men in their brocade coats and silk stocks leaned forward as the Speaker condemned the youth of today who cared neither for employment nor propriety.

Milly found herself being passed from one elaborately dressed blade to another. Her brother's friends were mostly in their twenties, affecting the style of

Regency dandies from England but unable to conceal their uncouth, island ways. Some of them, she realized, she had played with as a child. There was not a husband to be found among them.

She accepted a glass of punch which Dyce pressed into her hand. "I told them to put it on your account, my dear," he hissed into her ear. "I am really quite without resources at present."

"Dyce!" Milly smiled at him, drawing him away from his cronies. "This will not do. Your friends may be charming, but I cannot waste my time with them. Do you not know some influential people I could meet? Gentlemen of means."

As she spoke, Milly was conscious of someone watching her with an intensity which could not be ignored. She tossed her head with annoyance and red hair flashed as though alive. It was a gesture several of the men in the bar observed, raising their eyebrows at each other. This wench had spirit.

Milly turned her head sharply. She saw the boy on the bench stand up, his eyes frank in his appraisal of her.

"Who is that?" she demanded.

Dyce followed Milly's gaze, but the crowd closed around them before he could see. To Dyce's surprise, he found himself staring at the Governor. He clasped Milly's arm. "General Nicolay, I'd like to present my sister, Millicent."

The Governor, looking down his nose at Dyce, faltered when his eyes fell on Milly. His stern expression dissolved into a smile, and he lowered his head to utter pleasantries.

Dyce was pushed to the outside of the Governor's circle while Milly stood close to General Nicolay and her gay laughter trilled above the noise of the crowd. In spite of his hatred for the island's wealthy upper class who kept men like him down, Dyce smirked with

23

satisfaction. Milly was going to be his revenge.

The boy who had been watching Milly so intently moved away from his bench when he saw she was in the Governor's circle. Although General Nicolay had only recently arrived to relieve the Earl of Huntingdon, the Governor had established himself as an upright gentleman. The lady's immediate acceptance into his presence signified something to the boy.

"Hey, yo'!"

Cuffy snapped his head around as he heard the call. He glared in amazement when he saw that it was the boy who had called him. "Who yo' callin'?" he demanded with a scowl.

"Yo'," said the boy. "Ain' yo' de one what does be de slave 'round here?"

"Ah does be de buckras' slave, boy. But ah ain' yuhs."

The boy broke into a warm smile. "A'right, Cuffy. Don' get vex' fuh dat. Come here a while."

"Ah ain' got no time to dally wid yo'. Massa Gold does warn me 'bout gossiping wid niggers."

The boy chuckled. Only a foolish town slave would class himself above a mulatto. "Ah ain't no nigger, Cuffy. An' yo' does know mah massa could buy yuh Massa Gold an' dis hotel a hundred times. Besides, yuh massa eyes too full ob de *beké* wench to worry 'bou' yo' an' me talkin'."

Cuffy looked in the direction the boy indicated. Mr. Gold, the hotel proprietor, with a shape like a rum barrel, was elbowing his way into the throng surrounding the Governor and Milly. Cuffy grinned in agreement. "Dat wench sure got dem buckras hot."

"Who is she, Cuffy?" The boy sidled up to the Negro and tugged his arm.

"What fuh yo' does wan' to know? Yo' ain' nothin' but a plantation whelp fresh ou' de fields. De buckra woman like she, she ain' no concern of yuhs."

The boy smiled mysteriously.

"Wha' yo' schemin', Brett?" Cuffy's voice dropped to a whisper. He crouched down to bring his face level with the boy. "Yo' does know somethin', Brett?" he asked, a note of awe in his voice. "Yuh massa tell yo' somethin' 'bout her?"

Brett shook his head. "No, Cuffy. Ah don' know nothin'. But yo' tell me she name an' ah goin' tell yo' wha' ah does hear about her from mah massa."

"She name Milly. She does be born here in Roseau. Widow Dobbs dat done be de buckra seamstress does be her mam. She done be in Englan' fuh de time an' dat where she get her ladylike ways." Cuffy paused. "Hannah done shake her a'ready," he said, gloating.

The boy nodded thoughtfully. His bright eyes clouded over. Suddenly he smiled, raising his hand and patting Cuffy on his shoulder. "Yo' does be an obligin' nigger, boy!" he said, skipping away quickly.

"Ah gon' bam yo', boy!" Cuffy roared, lunging forward to catch Brett.

"Cuffy!" Mr. Gold's voice cut through the air, causing the slave to freeze in terror.

"Come!" Mr. Gold's voice had the icy tone of anger which Cuffy knew meant a lashing on his backside.

Cuffy raised his head reluctantly. He stared at the crowd. Mr. Gold was no longer in the group of planters and merchants around the Governor.

"Here, damn you!"

Cuffy peered in the direction of his master's voice, which came from the corner farthest away from the bar. It was a corner that afforded maximum privacy for those drinking in it. The high backs of the settles grouped around a low table prevented casual observers from seeing who sat there, while the lantern hanging nearby flickered with such a dim glow that it was impossible to see clearly. For this reason, the corner was

25

a favorite spot for the young dandies and their wenches.

No Negroes or slaves were allowed in the hotel bar. The only wenches Mr. Gold permitted were the free ones and, of course, whites. Cuffy assumed that Mr. Gold was calling him to escort a merchant and his wench up to a bedroom. He hoped it was for nothing more than that.

Cuffy shuffled nervously over to the corner where he could see the huge frame of his master spilling over the edge of the settle. To Cuffy's surprise, his master was sitting with a white man who was alone and there was no wench in sight.

"Cuffy, I've been talking about you."

Cuffy was relieved to hear his master's voice no longer contained the threat of a beating. In fact, it seemed to have a note of pride in it. Cuffy guessed what was coming.

"My friend here doubts my word, Cuffy."

"Yes, sir?" The Negro kept his voice level.

"If you are hung the way your master says you are, boy, you are wasted in this hotel for idle no-goods," the white man drawled. "You should be put to stud."

"Yes, sir." Cuffy recognized the white man. He was Carlton Todd, reputed to be the wealthiest planter in Dominica, although to look at him a stranger would think he dwelt in penury.

His coat was the brown of a tradesman, his trousers were patched and unfashionable, and his boots showed scars from years of service. He sported a shirt open to his waist, with neither stock nor waistcoat. He had no retinue of slaves with him as did the other planters when they stayed at the hotel. His only attendant was the white-looking boy, Brett.

Cuffy felt Todd's eyes appraising him. He drew himself up to his full height. He was proud of his

26

physique which, he knew, was revealed at its best in the livery Mr. Gold had designed for him.

"Place so dam' dark, I can't see you properly, boy. Step over here." Carlton Todd indicated the space directly in front of him, shielded from the drinkers in the bar by the settles.

"He has the finest dangler on him I ever saw!" Mr. Gold chortled. "Had him since he was a whelp, you see, so I know. Wife wanted him gelded. Said he would be a liability in the hotel with all the white ladies we have here."

"Be a crime," said Carlton Todd nonchalantly.

"That's what I'm saying. He ain't given no trouble at all. I have two wenches what drain him every night."

Cuffy listened while his owner and Carlton Todd discussed him as though he were not there. Mr. Todd beckoned him to his side and passed his hand across his chest and squeezed the muscles on his arms. His hand slipped around his shoulders and grasped his neck. Cuffy found the touch of Mr. Todd's fingers at the base of his hair vaguely disturbing.

"You got any whelps from him yet?"

"No," said Mr. Gold. "That's the puzzling thing. He's been mounting my wenches since the day he began to get a hard-on, but no whelp at all."

"What's his age?"

"Ah does be twenty, sah."

Cuffy reeled as Carlton Todd clouted him around his ear.

"Speak only when you are spoken to, boy!" snapped Carlton.

Cuffy glanced at his master, expecting him to protest. Mr. Gold glowered back at him, as though he had been hit instead of the slave.

"The guests encourage him to speak, Carlton. We get them straight out from England here. They are

27

full of ideas about how a Negro is a black human being, not a nigger animal. Sometimes I don't know what to do with him."

"Ban the wenches."

"What?" Mr. Gold's surprise had its echo in Cuffy's own whimper of concern.

"The boy is spoilt. Ban his wenches, he'll soon show more respect. And you'll thicken his juice that way. If he's mounting two wenches every night and probably pumping himself in the day, the juice will be too weak to get you a whelp. Keep him from the fillies for a week. Then put him to one filly at a time. When he gets one full, then put him to the next."

Mr. Gold's jaw dropped as he listened to Carlton. "I never thought of that."

"If he even looks like he plans to trouble a white lady, geld him, Gold. Don't hesitate!" Carlton's voice was thick with bitterness. Cuffy covered his crotch in anxiety. Seeing the gesture, Carlton grinned.

"Why, Gold, I only have your word for the buck's size. And the shadow of an outline under his britches, of course." Carlton chuckled and prodded Cuffy. "Ain't you going to let him strip off for me?"

"What, here? This is a respectable saloon." Mr. Gold's fat cheeks quivered with horror at Carlton's suggestion.

"Since when is it disrespectful to look at a nigger, Gold? Boy, roll down your britches."

"But the Governor is here, Carlton!" Mr. Gold flapped his hands.

"He is the Governor of slave breeders as well as hotel proprietors, Gold. You think our dandified General has never sighted a naked nigger? No one can see what's going on in this corner, as you know. Or are you squeamish because I have called your bluff?" Carlton leaned back, his eyes glinting.

"It's no bluff, Carlton." Gold heaved a sigh, his

tiny eyes darting around the room. All his customers seemed engaged in their own devices, the Dobbs girl being the main attraction. He nodded at Cuffy, waving his flabby hand to indicate that he should peel off his breeches.

Cuffy shrugged his shoulders imperceptibly. He loosened the tie at his waist, skinning the breeches down over his wide hips and thick thighs. He stood awkwardly as the garment hung at his knees above his stockings.

"A whopper," said Carlton laconically.

"Isn't it the darnedest dangler you've ever set your eyes on, Carlton?" Gold was slobbering.

Carlton reached out his hand. He cupped Cuffy's testicles in his palm, bouncing them expertly. He frowned, then a smile played on his lips as he gripped the slave's penis. He rolled back the foreskin to expose the purple glans. He could feel the monstrous appendage stiffening in his fist. He looked at the panting hotel owner, his eyes twinkling.

"I was wrong, Gold. There ain't nothing amiss with this buck's juice. You know why you ain't got a whelp out of him? It's because your wenches can't take him. He's too big. I'll wager they are sucking that thing instead of admitting it!" Carlton broke out into a loud chuckle, reaching across the table for the rum decanter and dismissing the slave from his mind.

Gold was perplexed, but he laughed politely. Cuffy stood uncertain whether he had pleased his master or not. He pulled up his breeches quickly, cramming his dancing penis between his legs. It was at that precise moment that Milly glanced over to the corner.

It was too dim for her to make out the scene clearly, but she had good eyes. They focused on Cuffy's nakedness, her brown eyes widening with disbelief. She leaned on her brother's arm as Cuffy strode away from the corner.

"Who is over there?" she demanded. "Talking to that awful Gold. He just had that slave naked in front of him."

Dyce peered in the corner where Milly was pointing. His voice was gruff. "Him? That's all he knows." He snorted disdainfully. "Don't bother with him, Milly. He's trash. I hate him."

"Why?"

"He has more money than he knows what to do with. The price of sugar is dropping and coffee is being ruined by the blight, and every planter is getting poorer, but that man gets richer and richer. He thinks he is smart, but he was not smart enough for me." Dyce smiled cryptically. "I'll tell you about that one day."

"What does he do?" Milly was intrigued by the vague outline of the man in the shadowy corner. Although she could not see his face, the way he was sitting revealed a lean, hard man of confidence and maturity. "My kind of man?" she wondered to herself.

"Do, Milly?" Dyce frowned at his sister's ignorance. "Why, he breeds slaves. He is Carlton Todd, the Bond-master of Roxborough."

Chapter 3

Brett raced up the stairs two at a time. He had been engrossed in his own thoughts when Carlton Todd had risen from the settle and made his way toward the staircase. Brett was supposed to keep his eye on his master so he could be ready when Carlton beckoned him. It was Cuffy hissing urgently from his post by the door who had alerted him. Brett glanced up and saw Carlton had almost reached the top of the stairs. He scampered after him.

"Mas Carlton, sir!" he called as he caught up with him.

Carlton did not look around. He continued to walk along the corridor to his suite, leaving Brett to trail after him. Pausing to unlock the door to the chamber, Carlton deigned to glance down at the boy who was panting beside him.

"What ails you, boy?" He sounded bored.

"Yo' does be goin' out tonight, Mas Carlton?" Brett's eyes blazed eagerly at the prospect of an evening following his master as he caroused through the Roseau casinos.

Carlton swung open the door and stepped into the room. It was a large room, the best in the hotel, filled with heavy oak furniture imported from England, but Carlton had hardly noticed the elaborate trappings of his suite all the time he had been staying there. He strode across the room to glance out of the window, which overlooked the small town square. In the dim light flickering from coconut oil lamps at the hotel entrance, he saw the shape of a Negro wench fastened in the stocks. Her cronies were gathered around her, laughing and joking amongst themselves. Carlton scowled. It seemed to him that these Roseau niggers had no respect. He raised his eyes to contemplate the opposite side of the square where the prosperous merchants had their homes, large wooden houses with balconies which had been built above their emporiums. He knew that in the shadows below those balconies whores lurked hoping to latch onto a passing sailor, a Roseau profligate, or an out-of-town planter like himself.

The whores were a sorry lot. He had already inspected them. Carlton smirked ruefully to himself. He must have seen every white whore there was in Roseau. He had invaded every whorehouse, inn, and casino, demanding to see all the wenches the proprietors could offer. He had even allowed himself to try out a doxy's charms when he had found one who appealed to him. The attraction had always been brief, and he had lost all interest in the wench once he had mounted her.

Carlton turned from the window in despair. When it came to pleasuring a man, no white whore could equal a Negro wench. He did not need whores. He needed a wife.

"Sah?"

Carlton focused on Brett with surprise. He had forgotten the boy was there.

"Sah. Yo' does want me to lay out yuh clothes?"

"What's the use, Brett? Every time I look for a woman, I only meet harlots. How am I going to find a wife in this town? Even the Governor is looking for a desirable white wench. I hear he is giving another soirée tomorrow." Carlton threw himself full-length on the bed, his dusty boots rucking up the counterpane.

"Sah?" Brett stepped forward nervously. He knew that if he were an ordinary slave, he would not dare to discuss such things with his master. But Brett did not consider himself a slave.

"What is it, boy?" Carlton sighed. "You are prancing around like a nigger on an ant's nest."

"In de matter of a white woman, sah." Brett blushed at his own boldness, twisting his hands in front of him.

"What is it, boy? Go on!"

Brett paused, recalling how Carlton had gripped his shoulders when his only white grandson had died not a month before. It was then that Carlton had fastened his bloodshot eye on Brett and vowed that he was

32

going to find a white woman as a wife to produce an heir. Although he was young, Brett could feel Carlton's misery. He raised his head. Carlton's eyes were watching him intently.

"Speak, Brett. You need have no fear of my anger."

Carlton sighed. He liked Brett. He was the only slave he had known who had guts. The boy did not whine and cringe or refuse to look a man in his eye when he spoke. Carlton remembered how Brett had once attacked a white man who was raiding the virgins in the Pen. He was five and gained the whip-scar which ran around his neck like a noose-mark as his reward.

"Dere is a lady recently arrived in dis hotel, sah." Brett spoke at last. "Did yo' not see her in de saloon?"

Carlton shook his head. What use was this charade, anyway? Perhaps he should go to Trinidad and try to buy a white wench there. Yet he knew he would never find what he really sought.

"She does be very beautiful, sah. She does be a virgin."

"What!" Carlton sat up abruptly, swinging his legs off the bed. He snatched Brett by his shoulder. "What did you say, boy?"

"De white lady. In de hotel. She is a virgin," Brett blurted out quickly.

Carlton snorted at his own foolishness. He kept his arm draped around Brett's neck. "How do you know that, Brett? You are not even old enough to have any sap in you, yet you can sniff out a virgin?" He clapped Brett's ear lightly.

"Ah does hear dat from de slave gal, Hannah, who done bathe de lady, sah. It does be true, sah."

"Indeed?" Carlton stood up, stroking his chin. "What a curious state of affairs." Of course, Carlton mused, there was always the possibility that the slave could have lied, but Carlton's experience taught him that slave gossip about the whites they attended was usually reliable.

"Beautiful, did you say, Brett? Have you seen her?"

"Yas, sah. Ah done watch her descend to de bar. She was be in de Governor's circle."

"So General Nicolay has launched an attack?" Carlton strode the length of the chamber, turning sharply to face Brett. "Tell me, youngster. Why do you say this lady, as you call her, is beautiful?"

Brett's eyes glowed. "She does have red hair, sir, de color de sun does have when it sets over de cane fields at home. Her eyes are a deep brown an' she does have clearest white complexion ah ever did see. She does move like a lady, sah, and her body is as proud as de liveliest wench yo' does have at Roxborough."

Carlton shook his head in amazement. "Seems like you'll need a wench yourself before long, boy. That's what your whore of a mother bequeathed you, eh?" He chuckled. "Prepare my blue coat and white trousers, Brett. With the yellow stock. It seems I may have to outflank General Nicolay and his preposterous Government House clique.

"Wouldn't that be something?" he mused aloud. "The Bondmaster of Roxborough stealing the Governor's lady?"

Chapter 4

Milly flounced angrily into her room. She was exhausted. She slammed the door shut and flopped onto her bed uttering a deep sigh of despair. Remembering not to crease her dress, she pulled herself reluctantly off the bed and unlaced her gown. She removed it and draped it carefully over a chair, returning to the bed with a groan. Finding a husband was not the easy task she had expected it to be.

"It is all very well," she thought, "for Dyce to talk about wealthy planters and merchants, but where are they?" It had not taken Milly long to realize that the swarm of popinjays and blades buzzing about the saloon of the hotel were not of the class her mother had intended. The merchants appeared to be bankrupt, the government officials were married, and the attorneys were worthless little men complaining about the high cost of slaves and the low price of sugar. She had found Dyce's set of knavish young men the most attractive, but what future lay in that direction?

She gazed up at the window. Stars were beginning to appear as night spread across the sky. She would have to call a slave to bring a lamp. She eased herself off the bed again, wondering what she would do that evening. Was she to bear her brother's company so he could escort her from casino to tavern in a search for the town's eligible bachelors?

Milly walked over to the open window and leaned

out. The stars were flickering in the clear tropic night. Below, the soft glow of the lamps cast shadows from the palm trees growing in the courtyard. Bougainvillea sprawled across the outside of the building, and the air itself seemed awash with the perfume of night orchids. Milly sighed.

Studying her curiously as he watched from the window of his dressing room, Carlton Todd sensed the yearning in the woman's troubled sigh. Her long, hibiscus-bright hair cascaded about her shoulders. In profile, Carlton saw her delicate nose with its slight upward tilt at its tip. Her small chin was trembling. She seemed on the verge of tears.

"*C'est triste, la nuit,*" he murmured softly, as though to himself.

"Oh!" Milly gasped. She turned her head in Carlton's direction. "You startled me."

Carlton smiled to give the impression that he was himself startled. "Forgive me, *ma'mselle*, I did not observe you."

"Are you in the habit of talking to yourself?" Milly asked with a giggle. The man was bare-chested, his silvery-gold curls haloing his tanned and rugged features. "And in French, too?"

"My mother was French," said Carlton, smiling. "Pray, what sadness caused a young lady to be sighing at the stars?"

"Perhaps the same sadness that causes a mature gentleman to be addressing them."

"You have a pretty wit, *ma'mselle*. I find it hard to believe that the same loneliness bedevils you as it does an old planter."

"I know no old planters, sir, with whom I may compare the depth of my feelings."

"Fie, lady. You are gazing through your window at one!"

"But I do not know him. Nor do I see him clearly

36

enough to know if he is old or merely pretentious."

Carlton could scarcely believe his ears. His experience with white women was limited to his wife, who had left him a widower seventeen years previously, and to his daughter, who had run off with a whoremonger. He frowned, turning to Brett who was listening eagerly behind him. "This lady of yours has a lively tongue in her head, Brett."

Brett rolled his eyes in mock disapproval.

"You look like a nigger when you do that." Carlton snapped. "Don't just stand there, polish my boots."

"Yas, Mas Carlton!" Brett grinned, knowing his master's anguish was at an end.

Carlton peered out of the window again. "Forgive me," he said, "a stupid slave I have here."

Milly raised her eyebrow sympathetically.

"May I say that your sadness appears to have lifted?" Carlton was feeling out of his depth with the curious female.

"Yours, too," she responded.

"If loneliness is a shared state, *ma'mselle*, could we not enjoy each other's company over dinner?"

"You are very kind, sir," Milly pouted. "But I am weary. Is there a place not too far from here where we could dine in private?" She stroked the bougainvillea petals under the window ledge, careful not to let the thorns snag her fingers.

"Indeed there is," chuckled Carlton. "Not five steps from your door. My suite. Shall we say in an hour?"

"Why not?" Milly's acceptance of Carlton's invitation was also a question to herself. She withdrew her head rapidly and felt her way across the darkened room to the bellpull. As she tugged the cord, she could hear the bell jangling outside the adjoining room as well. She wondered whom Cuffy would answer first. There was a knocking on her door within seconds.

"Who's there?" she demanded.

"Cuffy, ma'am."

"Did you bring me a lamp, boy? I am in darkness."

"Ah does have one here, ma'am."

Thus reassured, Milly opened the door. The slave stood outside, towering over her, his eyes half-closed with amusement at her precautions. Hannah stood by his side holding the lamp.

"Good night, miss," said Hannah, sweeping into the room. "We was be waiting fuh yo' to call. We done hear yo' talking, miss."

Milly clutched her bosom, remembering she was wearing only her petticoat, having removed her dress before she lay down. "That's all, Cuffy," she exclaimed, endeavoring to shut the door in the slave's face.

Cuffy halted the door with his hand for a few seconds. "Hannah does be stay here with yo' now, ma'am. Ah done fix it." He grinned, his right eye giving the merest suggestion of a wink.

Milly shuddered before she succeeded in shutting the door.

"Yo' does be a' right, miss?" asked Hannah, observing Milly's heaving breast.

"Oh, yes, Hannah!" Milly sat down. The planter in the next-door room was right. Slaves *are* stupid, she thought. She gasped, aware that Hannah was watching her. "Tell me, Hannah. The gentleman next door. Who is he?"

"He does be Mister Carlton Todd, miss."

Milly stood up, beckoning to Hannah to help her with her dress.

"Yo' does be going out this evening, miss?" Hannah was disappointed.

"I am having dinner with Mister Todd, Hannah. Next door."

38

Hannah's fingers faltered as she buttoned Milly's bodice.

"What is wrong, Hannah?"

"Nothing, miss." The girl pouted sulkily.

"I will not be out long, Hannah. You shall wait for me here."

The girl's face brightened a little.

"What do you know about Carlton Todd, Hannah?"

"Yo' does not be acquainted with the gentleman, ma'am?"

"Gracious, no! I met him out of the window but ten minutes ago. Here, girl, you can brush my hair." Milly sat in front of the shadowy mirror, watching Hannah's reflection as the girl began to brush and stroke her hair carefully.

"They does say Mr. Todd is very unsociable, miss. He does own two hundred slaves and a large plantation half a day's ride up de coast, miss. He does be very well off, miss, but he does not mix with society. They say he does not like de white people who live here, miss."

"Why ever not, girl?" Milly dabbed some perfume behind her ears as Hannah paused in her hairbrushing.

"They say he does believe dem to be feckless, miss. He does pay no heed to the island's laws, miss. He does be a good master until his slaves wrong him, miss, den he does be ruthless." Hannah brushed Milly's hair vigorously. "He does govern he estate and de village of Layou what does be near it with he own laws, miss. The authorities can't touch him, he does be so powerful."

Milly was restless. She turned to face Hannah. "What of the man himself, Hannah? Is he married?"

"No, ma'am. He has no woman."

"I am forty-four, Milly," Carlton murmured much later. They had finished supper and sat opposite each other at the small table in the parlor of Carlton's suite. A single candle burned on the table between them. Brett hovered at Carlton's elbow with the decanter of brandy.

"Put the decanter on the table, boy," urged Carlton. "You can tell that nigger to clear away the wares in the morning. You can go to your pallet and sleep."

"Yas, Mas Carlton." Brett grinned happily, as he backed away. "Good night, Miss Milly, good night, Mas Carlton."

"Good night, Brett." Milly acknowledged him with a slight nod of her head.

"He's only a slave, Milly." Carlton said reprovingly.

"Does that mean I should not be polite to him?" Milly's eyebrow arched a challenge.

"Of course, be polite if you wish. A slave does not expect it."

"That is surely my affair. I find your Brett quite a little charmer."

"He is that, all right," grinned Carlton. "His father was my son." He paused to see what effect this had on Milly.

She showed no surprise. Carlton remembered that Milly was Dominican-born herself and so would not be unfamiliar with the ways of planters. He would ask his lawyer about her own parentage tomorrow. From what he could see, she was pure white, but one could never tell with so much cross-breeding going on.

"You said his father was your son?" Milly smiled sympathetically.

"That's right. Caspar, my first boy. You never saw such a stout young fellow. I took him to England with me when he was Brett's age. He had a honey-colored complexion. The ladies loved him. We stayed there six years and when we returned he persuaded me to make him the overseer of Roxborough. He loved his work. . . ." Carlton's voice drifted away; steeped in sadness.

Milly put her hand out to grasp Carlton's as it lay on the table beside his brandy snifter. "What happened?"

"He was killed five years ago. He was only twenty-one."

Milly squeezed Carlton's hand to express her sorrow. "A slave uprising?"

"No. Whites." Carlton shook off his sadness, smiling again at Milly. He clenched her hand, chuckling. "The boy was a lady's man—took after his father, I suppose. He angered a set of white rakes and they hanged him one night. My daughter, Laura, ran off with one of his murderers."

Milly was aghast. She remembered hearing her mother speaking about the incident when she had been a young girl in the seamstress shop. "You never caught the killers?"

"No!" Carlton was scornful. "Who would help me? A slave gets killed by a gang of whites. It's nothing unusual. And it wouldn't bring back Caspar, would it?" He gripped Milly's hand tighter. "I know who did it, though, at least one of them. He was a ruffian called Fletcher. There were two others with him. Young Brett saw them both. He reckons he will recognize them if he ever sees them again." Carlton laughed.

Milly laughed with him. "Brett is a very determined boy."

"Oh yes. He knows what he wants. Since Caspar died, I've run Roxborough alone, breeding and selling slaves, shipping sugar, and distilling rum. One day, Brett will be the overseer, but I've no heir, Milly." He gazed into her eyes. "Milly, I'd like an heir."

Milly returned his gaze without flinching. With her free hand, she brushed away a strand of hair which

41

fluttered across her brow. A smile quivered on her lips. Carlton had captivated her. That a man so strong should have such a desperate need, a need she could fulfill, almost overwhelmed her.

Carlton was handsome in a mature and dignified way. His face was etched with experience, yellow eyes blazing out under a deep brow. His heavily tanned cheeks were lean, tapering to a firm jaw. He had an air of terrible strength and toughness which, Milly sensed, concealed a warm and compassionate nature. He had obviously dressed to impress her, discarding his tradesman's browns for a peacock blue coat which hung easily on his robust frame.

His eyes, still gazing at her, seemed to pierce her heart. She lowered her head modstly. "If only mother was alive," Milly thought. "I hope she will approve."

"You cannot have an heir without a wife, Carlton," Milly's voice was husky.

He stood up, releasing his hand from her grip. Suddenly she felt weak and helpless. Her bravado seemed to have led her into the situation she had most feared. Carlton's hands were on her shoulders as he stood behind her. His fingers were curling around her neck, feeling his way down onto her breasts. She twisted away from him, lifting her head.

Carlton curved his eyebrows at her reaction. Slowly, he raised his hand and gently stroked her cheek. As he bent lower, he held Milly firmly under her chin.

Milly's lips parted in protest. Carlton lowered his head, brushing his mouth against hers. Milly gasped.

Carlton swept his lips over hers again, sending a sudden sensation soaring through her body from her breasts to her loins. She held her mouth open, waiting.

Carlton withdrew. His face was kind, almost wise. "Milly," he whispered, still holding her chin between his finger and thumb, "will you marry me? Will you give me an heir?"

Now the moment had come, Milly quailed. Would he want her before the wedding? Would he want her tonight? Was this just his way to lure her to bed and deflower her? The smell of the brandy on his breath wafted over her. She gulped, trying to recover her senses.

"When?" she croaked unexpectedly.

Carlton's laughter surprised her. "You are supposed to blush and murmur your answer softly. But you say when?" He released her chin and spun around the room gaily.

"I do declare, Milly, you are a girl after my own heart. No nonsense, no false fluttering of your eye-lashes, no bartering of your charms. I believe you are a virgin, Milly?" He paused to judge the effect of his remark on Milly. The faint darkening of her cheeks confirmed what he already knew.

"Why are you in such a hurry, I wonder?"

"Is that wrong of me, Carlton?" Milly was nervous now.

"It's marvelous!"

Carlton was still capering around the room. Milly laughed timidly.

"You are an angel, Milly. Let us be married this very evening."

"Tonight?" Milly gulped.

"Why not?"

"Well . . ." Milly thought. It was all rather un-usual, but then wasn't this what she had planned? "You could not arrange it so quickly!"

Carlton raised his eyebrow. "Are you challenging me, Milly? I am not the Bondmaster for nothing. A cleric will rustle his skirts and be with us as soon as he hears the clinking of my money. A license is a formality I can arrange tomorrow. Damn it all, why should we wait?"

Carlton's impetuosity surprised himself. He had the

feeling that if he did not secure this woman at once, she would remain neither a virgin nor an eager bride for very long. The "When?" with which she accepted his proposal revealed rather more about this wench than he expected. Her hips were broad; she would bear children. What more did he require in a wife than white blood and an ability to breed?

He strode over to the door and yanked the bell cord.

The Reverend Newman was a pompous and doddering old fool. He raised every objection he could muster to express his reluctance at being asked to perform the marriage ceremony in the saloon bar of the hotel. He was seventy years old and a former member of the House of Assembly. In all his years, he assured Carlton, he had never known anything so bizarre and outrageous as this.

A few glasses of brandy and some gold pieces later, he was muttering what he could remember of the wedding ceremony while Carlton and Milly stood nervously before him.

Roseau's gentry, roused by slaves running through the streets in search of the rector, crammed into the saloon. Rum casks were broached on Carlton's instructions, and he invited all who could enter the hotel to drink with him. A loud huzzah marked the end of the Reverend's grandiloquence.

Carlton, fortified by the brandy he had consumed while awaiting the cleric, embraced Milly enthusiastically. The hotel was in an uproar. Slaves pushed their way through the crowd with mugs of rum. Attorneys drank with carpenters; merchants clinked their cups with sailors.

General Nicolay stumbled through the throng, his nose bright red, his eyes glazed. "Todd!" he spluttered. "Governor's priv'lege. Kish the bride!" He groped for

Milly, sloshing a wet slap with his lips on her cheek.

Carlton grasped Milly around her waist, squeezing her jealously. "You asked me when, Milly! Now you know."

Milly was in a daze. She clung desperately to Carlton, longing to escape from the uproar and run back upstairs to his suite.

"You ain't wasted no time, girl!" a voice hissed in her ear.

Milly turned away from Carlton to see who had addressed her.

Carlton felt someone tugging his coat. He released Milly and looked down. Brett, who had been dressed in his best breeches and shirt to act as wedding attendant, was grasping his sleeve as though he intended to pull it off.

"What is it, Brett? Can't it wait until tomorrow?"

"Oh, Mas Carlton, sah!" Brett's face was creased with worry, his eyes staring wildly.

"Are you drunk, boy?"

Brett stammered something in patois, the language of the field slaves which the Roxborough Negroes used when they spoke amongst themselves.

"Ah does not be drunk, sah. Ah beg yo', Mas Carlton. Dat man, sah. He does be one of dem."

"One of who, Brett?" Carlton was annoyed, but he knew through experience that it was foolish to ignore the words of a loyal slave. He bent down to listen closely to Brett.

"One of dem dat done kill Caspar, sah!"

"What!" Carlton's brandy-fogged brain cleared instantly. Of course, Carlton realized, all the rogues in Roseau were in the hotel tonight. With gallons of grog available at his expense, it was quite likely that the men who had killed his slave son were there, too. Brett had sworn that he would always remember them.

45

"Who's the man, Brett?" he demanded.

"Look, Mas Carlton. De one wid yuh wife."

Frowning, Carlton straightened himself up. Milly was whispering something into the ear of an ill-dressed man swaying at her side. Carlton glanced inquiringly at Brett. The boy nodded his head emphatically.

"Milly!" said Carlton, entwining his arm around his wife's waist and drawing her close to his side. "You have a friend you wish to introduce to me?"

"Not a friend, Carlton," said Milly as the man lurched in front of them, his hand extended to Carlton to offer congratulations. "My brother, Dyce Dobbs."

Brett, at Carlton's side, hissed, his eyes narrowing until they were slits glaring with uncontrolled hatred. "Dat's he, Mas Carlton. Dat's he!"

A sailor with a flourishing red beard jammed his huge hands around a concertina. The music squawked above the noise of the crowd. General Nicolay shoved Dyce Dobbs aside and, with a merry nod to Carlton, swept Milly away in a jig.

BOOK ONE

Brett

1827—1828

Chapter 5

The wail of a conch shell being blown in the slave quarters swelled through the silence of the pre-dawn. It sounded to Carlton like the cry of a slave in agony. In the subdued glow from his lantern, he completed his dressing, splashed his face with cold water from the jug, and passed a brush casually through his hair. He stepped out of the side door from his dressing room onto the balcony. He trod carefully on the creaking floorboards, hoping not to disturb Milly. When he reached the chair placed on the balcony in front of the house, he sat down to wait.

Every morning at Roxborough began the same way. A conch shell was blown by a Wagenie Negro an hour before dawn to wake the other slaves. While the Wagenies, who were fishermen, set out to row down the river to the sea in their canoes, the field slaves stirred. Carlton peered through the dark as *flambeaux*, the flaming torches which served the slaves for light, flickered between the shacks in the quarters.

From his vantage point on the balcony, Carlton commanded a view which, in daylight, encompassed the whole of the plantation buildings. The slave quarters were to his left by the river, located where the slaves could be observed but did not intrude on the consciousness of the occupants of the house. The breeding nursery, which he also called the Paddock because of the niggerlings who gamboled there, lay

48

between the house and the slave quarters in the grove of flamboyant trees.

As Carlton watched, a square of light appeared in the barrack-like building where the slave offspring slept. Miranda, the caretaker, had awakened and opened a shutter. Soon the children would be roused, and their cries would compete with those of the birds and chirping insects which signified the day had begun.

"Yuh coffee, sah!"

Carlton jerked his head up quickly. Brett was standing by his side. It would have been foolish for Carlton to tell the boy he had not heard him approach. With a slave, even a slave like Brett, no white man dared show any weakness. The way with slaves was to remind them continually who was the master.

"You're late, boy!" Carlton snapped. "I could lash you for that."

Brett mumbled an apology. He knew Carlton had not heard him arrive because he had trained himself to move with the stealth of a snake over sand. Carlton's threat of a whipping was an idle one. Brett, at fourteen, had no fear of the Bondmaster, nor of any white man. He had studied Carlton's weaknesses. Did the Bondmaster know, Brett wondered, that he was only the master of his slaves because Brett permitted it?

"It will be a fine day, Mas Carlton." Brett lifted his head to gaze at the slash of gray seeping through the night at the top of the mountains on the plantation's eastern boundary.

"Hurrumph! You think I don't know that?" Carlton cleared his throat and spat irritably over the balcony railing. He took up the dish of coffee Brett had placed on the table beside his chair and sipped at it. Soon, the slaves should be filing past the house on their way

49

to work in the cane-pieces. "And what do you propose that we do on this fine day, young Brett?"

Brett ignored the sarcasm in Carlton's voice. The old man was always touchy at this hour in the morning. Brett widened his eyes as though thinking. "I don't know, sir," he said meekly in carefully accentuated English.

The reply soothed Carlton. He sipped at the coffee again. "Come on, boy, use your wits. One day you will be the overseer. You'll have to decide the work to be done, not me." He reached up and patted Brett on his shoulder with affection. "You are the overseer, Brett. What would you do today?"

Brett frowned. He knew that if he answered too cleverly, Carlton might take offense. A slave was not supposed to be bright. He shifted his weight onto one leg and lifted his foot behind him, scratching it slowly. The gesture served to indicate his limited intelligence to Carlton.

"Well, sir. I know the cane-pieces need holing, so I would send the field gang to the flats to work there. It will be hot today, but niggers can stand the sun because of their black skins." He paused while Carlton nodded approvingly.

"The small gang must tend the livestock and the garden gang must gather ground provisions for the kitchen and nursery." Brett stopped, scratching his curls as though the effort of thinking had exhausted him.

"Not bad, Brett. You are learning." Carlton scowled. "But what you said is what happens every day. Can't you think of any special tasks which could be done today?"

"No, sir." Brett lied. Left to himself, he would repair the roof of the barracoon, which was leaking, burn the abandoned shacks in the quarters whose occupants had died or been sold, have the carpenters make beds for the children in the nursery, and attend to dozens of other small tasks.

"You see, boy, you must think." Carlton pounded his fist on the arm of his chair. "What about the road gang? They could clean out the drains on the trail from the village."

"They did that last week, sir." Brett blurted out before he could control himself.

"Huh! They did, did they? Well, they can damn well do it again!" Carlton drained the coffee and clattered the dish down onto the saucer. "Tell Caliste to saddle my horse, boy. And a pony for you. We are going to tour the plantation today."

Carlton watched Brett scurry away around the corner of the balcony toward the back stairs. The front steps, which were made of stone and gave access to the house from the courtyard below, were prohibited to slave use. It was a tradition started by Carlton's own father, who had built the house soon after his arrival in the island from America. His father had been a loyalist who fled from Alabama, where he was a plantation manager at the time of the war for independence.

His father had always been proud of the house, which he called Roxborough Hall but the slaves knew more simply as the *cou*. It was not one of the Great Houses of Jamaica or Barbados. The lower level was constructed of stone, dragged up the hill from the Layou River by slaves. This contained the food store, quarters for the house slaves, and the kitchen. The upper story of the house was wooden, distinguished by the balcony which girded it on all four sides.

Carlton smiled to himself as he recalled Milly's reaction when she saw the house for the first time nearly four years before. After their hasty marriage, Carlton was eager to bring his bride home to Roxborough. He endeavored to prepare her for the harsh realities of plantation life, but the house was a shock to her. She had clasped his arm in anxiety as she stood in the courtyard gazing up at her new home.

"You are teasing me, Carlton!" she exclaimed. "Surely this is the overseer's place?"

"No, my dear." Carlton suppressed his mirth. "This is the house of a hard-working planter, Milly. It was good enough for my father, and it is good enough for me."

Milly shot him a glance which seemed to doubt his sanity.

"Come," he said. "We are tolerably comfortable inside." He escorted her up the grand steps, freshly swept and scrubbed, onto the balcony.

Carlton knew she was impressed with the view in spite of her sulky expression. The panorama was magnificent. To the west over the cane fields was the shimmering blue of the Caribbean and the vast mouth of the Layou River with the village houses grouped along the coast. To the south, the plantation swept down the hillside to the river and the towering mountains beyond. As she walked around the balcony, Milly's eye took in the sugarcane growing around the house and the neat provision gardens running right up to the edge of the thick tropical forest. Everything, apart from the house itself, indicated a plantation of prosperity run with discipline.

Milly's shock at seeing the wooden villa, instead of the yellow-brick mansion she had expected, faded as she explored the inside. The house was furnished with quality pieces shipped out from England. The drawing room was large and airy with the dining room, containing a grand table, adjoining it at the back of the house.

"This is my chamber!" cried Carlton, kicking open a door. Milly peeped in, uncertain if she was being invited to enter or not. "Yours," said Carlton, taking her hand and steering her across the drawing room to a door at the other side, "is much prettier."

Milly was delighted. She had wondered if she would have her own boudoir or be obliged to share Carlton's quarters. The room was similar to Carlton's in size but furnished with all the necessities for a young wife.

"This was my daughter's boudoir," Carlton explained. "And my mother's before her. I was born in that very bed. See!" Carlton walked over to a door and pushed it open. "Here is a dressing room. Your maid can sleep in here. It has a door onto the balcony so you need not be disturbed by the wench coming and going."

Milly sat on the bed looking around her. "It is wonderful, Carlton. I expected to share your own chamber, though," she simpered.

"I know a lady needs her privacy, Milly," beamed Carlton. He thought it prudent not to mention that he needed his privacy, too. Even though he was married, he still had his responsibilities as Bondmaster to break in the plantation's virgins.

"We have two guest chambers with their own entrances from the balcony," Carlton added proudly. "My father designed the house with every convenience in mind." He stepped into the room and shut the door.

"Carlton, you have that look in your eye!"

Carlton closed the shutters and turned to face Milly. She pursed her lips, feigning annoyance. He advanced on her.

"Carlton, you are terrible!"

"I want a son, Milly." He laid her back gently on the pillows of the four-poster bed and lifted her skirts.

Since that day, Milly had fulfilled all his expectations, except one. She had become the perfect planter's wife. She transformed the house into a comfortable home, ordering furnishings and drapes from England.

She was adored by the house slaves, whom she controlled with discipline and concern. She was a lively and equal companion for Carlton, never interfering with his management of the plantation and slave nursery. Where Carlton had suffered loneliness as the only white man among two hundred black slaves, he discovered a delightful companionship in his young wife.

His sole regret was that Milly had failed to give him an heir.

Carlton sank his brow into his hand as he sat on the balcony, the dawn now bursting around him. "Why?" he asked himself, as he did every day. She was healthy. No less than three doctors had confirmed that there was nothing to prevent Milly's bearing as many children as she wanted.

"Am I to blame?" Carlton pondered the question yet again. True, he was getting older, but he was fit. Had he not sired a male whelp by his own slave daughter, Miranda, not four weeks before he met Milly?

Whatever the reason, Milly had lost two children before they were born. These two miscarriages had left Carlton distraught, his dear wife perplexed, and the future of Roxborough uncertain.

While there was sap in his loins, Carlton was determined to sire a son to succeed him as Bondmaster. His breed of slaves was the finest the Caribbean had ever known. A Roxborough nigger was stronger than the mightiest African and more docile than the meekest Creole.

Carlton sighed, acknowledging with a casual wave the shouts of greetings from the drivers as they marched the field gang to the cane-pieces. The burble of children's laughter wafted up to him from the nursery. He hoped Milly, asleep in her chamber, would not be disturbed.

It was Carlton's plan to show young Brett around the plantation today. The boy was keen and bright. Carlton wanted him to understand the regime at Roxborough. Carlton had decided to take Milly to Trinidad to be examined by the doctors there. He would have to hire an overseer to tend to the plantation and see that the slaves remained under control. Brett, if he knew the routine, would be able to help.

"Carlton!" Milly cooed. "What a beautiful day."

Carlton turned in his chair with surprise. Milly was standing in the doorway of the drawing room, wearing only her silk nightdress. Her long unbound red hair spread over her shoulders, drifting down onto her bosom. Against the vivid whiteness of her skin, it was like a flame devouring her face.

"The niggers will see you, Milly." Carlton was shocked.

"Fie, Carlton. Do you believe I will excite them? Their women are never as modestly dressed as I am now." She leaned on the doorjamb, her eyes yearning.

Carlton jumped up. "Milly, you are white. A nigger knows no restraint when he sees a white woman. You must be circumspect at all times." He strode across to her, slipping his hand eagerly around her waist.

"And so must you, Carlton!" Milly giggled, nestling her head against his lean, suntanned chest. "Do you have to attend to your niggers so early, Carlton?" she crooned. "Perhaps you could dally in my boudoir a while?"

Carlton felt his trousers straining at Milly's nearness to him; the heavy odor of her warm body fresh from her bed worked on his self-control. He gulped, bending his head to brush his lips against her cheek. He allowed himself to be led into her chamber.

Old Ella, who was setting up the table in the dining room for breakfast, glowered darkly.

"Mas Carlton ain't gon' hab no son to take away de

plantation from Brett," she muttered to herself. "He can mount he wife from now until de moon fall out de sky. Ain't no way de mistress gon' bear his whelp!"

Ella cackled evily when she heard the springs of the bed shriek in protest as Carlton clambered on top of his wife.

She knew what herbs to put in Milly's tea so she would lose her child. It had worked twice already!

Chapter 6

Brett was waiting in the kitchen for the Bondmaster to call him. He stretched himself idly on the bench, gazing around the room. There were two young wenches busy at the long table which filled the center of the huge stone-built kitchen. One of them, Ella's helper, was feeding wood chips into the stove. The other girl lifted her head from the table where she was grating a cocoa stick and glanced at him shyly. Brett pretended not to notice.

He raised his arms above his head and leaned back against the wall, flexing his body from his fingers to his toes. He could feel the girl's eyes on him as he lowered his hands and ran them slowly down his body. He let his hands rest on his thighs, outlining the bulge in his cut-off breeches with the thumb and forefinger of each hand.

Brett was proud of his muscular limbs. He was barefoot, and his naked thighs and calves were hard and tanned. It was said by the slaves that there was not a Negro of his age on the plantation who could match him. His shoulders, chest, and biceps were burgeoning under his torn shirt.

Brett exercised every day under the direction of Samboth, a free Negro who lived on the estate. Samboth used to be a friend of his murdered father. He had agreed to help Brett develop into a fighter so that when the time came and he met Caspar's killers, he could avenge his death.

"Yo' does look like yo' does be broodin' again, Brett."

Brett smiled grimly at Pip's voice. He lifted his hands from his thighs and ran them through his soft black locks. "Ah does be waitin' fuh de Bon'massa, Pip. He does say we must to ride on de plantation today. He trainin' me to be de overseer, Pip, so yo' sure got to show me respeck now!"

Pip put a jug of sangaree down onto the table. He frowned, cocking his head onto one side, squinting at Brett. "Aye!" he said. "Yo' does have de age." He stirred the crimson liquid in the jug with a wooden spoon and scooped out a spoonful. "Yo' wan' to taste de sangaree, Brett? Tell me if it does have enough syrup an' lime?"

"Not me, Pip. Ah does not take no rum-kind at all."

Pip nodded his head wisely and sipped at the spoon. He beamed, smacking his lips with approval. "Yuh da', Caspar, was be de overseer when he was sixteen an' done return from England wid Mas Carlton. He an' Ella done run dis plantation widou' no trouble." Pip chuckled.

"De Bon'massa don' have no cause lash anyone at all. He done t'ink de slaves just love him too bad. He don' know it was de fear ob Ella an' her obeah spells dat keep de niggers peaceful!"

Pip stared down at Brett as he stretched out on the bench basking in the glow of admiration from the

57

kitchen girl. Pip was pleased with Brett. He was a good boy. He loved Ella, who was his grandmother, and he was obedient and serious.

Pip had been house boy at Roxborough for nearly twenty years, from the days when Carlton's father was alive. In all his time at Roxborough, he had never known any slave with Brett's respect and willingness. Pip felt like a father to the boy.

"Yo' ain't got nothing to do, Brett, while yo' does be waitin' fuh Mas Carlton?"

Brett turned his wide eyes on Pip with amusement. He was fond of the man, even though he was the typical house slave with his fawning manners and servile smile.

"Dere does be one t'ing ah could do, Pip," said Brett mischievously. "Dat wench dere holding de stick. Reckon ah does have de nex' cocoa stick fuh her to grate right now!" Brett clutched himself, laughing when he saw the shocked expression on Pip's stolid face.

The girl at the table colored several shades darker and bent her head away from Brett's gaze.

"What de joke, Brett?" snapped Ella striding into the kitchen. "What, gal, yo' ain' made de cocoa tea, yet?" Ella slapped the girl on the cheek. "Yo' does be disruptin' mah kitchin again, boy?"

"No, ma'am." Brett looked serious. "Ah does be tired waitin' fuh Mas Carlton."

"He does be in his wife's chamber," muttered Ella. "Dat *beké* wench, she really loves Mas Carlton." She shook her head sadly.

Pip placed his arm around her shoulder. "She ain' got her no whelp, though, Ella." He tried to console her.

"Yo' does think Mas Carlton some kind of breeding nigger like de bucks, dem in de barracoons!" Ella snapped, twisting out of his grasp.

Brett raised his eyebrows, wondering what had caused Ella's fit of pique. The girl with the cocoa stick glanced at him again. He stared at her thoughtfully. It was about time, Brett mused, that Mas Carlton gave him a wench to breed with.

The sound of Carlton's boots as he stomped across the floorboards above their heads echoed down to the kitchen. Ella jerked her head at Brett, but he was already on his feet and trotting out of the kitchen into the courtyard. Ella smiled at Pip.

"Ah does know," Pip said. "Brett ain't a boy no more, Ella. Soon he does be de boss of all of us. Mas Carlton gon' make him de overseer!"

"Overseer!" Ella drew up her proud body, her back as straight as a deal board. She regarded Pip with disdain. "Brett ain't gon' be jes' de overseer alone, Pip. One day Brett gon' be de Bon'massa, self!"

Pip said nothing. There were certain questions a man never asked. Ella was an obeah woman feared by the slaves. She had her ways of making things come true. He gazed through the open door out into the courtyard. Mas Carlton had his arm around Brett's shoulder, chatting confidentially with him as they walked toward the stable.

Carlton had never felt closer to Brett than he did that day. Perhaps it had been Milly's loving that morning which had sweetened his mood. He was sure that he had at last planted a healthy seed in his wife which would grow into a son. Somehow, Carlton sensed that his heir had been conceived that morning. The feeling made him warm toward Brett and the boy responded eagerly.

Together they rode through the cane-pieces. Slaves were creeping across the soil digging holes for the new cane. Drivers lurked behind them to lash out at any slave who dropped out of line and disturbed the rhythm of the gang. The Roxborough slaves and their

59

drivers were experienced workers. Rarely was it necessary for a driver to lash his team. The crack of the whip above an idler's head was enough to make a slave move faster.

Carlton rode with Brett along the trails which led through the woods to the plantation boundaries, pointing out the imaginary line which divided Roxborough from the free land cultivated by the slaves up in the heights. In the depths of the forest with the giant saman trees towering above them, Brett marveled at the determination which had led to the creation of Roxborough.

"My father bought several estates from the French," Carlton explained. "It was against the law for one man to own so much land, but the French wanted to leave Dominica. Old Hayes bought the land and the slaves. He worked this land with his own bare hands, Brett, alongside the slaves."

"Did he start the slave breeding?" Brett asked as they descended the hill path down to the nursery.

"No," said Carlton. "That was my idea. Like other plantations, we used to buy our slaves from the ships that brought them over from Africa. Captain Loring, he was your mother's father, told us how the British were planning to stop the slave trade. My da' gave me some colts and fillies and told me to breed my own niggers.

"The Roxborough herd began then." Carlton halted his horse, letting Brett ride up beside him. They were at the fence outside the nursery. Young Negroes of all shapes and shades were frolicking in the acre of grass known as the Paddock. The older males and females squatted in the shadows of the flamboyant trees, while on the veranda of the nursery itself, slave women bounced babies on their knees.

"You are looking at the future of the Caribbean, Brett." Carlton pointed at the children romping in the grass. "Crops, be it sugar or coffee, are vital to the economy of these islands. Without slaves, no planter can grow sugar and coffee. Slaves are no longer shipped over from Africa, so the planters buy slaves from Roxborough. These are all Bondmaster breed niggers, Brett, the finest slaves money can buy."

Carlton's pride communicated itself to Brett. He had spent the first five years of his life penned in the Paddock. He, too, was a Bondmaster breed.

"Don't think those niggerlings just get born by accident, Brett." Carlton swung off his horse and tied the reins around a post in the bamboo fence. Brett did likewise, securing his pony beside Carlton's.

"First you have to pick a healthy wench, then find a first-class buck to cross her with. I have ledgers in the house with the pedigree of every slave at Roxborough. That way I can breed a Congo nigger with an Ibo. The whelp will be an ugly scamp, but he'll have a beautiful body with strong muscles and quiet ways, the ideal field slave. A Fulani wench with a reddish skin coupled with a Pawpaw buck can produce a good house slave. A nigger who works in a white man's house must be better-looking than a Congo monkey."

Brett learned with fascination that the whites controlled a slave's destiny even before he was born.

"Not one of the bucks here can understand why they can't mount any wench they please," Carlton snapped. "They think if they sire a whelp, the Bondmaster will be happy and give them a gold piece.

"Of course," grinned Carlton seeing Brett's interest, "I could sell any nigger whelp, but that's not the real Bondmaster breed, is it?"

"Am I the real breed, Mas Carlton?"

Carlton glanced at Brett, suspecting mockery. The boy's face was intense. Carlton sighed. "Your mother was a white whore, Brett. Your father had the best

61

nigger blood there is, Royal Watutsi, which he got from Ella. Her mother came from Africa. The Watutsis are the aristocracy of Negroes."

Carlton grinned as he watched Brett pull his shoulders back and stand proudly beside him. Children were crowding around them, shouting and jumping, eager to play. Brett brushed them aside carelessly and followed Carlton onto the veranda.

A young woman stood up quickly as Carlton approached. She handed the baby she was holding to an old crone who sat beside her. The woman's eyes eagerly sought Carlton's. She was barely twenty, tall and light-skinned. Her long black hair fell casually across her shoulders.

"Mas Carlton," she murmured politely.

"Miranda." Carlton kissed the woman briefly on her cheek. As they stood together, the resemblance Miranda had to Carlton was striking. He was her father, and the father of her child.

"How's Quentin?"

Miranda shrugged. "De chil' ain' strong, Mas Carlton!"

"Best thing is to leave him in the bush for the wild hogs to get him."

Miranda tensed, glancing quickly at Carlton. She pulled at her breast under her ill-fitting osnaburg shift. Under his stern gaze, her eyes lowered without protest.

Carlton chuckled loudly, clasping her around her shoulders and pulling her close to him. "Do you think I would do that to our son, Miranda? Who knows, he might grow up to sell for a small fortune!"

Miranda raised her face and smiled at him. Brett grinned with relief.

"I'm going to Trinidad soon, Miranda. I want to choose some bucks and wenches to sell there. Call your older whelps for me to inspect."

Miranda had been put in charge of the nursery when Carlton had brought his wife back to Roxborough. She kept a sharp eye on the youngsters. They stayed in the Paddock until they were assigned to the gangs to learn their work, sold to passing slave dealers, or set up as breeders.

The nursery had its own confining room and from the time a whelp was born until it was sent out to the gangs, it lived in the Paddock area. Care of all the babies was done by wet nurses, so a whelp never knew its real mother. In a good year, by rotating his breeding wenches and their studs, Carlton expected to have a new whelp in the nursery every week.

Brett watched as Miranda clapped her hands and beckoned the boys who were lounging under the flamboyant trees.

"Smart, Dale, Pompey, Lambert, York, and Winter," Miranda called.

The boys shifted uneasily, glancing from Miranda to the Bondmaster. Lambert rose first and trotted across the Paddock, followed by the others. Brett knew them all; he had grown up with them. He smiled at them, but each one averted his eyes and shuffled nervously as they stood below the veranda.

Carlton sniffed. "This is your best, Miranda? What's their ages?"

"Some have fourteen years, Mas Carlton. They work in the nursery gang already."

"Do you, my boys?" Carlton sounded avuncular. He moved off the veranda and eased himself down to sit on the top step. He gestured for the boys to form a semicircle around him. Brett, who understood from his gestures what he wanted, moved them forward. Carlton's eyes were level with the boys' faces.

Carlton gazed slowly in turn at each youth. "You see, Brett." He spoke conversationally as though the boys could not hear him. "Observe how some hang their heads, but others return my gaze."

Brett frowned.

"I'm telling you this, Brett, so you know how to pick a breeding nigger. You want one with spirit, not one who is likely to be idle and shifty."

The youths were clothed in the blue osnaburg short trousers which was the uniform of a male slave. The coarse linen was faded and worn from constant beating in the river. One boy's shorts were ripped so it resembled a loin cloth. His sex protruded from a tear in the front.

"What's your name, boy?" Carlton smiled.

"Ah does be Dale, sah!"

"Good," said Carlton. "See how quickly he answered, and correctly, too. Brett, we are looking for two niggers to take to Trinidad. Who would you choose?"

Brett stroked his chin thoughtfully, looking from Carlton to the boys grouped around him. He could feel their eyes watching them. Dale's eyebrows danced up and down in an effort to attract his attention. Brett realized the word would spread around the plantation that the Bondmaster asked him to chose slaves to be sold. His prestige would soar if he made the right decision. Suddenly he had an idea.

"I know who I would not sell, sir."

"Yes?" Carlton was intrigued.

"I would not sell the breeders, sir."

"Fine!" Carlton clapped his hand on his knee with pleasure. "A capital approach. Now," Carlton leaned forward toward Brett. "Do you know how to tell who is a breeder and who ain't?"

"Inspect them, sir?"

"Oy oy oy!" Carlton raised his head and grinned at Miranda, who was standing on the veranda behind him. "The boy knows everything. Go on!"

Brett faltered. He glanced at the old crones sucking their teeth as they bounced babies and watched him from the veranda. Brett realized he was being tested. In public, so all the slaves would know, Carlton was giving Brett the opportunity of proving he was part of the Bondmaster, not part of the slaves themselves.

If he did the Bondmaster's bidding efficiently, his influence and position at Roxborough would be secure. On the other hand, he could refuse so the slaves would know he was sympathetic to them, although he no longer lived in the Paddock. He pursed his lips.

Miranda smiled at him encouragingly. He turned back to face the youths.

"Wha' fuh yo' does all be standin' dere wid yuh mouths open like crab holes!" he shouted. "Drop yuh pants to de groun'. Fast, now!"

The youths stared at Brett in surprise. Lambert shrugged his shoulders and pulled off his shorts, stepping out of them swiftly. The others followed his example.

Confronted by the six naked boys, Brett scratched his head uncomfortably. He looked from one to the other. The boys were different shades, ranging from the black hue of Dale to the lighter-brown-skinned Lambert. Their *tulis* hung limply in front of them.

Brett glanced at Carlton. He was stroking the small stock whip in his hand with apparent boredom.

"Yo', boy," cried Brett quickly, pointing at the youth at the end of the line. "Stand back. An' yo' as well. An' yo'." he added, indicating another. He turned to Carlton. "These three—Dale, Lambert and Winter—does be breeders, Mas Carlton."

Carlton tugged at his chin, his eyes twinkling. "Bless my soul, Brett. How do you know?"

"I can see, sir."

"Oh!" Carlton chuckled. "The more inches, the more whelps, eh? Is that your theory, boy? Brett, you must inspect them thoroughly. Come here!" Carlton beckoned Lambert, who stepped forward smartly and stood in front of him.

Carlton gripped the boy's penis with his left hand and passed his right hand behind the boy. He slipped his hand between the boy's buttocks and deftly thrust his finger into the slave's anus. "See the prick dancing!" he exclaimed gleefully.

Lambert groaned, unable to prevent the stiffening Carlton's warm hand was causing.

"The grain, Brett," said Carlton, bouncing Lambert's testicles. "If it is large and well formed, the buck will produce the sap to breed whelps. Niggers with small grains ain't breeders."

Carlton released Lambert. The slave clutched himself and dropped back with the others.

"If you want those three for breeders, that's fine, Brett. I'll sell the others in Trinidad. Now let's see the wenches."

Chapter 7

Carlton strolled through the nursery barracks. It was a long open room, its floor covered with wooden trays. In each tray there was a naked niggerling, some sleeping, some kicking their legs and bawling. They were attended by elderly slaves who were no longer useful for plantation work or breeding.

"The whelps look good, Nana," said Carlton to

one of the slaves, an old woman with a face like a shriveled prune.

"Yassa!" wheezed the crone, her lips spreading in a toothless grin. She stuck a pipe in her mouth and puffed out smoke with pride. "Dey does be a bonny crop dis year, sah!" She cackled obscenely.

Carlton nodded his head in agreement. "It's true, Brett," he said pointing at different babies. "See, we have them from that small black pudding there, to that plump suckling pig yonder." He strode down the row of trays with Brett at his heels.

"It's a damn pity they take so long to mature, Brett. No animal takes as long as a Negro. He must be at least twelve before he is fit for a full day's work. That's twelve years feeding to be covered when I sell a nigger, plus my profit."

Carlton looked through the open shutters at a group of naked youngsters playing in the Paddock. "If we lose any through disease, Brett, that increases my production costs." He sighed.

"Breeding niggers is not an easy business, I can tell you. Wenches did not want to have children when I began. Up to now, I have to pay them bounties—a bolt of cloth for every whelp. A wench who gets me six whelps, I let her off hard labor for life. They are are queen bees of Roxborough!" He chuckled, clapping Brett on his back. "Come, boy, let's see what wenches Miranda has found."

There were five girls lined up in front of the veranda. Carlton glanced at them casually before squatting on the top step. Brett paused behind him, his throat tightening. He knew the girls as Phibba, Baddu, Hersey, Melia, and Empress. They were all friends he had played with as a young boy. He loathed what was coming.

"Five fine virgins, what!" Carlton waved Brett to step around in front of him. "Now what do you do?"

Brett decided it would be sensible to pretend he was as unaffected by the wenches as Carlton seemed to be. "Step ou' yuh shifts!" he shouted to the girls. They gaped at him blankly.

"Do as Massa Brett does say!" snapped Miranda.

Brett looked at her gratefully.

Sulkily, the five wenches removed their osnaburg dresses and stood naked in front of Carlton. He licked his lips.

Feeling the confusion mounting within him, Brett tried to assess each girl. Hersey and Phibba were small-breasted and too young for breeding. He told them to stand back. Phibba had a lithe, dark brown body with limbs which seemed designed to entwine around a man's waist. Brett squeezed his legs together uncomfortably.

Empress was staring with dark eyes that challenged him. Her proud head was crowned with hair laid across it in African-style braids. She had pure Negro features and stood with her arms on her lips, unashamed at exposing her beautiful body in front of him.

Brett coughed as he felt his loins stirring. Melia smiled demurely as though trying to encourage him. She was the lightest-skinned of the five, the color of brandy. Brett wondered if she had white blood in her. He sniggered. He would wipe that doting smile off her face.

"Come!" he said, squatting on his haunches as the girl walked over to stand in front of him. He placed his hands on either side of her hips the way he had seen Carlton do it. "She is wide-hipped, sir!" he said.

"Aye, boy, so she is. Fine conny on her, what!"

"Yes, sir."

"Pass her here, boy." Carlton held out his hands for Melia to step up to him. "Watch us, boy."

With deliberation, Carlton squeezed Melia's young

breasts. They were firm to the touch. He ran his fingers swiftly around the nipples, noting Melia's instant reaction. He slid his hands down her slender waist and placed his right hand on her crotch.

"Use your middle finger, boy," he croaked. Before Melia could resist, Carlton plunged his hand deep in between her legs, probing with his outstretched finger. His eyes closed. "Fine wench," he murmured, gasping.

"Check that black one, Brett. Let's see how you handle a wench."

"Empress! Come here." Brett dared not stand up. "In front of me."

The girl stared down at him haughtily. Brett gripped her hip with his left hand and placed his right hand on the tight whorls of black hair at the entrance to her crotch.

"Dig it in, boy!" Carlton chuckled. "The thing ain't going to bite you."

Brett jammed his fist between the girl's legs and jabbed his finger into her. Empress screamed, stumbling backwards in her panic. She grasped Brett's head to stop herself from falling. He toppled over with her and sprawled across her naked body.

"Oy, oy, oy! Miranda! See how the boy is hot!" Carlton reached over, grabbed Brett by his breeches, and yanked him to his feet. He patted his bottom affectionately and then paused in amazement. He had caught sight of Brett's breeches bulging out in front of him. He grasped Brett before the boy could protect himself.

Brett blushed deeply, but Carlton roared with laughter. "Miranda! See this! The young buck wants to breed a whelp himself." He released Brett. The boy staggered back clutching his hands over his crotch.

"Don't be ashamed of a hard prick, Brett. That's

currency for the Roxborough coffers. You think you could sire me a whelp?"

Brett lowered his eyes, conscious of the girls around him. He nodded his head with embarrassment.

"Of course you could. That Empress might be the wench to give you, Brett. You can wash the blacka-moor white, boy. A light-skinned whelp would be a nice fancy to sell as a house slave."

Carlton looked at the girls grouped around him. "We'll keep these two you picked out, Brett, and I'll sell the others. Melia can breed with that Lambert buck. Do you think you can handle Empress? She is a fine filly; built like a plow horse."

Brett stole a glance at Empress. She was watching him with a haughty grimace as though trying to make him feel small. "If she can take me, sir!"

"Whoa!" Carlton guffawed, standing up and pulling Miranda over to him. "What do you think of young Brett's pretentions, eh, Miranda?"

Miranda appraised Brett. She had liked him since she first saw him, some six years before when Carlton brought her back to the plantation. He had grown fast. He was no longer the wide-eyed child, eager to please. There was determination about his eyes, as though he was aware that he had a destiny to fulfill and he was preparing himself for it. Even his smile, when it lit up his normally serious face, seemed to be carefully measured.

"He does be a very proud young man."

"Aye," said Carlton, "but he is a slave, for all that. Take him in hand, Miranda. Shape him up. Show him what to do. I'll put him to stud with Empress when you say he's ready."

Miranda's heart soared. As Mas Carlton's mistress and daughter, she had not dared to take a buck for herself in case Carlton found out.

Brett was her nephew. He was a buck she would willingly teach.

Milly watched Carlton stride across the cobblestones of the yard in front of the house. Each day, while she waited for him to come for his dinner, she tried to judge his mood. When it was crop time, his manner was often irritable if he had been irked by the slothfulness of the slaves grinding the cane. Carlton preferred slave rearing as a more profitable crop, but Milly liked it better for the time it gave him to spend with her.

Carlton's walk was jaunty this afternoon, which Milly hoped was a sign of his good humor. His full shirt fluttered open in the breeze, exposing his hard muscular chest to the sun. His breeches hugged his sinewy legs, accentuating his manliness. He never wore a hat, which had allowed the sun to bleach his thinning gold locks to silver. He reached the steps, glanced up at Milly waiting at the top, and ran up the steps two at a time.

Ella, who was watching Carlton's progress across the yard from the stables, clucked brusquely at the slaves in the kitchen. "Pip, Mas Carlton done return. Upstairs now, an' see what he does want."

"Ella, why de fuss? Miss Milly does be dere to attend he."

"Yo' want she do yuh job, nigger!" Ella's eyes blazed. "Pip, how yo' think we does know what dey does be sayin' if we not dere listening. Something does be in de air. Ah does feel it in me bones."

Pip shot a glance at Ella and scowled. The old cook was usually right. "Yo' know, Ella," he said, walking toward the back door and pausing at the foot of the stairs. "All de cooks ah ever done see does be fat like a butter barrel. Yo' does be thin like a snake. Sly like one, too!"

He dashed up the stairs as Ella picked up an orange from the basket on the table and threw it at him.

Ella scowled at the two girls in the kitchen. "Lucy, put de callaloo on de fire. Pallis, spread butter on de ground provision." She cast her eye over the tureens which were set out on the long table ready to be carried upstairs as soon as Miss Milly rang the bell.

When she was satisfied everything was prepared, Ella returned to the front door and leaned out over the closed lower half, watching the slaves drift down to the quarters from the fields.

She answered their greetings casually. All the slaves knew her and respected her for her powers. Since Miss Milly had arrived at Roxborough, her influence had not lessened, although she no longer enjoyed the confidence of Carlton the way she did before. In the old days before he married Milly, Carlton spent his evenings telling her his plans. Now she had to send Pip to eavesdrop. She raised her head, hoping that Pip would listen carefully.

"Thank you, Pip, you can go downstairs now." Milly took the tray of punch which Pip proffered her. She turned her back on him to take the tray over to Carlton.

"Downstairs, mistress?" Pip gaped.

"Yes, yes. We don't need you here, Pip. I'll ring the bell when we are ready for dinner." Milly sensed Pip's hesitation. She ran her eye quickly up and down the slave's body. His livery was tidy, and his black breeches tucked into his white socks were clean. He wore a freshly laundered silk shirt and a bright red sash around his waist. His heavy face, black like a mask, was creased with concern.

"What is wrong, Pip?"

"Nothing, mistress. Ah does stay an' mix de nex' punch, Miss."

"Mas Carlton does not have the first one yet, Pip.

You may go." She swirled away from the dresser, leaving Pip gawking miserably. He picked up a glass and began to dust it.

"Your punch, Carlton!" Milly bent down to kiss her husband on the cheek.

"And you?" Carlton smiled gratefully.

"I have tamarind juice, Carlton." She settled in the chair beside his. "We have a splendid dinner. The yard boy collected crabs last night. They were simply swarming everywhere. I sent for some dasheen leaves and ochroes from the provision grounds and we've made a callaloo for you." She leaned forward. "There is wild pigeon, too, and slices of that new coarse food you've been growing. You know, the breadfruit."

Carlton's eyes showed his appreciation. He sipped at his punch quickly and raised his feet onto the balcony rail. He nodded with contentment. "You are good to me, Milly."

"That's what a wife is for, Carlton."

There was a crash from the dining room. Milly was on her feet instantly. She saw Pip staring at the broken glass which lay at his feet. Milly turned to Carlton. "Don't disturb yourself. I'll deal with it."

Carlton sighed. He had no intention of moving, anyway. He listened as his wife scolded Pip and the slave replied with the usual answer. "It wasn't mah fault, miss!"

It never was a nigger's fault, Carlton mused. The niggers always blamed some unknown force which caused them to make mistakes, break things, sleep late, or cause any calamity. It wasn't my fault! If a slave ever realized he had in his hands the power to mold his own destiny, to accept responsibility for everything that happened to him, Carlton's position as a slave owner would be perilous indeed. To hear a slave mutter shamefully "It wasn't my fault" was reassuring.

"He's gone," said Milly, returning to the balcony. The sun had spent itself and was cowering behind clouds which hung over the sea where soon it would set. The afternoon stickiness was being bounced away by the breeze bounding down the valley, shaking the tops of the coconut trees and fanning out the bamboo branches by the river.

"Pip seems edgy tonight." Milly sipped at her juice.

"The house slaves are worried," muttered Carlton casually.

"Whatever for?"

"They hate change. They can't understand it. They wonder how it will affect them."

"What change?" Milly put down her glass and turned away from the scenery to look at Carlton.

"They sense things, Milly. Before we do. A good house slave is better than a guard dog or a spy. Just by their attitude I can tell if something is wrong on the plantation." He chuckled, standing up and walking to the end of the balcony.

"My old father could tell by his nose. He stood here every night sniffing the smells from the slave quarters. He could tell if the niggers were out in the dark or if they had shuttered up their shacks and gone to bed." Carlton sniffed, shrugged his shoulders, and walked the length of the gallery to his seat.

"If they were sitting outside, they were fretting over something. He would get ready for trouble by stringing up a few niggers by their ankles and lashing them!" Carlton grinned as he sat down.

Milly shuddered. "It sounds horrible. I've never seen you do that."

"I don't have to. My drivers keep order in the field. The slaves are content. I give them enough food, and they have their own provision gardens. They even sell their produce in the village on Sundays so they

74

can earn some money to buy baubles and knick-knacks."

Carlton put his feet up on the rail. "It's a regular life. That is why they are terrified of any change."

"You mean Pip breaking that glass?"

"Yes. Ella is an obeah woman, Milly. She knows the spirits. Sometimes I think she knows more about me than I know myself. Somehow she knows what I am planning. She must have told Pip to listen to us talk. That's why he was nervous."

"What are you planning, Carlton?" Milly frowned. It had taken her considerable time to adjust to life on this isolated plantation after the civilization and security of town life. She could not share her husband's belief in Ella's powers: it sounded so old-fashioned to her.

"When we go to Trinidad, Milly, we may stay a few weeks. I don't want to leave the plantation without a white man here."

"You can get an overseer, can't you?"

"I will have to do that, Milly. I don't like it, though."

"Why not? All the other plantations have overseers."

"Yes. I should have one here, according to law. Dam'me, with two hundred niggers, I am supposed to have about ten whites living here. It's preposterous!"

"But you will need an overseer if we are going away."

"I know. It worries me, and I think that's what is worrying Ella, too. I've never known a white overseer with a lick of sense. It's the lick of the whip they think with. The slaves don't belong to them, you see. An overseer don't care how many niggers he lashes to death."

"Surely you can find someone who'll look after the

75

slaves properly. Someone with your own interests at heart."

Carlton frowned. "Like who, for instance?"

"What about a relative? Someone with family connections who would have an interest in Roxborough."

"Family? I don't have any family." Carlton pulled his feet off the railing and sat up in his chair to look at his wife.

"Yes, you do, Carlton. There's someone we haven't seen since we were married. He would be ideal."

Carlton's eyes narrowed, a chill hand of apprehension gripping his heart. "Who's that?" he asked with reluctance.

Milly smiled warmly. "Who else, dear, but my brother, Dyce?"

Chapter 8

"No."

"Yes, yes."

"No!" Miranda was emphatic. She pulled away from him. "Yo' ain't no cock, chasin' a hen, Brett," she said. "Dis does be de t'ing dat yo' got to do slow."

Brett scowled. He was lying in the grass behind the nursery. He was naked. Miranda lay beside him, her shift bunched up around her waist, her naked thighs gleaming in the moonlight. He reached for her again, sliding one arm under her neck.

Miranda turned her head toward him. "Yo' does be de cutest little buck ah ever did see!" she drawled.

"Yo' like quicksilver." She ran her fingers down his chest, over his flat stomach, and onto his sex. "Dis de t'ing dat give de pleasure, Brett. When yo' does put it in de pot, stir de honey widou' de hurry."

"Ah does know what to do, Miranda!"

"Of co'se," she breathed into his ear, "an' yo' does do it good." She rolled onto her back, clutching Brett around his waist so he rolled over on top of her. She guided him with her fingers. "Dere ain't no driver cracking he whip over yuh backside, Brett," she whispered, fingering his bottom. "Yo' does be de driver!"

Miranda lifted her legs, linking her ankles around Brett's slim body. She reached down and fondled his tiny grain as he bucked on top of her. The moon was poised overhead, its brilliant glow stealing through the fronds of the coconut trees and dappling Brett's back with gray shadows.

His head was on Miranda's chest. His teeth were biting through her shift, nipping her flesh. He stirred Miranda. She arched her waist in response, churning her limbs and clawing at his back. His slender body pulsed life into her, and she flowed with a sudden passion which made her gasp.

Brett prepared to roll off.

"No!" She gripped his tousled hair with her hand. "Stay!" she panted. "Leave me slowly. It does be sweeter so."

Brett raised his eyes to look at Miranda's face. Her own eyes were closed in happiness. He realized then that she had enjoyed it as much as he. He frowned. It had not occurred to him before that wenches derived as much pleasure from rutting as bucks did.

Slowly, as Miranda suggested, he eased himself off. He kissed her cheek.

The impatient *crack-crack* of crickets crying in the plantain walk broke into his thoughts. They were lying

77

in a clearing in the undergrowth beyond the bamboo fence surrounding the nursery. It was uncomfortable.

"Ah gon' tell Mas Carlton to give me de key fuh de overseer's cabin," Brett said, sitting up. "We does be rutting like niggers here."

Miranda smiled wisely. "Yo' think Mas Carlton gon' give yo' dat?"

"He done say he gon' make me de overseer."

"Mas Carlton does say plenty things, Brett. He done tell me our child Quentin gon' be free, but ah ain't see it yet."

"Yo' want we to come here in de bush every time?" challenged Brett. "De breeding niggers demselves does have a pallet in de quarters. How yo' gon' learn me 'bout wenches 'less we does have a schoolroom?"

Miranda giggled. "Yo' don' need no learnin', Brett." She reached across and laid her hand on his hard stomach. "Yo' does be a man already." She lapsed into silence, curling his sparse pubic hairs around her finger.

The gigantic fern trees spreading over their heads rustled as the night breeze twisted the leaves. Miranda felt protected lying in that cocoon of night with Brett, even though he was so young. Perhaps it was his white skin which gave him an air of authority. He was lying back with his hands clasped behind his head, watching her as she played with him.

"Brett?" she whispered.

"Huh?"

"Brett, what yo' does be thinking?" She tugged at his hair, pulling a strand from his body. He winced.

"Why yo' ax dat?" Brett gripped Miranda's waist.

"Yo' don' act like a young buck somehow, Brett. Yo' is always tensed up 'bout something."

"If yo' telling me ah does have more sense dan a nigger, yo' does be correct, Miranda."

"Ah mean even when yo' was be doing it to me,

Brett, yuh heart don't give nothin' away. Yo' work on me like it is trainin' yo' does be doin'."

"Come, Miranda, let's walk." Brett released her waist and stood up. His naked torso was outlined briefly in the bright moonlight. Miranda sighed at the sight of his compact young body, muscles already hard and firm. His *tuli* stood out in front of him, his grain bouncing against his solid thighs.

Brett reached down for his breeches. He pulled them on quickly and picked up his shirt, which he slung over his left shoulder, looping his thumb in the collar to hold it in place. He began to walk without waiting to see if Miranda was following.

Miranda frowned, scrambling quickly to her feet. She brushed her petticoat down over her thighs, shaking out the twigs which had caught in it. "He does be right," she thought. "Mas Carlton must give us a cabin." She pushed her way through the trees and ran to catch up with him.

Brett was standing at the edge of the trail which led up the hill to the house. The royal palm trees which lined the road towered above his head. Mas Carlton, he had heard, planted those trees himself when he was Brett's age.

"Wha' yo' watchin'?"

"De *cou*," he said shrugging his shoulders. "See how de moon shines on de shingles of de roof. Ah don't like de moon."

"Why not, Brett? It does make de night day."

"Oh, ah does like de night, Miranda. Ah can move t'rough de plantation an' nobody does see me. De moon does want to betray me sometimes."

Miranda slipped her arm under his, trying to understand.

"Ah does see things at night, Miranda. When all de slaves does be shut up in de *ajoupas* in de quarters,

79

ah does prowl through de shadows an' listen to dem. Dat's what Caspar done do."

"Ah never knew Caspar, Brett. He was mah brother, but he died before Mas Carlton brought me here."

"Dere was a moon de night dey hung Caspar, Miranda." Brett sought her eyes in the moonlight, staring into them. "Ah done see de t'ree men who beat him. One of dem, de one dey call Fletcher, rode off with Miss Laura. De other two hung Caspar from de flamboyant tree by de overseer's cabin. Ah gon' kill dem white men one day."

Miranda squeezed Brett's arm in surprise. "Yo' can't do dat!"

"Why not?"

"How yo' gon' kill a white man?"

"Dat de easiest t'ing." Brett turned his head away, but she raised her hand to his cheek and slowly turned him back to her.

Miranda gasped. "Ah does see de resolve in yuh eyes, Brett. Yuh time will come."

For the first time that night, Brett smiled. His face softened as his lips curled. He let his arm slide around Miranda's waist. "I'm sorry if I disappointed you tonight," he said dropping the slave tongue to speak in English. "Sometimes, I don't know what I am."

"How yo' mean?" She snuggled closer to him as he led her up the path.

"My mother was a white whore and my father was a half-breed nigger. My grandfather owns me. So I must be a slave. But am I a slave like those niggers who work bent double in the cane fields all day?"

"Yo' does be a slave like me," said Miranda softly. "Mas Carlton controls us so he puts us in positions that make us better dan de niggers. He done give me de nursery and de whelps. He gon' give yo' de overseer when yo' does be more old."

Brett spat angrily on the ground. "I don't want Mas Carlton's privileges." He glared at Miranda. "Don't you see, I'm a man without Mas Carlton!"

Miranda slipped out of his grasp. "Yo' does be like one spoilt nigger when yo' take on so!" she sneered. "Mas Carlton loves yo'. He wants yo' to be de overseer. But yo' does be vex' jus' like de field slave who believes Mas Carlton does hate him because de drivers lash he fuh idlin'."

Brett shook his head slowly. "It's not that, Miranda. You see, I must prove I am a man, then Mas Carlton will believe in me. I am his creation now, just like your whelp, Quentin. He sired you, then he sired your child. I don't want everything because Mas Carlton commands that I have this or do that! I have to do something for myself!"

Miranda sniffed. She was completely devoted to Carlton and resented criticism of him. It was tantamount to insurrection as far as she was concerned. "What will yo' do?" she demanded sarcastically.

"Oh, Miranda!" scolded Brett when he noticed her tone. "I've told you. I'm going to kill the men who murdered Caspar." He stared up at the house, his voice steady.

"Yo don' know who dey does be!" Miranda snorted. She was not as confident as she felt. Brett's eyes had a sheen of conviction that frightened her. She gripped his arm. "Walk me back to de nursery, Brett."

"I saw one of them at Mas Carlton's wedding, Miranda," Brett replied softly, turning onto the path back to the paddock. "His name is Dyce Dobbs. He is Miss Milly's brother."

"Your brother is not coming here, and that's final!"

Carlton banged his empty glass down on the arm of his chair. He and Milly had been arguing throughout dinner about finding an overseer for the plantation. Carlton had slurped his soup hurriedly, stabbed without interest at the wild pigeon so lovingly prepared by Milly, and growled his way back to his seat on the balcony.

"Pip!" he bellowed, ignoring Milly as she slipped into the seat beside him. He rapped on the floor of the balcony with the heel of his boot.

"Yassa!" The answering shout came quickly as Pip scurried up the back stairs. Ella, regarding the uneaten food on the plate Pip had carried down to the kitchen, smiled. The slaves understood Mas Carlton when his voice was edged with anger. They got too lazy when all was quiet. If her master had a problem, thought Ella, he might ask her to help solve it.

"What do you want, Carlton?" Milly demanded.

"I want a slave with a civil tongue in his head to bring me a decanter of old rum! I don't want any more of your endless nagging!"

"I didn't nag you, Carlton. I don't see why you can't even invite my brother here. You will like him much better when you know him properly. He would be very good discipline for the slaves."

"What does that mean?" Carlton glared at Milly.

"What yo' does wan', sah?" Pip poked his head around the door of the drawing room, frowning anxiously.

Carlton raised his eyes in relief. "Pip! A decanter of old rum from the cellar."

"De aged rum, sah?" Pip tried not to sound surprised. "Wid de meat an' peppers in it, sah?"

"Exactly, boy. And draw some water from the cooler."

"Yassa!" Pip almost ran through the drawing room and down the back stairs. Mas Carlton had not called for the aged rum for months. The last time was when he heard his friend, Reverend Audain, the privateer, had died in St. Eustatius. It was like the old days before Miss Milly came to Roxborough.

"De aged rum!" Pip said breathlessly to Ella waiting for him at the kitchen door. "De rum wid de peppers!"

Ella gaped at Pip's excitement. "Where's Miss Milly?"

"She does be sitting dere wid he. He sure does be vex' about something."

Ella lifted her head at the sound of Carlton's boots as he stomped across the balcony. His voice drifted down faintly to them in the kitchen.

"Don't you say anything about the way I treat my slaves, Milly." Carlton shook his finger at his wife. "You've only known one side of me since you have been at Roxborough. The sweet side, Milly. But there's a side to me that's ruthless. The niggers know that even if you don't!"

"I don't know why you are getting so excited, Carlton." Milly pouted. "Just because Dyce was drunk at our wedding and brought all his cronies to drink your rum. All he did was throw up over the Governor and pass out."

"Thank God, Pip!" Carlton grabbed the decanter off the silver tray Pip was holding in front of him. He pulled out the glass stopper and dashed the dark rum into a glass. He held back his head and let the fiery liquid drain down his throat. The rum burned his lips, and he could feel it scorching his gullet. He took the glass of water Pip offered him and gulped it down to chase the rum.

"Boy, that's good!" he beamed.

"Thank yo', sah!"

"Leave the decanter, Pip. And tell Miss Ella I want to see her this evening."

Milly's eyes clouded over. It was one thing Carlton deciding to drink his rum, but another when he sent for his slave wench in front of her. Although she could not believe Carlton would still make love to the old cook, Milly was intensely jealous of the black woman's influence over him.

"What do you want to see Ella for?" she demanded.

"Don't start again, Milly!"

"I'm not starting again. I asked a simple question."

"And I'm giving you a simple answer. Woman, leave me in peace!"

"What's happened to you, Carlton? I've never seen you like this before." Milly's shoulder shook with her sobs.

Carlton swallowed uneasily. He pinched his nose and poured a measure of rum into his glass. He sniffed it, savoring the pungent odor before sipping the rum slowly, letting it scour his gums and his throat.

Milly's shoulders still quivered. She raised a dainty hand to her hair and brushed it back behind her ear. "I'm sorry, Carlton," she blabbered. "I did not mean to disturb you."

He glanced at her haughtily, taking a second sip from his glass. He swallowed the rum, feeling himself mellowing under its influence.

"It is not your fault, Milly. Please understand that. There are some things I cannot explain to you, Milly, so don't ask me." He reached out his hand to grasp hers.

"About your brother. If he ever comes here, Milly, there will be trouble I would not be able to control." He held up his hand. "Believe me, Milly. I know."

Milly peered at him through her tear-filled eyes. "All right, Carlton," she sighed. "But what about Ella?"

"Is my little wife jealous of a nigger?" Carlton grinned, pouring another shot of rum in his glass.

"Fie, Milly, have I ever neglected you? I am too aware of my good fortune in having you as my wife to do such a thing." He squeezed her hand soothingly.

"I need Ella's advice, Milly. About the slaves I should sell."

"That's all?" Milly's lips trembled.

"Yes, Milly, that's all."

Chapter 9

Ella slipped quietly out of Carlton's chamber and padded in her bare feet around the balcony of the house. There was at least an hour before the morning conch shell would wail over the plantation to wake the slaves. Ella had time to rake over the dying embers under the grate and start a new fire to heat up a pot of coffee. Carlton liked to have his dish of strong coffee as daybreak seeped over the mountain ridge and the slaves shuffled out to the fields.

Ella hitched up her bosom as she stood on the balcony at the back of the house and stared into the darkness. Last night's moon lingered in the north, bathing the back yard with its pale glow. Ella gripped the railing and stood up straight, trying to read the night and Carlton's concern.

He had taken her quickly, even viciously. When he plunged into her, it was as though he was trying to recapture the atmosphere of their youth together. Each thrust grew more desperate until he collapsed, spent, in her arms. But she knew he was dissatisfied.

He rolled away from her with a sigh and fell asleep quickly, relieved that he had performed his duty.

Ella was puzzled. Why? What was Carlton trying to prove? Ella had been his bed wench for thirty years. She did not need Carlton to mount her to maintain her loyalty to him.

Although Carlton frequently said Negroes did not think like whites, he himself treated them as though they did. She would always be loyal to Carlton, Ella knew, not because he mounted her occasionally or because she was a slave he owned. She was his in the same way that he was hers. There was no way that it could be otherwise.

Ella touched the amulet she wore tied around her upper left arm. It had been given to her by her mother, an obeah woman who had crossed the sea from Africa. She had never opened the plaited reed purse which protected it. It contained grains of soil from the grave of the Grand Obeah of her mother's village. It decreed Ella's status on the plantation as much as the Bondmaster's whip signified his.

If Carlton knew that, he would not have to strain himself to please her with his declining ardor. All he must do was share his thoughts with her so she could influence the slaves to support him. Without her obeah to keep them docile the slaves could follow the maroons, the runaway slaves who lived in the hills in the island's interior.

Ella clenched the railing and glared at the dark. The gulping of the frogs high in the valley and the whistling of the night insects answered her. She sighed heavily. Ella sensed trouble coming to Roxborough, and she did not know how to prevent it.

Joel Puttock was pleased with what he saw as his horse trotted along the trail from Layou Village. The hedgerows were freshly cutlassed, the drain alongside the trail was clear, and even the wheel ruts in the road had been filled in and leveled out. The care of the track indicated industrious niggers working under a stern taskmaster.

Puttock valued hard-working blacks. Give him a gang of willing slaves and he could turn a barren hillside into an orchard. He respected slaves who did their work. With such slaves, Puttock boasted, he could earn any planter a fortune.

A fork in the road led him, Puttock assumed, either to the river on the right, or up to the house on the left. Thick foliage and bamboos obscured his view of the river. Puttock took the left fork, observing the gradual uphill climb of the path. The tangled bush gave way to an avenue lined with royal palm trees. On either side, cane fields stretched as far as the eye could see. At the head of the imposing boulevard, on the crown of the hill dominating the cane-pieces, was Roxborough Hall.

Puttock reined in his horse to contemplate the scene. He had heard so much about the Bondmaster breed of slaves, it was a meaningful moment for him to be gazing at the house of the Bondmaster himself. The fact that the house was singularly unimpressive did not worry him. The plantation itself was immaculately kept. More important were the slaves.

A line of them stretched across the hillside in the blazing sun. Brown like the soil they were hoeing, if it weren't for their steady movement, they would have been invisible. Joel was surprised at the silence. The driver advancing behind the line had his whip curled under his arm. There was no whip crack and slash, no shouts of pain.

Puttock raised his hand to wipe away the sweat trickling down his neck. "It's a damn rare breed of nigger if they're not complaining in this heat," he mused aloud. He jogged his horse to stand in the shade of the trees at the side of the trail. A gang of wenches was walking down the road toward him. They were carrying bed sheets and other pieces of laundry under their arms.

"Good day, massa!" they chorused cheerfully.

Puttock touched his cap in mock politeness at their greeting. The wenches giggled among themselves.

"How de day does be, massa?" said one, bolder than the rest. She grinned from ear to ear under her large squashed nose.

"Tolerable, wench, tolerable," Puttock retorted. "Whose slaves are you?"

His abrupt manner silenced their giggles. He saw their eyes widen and felt the fear with which they now regarded him. He smirked. This job, he was sure, would be easy.

"We does be Roxbruh niggers, sah!" The stout wench seemed to be challenging him. "Yo' does be on Roxbruh land, sah."

Puttock appraised the woman, staring at her under his lowered brows. His fingers tightened around the supplejack he held in his hand. "Indeed?" Puttock spoke between clenched teeth, his voice rumbling at the back of his throat.

Sensing his authority, the woman backed off. "We does be gon' to de river, massa!" the stout one muttered hastily.

Puttock nodded his head as the women waddled away from him. No laughter drifted on the air now. His lip curled in a satisfied snarl of amusement. "Fine slaves!" he snickered. "Gutless and mindless!" He thwacked his horse with the supplejack and galloped up the trail to the house.

Carlton watched Puttock with interest as the man jumped off his horse and handed the reins to Caliste. Puttock appeared to address the stable boy, seemed satisfied with the response, then turned to gaze at the house. Observing Carlton watching him, the man waved genially and strode over to the front step.

Carlton put his age in the late thirties. He was a short man and walked with his legs slightly bowed, rolling from side to side like a sailor. His dark hair was close-cropped, revealing that the man had no eye for fashion. He was wearing a coat and brown trousers, and his boots looked well worn. His face, Carlton noticed as the man drew closer to him, was pockmarked.

His hand grip was firm. "Joel Puttock, sir."

Carlton shook his hand without any unnecessary enthusiasm and indicated the chair beside him on the balcony. Carlton glanced into the drawing room before sitting down himself, to make certain that neither Pip nor Ella was lurking there hoping to overhear the conversation. His wife, he knew, was in her boudoir with her maid, preparing gowns to wear in Trinidad.

Carlton observed with pleasure that Puttock remained standing until he had seated himself. "Well," Carlton began uncertainly, "Mr. Puttock, let me welcome you to Roxborough."

"It is an honor to be here, sir. I've heard about the Bondmaster breed of slaves throughout the Caribbean. I have always wanted to meet their . . . er . . . trainer."

Carlton acknowledged Puttock's compliment with a wry smile. The man's accent intrigued him: he was a Creole. Carlton had not expected that.

"Have you ever had Roxborough slaves under you, Puttock?" asked Carlton, deliberately dropping the "mister."

Puttock noticed the slight, but let it pass. His accent had given him away again. Being born a poor white in the Caribbean was sometimes worse than being born a slave, he thought.

89

"Indeed I have, sir. Splendid blacks, the lot of them."

"That's because I breed them to meet planters' requirements, Puttock. I don't bully them. I believe in firmness, with immediate punishment appropriate to the crime. Sickness, or pretended sickness, is dealt with by my dispensers. Laziness is cured within the slave's gang by the other slaves, who are kept back by their lazy brother. And by the driver's dusting, of course."

"I understand." Puttock's eyes glinted.

"You come here with a good reputation, Puttock. James Macreary, my agent in Trinidad, recommended you as the best overseer in the region."

"I have that reputation, sir. There is not a plantation I have not left in a better state than when I arrived. Niggers are bound to respect me, sir."

Carlton sniffed. "Any man can get respect with a lash, Puttock. I don't like whipping. My slaves are property to sell, Puttock; they are not beasts to be beaten to squeeze profits out of the soil."

Puttock leaned forward to interrupt.

"Let me finish, Puttock," said Carlton, brushing him aside. "A scar on the back of a nigger lowers his price. Of course, we grow sugar here, Puttock. This used to be a major sugar plantation. Slaves are my crop now. I keep up the sugar to absorb the niggers' energy until they are sold." Carlton pursed his lips, eager for a drink. He sat back in his chair.

"You were going to say something?" He raised his eyebrow politely.

"The matter of discipline, sir. It is my *métier*. With respect, sir, if you are away from the plantation, the slaves may be inclined to take advantage of your absence. Were that to happen, would I have your permission to punish the recalcitrant niggers as I think fit? It is the only way I can work, sir."

Carlton frowned. "Providing you give me your word as a gentleman to neither scar, maim, nor kill my slaves, Puttock, then I must let you have a free hand. If they have no fear of you, Puttock, the niggers will please themselves."

Carlton studied Puttock carefully. The man's wrists appeared to be thick under his coat sleeves. His hands were wide, with fat fingers which, bunched together, formed a colossal fist. Puttock was tough, of that there was no doubt. Even without Macreary's recommendation, Carlton would have employed him.

"Puttock, you do understand, I trust, that niggers are my business. They must not be treated in any way which would lower their price."

"Niggers are my business, too, Mr. Carlton," smiled Puttock, his dull gray eyes fixed on Carlton's. "After I have handled them, your niggers will fetch more money, not less, sir."

"Splendid. We will talk terms after dinner. How about some sangaree?" Carlton tapped his boot rapidly on the floor to summon Pip.

"Excuse me, sir, I do not drink." Puttock's face was stern.

Carlton raised his eyebrows in surprise. "What, no rum! You are hardly a Creole, Puttock."

"My mother was a poor white who died in the gutters of Port-of-Spain because of her taste for rum, Mr. Carlton. I never knew my father. He was a seaman on the middle passage, transporting slaves. They killed him."

"Oh, I see." Carlton coughed to hide his embarrassment. "A pipe, then?"

"I do not smoke, sir."

Carlton was puzzled. "Ah," he said breaking into a grin. "I know something you can not refuse. I have many wenches here, Puttock. I will send my housekeeper to round up a selection. You shall take your pick."

"You are very kind." The gray eyes stared at Carlton without expression. "I do find it does not aid discipline to ride a slave wench, sir. She tends to lose respect afterwards, sir. The wench becomes difficult to control. I prefer not to have any favorites where niggers are concerned."

"Humph! Just as you say." Carlton growled uneasily, taking the glass of sangaree from Pip with a sigh of relief. "You wouldn't find it makes any difference here, Puttock. Like I've told you, my fillies and colts are breeders. That's their work, Puttock, to get whelps. Would you care for a glass of tamarind juice, perhaps?"

Puttock accepted, ignoring the note of mockery in Carlton's voice. He gazed out at the palm trees, plantains, and cane fields which stretched to the cliff edge overlooking the sea. In the distance, he could see the inter-island schooners anchored in the river mouth, and the roofs of the casinos and shacks of Layou. It was this little kingdom which Carlton Todd was giving him for three months.

No black would smile at a white man after he had finished with the Bondmaster's niggers, Puttock thought.

A white youth was running across the courtyard, laughing as he chased after a puppy. The youth caught the dog, picked it up, and turned. Joel Puttock leaned forward in his seat and gasped. The boy was beautiful!

Carlton looked at him curiously.

"Your son?" Puttock's voice trembled.

"No!" snapped Carlton, then paused as an idea occurred to him. "But he is my grandson, Puttock. I want him to be your apprentice while I'm away. Teach him how you handle niggers." Carlton spread his hands in front of him expansively. "Educate him!"

Puttock shielded his face with his glass of juice and leered. The boy, as he came trotting up the front steps, stared at him carefully.

"Brett!" Carlton exclaimed. "This is Mr. Puttock. He is going to be the overseer while I am in Trinidad. He will teach you his job."

Brett studied the stranger's face, searching it to see if he looked familiar. The man's blank eyes stared back at him coolly.

Brett's nostrils quivered, then abruptly he bowed his head in greeting.

Chapter 10

Brett sat with Ella in the kitchen. It was night. Carlton and Milly had retired to their chambers. Pip and the other house slaves were already in the quarters under the house. Brett stared moodily at the single lamp Ella had placed on the table where it fluttered grotesque shadows on the stone walls of the kitchen.

Ella's eyes were also fastened on the flame.

"Mas Carlton does leave fuh Trinidad tomorrow, Brett. Mr. Puttock does be in charge den. What he does be like, Brett?" Ella's tired black face creased in concern.

Brett shrugged his shoulders. "I don't know, Ella. He doesn't drink and he doesn't pester the wenches. He's tough and he has a stern voice and a way of looking at the slaves which makes them work."

Ella frowned. It was exactly what she had heard

from the slaves. Usually when a new white man visited the plantation, the bolder slaves would test him to see what liberties they could take. Not with Mr. Puttock. His manner alone had been enough to forestall them.

"Mas Carlton has shown him everything on the plantation. He seemed impressed." Brett pursed his lips doubtfully.

"What's wrong?" Ella turned away from the light to face him.

"He said something about Mas Carlton's slaves having the easiest life of any he had ever seen."

"What Mas Carlton done say to dat?"

"He laughed the way he always does. Then he said that if the niggers did what he required, that was enough for him. Mister Puttock said Mas Carlton should train his field slaves better than that. He said the buyers wanted niggers to work harder than Mas Carlton did, because they have real plantations."

Ella nodded her head slowly, sucking in air between her teeth with a hissing sound.

"Mas Carlton told him to see what he could do."

"Yo' like dat white man, Brett?"

Brett turned his yellow eyes onto Ella, opening them wide in an expression of surprise. "A white man gave me this scar, Ella," he said softly, touching his neck. "And white men killed Caspar."

"He does like yo'."

Brett's eyes narrowed. Ella was always right. He shrugged his shoulders, then rested his chin on his hand to stare at the flame. He considered Ella's remark.

In the two weeks since Puttock had arrived, Brett had spoken to the overseer only when necessary. He had accompanied Mas Carlton as he rode around the plantation with Puttock. He had supervised the opening up of the overseer's cabin and directed the women who cleaned it out so Puttock could live in it. Apart from that, he had done nothing to draw Puttock's attention to himself.

"Of course!" Brett exclaimed suddenly, turning again to Ella. "Mas Carlton told Puttock I am his grandson. He thinks I'm white, you see, not a slave at all. That's why he likes me."

"Maybe." Ella sounded doubtful. "He does be watchin' yo', Brett. He eyes does be on yo' all de time yo' does be wid he. Beware of him, Brett!" Ella's warning echoed in the silence of the kitchen. Outside the closed doors, a rat squealed its life away as a cat pounced on it.

Brett tried to turn his head away from Ella's stare. A chill had descended on the room. He shivered. The lamp flame dipped and almost died, causing Brett to feel he was being enveloped with Ella in a cloak of darkness. The flame recovered and reflected in Ella's eyes as they peered into his.

"Ah does wan' yo' to wear dis, Brett." Ella's voice was husky. She reached inside the bodice of her dress and pulled out a small sachet made of *vetyver* grass.

"What is it?"

Ella glowered at him silently.

Brett shivered again. "I must know," he pleaded.

"It does be soil from de grave of Caspar, an' some blood. It will protec' yo', Brett.'

"Whose blood, Ella?" Brett's voice cracked as he spoke. He knew it was wrong to question the power of obeah.

Ella's lips parted, spreading across her teeth. Her mouth opened. There was silence. Suddenly she uttered a sharp, inhuman cackle which appalled Brett. He tried to move away. Ella had a small silver knife in her hand. She lunged at Brett quickly.

The knife sliced into the flesh above his right breast. He stared into Ella's eyes, flinching, as she made two quick incisions in the shape of a cross. She slapped the fetish onto the cut and held it there as it soaked up blood. Her lips were murmuring silently. From a pot she had on the table in front of her, Ella dipped a handful of paste. She removed the bloodied sachet from Brett's chest and applied the paste to the cut. She smiled reassuringly at him.

"Dis unguent will stop de bleeding, Brett." She threaded the sachet onto a thin leather thong. "Here, bend yuh head forward." She tied the leather lace around his neck. "Wear dis always, Brett, an' yo'll be safe."

"Yes, mam." Brett raised his eyes and nodded his head obediently.

Brett stood at the bottom of the grand steps as the wagon pulled away from the house. Mas Carlton and Miss Milly sat on the front bench with Caliste, the groom, holding the reins. Pallis, Miss Milly's maid, sat in the back of the wagon with the trunks.

The eight slaves they were taking to Trinidad to sell were fastened to the wagon by a light chain linking their ankles. As the wagon rolled forward, the slaves in the coffle broke into a trot. Asaph, the driver, rode behind them, his whip unfurled. Two field slaves jogged behind Asaph's horse. They were to help load the trunks onto the schooner.

Brett wanted to run alongside the wagon all the way to Layou. He was disappointed not to be attending Mas Carlton on the voyage. He bit his lip, remaining motionless on the step. Mas Carlton waved to him. He bowed his head somberly. When he looked up, the carriage was already enveloped in a cloud of dust as it bounced down the hill. Brett was aware of someone watching him.

Raising his head, Brett saw Mr. Puttock leaning over the balcony rail, The man had an odd expression on his face, a dour sneer which Brett supposed was Puttock's way of smiling. Seeing that Brett had observed him, Puttock beckoned to him with his whip. Brett scowled, then quickly ran up the steps.

"Yes, Mr. Puttock?" Brett was determined not to call the overseer "Master."

"Sit down, boy." Puttock gestured to the chair Miss Milly usually sat in. He plonked himself down in Mas Carlton's chair and stared at Brett, who was still standing. "Sit down, boy, I said. You're standing there like a nigger about to shit himself!"

Brett lowered himself onto the edge of Miss Milly's chair. He wondered what Mas Carlton would say if he knew Puttock was in the Bondmaster's chair.

"You look like a bright boy, young Brett," Puttock was saying. The man leaned forward and put out his hand, tapping Brett on his thigh. Brett shifted uneasily, but Puttock kept his hand on his leg.

"Your grandfather has asked me to make you into a good overseer, boy. An overseer demands obedience from his niggers, boy, you understand?"

Brett nodded his head. Puttock's gray eyes were probing his.

"You have to be obedient, too, boy. When I tell you to do something, you must do it. A nigger has a nose for weakness. If a slave sees that you and me ain't pulling well, he could be troublesome. You understand?"

Brett felt Puttock's bony fingers squeezing his thigh like a fetter. He refused to flinch and returned his gaze without blinking.

"You're a strange lad, and no mistake," muttered Puttock, withdrawing his hand. Brett saw Puttock's Adam's apple leap up and down as he swallowed dryly. "Your grandfather has given me a free hand to run the plantation the way I want it, Brett. If I am to live in the overseer's cabin, I need two house boys."

"House boys?" Brett looked startled. "What for?"

Brett saw Puttock's face tighten, his cheeks drawing in as he sucked air through his thin lips. He paused and peered at Brett as though disconcerted.

"Obedience, boy!" he snapped. This time Brett did flinch as Puttock's hand slapped down suddenly on his thigh. His skin reddened from the blow, but Brett stopped himself from crying out.

"I say I want two house boys, Brett. You have to tell me how to get them, not question why I want them."

Brett wanted to sulk. He glared back at Puttock, then cowered his eyes down in the face of Puttock's own defiant gaze. "The nursery, sir. We have boys of all ages there."

"That's the way, Brett. You can go there and pick out two. Your grandfather says breeding is all the niggers think about. Any two should be lively enough. Mas Carlton should be pleased when he sees the extra training I've given his slaves."

"Yes, sir."

"Go on, boy. You can go now."

Although Brett had decided he was not going to let Puttock order him about as though he was his personal slave, it was impossible to ignore the command in the overseer's voice. Everything he said carried a menacing tone.

Brett did not find out until he crept, exhausted, into the kitchen late that night, how Puttock had already changed the routine in the *cou*. Ella was waiting for him.

"Where yo' been, boy?" she demanded.

"Puttock!" was all Brett could answer. He sat down on the bench and pulled the plate of ground provision and gravy toward him. He began to scoop the food into his mouth.

Turning a lump of dasheen over with his spoon,

he prodded at the other vegetables on the plate. "There's no meat!" He looked at Ella in surprise.

"Dat so, Brett?" Ella sighed. "Puttock!" she retorted.

"What do you mean?"

"Puttock done say no meat. He say meat ain't good for niggers cuz it does get de blood too hot. He say we got to live on our rations an' salt fish once a week."

Brett raised his eyebrow. "He has meat. He has taken a wench from the quarters to cook for him. He had me supervising a gang to build him a kitchen outside his cabin the whole day. We finished a half-hour ago." Brett grimaced as he chewed more of the dry dasheen.

"The slaves are vexed because they finished work so late they had no time to go to their gardens."

"What!" Ella was astonished. Every able-bodied Negro at Roxborough cultivated his own piece of land where he grew vegetables to sell in the village market on Sunday. The vegetables also supplemented the rations given out to them each week.

"Mas Carlton ain't never stopped de people gon' to deir gardens!"

"Puttock says slaves get too much freedom here. He says they will only go to their gardens when he tells them. And that's not all." Brett pushed away his plate, watching for the effect his words would have on Ella.

"He says that everything they grow in their gardens must be brought to him. He says he will choose the slaves who will sell in the market on Sundays. The money must come to him. He says Sunday is the Lord's day!"

Ella sat down wearily on the bench beside Brett. "An' he does be de Lord? Whoa, Brett!" Ella wailed. "Dis overseer does want to be overall. He done sen' Pip to tend de niggers in de sickhouse. He done say ah does have no need to be here. He done sen' 'way de

99

wenches, too. Dey gone to de quarters to join de mill gang!" Ella buried her head in her hands.

"Seems dat Puttock does want we niggers' blood more dan an obeah vampire!"

"A lougaroo!"

Brett and Ella glanced at each other at the same moment. The thought which had entered their heads simultaneously electrified Ella. She sat up, her back straight and her eyes blazing. Even Brett allowed himself a wry smile.

"Do you think you can do it, Ella?"

Ella looked at him scornfully. "Of course, boy. Ain't yo' know ah does have de mos' powerful obeah dere does be outside Africa?" She fell into a thoughtful silence.

Brett chuckled to himself. Puttock was supposed to be with them for three months. Ella's magic obeah would finish him off in three days.

Chapter 11

Brett's prediction did not come true. Three days later, Puttock was not only there, but had demonstrated quite plainly that there was not a slave on the estate who could defy him, not even Ella. The slaves were even beginning to believe he was an obeah man himself.

Brett had picked out Lambert and Dale to be house boys for Puttock. He thought that they would work for Puttock during the day and return to the nursery at night. Puttock seemed pleased with Brett's choice but stipulated that the boys should sleep in his cabin. Brett was kept busy checking the slaves in the tasks which Puttock wanted done and did not have time to discuss Puttock with the two boys until the third morning. Puttock had ridden off to the slave gardens in the heights.

"He does be smart, Massa Brett!" confided Lambert. "Dat man ain't gon' be fooled by no one, Negro nor spirit."

"What do you mean by spirit?" Brett sat on the veranda of the overseer's cabin while Lambert leaned on the broom with which he was supposed to be sweeping.

"Yo' don't see de sand?" Lambert pointed to the sand he had brushed up on the veranda. It was black and came from the strip of beach bordering the village at Layou. "Every night Mas Puttock does throw de sand down in front he door."

"What for?" Brett was bemused.

"Dat's what we Negroes does do to keep out de spirits, Brett. When a lougaroo sees sand in front a house, she bound to count every grain. Daylight must catch she 'foh she finish so dere ain't no way she can enter de house."

"He believes in obeah?" Brett was appalled.

"Dat man knows we ways moh dan we, Brett. He does be taking precautions, he say."

Brett frowned. He had not expected Puttock to be so smart.

"Yo' know why he not gon' eat he dinner at de *cou*?" Dale had been cutlassing the grass which grew around the cabin. He rested his cutlass down on the deck of the veranda. "He say he don't want no nigger to poison he!"

"Huh?"

"Is true," said Lambert. "Ivonia does cook he meals

101

in de kitchen here an' den Mas Puttock does make Dale taste every t'ing on he plate befoh he does eat it."

"An' he drinks, too," chipped in Dale. "Yo' fuhgot he drinks."

"Dere does be something else, Brett." Lambert sounded glum.

"Yes?" Brett noticed the youth was nervous.

"He done tell we not to say anything 'bou' dis to yo'."

"Why me?" Brett was puzzled.

"He does believe Mas Carlton done put yo' to spy on he."

"What does he have to hide?" Brett stood up and turned his eyes onto Lambert. The youth faltered.

"Ah don't know." Lambert paused, continuing uncertainly. "Brett? In de evenin' when we does serve he dinner an' juice, he does make we remove we clothes."

"We does wait on he at he table, *tu-tu-ni*." breathed Dale.

"Completely naked!" added Lambert.

"Hey! You there!" Puttock's voice bellowed almost at Brett's ear.

Brett's heart sank. He had been so engrossed with what the two boys were telling him, he had forgotten to watch the trail for Puttock's return.

"Not sweeping, Lambert? Tired cutlassing, Dale?" Puttock drawled ominously.

"Yes, sir!" Lambert dashed the broom over the veranda.

"No, sir!" Dale snatched up his grinding stone and started rubbing it against his cutlass blade.

Puttock ignored the two boys and put his arm around Brett's neck, leading him away. "Always surprise your slaves, Brett. Condition them so that they expect you to creep up on them at any moment." He squeezed Brett's shoulder. "That way they will work

102

even if you are a mile away. How do they know where you are, unless you tell them?"

Puttock cupped his hand around the neck of Brett's head, ruffling his curls. He tilted Brett's head up, forcing him to look into his own face which he brought within an inch of Brett's nose.

Brett smelled the odor of Puttock's foul breath wafting over him. He blinked as the man's dull gray eyes probed into his. "Obedience, Brett, then surprise," Puttock hissed. "Remember?"

"Yes, sir!" Brett answered sharply.

"Fine, now what are your niggers doing now?" Puttock scowled, releasing Brett's head and pulling away from him.

"The carpenters are finishing the stocks, sir."

"Of course they are. That's what I told you to do. Go and creep up on them, Brett, and surprise them. If they are not working as you told them, they must be punished, not so?"

"Punished?" Brett backed away from Puttock.

"Some wretched nigger will do something wrong soon, Brett. Thirty-nine lashes is the punishment allowed by law. We'll try something new. As an example!"

Puttock walked with Brett to the coppice in front of the house. Brett crouched down to worm his way through the undergrowth up to the courtyard where the carpenters were constructing stocks on Puttock's instructions. Puttock eyed Brett, licking his lips. The boy's breeches hugged his slender frame enticingly. Scratching himself, Puttock turned his thoughts to the two tykes he had waiting for him at the cabin. He decided to creep up on them to see if they were idling again.

Threading his way into the plantain walk beside the path, Puttock edged his way up to the kitchen at the side of his cabin. The kitchen itself was constructed of round wood posts with a roseau reed thatched roof and one wall of bamboo to serve as a windbreak. As he approached this windbreak, Puttock heard voices. He knelt down stealthily to listen.

There were two women, both of them talking hastily in patois. Puttock knew enough from his youth when he worked as a porter with the Negroes on the wharf at Port of Spain to get the drift of what was being said. He heard his cook, Ivonia, protesting at the demands of the other woman. The second woman spoke with a harsh voice which he identified as Ella's.

Puttock sidled around the bamboo with a snarl, reaching out in time to grasp Ella's wrist as she forced something into Ivonia's hand.

"A powder for me, Ella?" Puttock's voice was sinister. "Are you sure?"

Ella shrieked. "Ah does not know what yo' mean," she gasped, glaring at him defiantly. She tried to shake his hand off her wrist. "Yo ain't got no right to touch me!"

Puttock crooned gleefully. "Oh no, my proud wench? I don't believe Master Carlton exempted you from my management." He looked toward the cabin. "Dale!" he called sharply.

The young slave ran around the corner of the cabin and stopped, his eyes widening at the sight of Mas Puttock with the two cooks.

"Run, boy! Tell Asaph come quickly with a tether."

"Who yo' gon' tether?" demanded Ella, trying again to wrench her arm free of Puttock's massive hand.

"Oh, do keep still, Ella," drawled Puttock. "You are being very tiresome. Now, Ivonia. That powder, if you please!" He held his free hand out toward his cook. "Do not do anything stupid, Ivonia," he hissed slowly.

"I know that powder is for me, so give it to me."

"No!" shrieked Ella speaking in patois. "Don't let he have it!"

"*Oui!*" Puttock spoke in patois himself, his eyes glinting. "Do let me have it, if you please!"

Ivonia's eyes bulged with terror. Timidly, she dropped the twist of paper into Puttock's outstretched palm. Ella cursed.

"Tut, tut, Ella! How could you? Come, let us go to my veranda, shall we? You are an intelligent nigger; I am sure you won't try to run. Indeed, where would you go?" He jerked Ella by her wrist, forcing her to follow him to the cabin.

"Lambert, your broom and a cord, please."

Lambert handed over the broom without a word and dashed inside the cabin for a piece of cord. If Puttock could hold Ella, he could do what he liked with any of the slaves, he thought. He grabbed twine where it hung on a nail and hurried back.

Puttock told Ella to stand with her back to the corner post of the veranda.

"What yo' doin'?" Ella snapped. "Loose me."

"For a dignified nigger, Ella, you really are behaving in an irksome manner. Do you wish me to strip you down and lash you?"

Ella paused in her struggling.

"Right, now pass your other hand around your back like so." Puttock caught both of Ella's wrists in one hand while looping the cord around the handle of the broomstick with the other.

Lambert steadied the handle as Puttock told him, then stood back. He watched fascinated.

Puttock released Ella's wrists. She moved forward but discovered she was pinioned behind her back by her hands which were bound to the broom handle on the other side of the post. She was trapped.

"Now, Ella, let's not have any foolishness at all."

Puttock's voice was cool without anger. "What are you doing here and what is this powder?"

"Loose meh, yo' hear." Ella spat on the ground.

"Not very dainty, Ella! An angry Negress is a rather fearsome sight, especially one as wild and ugly as you." Puttock looked up at the group of slaves rushing down the path toward him. Brett was leading thcm.

"Ah warn yo', Massa Puttock. If yo' don't loose me, yo' gon' have all de Roxbruh slaves at yuh t'roat!" Ella kept back the tears of rage which were threatening to burst out of her eyes. How could she have been so careless? What would Brett and the slaves think of her now?"

"Why are you holding Ella?" Brett stood in front of Puttock, his arms on his hips. "Release her!"

Brett hoped the fear in his voice wouldn't show. He drew strength from the twenty slaves who stood behind him snarling with menace.

"Oh, Brett," purred Puttock, sitting down on the veranda step so his eyes were level with the youth's. "If you are to be the overseer, you must have reason for your actions. A slave really does not like to be punished unfairly.

"First you ask me why am I holding Ella. I will tell you. Then *you* decide if I should release her, or if she should be punished. Yes?"

Brett took a step back. He looked up and down at Ella, who stopped pulling against her bonds and glared at Puttock. Then he stared at Puttock himself.

The slaves behind Brett murmured angrily. They wanted to hear what Ella had done.

Brett nodded in agreement.

"Right. What is this?" Puttock tossed the twist of paper at Brett. Brett caught it and opened it cautiously, glancing at Ella.

"A powder."

The Negroes who were crowding around Brett

106

stepped backwards smartly. They knew the power of such things.

"Ah," said Puttock. "A powder. Say no more. Ask Ivonia where she got that powder."

Brett and the slaves looked at Ivonia, who was still blubbering in the corner of the cabin. Ivonia shuddered, raising her finger slowly to point at Ella.

The slaves gasped, swiveling their eyes back to Ella.

"What did Ella give you that powder for, Ivonia?" Puttock's voice sounded calm.

"Ah done give it to she fuh she man!" shouted Ella. "She man not lovin' she, so she ax me fuh a love powder. Now loose me so ah can go 'bou' mah business!" Ella tossed her head haughtily.

The slaves laughed with relief, crowding around Brett, pushing him forward to free Ella.

"Wait!" Puttock stood up, idly patting his belt, making them aware of the pistols at his waist. "I heard Ella tell Ivonia to put the powder in my food to poison me." A jeer went up from the slaves.

"Mayhaps I was mistaken." Puttock drawled. "Perhaps we should have a test. Just to make sure. Let us see who is right. Brett, if this is a love powder, could it harm the person who swallowed it?"

"No," said Brett doubtfully. "Might give a buck an itch, that's all."

The slaves laughed, reaching over each other to clap him on his back.

"Very well, then," said Puttock, stepping down off the veranda. "Let Ella take her own powder!"

A hush fell over the slaves. A single blackbird whistled mockingly from the flamboyant tree. Brett's face clouded with concern as Puttock walked toward him.

"You were so anxious to involve yourself in the affairs of your slaves, young Master Brett. Why don't you administer the powder to Ella yourself?" Puttock's voice grated evilly in the silence.

The slaves fell back, leaving Brett standing alone outside the cabin. Ella looked at Brett, then at Puttock. She gazed around at the black faces of her people. They turned their eyes away as she searched their faces for help.

She had failed them.

Brett walked toward her, the powder in the palm of his hand.

"It ain't no love powder," she blurted out. Her voice dropped to a whisper. "But it ain't a poison, Mas Puttock."

"Indeed, then I'm sure you would not mind taking a little of your medicine to show us all what it does do?" Puttock gestured at the slaves to show how reasonable he was. They murmured in agreement.

"No!" said Ella. "No!" She hung her head in shame, her shoulders shaking as she sobbed.

Puttock flicked his fingers contemptuously.

Asaph moved over to Ella. In his hands he carried a heavy iron ball at the end of a chain. He looked at Puttock, who nodded. Asaph knelt down and slowly fastened the shackle to Ella's ankle.

Chapter 12

The news about Ella's humiliation at the hands of the new buckra spread like a cane fire through the plantation. Those slaves who had witnessed the confrontation between the *beké* and Ella were heroes to the others. As soon as the slave gangs drifted back to the quarters from their work on the far boundaries of the estate, they gathered around the eyewitnesses to hear the details. At first, the slaves found it difficult to believe. For thirty years, Ella had been the Queen of Roxborough. Her knowledge of herbs and powders and her position as the Bondmaster's first bed wench had made her seem invincible.

"We does see how good she obeah does be when she flies out dem chains!" chuckled an old slave in the crowd gathered outside the sickhouse where Ella had been taken.

"Why de *beké* not put she in de cell?" asked another slave.

Miranda pushed her way through the crowd and rapped on the door of the sickhouse. An eye peered at her through the bars covering the narrow opening on the door.

"It does be me, Miranda," she called. "Let me come in to see Ella!"

The eye peered at her briefly; then the crowd heard the withdrawal of the bolt. The door opened slightly and Miranda edged inside.

The slaves called the building the hot house. Its walls built of large river stones made it seem like a dungeon. The windows were all shuttered, and the main room was airless. Pip, who had been put in charge of the sickhouse by Puttock, had a pallet in a corner. The inmates were forced to sleep on mats on the mud floor. Ella sat mournfully on Pip's pallet, the heavy iron ball on the ground in front of her.

Miranda rushed over to her and took her in her arms. "Oh, Ella, ah does be so scare' fuh yo'!"

Ella took a deep breath and drew herself up. "Ain't no cause, Miranda. Ah ain't scare'."

"Yo' not scare'?" Miranda released Ella and looked

109

at her in amazement. "Dat Puttock does be a wicious man, Ella. Ain't no knowin' what he does be gon' do to yo'. Ah hear Constance does be lightin' he fire an' forgin' some kind of piece dat Puttock done ax he fuh."

Ella sniffed. "Ain't no never-mind to me, Miranda."

Pip squatted down beside Ella. "Yuh mam ain't 'fraid, Miranda. Puttock heself done tell Mas Carlton he ain't gon' maim we slaves. De niggers gon' rise up an' lynch Puttock if he does hurt Miss Ella!"

Miranda scrutinized Pip scornfully. "Yo' ain' hear dem niggers ou'side, Pip? Dey *pleased* Ella does be here. After all she done do fuh dey! Niggers does be stupid, jus' like Mas Carlton does say."

Ella shrugged her shoulders. "Ah done fail, Miranda." She lowered her head away from the gaze of the sick slaves who lay on the floor watching her. Some of them were there because she had obeahed them at the request of other slaves. She raised her head again and smiled bravely.

"Tell Brett he must do what Mas Puttock does tell he."

Miranda frowned doubtfully. "Brett does be like de little massa, now, Ella. Puttock was be teachin' he how to lash a nigger so he don't leave no scar!"

"Small matters, Miranda. Puttock ain't gon' do me nothin'."

Ella was wrong. It was late afternoon just before sunset when Puttock approached the sickhouse. He was attended by Brett carrying a driver's three-thonged whip in his hand, and by Constance, the blacksmith.

Constance was as black as rage, a giant with a shaved skull and massive hands which could throttle a man in seconds. He lumbered along behind Puttock, honking gleefully. Constance was deaf and dumb, an asset, Mas Carlton always said, as he could not hear the cries of those he was punishing. In his hand, Constance clutched a leather sack. The slaves who were grouped around the hot house eyed it warily, falling back to let Puttock pass.

Pip opened the door quickly. Puttock stepped into the sickhouse and glanced at the Negroes lying on the floor. Brett sought the eyes of Ella. She smiled at him, nodding her head gently.

"Pip," demanded Puttock, "open these shutters. Let some air in the place. Everybody here is sick. No one is going to jump out the windows and run away."

Pip unfastened the shutters hurriedly. Black faces immediately peered into the hot house to see what was going to happen. Puttock swaggered down the length of the building, stooping beside each slave to ask him what ailed him.

"We must look after the sick, Brett. I promised Mas Carlton that no slave would die while he is away. These are special slaves to be treated properly." As he spoke, Puttock forced open the mouth of an old Negro woman with his fingers. He put two tablets in her mouth and ordered her to swallow.

Brett translated the command in patois, and Pip gave her a mug of water. The process was repeated with every slave whether he had sores on his legs, the flux, or bleeding gums.

Brett was curious. "What are those tablets?" he asked.

"Placebos." Puttock answered curtly. "The niggers will cure themselves." Puttock turned as he reached the end of the room and swaggered up to the door. He paused by Ella.

"How are you, Ella?" His voice had that underlying threatening note in it which made the watching slaves cringe with fear.

Ella stared up at him without speaking, her eyes filled with loathing.

"The venereal? Locked jaw, perhaps?" Puttock did

not smile. "I could have been laid out in here tonight, Ella. Or would I have gone straight to the carpenters for a coffin?" He turned to gaze at the slaves in the doorway. They flinched, shuffling awkwardly.

"Are you suffering from constipation, Ella?"

Ella remained mute, refusing to give the white man the pleasure of ridiculing her in front of the Negroes.

"Doctor Constance here has constructed a device to my design, Ella, which is ideal for clearing out the system. It's something much in vogue in Trinidad. I'm sure it will give you relief!"

The slaves gaped as Constance removed the contraption he carried in his leather sack. It was shaped like a funnel with a pointed end and a tube attached to it. The tube had a rod projecting from it.

Puttock took the gadget from Constance and pulled out the rod. There was a wad of coconut fiber on the end.

"Water!" Puttock commanded.

Pip moved a pail of water to Puttock's side. He passed a mug to Puttock to serve as a dipper. The overseer put a finger over the small end of the funnel to block it and poured water into the tube. He poured in four mugs full before he was satisfied. He replaced the rod at the top of the tube and pressed it down like a plunger. He nodded his head with satisfaction at Constance.

"Ella," he rasped. "A simple treatment. Kindly lie down on the pallet, raise your skirt and expose your bottom."

An expectant hush gripped the slaves. Brett looked at Puttock dumbfounded. Ella sat back as though shocked.

"Get on with it, Ella. Do you want Doctor Constance to aid you?"

"No!" whispered Ella in horror and disbelief. "No!"

112

"Ella, my patience is exhausted." Puttock's voice was flat without emotion. He gestured with the contrivance at Constance, who picked up Ella off the mattress as though she was a whelp.

Constance dropped Ella, face downward, on the pallet and sat beside her, pinioning her shoulders to the bed with his huge arm. Asaph wrapped the chain around her ankles. Ella was trapped.

"Brett! Why don't you raise the wench's skirt for me?"

Brett was mesmerized by Puttock's toneless voice. He moved toward the bed slowly and grasped the hem of Ella's skirt.

"That's right, Brett." Puttock spoke almost soothingly. "Raise it to her waist."

Brett pulled back the skirt until he exposed Ella's naked bottom. It was firm in spite of her age. Ella tried to squirm, but the chain held her ankles fast to the pallet. Puttock advanced on her.

"This is a simple technique to clean out a slave whose bowels are blocked," Puttock explained, placing the nose of the funnel in between Ella's buttocks.

He prodded the crude syringe into her until he was satisfied.

"Ah!" Puttock exclaimed with relish. "It's in!" Gradually he drove down the plunger, forcing water into Ella's rectum.

The slaves chuckled gleefully as Ella howled.

The weeks of Carlton's absence from Roxborough passed quickly. After the example he made of Ella, Joel Puttock had only minimal trouble with the slaves. Ella herself was soon released from the hot house and spent her time brooding in the kitchen. Brett, ashamed of his part in her downfall, rarely visited the *cou*. He slept instead in the nursery with Miranda.

Brett became an eager disciple of Puttock's ways

of enforcing discipline. Because of the novelty of his punishments and the degradation the slaves felt when exposed to them, Puttock was feared wherever he went.

Slaves could understand the lash. In fact, the older Negroes were afforded respect according to the number of stripes they had on their backs. Puttock's methods, which subjected recalcitrant slaves to the ridicule of their brothers, were less severe but far more humiliating.

It became so that Puttock need only cast his eye on a gang of boisterous slaves for them to fall silent, meekly listening to his commands. Puttock taught Brett about the constant vigilance necessary to stay ahead of the slaves, knowing their feelings before they knew themselves.

"Slaves need a master!" he told Brett one day as they rode to the upper cane-piece where a gang was hoeing the ratoons. "Some planters think Negroes are animals. I don't believe that, Brett. A Negro is a black human being, but an inferior one to you and me. He has a mind."

Puttock reined in his horse in the shade of a calabash tree. Through the trees ahead of them they could see a line of slaves working its way slowly across the field like a snake.

"The obeah men work on a slave's mind, Brett. Niggers fear obeah, but what is it? Potions and herbs and a receptive mind.

"It's in a slave's mind that he must have a master. The Bondmaster's slaves were bred in captivity. Their minds tell them they need a white master to make them work well. I merely oblige their desires." He chuckled cruelly.

"Africans need rougher handling, of course, but you don't get Africans in these islands since the British banned the trade twenty years ago."

He moved his horse forward out of the shade. "Captitalize on that, Brett, work on a slave's mind."

The gentle murmur of the slaves toiling in the heat ceased as Puttock and Brett broke cover. The driver ran over quickly and saluted.

"Any problems, Cudjoe?" asked Puttock.

"No, sah!"

Brett eyed Cudjoe. He was in his late twenties, a tall, thin Negro with a shifty eye. Brett had never trusted Cudjoe, but had been unable to decide why. He always seemed to get his gang working well. There were six males and four females in his gang. They were usually assigned the easier jobs in the fields.

Puttock dismissed Cudjoe with a wave of his hand and turned his horse to leave. Brett was about to follow him when he paused. He glanced at the slaves again, counting quickly.

"One of the fillies is missing, Mr. Puttock. She was here this morning, because I checked the gang myself."

"Indeed!" Puttock's voice, pitched slightly higher than usual, was the only sign that he was concerned. "Could the female in question have slipped away without the driver knowing, Brett?"

"Oh, no, sir. She is Cudjoe's wench. Tency is her name. The other three are all there working."

"Collusion, Brett. Cudjoe is involved. What do you do?"

"Punish both of them, sir?"

"Perhaps, Brett. Is Cudjoe a good driver?"

"Average, sir."

Puttock stroked his chin. "And Tency? Is she a good hand?"

"I would say so."

When they questioined Cudjoe, he denied any knowledge of Tency's disappearance. Puttock told him to carry on with his driving while he and Brett settled

115

down in the shade to wait. It was not long before Tency appeared, grumbling loudly in patois.

"Ah does be tired running down de still fuh muh rum fuh yo', Cudjoe!" she muttered. "Oy! Why yo' lash me? Ah done run fast as mah legs gon' carry me in dis hot sun."

Tency shrieked as Cudjoe's whip cut into her cheek and Puttock and Brett emerged from their hiding place in the undergrowth.

"Your whip, if you please, Cudjoe!"

The driver looked at Puttock in surprise.

"For Tency, of course. Brett," he said when Cudjoe handed the whip over to him, "manacle Cudjoe." He turned to Tency, who was cowering under the front of his horse. "Here is the whip. Take it!"

Tency bent her head, covering her face with her hands as she waited for the slash of leather across her back.

"Wench. Take the whip!" Puttock thrust the handle at her. She peered through her fingers nervously.

"You are to be the driver of this gang, Tency. You will let no one leave the field without my permission." He turned his horse around and trotted off, followed by Brett.

Cudjoe, attached to Brett's horse by a chain around his manacled wrists, scampered after them. That night he was locked in the stocks, where he stayed without food or water for two days until Carlton and Milly returned to Roxborough.

Chapter 13

Carlton drew on the pipe which he had acquired from Trinidad. The tobacco had lost its flame, and he was tired of summoning Pip for fire. He sucked thoughtfully on the dry stem instead. The green jewels of the fireflies were already twinkling in the flamboyant trees that edged the courtyard. Carlton put his feet up on the balcony railing, competing for resting space with the bougainvillea which crawled over the latticework like an irrepressible creeper. Wind whipped around the house, heralding an evening shower of rain.

Carlton smiled to himself. The driver Puttock had put in the stocks would get the water he had been crying for, Carlton decided.

Contrary to Ella's belief and the slaves' hopes, Carlton did not intend to dismiss Joel Puttock and let the plantation slip back to its old routine. Following his return to the estate that afternoon, he had heard Mr. Puttock's report, Ella's shrill complaints, and Brett's measured comments. Milly, tired after the voyage, had taken to her boudoir to rest.

Of course, thought Carlton, it was reprehensible of Ella to try her obeah nonsense on Puttock. Carlton did not believe Ella would really poison him. The punishment meted out to Ella seemed appropriate. Carlton chuckled again. Ella had been humbled at last. The stocks in the courtyard Carlton saw as an excellent innovation. It would be fun to put shirking niggers there and let the slaves pelt them with rubbish and abuse.

Brett pleased Carlton. The youth had matured in the three months of Carlton's absence. He would make a first-class overseer when Milly's son was the Bondmaster. Carlton leaned forward and studied the purple leaves of the bougainvillea at his feet. The Trinidad doctors had found no reason why Milly should not have a child. And she was pregnant! Soon her stomach would round out, and then, in six months or less, there would be an heir for Roxborough.

In the weeks which followed Carlton's return, the tempo of life at Roxborough took on a new pace. The slaves realized there was no appeal to Carlton against Puttock's peculiar but utterly effective punishments. Carlton was content to leave the management of the slaves to Puttock and Brett.

Carlton knew that Brett had taken to his task of mounting Miranda with zealousness. With Brett occupying Miranda, Carlton had solved the problem of how he could do it himself. He wondered idly what color whelp his daughter and his grandson would produce. His concern, however, was for Milly. He loved Milly with a proud affection which, incredibly to Carlton's mind, she reciprocated.

Milly had relished the balls and fetes they had attended in Trinidad, but now they were back at Roxborough, she settled down to be, she told Carlton, a dedicated wife and *mother*. The forthcoming birth of their child was their only concern. Carlton shielded Milly from everything else as though she were an invalid.

He forbade her to ride her horse or take the wagon to Layou. When she wanted exercise, Carlton walked by her side, with a slave wielding a parasol over her head. He ordered Ella to prepare especially nourishing dishes and sent for whatever Milly craved from the merchants in Roseau.

When Milly, after weeks of not mentioning her brother's name, confessed to Carlton that she would dearly like to see her brother, Carlton was forced to relent. He permitted her to write to Dyce. He was living in Antigua, so Milly invited him to come and spend a few weeks at Roxborough. He would be company for Milly, Carlton reasoned, hiding his own misgivings for his wife's sake.

Joel Puttock appreciated the Bondmaster's confidence in his ability. It had always been his policy to repay a good master with dedicated service. It was the way he had won his reputation. However, if a master tried to harass him, he repaid him with the same coin. Puttock understood slaves. The severity of the overseer was a kind of affection the slaves craved for.

In his cabin at night, Joel Puttock craved for affection too. He was a lonely man, isolated by his calling from the company of other white men. As a poor white he was not fit to dine at his master's table, and as an overseer he could not expect to find companionship in the slaves under him. On some plantations where he had worked there were other whites such as bookkeepers and managers. Puttock had always been restrained in their company, however, as his tastes were not for rum and wenches like theirs.

Puttock sighed that evening, putting down the glass of guava juice he had been sipping. Lambert glided up to the table to remove it. The youth was completely naked, his skin, the light brown of cinnamon bark, glowing in the rays from the lantern hanging from the beam overhead.

Puttock tugged the boy's penis playfully. "Did you bathe this afternoon, boy?"

"Yassa!" Lambert replied quickly, remaining motionless beside the overseer. He was fourteen, his slim body showing the outline of the muscular frame he would soon be developing.

Puttock, sitting at the table, had his eyes level with the boy's chest. He tugged the boy's penis again to make him stand closer. Putting his nose under Lambert's arm, he sniffed.

"Hmm!" he said with a grin. "That's a clean nigger smell!" He lowered his face to Lambert's crotch rubbing his nose against the boy's thigh.

"Boy, you have hair sprouting there." Puttock slapped Lambert's stomach. "You'll be too old for me soon. I'll have to look over those young bucks in the nursery and find a replacement. You'll have to start breeding for your master."

Lambert's penis leaped. "Yassa!" he said eagerly.

Brett had been visiting the cabins in the slave quarters by the river bank. There were about thirty cabins which formed the compound. The original cabins had been built by Carlton's father around an open square. As the number of slaves had increased, more cabins had been added, so the compound was no longer neatly laid out.

The skilled slaves like the coopers and sugar boilers who were part of the plantation's slave aristocracy had contrived to make their cabins into regular homes. They were furnished with beds and chairs and eating utensils. The slaves who graduated to the quarters from the nursery while they waited to be sold eked out an existence in makeshift cabins and thatched *ajoupas*.

In the soil surrounding each sad cabin, the slaves cultivated plantains and ground provisions. The proximity of the Layou River assured that the soil was fertile. On even the hottest days, with the gardens jammed with plants and the thick foliage of the trees growing around the compound, the quarters was a cool and shaded spot.

The slave routine required all those slaves who believed they were sick to report to the overseer every morning. They were then sent to the sickhouse, where they would be dosed by the keeper according to Mr. Puttock's orders. The old slaves who were no longer fit for field work were allowed to remain in the quarters. They were expected to perform the small tasks of rolling cocoa sticks, putting cinnamon and coffee out to dry, shelling peas for the house, or anything else assigned to them.

The breeding fillies were billeted in the quarters where each wench was put under the control of one of the old crones. The colts who had been stabled in the barracoon were sent to the wenches by Carlton Todd himself. Each buck was ordered to mount only the wench given to him, and the crones were ordered to see that the buck mounted his wench every night.

It was a precarious process, Brett soon realized. Many of the bucks lusted for wenches other than the ones they had been allotted. To obtain their freedom to roam at night, the bucks were forced to satisfy the wenches' guardians first. With only their bodies to barter, sex was the currency of the slaves.

Brett had been trying to make some sense out of permutations of the quarter's inhabitants. Mas Carlton would be pleased, he knew, that four of the breeding wenches were pregnant. But what would he say about Norah being full for Hamlett instead of Stewart, and Thames being the father of the whelps expected by both Sarah and Eliza?

Brett shrugged his shoulders as he wended his way up the hill path back to the house. One day he was going to sire a child of his own, perhaps with Miranda or even with the charcoal-black Empress. His thoughts must have distracted Brett's attention because he was nearly into the courtyard in front of the house before he looked up at the balcony.

Brett froze.

A feeling that his heart had leaped into his throat overwhelmed him. Brett stared up at the balcony, blinking in the sunlight in case he was mistaken. But there was no mistaking the profile of the man whose image had haunted his mind for nearly ten years!

Brett stepped off the path and ran quickly through the flamboyant trees to the kitchen door at the back of the house.

"Ella! Ella!" he shouted, tumbling into the room.

"Lor! What's happened, boy!" Ella dropped her ladle at the side of the stove, wiped her hands on her apron, and caught Brett by his shoulders. "Yo' done see a jumbie, boy?"

"No, mam," he gulped, grateful for Ella's firm hands clenching him. Suddenly the remorse he still felt for Ella's shame at Puttock's hands welled up in him. He sank to his knees like a child, wrapping his arms around Ella's legs. He whimpered.

"Dere, dere, Brett!" Ella placed her hands in his ringlets, caressing the back of his neck as she smiled to herself with relief. Ella had been waiting for the masquerade of being a man to prove too much for Brett. She was soothed now that his hard façade had cracked and she could speak to the boy who dwelt underneath the mask.

"Dat Puttock done bugger yo', boy?"

"No, mam!" Brett choked. "Ah done see he," he stuttered in patois.

Ella rolled her eyes at Pip who quickly poured a brandy into a glass and drained it down his throat himself.

"Sit down, Brett!" Ella pulled Brett to his feet and steered him to the bench. She forced him to sit, straightening the torn collar of his shirt. "Everyt'ing does be a' right, Brett. Now tell me slowly so we can know what to do. Who yo' done see?"

Brett stared at Ella. "Dyce Dobbs!" he said, waiting for Ella's reaction.

"De mistress brother," said Pip.

"He done come fuh six weeks." Ella spoke calmly. "Dat de man yo' does be 'fraid fuh?"

"I'm not afraid of him or any white man!" Brett shouted indignantly, recovering his arrogance.

"Yas, yas." Ella put her hand on his shoulder again.

"Don't you remember, Ella? Dyce Dobbs is one of the men who killed Caspar."

Ella gasped. "Yo' sure?"

"I will never forget his face." Brett paused gazing at Ella. "As long as he lives."

Ella felt tears pricking her eyes. Brett's face was turned upwards to hers, watching her with such confidence she wanted to weep. She knew her failure had been forgotten. Brett was asking her to be his ally.

Brett bounced off the bench; his tough little white body which had seemed so fragile only minutes before now radiated strength. He pounded his small fist into the palm of his hand.

"What can we do, Ella?" he pleaded.

"Ah gon' tell yo', boy," Ella said, leaning back against the table, crossing her legs comfortably. "We ain't gon' do nothin'. At first. Wait, Brett." She held up her hand. "Let me explain."

"Go on!"

"Mas Carlton does know dis man does be one of Caspar's killers?"

"Yes."

"An' he does know yo' want yuh revenge."

"Yes."

"So if de man dies, Mas Carlton sure yo' done do it. He gon' hang yo'!"

123

"I don't care, Ella."

"Now, Brett, t'ink of de t'ing good. Dere was be t'ree men. Dis one is but one of dem. An' dis one does be de brother of Miss Milly. Mas Carlton does love Miss Milly moh dan he loves yo', Brett. An' she does be full fuh him, too," she sniffed. "If yo' does kill Dyce Dobbs an' Mas Carlton ain't gon' spare yo', how yo' gon' get de oders?"

Brett stared at Ella, his eyes wide.

"Yo' got to act like yuh fuhgit all dat business 'bou' dis Dobbs, Brett!"

Brett cocked his head on one side as he listened to Ella outline her plan. When she had finished, he stared at her without expression for several seconds. Then gradually his young face lit up into a boyish smile of such innocence that Ella herself was surprised.

"Mam," he said proudly, "yo' does be de mos' wicked *soucoyant* in de whole of Dominica!"

Pip lifted the bottle of brandy to his lips and poured the contents rapidly into his mouth.

Chapter 14

Dyce had been at Roxborough for a week. His exemplary behavior made Carlton think he had been too hasty in judging him. He was well-behaved although arrogant in his manner toward the slaves, the usual reaction of someone not used to having servants.

That Dyce was a rogue and a spendthrift was obvious, but he was an entertaining companion. The West Indies was full of such characters. They were the descendants of the white settlers who had not made the fortunes they sought. They were condemned to drift through the islands picking up work wherever they could. Some became overseers; others found minor government posts. Most, however, engaged in questionable business deals, spending their money when they had any in the grog shops and casinos of Roseau, St. Johns, or Port-of-Spain.

If such a knave could read and write, he might obtain a post as attorney for an absentee plantation owner. The practice of having attorneys running plantations while the owner lived in England was widespread. In many cases, the owner never even visited his property but left its management completely in the hands of his attorney. It was not unusual for an attorney to retire with his own small plantation and a substantial number of slaves, all acquired out of swindling the proprietor who had engaged him.

"I'm not against that," said Carlton as he sat on the balcony with Dyce at the end of Dyce's first week at Roxborough. Milly sat with them working on a sampler, straining her eyes in the faint glow from the lantern. She listened with satisfaction as her brother and Carlton exchanged their views. She was pleased that Carlton had lost his original distrust of Dyce.

"It seems to me," Carlton continued, "that any proprietor who is foolish enough to live in England and let an attorney run his plantation deserves to lose some of his profit. An attorney, even if he is not a rogue, could never have the interests of an absent proprietor at heart."

"Not all attorneys are rogues, Carlton!" Dyce spoke charily. "Blood or marriage ties could be the bond to

125

ensure that an attorney did well for his proprietor. Maybe better," he added wryly.

Carlton raised an eyebrow, peering closely at Dyce. He was about ten years older than Milly. His lean cheeks were already lined and his eyes were sunk deep into a hard and sneering face. His dark hair hung straggling down his neck and his complexion showed the ravages of haunting casinos and whore-houses. What appeared to be his only suit, with its high-waist trousers and ill-cut jacket, was shabby. Dyce had the air of being a permanent loser.

"What are you suggesting, Dyce? That you would make a good attorney for Roxborough?"

"Why not, Carlton?" Dyce moved forward in his seat, putting his hand out to tap Carlton's bare arm. "Look at the advantages. I know the work, and I am your wife's brother."

Carlton sniffed, withdrawing his arm. "I have no intention of being impolite, Dyce. I am sure you have admirable qualities. However, I have no need for an attorney. Milly is soon to have our child. He will be heir to Roxborough. I trust I have plenty of years ahead of me to guarantee the boy has a thriving plan-tation to inherit."

"You may want to take a holiday." Dyce glanced at Milly.

Carlton saw the look. So, he thought, he and Milly were brewing up some kind of plan? "A man like me, Dyce, who is dedicated to his work, does not take holidays."

"A trip to England would be nice, Carlton," Milly simpered.

"Indeed it would, Milly," Carlton grinned. "So would another rum." He poured a drink for Dyce and filled his own glass, dismissing the matter from his mind.

"I told you so!" Milly mouthed soundlessly to Dyce behind Carlton's back.

Dyce tried again. "Perhaps, Carlton, you have a place for me on the plantation? I am admirable in dealing with niggers, and I can keep books with a professional flair."

"Doubtless, Dyce." Carlton put down his glass and glanced at Milly. "I am grateful for your offer. I appreciate it, I really do, Dyce. I will look into the possibilities."

"What Dyce needs," said Milly, seeing they were getting nowhere, "is a sinecure. I am sure he would settle down if only he could find some regular basis for his life. He would not interfere with your slave rearing, Carlton, or anything like that."

Carlton sighed. "I've said I will consider it, Milly." He lapsed into silence, staring out into the night.

After a few minutes, when she saw Carlton was not going to say anything else, Milly rose to her feet, clutching her sampler in her hand. "The lamp is low, Carlton. I think I'll go to my boudoir."

"Yes." Carlton leaped to his feet and kissed his wife. "You must rest. For the baby."

Dyce scowled as he watched Carlton. He hated him. Carlton had everything but refused to help him, his own brother-in-law. Dyce pulled himself to his feet, reluctant to remain on the balcony with Carlton. "Let me accompany you," he said to Milly.

"To my boudoir?" Milly queried. "Why, it's only beyond this door." She smiled up at Dyce as they walked off the gallery into the drawing room. She paused outside her chamber. "Good night, Dyce."

"Milly, do you have some currency? I am most discouraged by your husband's answer tonight. I would like to go down to Layou to bolster my spirits."

Milly frowned. "Don't worry about Carlton. I will

127

speak to him again on your behalf. Good night." She opened her door.

"But Layou, Milly. If I go there I am sure to feel brighter. A few pounds in currency, Milly?" Dyce put his hand out to touch his sister's waist.

"No!" Milly's voice was firm. "I am not the one to pay for your gambling."

"Just a loan, Milly. I have a feeling I will win tonight. I can pay you back tomorrow."

"I said no!" Milly wiggled uncomfortably at the pressure of his hand as it drifted down to her hip. "Carlton would disapprove."

"Carlton!" Dyce spat with disdain. "Your precious Carlton has been known to gamble niggers when he had no currency with him. Please, Milly. Until tomorrow."

"Oh, very well." Milly sighed. "Just this once. Wait there!" She slipped into her room while Dyce paced the drawing room floor, smirking to himself.

"Here!" Milly thrust some coins into his hand. "You'll pay me tomorrow?"

"Of course, sister Milly. I love you." He kissed her quickly on her cheek, then strode back onto the balcony.

Carlton acknowledged Dyce's departure with a wave of his hand. He rarely went to Layou himself, unless it was on business during the day. Carlton's nights spent carousing with the seamen and young planters in the casinos were gone long ago. He watched Dyce strut across the courtyard to the stables, calling for Pip to come with a lantern so he could saddle a horse.

To Carlton's surprise, he saw Brett run out from the kitchen. The boy trotted eagerly after Dyce, the sounds of his carefree chatter drifting up to the balcony. Carlton's gaze followed the lantern until it disappeared into the clump of trees surrounding the stable. Carlton shook his head with puzzlement when he recalled his doubts that Dyce's presence at Roxborough might have provoked Brett.

"Hey, boy, come here!" Carlton shouted when he saw Brett jogging back across the courtyard. Brett ran up the steps quickly. He was smiling.

"Yes, sir?"

"Your eyes are bright tonight, Brett." Carlton was puzzled. "When a slave who sulks suddenly seems cheerful, Brett, there is some mischief abroad. I've learned to watch the signs. So will you."

"Yes, sir?" Brett placed the lantern on the floor and stood before Carlton with his hands behind his back and feet apart. He resembled a young soldier at ease before his commander. His face was trusting and innocent.

Carlton frowned. "There's a change come over you, boy. What's afoot?"

"Nothing, sir!" Brett's normally husky voice was crisp. The lantern at his feet threw a shadow of his legs onto the deck of the balcony.

"Hmm!" muttered Carlton. "You tell me nothing, but look at you, boy. A week ago you could not stand and look me in the eye and smile! Did you know how to smile? You had Caspar's dedication, but not an ounce of his charm. Now you are bouncing about with the grin of a foolish nigger."

"Yes, sir." Brett paused as though thinking. "It's Master Dyce, sir."

"Indeed?" Carlton snapped suspiciously. "What about him?"

"I was wrong, sir."

"How do you mean?"

"You see, I believed he was one of the men I saw killing my father, sir. I've been unhappy since you married Miss Milly, sir, thinking that her brother killed Caspar. But I was wrong." Brett shifted his foot.

"You were wrong?" repeated Carlton, his eyes narrowing as he studied Brett's face.

"Yes, sir. I was mistaken. Now Master Dyce is here, sir, I can see he wasn't the man who did it, sir."

"You like him, Brett?" Carlton was confused. If Brett was right, then Carlton himself had no reason to be suspicious of his brother-in-law.

"Oh, yes, sir. He makes me laugh, sir. He is not humorless like Mr. Puttock."

Carlton considered Brett. The boy sounded genuine. He had certainly changed since Dyce arrived at Roxborough. "And what will you do if you chance on any of Caspar's killers, Brett?"

For a moment, the twinkle left Brett's eye. He folded his hands across his chest. Then the ready smile returned as Brett answered apologetically. "I'm not sure I would recognize them now, sir."

"Nor will you see them, boy." Carlton sat up. "Be sure they will never come here again. It's a relief you have abandoned those thoughts of revenge. They were corrupting you, boy." Carlton beamed at Brett, standing so straight and upright in front of him. His black ringlets framed his sunburned face, and his yellow eyes shone with youth's vitality.

It would be impossible, Carlton thought, for a stranger to know that Brett had black blood in him. In the States, Brett would be considered black even if he had only one-sixteenth Negro blood in his veins. In the Caribbean, he was a mulatto. He could never inherit Roxborough, of course, nor could he be free, but he was growing into a man who would command respect.

"What's the name of that wench in the nursery I promised you, Brett?"

"Empress, sir."

"You want her, boy?"

Brett's smile became a broad grin. "Of course, sir. But Miss Miranda, sir, she does get powerful jealous."

"Jealous, boy?" Carlton wrinkled his brow. "She's more nigger than you, Brett. Where did she learn jealousy? I'm ordering you to mount that Empress wench and get me a whelp. When I was your age I had two wenches full for me already."

"Yes, sir," replied Brett, grinning. Ella was right, he realized; a smile was easier than a frown. And it brought an early reward.

Brett's newfound smile began to captivate Joel Puttock. He had been deterred by the boy's sullen expression and had made no effort to establish more than the conventional relationship between an overseer and his employer's grandson. Brett's earnestness had made him a quick learner, and he was respected by the slaves. The same quality had kept Puttock from pestering him.

But Brett began to hang around his cabin. When the slaves had been brought in from the fields at night, Brett joined him on his veranda to talk about the day. Sometimes he wrestled with Lambert or Dale in the sand in front of the house.

"You see, Mr. Puttock, I can lick those niggers!" Brett boasted one evening as he sat on Lambert's chest. "These slaves of yours aren't good for anything!"

"Dat's all yo' know," laughed Lambert wriggling away. "Ax Mas Puttock, Brett, what we does be good fuh!"

Brett looked at Puttock curiously, flashing his eyes. He grinned. "I am sure there is nothing these nigger boys can do which I cannot do better!" he challenged.

Puttock raised his eyebrows and groaned. Brett

131

was standing in the center of the glade, his bare chest heaving with the effort of besting Lambert. His breeches were short, tight, and ripped provocatively up his thigh. He brushed his locks out of his eye and smiled at Puttock.

"Damn you, Brett!" muttered Puttock, pressing his crotch.

"Puttock. I've come for a rum!"

Puttock was about to beckon Brett to come to him when Dyce strode into the glade.

"I'm dying of thirst and bedeviled by righteousness. You'd think a man could live as he pleased as guest of the Bondmaster. Not me! Mine host eyes me for shouting at his niggers, and my sister scolds me for losing at *brelin!* A rum, Puttock, for a benighted house guest."

Puttock nodded at Dyce sympathetically, pulling forward a chair for him to join him. Dyce had become a daily visitor to sip rum and swap stories. Each man recognized a kindred spirit in the other.

"I'll get the rum, sir," said Brett, dashing onto the veranda and into the cabin. Lambert, still on his haunches on the ground, lolled back lazily. Dale snorted with disgust.

"Fine lad, that," said Puttock, nodding after Brett. "He'll make a good overseer."

"Yes." Dyce was thoughtful, sinking into the chair with relief. "You have a damned good life out here, Puttock. More freedom than being in the house. I have the guest room at the back, but I'll wager if I tried to smuggle in a wench, Mas Carlton would turn her out."

"He hasn't offered you one?"

"No, more's the pity. Perhaps he thinks I'll accept and offend my sister."

Brett carried a tray out onto the veranda. There was a glass of rum on it which he offered to Dyce before presenting the tray with the juice on it to Puttock. He stood between the two men holding the pitcher of water ready to pour into Dyce's glass as soon as he gulped back the rum. He also wanted to hear their conversation.

He was aware of Dyce appraising him.

"Yes, yes," muttered Dyce, sending the rum down his throat. He held his glass out for Brett to fill it with water. "He is a fine youth, Puttock. Jepson, my partner in Layou, would crave him." He chuckled, raising his eyebrow to see if Puttock understood him.

"Oh, aye," said Puttock, casually brushing Brett's backside with his hand. "There are men who like youths such as this one."

"Jepson!" thought Brett, returning to the interior of the cabin. "Jepson! He must be the man who was with Dyce that night." Brett stared around the cabin. He shuddered as he recalled the night when he had crouched in the cane and watched Dyce and his partner drag Caspar out on to the veranda. He remembered how the two men had attached the noose to Caspar's neck and then swung his body from the flamboyant tree. By the time the men had ridden off and Brett had cut the rope holding his father, he was dead. "Dyce," thought Brett engulfed with a blinding hatred. "And Jepson."

Brett placed the tray on the table and walked back to the veranda. He smiled at Puttock, fluttering his eyelashes.

"Excuse me, Mr. Puttock." he said. "I must go to the *cou*."

Puttock nodded his head. "Sure, boy. I'll see you tomorrow."

"Yes, sir!" Brett winked suggestively, then turned and jumped off the veranda and ran across the glade and into the trees. Ella would be waiting. He would tell her everything was ready.

Chapter 15

Milly was irritated by Carlton's fussing. He patted her belly proudly as they lay on the bed together. It was early evening. Milly had been reading when Carlton had knocked on her door and entered the boudoir.

"The baby will be all right, Carlton," she scolded. "You fret too much."

"As long as you do not exert yourself, dear. You have no need to supervise the cooking, for instance. Ella is quite capable. And you must leave everything in your chamber for Pallis to do for you."

"For heaven's sake, Carlton!" she snapped. "I am not an invalid." She put her book down on the bed and faced Carlton. "There is another three months to go yet. I'm not going to be stuck in here all that time!"

"Of course not, dear." Carlton stroked her arm. "This baby is so important to me." He placed his ear to her stomach. "Do you think I can hear him?"

"Oh, you make me laugh, Carlton! Anyone would think you have not fathered a child before. You had Laura and any amount of slave whelps. I know Caspar is dead, but what about the boy Hayes? And Miranda and Quentin?"

Carlton drew back in surprise. "Who told you about them?"

"Ella. But does that matter? Ella said you sent

Hayes to Trinidad to be an apprentice. Why did you do that?"

"He was a slave whelp," Carlton said irritably.

"But so were the others." Milly teased her finger down Carlton's cheek. "You are strange sometimes, Carlton. You like the niggers to believe you are tough and ruthless, but I don't believe you are."

"I thought Hayes was my wife's son," said Carlton bitterly. "But he wasn't. I've never had a white son. That's why your baby is so important to me."

"Dear Carlton," Milly murmured, snuggling her head into the crook of his arm. "He is important to me, too. Don't worry."

He kissed her. She opened her mouth in response and forced her tongue between his lips. He pulled away from her.

"No, Milly! You'll start me off."

"That's what I want to do, Carlton." Her hand slipped down his chest under his open shirt. She rubbed his stomach slowly.

"But you can't. It would harm the baby." Carlton felt his flesh stirring as he spoke. He would summon one of the wenches from the nursery. What about that one he had given to Brett? Empress! That was her name.

Milly's head followed her hand. She lay with her cheek pressed close to Carlton's belly, teasing his navel with her tongue. Carlton squirmed.

"No, Milly!" he murmured breathlessly.

Her fingers clutched him and her lips slipped lower.

Carlton lay back and scratched his armpit thoughtfully. Empress would have to wait until another day.

"I came to tell you about Dyce," he whispered into Milly's ear when she snuggled into his arms again.

"You must stop giving him money."

"Just a few pounds, Carlton. You can't expect him to stay cooped up here without going down to the

135

village to enjoy himself. Dyce is used to company. He'll repay me sometime."

"With what? You know him better than I do, Milly. If he was ever going to be worth anything, he would have his own business or have leased a plantation by now. Instead, he feels I owe him a living because I married you. He is using you, Milly."

"No, Carlton. You don't understand him."

"I don't?"

"If you helped him to make a start, I am sure he would surprise you."

Carlton nodded his head, smiling ironically. "I'm going to, Milly. For you." He turned his head to one side as Milly bounced onto him.

"Careful!" he spluttered.

She released him. "I know," she pouted. "The baby."

"There's about thirty acres of land the other side of the river, inland from the slave quarters. It's uncleared bush, but it's flat and fertile. I'll lease that to Dyce if he wants, lend him some slaves, and let him work it. If he is serious, he could raise sugar. That will earn him a small income."

"He's serious, all right, Carlton. I'm so pleased!"

Brett placed the rum decanter on the table beside Puttock and smiled at him. "I've squeezed guava juice for you, Mr. Puttock," he said, indicating the pink liquid in the jug. "Do you think you will need more rum for Master Dyce?"

"No, you young rascal!" Puttock cuffed Brett in his stomach, just missing the boy's balls. "He's bound to head for Layou after he has quaffed his fill here."

Brett danced away as Puttock made a playful grab for him. "Do you want me to stay down here with you tonight, sir?" Brett grinned impishly.

Puttock swallowed, looking beyond Brett to where

Lambert was watching. Lambert lowered his eyes. "What's the matter with you, nigger?" he shouted. "Yes, Brett. You stay here tonight if you want."

"I must go to the house first, sir. For my supper."

Puttock nodded, leering after Brett as the boy bobbed off the veranda and disappeared into the undergrowth. Puttock stroked himself reflectively, then reached for his glass and the jug of guava juice at his elbow. He looked around for Dale.

"Here, boy, taste this juice for me."

Dale cast his eyes upwards to indicate his annoyance at the overseer's finicky habits. He shuffled across the veranda and poured some juice into a spoon he carried with him. He sipped it with distaste.

"Well?" snapped Puttock, irritated by the boy's attitude.

Dale shook his head.

"I suppose you'll be happier when you try the rum!" Puttock poured himself a measure of the juice while Dale dripped a drop of the rum in his spoon and sipped it.

He smiled. "Dat does be good, sah!"

"Pah!" muttered Puttock, peering out into the night and wondering when Dyce would turn up.

Brett, who was crouched at the back of the cabin, wondered the same thing. He had not gone to the house as he told Puttock. Ella was sitting silently in the grass beside him. She sniffed the air and touched Brett on his arm. A minute later, they heard Dyce walk along the path and step onto the veranda.

Brett stood up to go.

"Let he drink de first rum," warned Ella. "Make sure dat Puttock does be relax. Sit on he knee if you like. Let he feel you." Her eyes glinted.

"Give me the poison." Brett's voice was hard. He held out his hand. Ella gripped it in the dark. He felt her dab his little finger with a liquid.

137

"De poison gon' stay under yuh nail, Brett," she whispered. "Just dip yuh finger in de rum when yo' serve he." She patted his leg as he stood above her. "Go, Brett. For Caspar!"

Puttock's face brightened when he saw Brett enter the circle of light from the single lantern burning on the veranda.

"What's that whippersnapper doing here?" asked Dyce mournfully.

"You know he likes to spend his evenings with me, Dyce."

"I'm not surprised, really. It's unbearable at the house. Carlton insists that Milly rest all the time, and he watches me like a missionary. Perhaps he thinks I'm going to run off with his silver! Wouldn't mind getting my hands on his gold, though, instead of that piece of land he wants to lease me."

Brett stretched out on the veranda floor at Puttock's feet, resting his head on the overseer's knees. He saw that Dyce's glass was full.

Puttock allowed his fingers to stray down to Brett's head. He tickled his ear, then ran his fingers through his ringlets while Dyce continued his tirade against the Bondmaster.

Brett gazed up at the young moon. "It was a moon like this," he thought, "the night Caspar died."

Dyce downed his rum. Brett eyed him surreptitiously, pressing his head back against Puttock's thigh.

"My friend would give a purse of gold for a colt like that," observed Dyce. "White, too!" He reached across for the decanter on the table.

"Let me, Master Dyce!" said Brett, leaping up from the floor. Puttock sat back in his chair, covering himself awkwardly with his hands.

Brett picked up Dyce's glass in his left hand and deftly poured rum into it from the decanter. He put his hand over the top of the glass as he passed it back

138

to Dyce, letting the tip of his little finger dip down into the rum. He poured a juice for Puttock, then sat down again at the overseer's feet. Lambert and Dale were curled up together at the other end of the veranda.

Dyce was speaking for so long that Brett thought he would never drink the rum. Puttock's hand had crept around Brett's neck and he was groping down his chest. Brett tried not to fidget. He raised his head and smiled brightly at Puttock.

At last Dyce lifted the glass to his lips. "I'm off to Layou after this rum," he said. "Sure you don't want me to take that buck with me?"

"No," grinned Puttock, gripping Brett's shoulder. "He stays here."

Dyce tipped the rum down his throat. He lowered his glass and leaned forward for the water jug. As Brett watched, Dyce seemed to hover in mid-air: he gasped, then toppled slowly out of his seat. He slipped to the deck of the veranda, twitched once, then lay very still.

Carlton was not satisfied.

He had listened very carefully to the events recounted by Puttock, Lambert, Dale, and Brett. And now he looked at the lifeless body of Dyce as it lay on the floor of the veranda. Someone was lying.

One of the four had put poison in Dyce's rum, of that Carlton was certain. In spite of Carlton's doubts, the only person who could have done it seemed to be Puttock. Puttock had been alone with the rum between the time Dale had tasted it and the time Brett served it. Brett swore he had no knowledge of the poison, and both Puttock and the slaves said Brett could not have put poison in Dyce's drink without them seeing.

Carlton glared at Dyce's body. He was an unattractive character. His lip was curled back in agony. Carlton was not sorry to see him dead. Now he must break the news to Milly, he thought ruefully.

Milly had her miscarriage two days later.

Ella passed on the news to Brett with a shrug of her shoulders. She was elated. "Mas Carlton should be grateful to me," she sniggered. "De whelp was be a wench."

BOOK TWO

Vengeance

1829—1830

Chapter 16

Laura brushed aside the branch of the flamboyant tree blocking her path. If she had been riding fast, she thought, the branch could have swept her off her horse. She glanced down at the trail that meandered through the plantation from Layou. It was clotted with puddles and loose stones, and long lemongrass bunched up on the side blocking the drains. It must have been months, she thought, since the path had been cleaned.

Laura stared at the house ahead of her as she rounded the curve and took the uphill path. It looked the same. The weather-worn balcony still girded the house like a strap holding it together. The shingles of the roof were bleached gray by the sun; some of them, Laura noticed, were ripped and needed replacing.

Fallen palm branches were scattered across the main trail up to the house. The royal palms had grown proud and straight and were taller than she remembered them. Laura gazed over the unclipped hedgerow of crotans between the trees to the cane fields beyond. The cane was overgrown, waving uselessly in the breeze wafting down the valley from the hillside. Laura raised her eyes to the mountain on the distant plantation boundary. Smoke drifted skywards from a thick mass of trees high on the hillside. Laura wondered why slaves were working so far up in the heights.

Slaves! Laura was so shocked she jerked the horse's head in surprise, jolting to a stop and almost throwing herself off. She gazed around quickly. There was not a slave to be seen. She cocked her ear to the breeze to see if she could hear the low rhythm of a work chant, or the shouts of slaves calling to one another across a cane-piece. Apart from the cawking of the birds and the scraping of branches in the wind, the plantation was silent.

Laura spurred her horse and galloped swiftly up the hill to the house.

She was relieved to see a Negro ambling out of the stables as she approached. She squinted at him. "Caliste?" she asked as he gripped the bridle in his hand.

"Yas, ma'am." The slave answered dutifully without taking his eyes off the ground to look at her.

"You've grown thick-waisted since I saw you last, Caliste. Any whelps?"

"Yas, ma'am." Caliste raised his head and peered at the lady as she dismounted. He frowned. "Miss Laura? Ah done breed four fuh Mas Carlton. He done sell all dem." He snapped his mouth shut suddenly as though he was frightened of having said too much.

"That's good, Caliste. I'm sure you have more in you."

"Yas, ma'am." He steadied the horse, bowing his head again.

Laura smoothed down her ruffled gown and unlaced her bonnet, shaking out her hair. It fell to her shoulders. She patted it and turned to look up at the house. "Where's Mas Carlton?"

"He done go by de quartahs," Miss Laura." Caliste stroked the horse's neck. "Wid Brett," he added.

"Brett?" Laura tried to put a face to the name. It would be difficult for her to remember every slave after being away from Roxborough for nine years.

She nodded curtly at Caliste and walked across the courtyard to the kitchen. She could not help noticing that weeds were springing up through the cobblestones. The bougainvillea trailing up the columns supporting the house needed pruning. The barrel placed at the corner of the house to catch water when it dripped off the roof during rain was lying on its side. Laura righted it, wondering to herself why her father had let the plantation get so neglected.

She looked over the open top half of the kitchen door. The kitchen seemed to be empty. She unlatched the door and stepped through.

"Miss Laura!" a loud voice squawked at her in surprise.

Laura peered into the distant corner of the kitchen. As her eyes became accustomed to the gloom, she made out the figure of the tall Negress rising from her chair.

"Ella!" Laura rushed over to the slave and hugged her. "Ella! How wonderful to see you again!"

"Miss Laura! Ah done swear ah does be dreamin'! Ah done sit down in de chair to rest mah feet an' mah eyes does close. Ah hear de latch on mah door an' ah does see yo' standin' dere. Is yo', Miss Laura? In trut'?" Ella sounded as though she was on the verge of tears.

"In trut', Ella," Laura mimicked. "Heavens, Ella, don't cry!"

"Ah done t'ink ah never gon' see yo' again, Miss Laura."

"Well, I am really here now, Ella." Laura held Ella at arms length and scrutinized her. "You look just the way I remember you, Ella."

"Indeed, Miss?" Ella sniffed. "Yo' done grow moh lovely, Miss Laura."

"Don't lie, Ella. In two more years I will be thirty.

144

After what I have been through, Ella, I feel twice as old."

"Yes, Miss Laura, but yo' sure have de beauty to make a buck spark, if you' fuhgive me sayin' so, Miss."

Laura laughed gaily. "Oh, it is so good to be back here, Ella." She twirled around the kitchen. "But where is everybody? Mas Carlton, Caspar, the slaves?"

"Caspar, Miss Laura?" Ella's voice faltered.

Laura saw Ella's hesitation. "What is it, Ella?"

"Caspar done die, Miss Laura."

"Caspar! My Caspar! I don't believe it!" Laura sat on the bench with a thump, shaking her head mournfully.

"Ah t'ought yo' does know, Miss."

Laura hissed with exasperation. "How could I know, Ella? I have been in Jamaica these nine years. I sailed away the very night I left here with Fletcher."

"Miss, de night yo' done leave Roxbruh, Caspar does be killed."

Laura stared at Ella, blinking her eyes with disbelief.

"It does be true, Miss. Brett done see yo' ride off with Fletcher, den two of he cronies hung Caspar from de flamboyant tree. One of dem does be Dyce, but he done die dis year." Ella smirked proudly.

"Oh, Ella. I'm so sorry. I'm sure Fletcher did not know. He told me Caspar would be all right, I swear it."

"Don't fret, Miss Laura." Ella placed her hands on Laura's shoulder, comforting her. "It does be a long time now."

"What of my father, Ella?" said Laura after a moment.

"Mas Carlton?" Ella raised her eyebrow. "He does be gettin' on now, Miss Laura. He ain't what he used to be. He an' Brett does run de plantation demselves now."

Laura nodded. Perhaps that was the reason for the ill-kempt appearance of Roxborough.

"Mas Carlton done sell plenty slaves, Miss Laura. Only a score of whelps does be in de nursery, an' we ain't got no moh dan fifty slaves on de whole plantation!" Her tone reflected her disapproval. "Jus' me an' Pip an' a boy to run de house. Miss Milly has her maid, Pallis."

"Miss Milly?"

"Lor'," said Ella. "Yo' don't know Mas Carlton done marry 'gain."

Laura shook her head.

"He took a young wife fuh heself, Miss Laura. Why, she does be moh young dan yo'! Don't help him breed no son, dough," Ella cackled hoarsely.

Laura eyed Ella. "What's wrong?" she demanded.

It was Ella's turn to look carefully at Laura. Times had changed since Miss Laura had been Mistress of Roxborough. Ella was the queen who controlled everyone on the estate, whites and blacks. Laura could not harm her. Ella spoke freely. "She done lose she whelp t'ree times, Miss Laura. Mas Carlton does be tired of her now."

Ella's lips curled downward in a sneer. "She don't have no nigger, dough."

Laura's eyes flared. "Ella, that's a wicked thing to say!"

"Sorry, Miss Laura. It not mah fault." She wiped her nose on her apron. "Mas Carlton does spend he evenings on de gallery wid Brett. He does believe dat boy does be he heir, Miss Laura. He don't want no oder now." Ella's last words contained a note of menace as she stared defiantly into Laura's eyes.

Laura blinked and stood up. "I've come back, Ella. My baggage is down on the wharf. Could you organize some slaves to carry it up, please?"

Ella sniffed. "Is Brett who does be in charge de

slaves, Miss Laura. When he does return from de quarters ah gon' tell he."

"I think I'll go and say hello to my stepmother."

Ella looked puzzled. "Who dat?"

"Miss Milly, of course," Laura explained patiently.

"Whooo!" Ella clasped her belly as the howl of laughter erupted from her. "Dat Miss Milly yuh stairsmoder? Whoo! Yo' is de mudah and fadah of her, Miss Laura, an' no mistake."

Brett carried the ledger under his arm while Carlton rode slowly up the path ahead of him. Brett wished he could read. The ledger contained the names of all the slaves who had ever lived at Roxborough, including his own. When they reached the quarters, Brett made the slaves gather around them while Carlton called out names from the ledger. Brett would like to have done that.

"This is called stock-taking, Brett," Carlton explained.

The slaves stood in meek groups around Carlton, who peered at them from his horse, then back at the ledger. Every adult slave on the plantation knew that ledger. For them it was the symbol of their bondage. As long as their names were entered in that heavy, leather-bound book, they were owned by the Bondmaster.

Carlton read the names out slowly. Each name had the slave's date of birth written beside it, together with parents' names and the names of their children. A second date appeared by the names of those slaves who had died or been sold. Carlton had other registers which recorded his slave sales and the price he received for each Negro. There was also an annual workbook with the names of the slaves actually working on the estate and the jobs they performed.

"Because I've sold so many of the niggers these

past few weeks," Carlton explained to Brett, "I want to see the quality of what we have left."

As he called the names, the slaves shuffled around and answered softly. The preceding months had been unsettling for them. Since Puttock had left and Mas Carlton's wife had lost her baby, the slaves did not know what to expect from the Bondmaster from one day to the next. Mas Carlton had sold so many of them, the quarters were almost deserted.

"There's not many now," sighed Carlton as he closed the book and handed it back to Brett. "But the stock we've got is good." He waved his hand to include the cluster of slaves.

"It's a small herd that you can handle. The old mammies serve in the nursery, and the old men who can walk tend the quarters. The useless old niggers will soon die, so you don't have to worry about them." Carlton pointed to the group of males and females who formed the nucleus of the slaves.

"You have Asaph and Mercury there as your drivers. Tency, too, if you want her. There are enough strong colts and fillies here for two gangs."

The slaves stared listlessly at Carlton and Brett as he spoke about them. Just as he looked on them as dim-witted creatures unable to comprehend his meaning when he spoke about them, they accepted him as the power who controlled them.

"We ain't gon' have no outside overseer on the plantation again," Carlton shouted. "You niggers must do what Brett tells you. He is young yet, but he's my grandson so you bound to do the tasks he gives you. If not, then Constance is going to flay your stinking hides with the cat-o'-nine-tails!"

A lowing spread through the slaves. Carlton listened with satisfaction. He did not know that the slaves would give Brett respect because he was the grandson of Ella. Ella's obeah was more terrifying to them than the Bondmaster's whip.

But Brett knew. It would be Ella's power coupled with his white skin which would bind the slaves to him.

He stared in front of him studying the Bondmaster's back as the two rode up the path to the house.

Carlton's shoulders drooped; no longer was his bearing that of the proud slave holder who had built the finest herd in the West Indies. Since the night Milly had fallen to the floor of the boudoir, clutching herself and screaming while blood seeped down her thighs, Carlton's demeanor had changed.

As Ella had taken the bloodied fetus from Milly, so Carlton's spirit had been snatched from him. For weeks he brooded, losing all interest in the plantation. The sugar crop went to seed. He emerged only to sell parcels of slaves to itinerant slave peddlers who called in the hope of picking up Roxborough rejects.

Gradually, encouraged by Brett, who sat with him on his balcony at nights, Carlton's depression lifted. But his strength and enthusiasm were gone. His shoulders slumped as he rode his horse, the torn shirt clung to his back in the humid afternoon, and his tangled, uncombed hair reflected his broken heart.

"Mas Carlton!" Brett urged his horse forward as they approached the avenue leading to the house. "We have a visitor at the *cou*."

"Heh, boy?" Carlton roused himself from his thoughts. "How do you know?"

"That's fresh horse dung we just passed." Brett smiled. "I'm going to get those niggers to clean up this trail tomorrow. It needs cutlassing too bad."

Carlton ignored the reproachful sound in Brett's voice. The boy was right. "I don't want no more slave peddlers here, Brett. I've sold enough niggers now."

Caliste was running toward them as they rode into

the courtyard. Carlton slipped off his horse and ambled up the steps, shouting for Pip to bring rum. Brett noticed the nervousness in Caliste's eyes. He questioned the groom about the visitor, raising his head in awe to watch the scene on the balcony.

Carlton threw himself into his favorite chair, hoisting his feet in their muddy boots onto the balcony railing. He closed his eyes, waiting for Pip to bring him his drink.

Brett watched Laura glide along the balcony carrying the tray with the rum decanter on it. Suddenly, Brett was apprehensive. He watched Laura shyly. She was tall with a straight back and a determined manner. She paused in front of Carlton, waiting.

Brett felt his heart going out to Laura. He willed Mas Carlton to open his eyes and accept his daughter back into the home. A feeling as though he was out of breath gripped Brett's chest. His heart thumped loudly.

Laura placed the tray quickly on the table beside Carlton. "Daddy!" she whispered uncertainly.

Carlton's eyes twitched but remained closed. He heaved a sigh.

"Daddy, look, it's Laura."

Slowly Carlton opened his eyes. His first view was of a long dark blue gown which was positioned between himself and the sun. He frowned, trying to understand. When he raised his head the sunlight dazzled him.

"Laura?" The word dropped from his lips before he could control it. He shook his head. "Can it be true? Laura?" His voice grew bolder. He struggled to rise, pushing himself up from the arms of his chair.

Laura stood quietly. She turned her face to the sun as Carlton stared at her. She bit her lower lip anxiously.

Carlton stumbled and gripped the balcony railing

for support. He drew himself up to his full height. His eyes searched Laura's face eagerly. He took in the angular cheeks and the firm Todd chin, the blue eyes which watched him from under a brow flecked with concern. Suddenly Carlton felt tears pricking his eyes.

"Laura!" he croaked. "You have come back!" He opened his arms, and Laura fell into them.

Watching from the courtyard, Brett breathed with relief. He sprinted into the kitchen to tell Ella.

Chapter 17

Milly spread the pulp from the avocado pear onto the thick slice of toast she held in her hand. She listened to the sound of the wind rushing through the trees around the house. "Rain," she said conversationally to Laura. "You can always tell when the wind starts to howl through the valley like that."

"I know," said Laura, ladling pigeon peas onto her plate. She put down the ladle and reached across the battery of dishes in front of her for the beef, piercing a large slice with her fork. "I used to be so frightened of the rain when I was a child. The way it pounded on the roof, especially when there was lightning." She attacked the pile of food on her plate.

Carlton munched on a cassava cake, comparing the two women as the three of them sat around the dining table at breakfast. Milly had taken trouble with her appearance this morning; her red hair glistened, and her gown was a newly laundered one. Laura, in contrast, was dressed more practically in a plain outfit. Her hair was tied with a ribbon behind her ears.

"That reminds me, Daddy." Laura spoke with food stuffed in her mouth so Carlton had to lean forward to understand her. "There are some shingles on the roof that need repairing. The rain will leak into the house soon."

Carlton raised his eyebrow, glancing at Milly. She was sipping her chocolate as though she had not heard the remark. Carlton knew that the state of the plantation did not interest Milly at all. She was quite happy as long as she had money enough for clothes and books from England. What did she do all day, Carlton wondered, shut up in her boudoir?

There was a brief rush of cold air through the dining room before large drops of rain began to splatter the sides of the house. Pip and Brett dashed up the back stairs and began to close the shutters of the rooms on the northeast to keep rain from drifting in.

"You see," smiled Milly, pleased, "I knew it was going to rain." She gazed out the door to the balcony. The rain began to hurtle down, slamming onto the roof with a clatter.

"Damn!" said Laura, raising her voice to make herself heard.

Carlton grinned at Milly's scowl of disapproval at his daughter's unladylike language.

"I wanted to ride around the plantation with Brett today! This bloody rain is going to stop me."

"It's the rainy season now, Laura." Milly munched her toast daintily. "Whatever do you want to see the plantation for?"

"Why?" Laura looked askance at Milly. "Don't you take an interest in the estate, Milly? I want to see what is growing, what the slaves are doing—oh, everything!"

"Carlton doesn't like interference in his business,"

sniffed Milly with a frown, hoping to put Laura in her place.

"I'm sure Laura has no intention of interfering," snapped Carlton. He wondered why he always snapped at his wife these days. He swallowed and continued in a softer tone. "She might see what needs to be done, Milly. I never noticed that the roof needed repairing."

"I did," said Milly sulkily.

"Why didn't you tell me?" Carlton stared at his wife.

"If I told you, you wouldn't have done anything, would you? So many things I ask you, and you just ignore me." Milly stabbed the pear on her plate, scooping its inside viciously.

Laura looked at Carlton and Milly glaring at each other from opposite ends of the table. "Well, we're going to do something now. What do you say, Brett?" She shouted above the heavy pounding of the rain to call Brett as he stood with Pip watching the streams of water gushing around the house.

"Yes, Miss Laura?" Brett turned on hearing his name. His eyes were eager as he looked across at her.

Milly noticed his quick response, and sipped her chocolate miserably. Carlton seemed to hate her, she thought, his slaves took no notice of her, and now his daughter seemed to want to take over as Mistress of the Plantation.

"When the rain stops, Brett, we'll take a good look around the estate. I'll make a list of all the tasks that need doing."

"That's no use," countered Milly. "He can't read. He is a slave, you know."

"He is also my half-brother's son, Milly dear," Laura leered, pushing her plate away from her. "A marvelous breakfast! I'm so glad to be home."

"Are you staying long?" Milly's voice was bitter.

Laura looked at her curiously. "Why, yes, Milly. Like I said, I've come home now."

"Huh," Milly rose from her chair. "I suppose that's because the man you ran off with has gotten tired of you!" She turned her back on Laura and swept through the drawing room, tossing her head arrogantly so that her hair swirled around her shoulders like a fire. The rain thundered down, swirling over the landscape and engulfing those in the house.

Laura stared at Carlton. He shrugged his shoulders. "It didn't take long for you two to sharpen your claws," he drawled.

"Why?" Laura sipped at her coffee. "I've done nothing to her."

"Perhaps she thinks you will. I love Milly, Laura, make no mistake about that. She is my wife. I wanted her to be the mother of an heir for Roxborough, but that was not to be. Sometimes life here must be lonely for her. And the rain!" He gestured outside. "It gets on her nerves. Try to be friends with her, Laura. Please."

"Of course, Daddy." Laura stood up. "She's right, you know. Fletcher did get tired of me."

"Laura, I don't want to know what happened. You are here now, and I am so pleased to have you back. This is your home."

Laura stepped over to Carlton and kissed him gently on his forehead. "I never dreamed it would be as easy as this, Daddy. Thank you." She beckoned to Brett. "Come, Brett, let's go down to the kitchen. You can tell me what you think needs to be done on the estate first. I'm going to help you, Daddy."

Milly slammed the door of her boudoir so that it shut with a crash. She squeezed her eyes closed, fighting back tears.

"What does be de matter, Miss Milly?" Pallis was at her side, her arm twining around her waist.

"I'm all right, Pallis," Milly said wearily. She lifted her head and glanced around the room. "Open those shutters, Pallis!"

"But the rain, ma'am."

"I want to see the rain, Pallis. Would that it would wash away Laura!" She sat down heavily on the couch and gazed through the shutters that Pallis opened onto the balcony. The sky was aswamp with the rain that poured down ceaselessly. The slaves, Milly supposed, would be huddled in their shacks, trying to dodge the drops plopping through the thatch roofs.

"What do the niggers think of Mas Carlton, Pallis?"

The maid turned from the window. Milly saw the fright in her eyes as her face tightened.

"Now, Pallis," crooned Milly, "you don't have to be shy with me. Haven't you been my maid these five years since I came to Roxborough? I am not testing you, Pallis. Just the opposite. You can tell me what you like about Mas Carlton, and I'll not be vexed or report you. Besides, he gave you to me, so he has no power over you at all. You understand?"

Pallis nodded her head glumly.

"Very well, then. What do the slaves think of Mas Carlton?"

"De slaves, Miss? Dey don't t'ink nothin' of Mas Carlton, Miss Milly." Pallis bowed her head.

"That's nonsense, Pallis, and you know it. Do they like him, Pallis? Do they fear him? Do they plot against him?"

"Oh, no, ma'am!" Pallis was alarmed. "No plotting, Miss. Ain't none of de slaves does do dat, Miss!"

"Then they must like him, then," concluded Milly, not noticing the panic she had inspired in her maid.

"I suppose I like him too, really. But that daughter!" Milly watched the rain, her spontaneous feeling of compassion for the slaves drenched in their hovels

155

safely forgotten. She patted the couch beside her.

"Come sit with me, Pallis."

"Yes, Miss Milly." Pallis was relieved that her mistress's questions had probed no further. She seated herself down on the couch in the manner she had learned from her mistress. She decided to be extra loving to Miss Milly so her mistress would forget those dangerous questions. She wondered how Miss Milly had heard about the plot. She would have to warn the others.

Milly put her hand in her slave's lap, squeezing Pallis's hand. Pallis smiled sweetly, laying her head on the back of the couch and opening her mouth expectantly.

It was mid-afternoon before the rain stopped. Huge puddles pocked the courtyard, and channels of dark, muddy water swirled in gullies across the main drive. The vast leaves of the plantains, bananas, and giant ferns dripped with water while raindrop pearls slithered on the swaying ribbons of the cane plants. The haze over the rolling lowland lifted, and the sun sparkled in the sudden green flush of the valley. Laura looked at the scene and smiled.

"I ain't seen rain like that in years, Daddy. The whole plantation has burst into life. The birds are calling. You can almost see the plants growing."

Carlton raised his head from the ledger he had been studying. "It's getting so it's too much for me to handle now, Laura."

"Don't even think about that, Daddy." Laura patted his hand. "I'm going out."

Brett was waiting for Laura as she ran down the steps. She carried her skirt high up to her knees so it would not get splashed as she stomped on the rain-sodden path to the stables. Brett caught a glimpse of her knees, a flash of white flesh above her riding boots. He was strangely moved.

Caliste quickly saddled two horses for them and they set off down the avenue. In the distance they could hear the roar of the river swollen by the rain as it tore down the crotch of the valley to the sea.

"This rain has done some good, Brett," Laura called, pointing to a rivulet running across the trail. "You can see where you must get the gang to clear the drains." She rode on in silence for a few moments.

"Brett, what really happened here? Why have the slaves not done any work for months?"

"Mas Carlton, Miss Laura. It was just like he didn't care any more. I tried, Miss, but every day slaves would be sold or disappear. I could never succeed."

"Disappear. Do you mean run away?"

"Some did, Miss Laura."

"No one went to look for them?"

"Mas Carlton cursed them, Miss Laura, but he did nothing about it. Since Miss Milly lost the child."

"We'll get things going again, Brett."

"We, Miss?"

"Of course, Brett. You want to work with me, don't you? We can't let the plantation go to ruin."

Brett pulled his ear. "But you're a woman, Miss."

"Hah!" Laura's laugh was so loud that a parrot crashed out of the forest tree over her head and set off up the valley with an angry shout. "I wondered if you were old enough to notice."

Brett lowered his eyes.

"Boy, I believe you are blushing!" Laura guided her horse over to Brett and put out her hand to touch him under his chin. She raised his face and stared into it. "You have your father's eyes," she whispered huskily. She brushed away a lock of his hair which the rain from the trees had stuck to his brow.

She leaned over toward him and kissed him quickly on his cheek.

His arm snaked around her waist before she could withdraw. Surprise fluttered in her eyes. He turned his face toward her and slowly placed his lips on hers, grasping her firmly with his hand. She flickered a protest with her eyebrows but his tongue tore into her mouth. She tightened her grip on her horse as her loins swam with an unexpected warmth.

"Brett!" she stammered in surprise. "But you're a boy!"

"I wondered when you would find out!" he laughed, reaching out for her bridle. "Follow me."

"Where are we going?"

Brett turned his large eyes on her without speaking.

They rode cautiously along the narrow path through the overhanging bush, bowed low with the weight of the rain on its leaves. Brett halted his horse at the edge of the glade. The cabin was just as she remembered it, nestling under an enormous flamboyant tree, acres of tall waving cane growing into the distance beyond it.

Brett put up his hand to help her as she slipped out of her saddle. He tied her horse and walked on in front of her to unlock the door of the cabin.

Laura was puzzled. Brett walked with a swagger and appeared to know his own mind. Yet he was not much older than a child. By his kiss, Laura knew he understood how to use his body. She had not been stirred like that for years! He was tough with muscles bulging on his legs and arms like a blacksmith. He wore a loose smock soaked by the rain, and breeches which stuck to his skin intriguingly. Laura hurried after him onto the veranda.

He opened the door and went through, not looking to see if she was following. He walked straight over to the bed and sat down. She stood in the doorway glancing around.

"Shut the door," he said.

Laura's throat dried. She wanted to reprimand him for his boldness. Instead, she quietly closed the door, groping her way in the darkened interior over to the bed.

Laura felt Brett's hands gripping her waist. She wanted to stop him, but it was impossible. His hands were firm. They slid up her body to caress her breasts through the stiff fabric of her dress. She pounded the floor of the cabin with her boots in excitement as Brett began to gnaw at her neck.

"No!" she said, meaning yes. "No! No!"

Brett did not answer. He nibbled his way up the side of her ear, prodding his tongue inside, making her cringe.

Laura groaned and laid her head back on the pillow. Brett's fingers fluttered over her breasts and descended to her waist, rubbing down the material of her dress and petticoats. She twisted away from him, raising her skirt to help him. She put out her hand to grasp him and guide him toward her.

But he was not there.

She opened her eyes, patting the bed beside her. "Where are you, Brett?" she laughed.

There was a crash as he opened the shutter and light bounded into the cabin like a caged dog. Brett stood in the center of the room staring at her. She was lying on the overseer's bed wtih her legs parted expectantly. Her flesh from the tops of her wet riding boots to the damp mystery of her crotch was a vivid white against the grime of the sacking of the plantain leaf mattress.

Brett walked over to the bed and stood above her. His hardness showed through the rough osnaburg of his breeches. The tenderness had left his eyes as he studied her.

"What's the matter?" she demanded. She let him feast his eyes on her body. "You've never seen a white wench before, I suppose?"

"Caspar was whipped until a pool of blood from the lash spread across this floor," snapped Brett. "You saw him here!"

Laura licked her lips, eyeing Brett anxiously. "What are you going to do?"

"That depends on you!" He spoke evenly, without a smile. Laura was frightened.

"I had nothing to do with it, I swear." She raised her head off the pillow. "I stopped them thrashing him. Fletcher told me he would be all right. I made Fletcher take me away."

"I know." Brett put his hands on his hips. "The other two, they hung Caspar from that branch outside. One of them was Dyce Dobbs. I've killed him already. I believe the other was called Jepson. Do you remember him?"

Laura could not believe the chill in Brett's voice. "I think so," she whispered.

"Would you recognize him?"

"Yes."

Brett walked to the side of the bed and put his face close to Laura's. "I'm going to kill him, Laura. Will you help me?"

Laura stared back at Brett. It was like looking into the past, as though it was Caspar there beside her. She reached up and clasped him around his neck, pulling him down onto her.

"Yes, Caspar! Yes!" she whimpered.

Chapter 18

"Jepson!"

The man sitting in the darkened corner of the rum shop pulled his head out of the embrace he was engaged in. The black arm hooked around his neck slithered out of sight as the Negro merged into the blackness. The man wiped his mouth on the back of his sleeve and peered at the woman standing over him.

He saw a blond wench with a smile of old friendship on her face. Jepson frowned as he considered her. Her gown was well-tailored, with a minimum of finery. She carried a short riding whip in her hand, holding it like a wand of authority. She looked amused.

"You don't remember me, Jepson?"

Her voice did not carry a threat of trouble, but Jepson decided to be cautious. Quickly, in his mind, he reviewed his recent deeds. Finding none that could have involved such a woman, he acknowledged her presence by shaking his head gruffly.

He wondered whether the Negro cowering in the corner would be any use in a scuffle in case he had to clear out of the tavern quickly. His eyes darted past the woman to see if ruffians were lurking at the bar waiting to attack him at the woman's signal. The only stranger in the tavern was a white youth with black hair tumbling down his neck in ringlets.

"I'm Laura, Fletcher's wife."

Fletcher's wife! Jepson gasped, pointing to an upturned barrel beside the table. "Sit down!" he said thickly.

"I wasn't sure. I have to be careful." He frowned as Laura pulled the barrel closer and settled herself on it. "What does Fletcher's woman want with me?" he thought to himself.

"It's been a long time, Jepson. I hardly recognized you." Laura spoke the truth. It had taken over an hour visiting the various casinos and taverns in Layou to find Jepson. She had asked for him at each one, only to receive evasive answers. It was John-James, the mulatto owner of this tavern, who had been quick to point him out, snatching up the money Laura had placed on the counter for him.

Jepson had grown stout. He had been stocky and tough before, but now he had fleshed out, his short body flabby with decadence. He spoke with a lisp. "Ith Fletcher here?"

"He is in Jamaica."

"You are alone?" Jepson was puzzled. The only white wenches to be found alone in a Layou rum shop at night were whores.

"It depends," smirked Laura, baring her teeth in a smile. "Fletcher is far away."

Jepson picked his nose with his thumb. He glanced at the black boy sitting behind him in the corner, then looked back at Laura. He wiped his thumb on the collar of his coat. "Fletcher wath a good friend of mine. A weal terror!"

Laura nodded her head. She understood Jepson. "John-James," she shouted, "where's my sangaree?"

Jepson raised his eyebrow. The rum shop was deserted except for the white youth at the bar. It was a small square room, lit with a single lantern behind the counter. John-James, his face shrunken like a dried-up pomegranate, could be trusted to keep his mouth shut. Jepson would not like it known that he had been drinking with Fletcher's wife.

"A rum, John-James!" he called, leaning forward and gripping Laura by her elbow. "I'll join you."

"Of course," smiled Laura, "for old time's sake." She looked in the direction of the boy in the corner. "I would like to talk to you. Privately." She saw Jepson frown suspiciously. "It's about my nephew." Laura gestured to Brett at the counter.

Jepson gaped. "He is your nephew?" His voice was husky with greed.

Laura nodded. "Perhaps you can help him?"

"Mayhap I can. You!" he said to the black boy. "I'll see you tomorrow. Move!"

The Negro uncurled himself from his position in the corner and minced out of the shop. Jepson cleared his throat and spat on the floor. He stared at Brett again as though unable to believe what he was seeing. The youth's breeches were split up one side revealing his tanned and muscular thigh. His smock hung loosely about his shoulders. Aware of Jepson's gaze, the youth turned to face him. His smile was exquisite.

"Brett, come here!" called Laura as John-James delivered the sangaree and put Jepson's rum on the barrel that served as a table. "This is Jepson, a friend of my husband!"

As he watched Brett strolling across to him, Jepson squeezed his thighs together with desire. He was fired by the boy's swagger and slender, provocative limbs.

"Sit down, Brett!" ordered Laura, playing her part as the concerned aunt. "I'm desperate to find something for Brett to do, Jepson." Laura confided. "He needs discipline, guidance. I can't give him that."

Jepson was going to ask who were the boy's parents, but he could not take his eyes off him. His face had a feminine beauty, but it was not difficult to see that

163

this was an illusion which concealed a tough manliness.

Brett sat straight, his palms pressed down on his thighs. He watched Jepson as though worshipping him.

"How do you think I can help?" Jepson sipped his rum, gazing at Brett over the rim of his glass.

"It's difficult for a woman, Jepson. You have traveled all over the islands. You know so many people. I wondered if you would know anyone who would like a boy like Brett."

"I can do anything!" Brett winked. He put his foot around the barrel and pressed it against Jepson's in case the man doubted his meaning.

Jepson gulped, quickly swallowing his rum. It helped him concentrate. "I could look around," he said.

"That would be wonderful. Fletcher would be pleased when I tell him how you have helped." Laura stood up.

"I can't promise anything," Jepson added hastily, cowed by the mention of Fletcher's name. "You're not going?"

"I have a friend to see." Laura bared her teeth again as though smiling. "Can I leave Brett with you for a while? I'm sure you want to ask him questions and so forth to discover what he can do."

Jepson was speechless. Laura left some money on the counter for John-James, who nodded his head like a delirious puppet. She swept out of the cabin. Jepson was alone with Brett.

"My aunt believes I'm still a child." Brett smiled apologetically. "I'm not."

"I can see that." Jepson rested his hand on Brett's knee, squeezing it emphatically. "You could do well for yourself, boy. There are gentlemen in Barbados would give five niggers to have a white lad like you attend them."

"How do I get to Barbados? I have no money."
Brett pushed his knee closer to Jepson.

"I could help you do that." Jepson fingered Brett's
thigh. "It's up to you."

"I don't know how I could repay you."

"You don't?" Jepson croaked. "Come, boy, let's
take a walk."

John-James bowed his head as Jepson and Brett
stepped down out of the cabin. The narrow street,
which wound its way through the taverns, rum shops
and casinos of the wharfside village, was lit by lanterns
hanging from the verandas of the larger houses. The
sea was on one side of the street behind the cabins,
while the forest which separated the village from Roxborough Plantation pressed down on the houses at the
other side.

Jepson paused, looking up and down the street as
he stood in the shadow between two cones of light,
careful that the wandering groups of sailors and trades-
men should not see him.

"Come, we'll go to my lodgings, boy." Jepson
gripped Brett by his shoulder.

"Oh, no," said Brett. "Look at the moon. See, it
is like a ghostly sun with its glow haunting the sky. Let
us sit by the sea." Brett raised his head and gazed
deliberately into Jepson's eyes. "It is very romantic. I
know the place."

Brett put his arm under Jepson's and hurried him
down the narrow passageway between John-James'
cabin and the neighboring shack. It was darker there.
Jepson trod carefully, feeling refuse and stones under
his feet.

"Where you taking me, boy?" he asked, suddenly
suspicious.

"It's all right," whispered Brett, grasping Jepson's
hand and squeezing it. "Down here."

The moon lit up the spot where Brett was leading

him. It was at the top of a wall, built behind one of the casinos to prevent the sea washing away the building's foundations. Jepson glanced down. The sea splashed the boulders about twelve feet below. Above him towered the rear of the casino, holes of light leaking out of the cracks in the wooden wall. Inside the building people shouted to make themselves heard above the jangling of a squeeze box and the thumping of a drum.

"No one can know we are here," smiled Brett. "And no one can hear us."

Jepson looked around him carefully. He seemed satisfied. He pulled Brett to him roughly and grasped his hair at the nape of his neck. He snatched at his head and forced his lips onto his mouth in a thirsty kiss.

Brett choked back his disgust and responded as best as he could.

Jepson relaxed.

"You're as good as you look, boy. Lie down with me here." Jepson eased himself to the ground, pulling Brett down with him. He could hear the sea pounding below him. The boy was right, it was romantic, he thought. The moon silhouetted the boy's profile, his straight nose and firm chin haloed by his ringlets.

Jepson pulled Brett's head close to his chest, letting his hand slide down his back. He squeezed his buttocks, hugging Brett closer to him.

Brett gagged on the smell of rum and sweat from Jepson's body.

"Let me help you." Brett smiled at Jepson, the moon catching the flash of his white teeth.

He fumbled with the strap holding up Jepson's trousers. Jepson laughed and unfastened it himself. Brett eased down Jepson's trousers until they were caught around his knees. He forced himself to grasp Jepson, stroking him briskly.

166

He pulled himself away from Jepson as though to remove his own breeches. "You want to do it to me?" Brett whispered reassuringly.

"Yes, yes!' Jepson reached out his hands to draw Brett back to him.

Laura slid out of her hiding place in the shadow behind the casino. Brett saw her move. He separated himself from Jepson, pretending to unfasten the tie at his waist.

"Let me shed my breeches," he breathed.

As Jepson put out his hand to touch Brett, he felt hands pushing at his waist. He looked up in alarm. It was too late.

Laura and Brett roughly rolled him over.

He plunged off the wall into the water below, his shriek of comprehension drowned by the commotion from the casino.

Brett peered over the wall as Jepson slapped onto the rocks and the sea gushed over him. "Perhaps he can swim!" He glared at Laura in panic.

"No, Brett, men like him are scared of water. He's dead." Laura took Brett's hand.

"Help me to the road, Brett. We must get back to Roxborough before anyone sees us."

Milly could not sleep. She must have been lying in her bed for over an hour. Pallis had fallen asleep immediately and lay beside her breathing deeply. Her arm was thrust across Milly's chest. Milly opened her eyes. The curtains of the bed were drawn. A firefly had entered the room and dived about, its luminous green light brightening the shadows. Milly stared at its erratic progress and sighed.

The firefly is like me, she thought. A bright light trapped in this Roxborough boudoir, with no way out, flitting hither and thither. She sighed, lifting Pallis's arm off her breast and easing herself out of the bed. She wondered whether if she opened the window the firefly would be able to escape.

She moved over to the window, hugging her nightgown around her shoulders. She snapped down the wooden bar fastening the shutters and creaked the windows open. The night air rushed into the room, chasing out the staleness of the hot evening with the fragrance of the forest trees and flowers. Milly breathed in and sighed sadly to herself.

She looked for the firefly. It was perched on top of the bedpost, its tiny flame almost extinguished. He's too scared to fly away, Milly thought. Like me.

The moon shone brilliantly out at sea, its light flooding over the cane fields and probing the shadows of the old house. Somewhere, a board creaked. A dog snuffling in the rubbish yelped with surprise. A lonely night creature whistled plaintively while from the plantain walk at the other side of the house, the crickets cracked busily.

Milly caught her breath. She could hear the sound of horses. Yes. There was a neighing of a horse and the soft response of someone talking to it. She strained to see through the moonlit dark, but could only hear the noise of some kind of activity. A door banged somewhere on the plantation. There was the sound of a man's voice and a woman's strident laughter.

Milly bit her lip bitterly. As she watched, she saw Laura emerge from the darkness and walk across the courtyard to the steps. She was accompanied by Brett. Milly was not surprised. The two of them had been conspirators since Laura had arrived. Milly saw Laura pause at the steps. She spoke to Brett as though asking him something. He shook his head, patting her waist with obvious tenderness.

Milly stared in disgust as Laura lowered her head and Brett kissed her passionately on her lips. After an agony, they broke apart and Laura climbed the steps to the house while Brett walked under the veranda to his bed in the cellar below the house.

Pulling her hair in frustration, Milly sank slowly to her knees. Was there no way she could recapture the life she had once enjoyed with Carlton? she wondered. She was the Mistress of Roxborough but even the slaves like Ella and Brett had more influence than she did. If she had been a slave, Carlton would have sold her. He regarded her as useless. He did not even sleep with her any more.

She rested her chin on the window ledge, tears filling her eyes as she gazed at the moon. The sea in the distance shimmered below it. The stars scattered in the pale blue of the sky seemed dulled by the moon's brilliance. Through her tears, Milly saw the coconut trees, the breadfruit, the mangoes, the cane, the bananas, and all the trees and plants which seemed about to sweep over the plantation. One moonlit night, Milly dreamed, the forest would choke them all, and the Roxborough plantation would go back to bush.

Milly jerked herself awake. She was lying on the floor, her head leaning against the wall. The distant blare of a conch shell being blown in the slave quarters roused her. She rose awkwardly from the floor, stretching her body and trying to smooth out the aches caused by her unhappy night.

After using the utensil under the bed and splashing herself with water from the basin on the dresser, Milly dressed quickly. She had resolved to force Carlton to accept that she did belong at Roxborough and could do whatever Laura was doing.

Dawn's early light was creeping over the mountain range ringing the valley when Milly slipped out of the house. She trod carefully down the steps and gathered up her skirts as she ran to the stables. Caliste was washing himself when she appeared. He wiped the water from his face and opened the stables to saddle a horse for her. She mounted quickly and urged the animal down the path. She wanted to ride around the plantation before breakfast so she could surprise Carlton with her report on what should be done.

Milly took the fork leading down to the hill. She decided to branch off for a look at the overseer's cabin. She was surprised to see that someone had tethered a horse in the glade in front of it. She did not know Carlton had hired a new overseer. "He might have told me," she thought angrily.

As she stared at the cabin, the door opened. A man stepped out and stretched his arms above his head, chasing sleep from his body. Milly watched him with amazement. He was about her age, naked except for the linen drawers which clung to his body. His hair was dark and bushy, while his skin had a golden glow to it, as though he had spent his life lying in the sun.

Milly gasped.

Without looking in her direction, the man dived back into the cabin. A window crashed open and Milly found herself staring into the muzzle of a pistol. The man's halo of hair peered over the top of the casement.

"I have you covered!" the man shouted. His voice was deep and steady. "Advance and show yourself. No false movement, or I'll blast you to Hades."

"Goodness!" Milly exclaimed without being able to stop herself. "What a way to welcome your Mistress!"

"Mistress?" The voice slurred with anger. "I have no Mistress! Who are you? Advance into the clearing so I can see you!"

"If you yield that weapon you have pointing at me. I shall report this to my husband!" Milly saw the man remove the pistol from the window ledge. His eyes, which even from that distance seemed strangely

170

familiar, appraised her coolly. She jogged the horse up to the cabin and slid quickly out of the saddle.

"Are you alone?" the man demanded, standing upright so his naked torso was framed by the window.

"Yes," Milly answered equally coldly. "And you?"

The man nodded. "What do you want?"

"You ask me that? This is preposterous. I am the wife of the Bondmaster, the man who hired you. I expect a little more civility from you. Put on your clothes and come here." She stamped her foot on the veranda, astonished by the man's cheeky grin.

He threw open the door and stood before her, still clothed only in his drawers. He was her height, his body lithe and exciting. "I am the hireling of no man, and no man is my Bondmaster, ma'am." he answered curtly.

"Then what are you doing in the overseer's cabin?" Milly felt less confident now.

"I arrived too late last night to disturb the household," he answered glibly. "So I slept here."

"Who are you?" Milly asked softly, feeling her heart weakening as she faced the young man with his familiar features.

"Me?" The man smiled wryly. He crossed the veranda and seized Milly in both his arms before she could move. He latched his lips over her mouth in a kiss which choked her cry of protest.

As his fingers played at the base of her spine and his lips devoured hers, Milly was unable to resist returning his embrace. She clung to him frantically, her fingers tearing into the hard flesh of his bare shoulders.

She gasped as he lifted his head away. "I needed that!" he exclaimed. "So did you! What's wrong—my father too old to satisfy you?"

"Your father?" Milly gripped the man's waist to keep herself from falling. "Who are you?"

171

"Hayes," he smiled, licking his lips. "The Bond-master is my father. That makes you my stepmother." He swept Milly off her feet and carried her inside the cabin.

Chapter 19

"Oh, Hayes, I love you!"

"No, no, no! Tell me you loved the way I made love to you. But don't say you love me. I'm a nigger, Mistress Todd. Nice white ladies like you don't love niggers."

Milly was confused. She sat on the edge of the bed in the overseer's cabin, smoothing down her hair and wondering if there was a glass anywhere. She was sure she looked a fright. Outside, daylight had taken over the plantation. In the distance, she could hear the tramp of slaves and the shouts of the drivers as they ushered them to their work. She laughed nervously at Hayes's remark.

"A nigger?"

"Of course, ma'am. Mah mam does be a black wench de Bon'massa done mount when he was be tired of his wife." Hayes, stretched out naked on the bed, watched Milly mockingly.

Again Milly giggled. "Why are you telling me these things?"

"Because it's true." Hayes shrugged his shoulders.

"But you look so white. You skin is fair."

"My mother is a Fulani. I've heard whites say she

172

looks like a peasant from the Mediterranean. She has straight hair and a straight nose. But she's a nigger and a slave."

"That makes you a slave, too?" Milly gasped.

"No, Milly. Your virtue hasn't been sullied by a bondsman!" Hayes grinned. "Mas Carlton manumitted me before I was apprenticed in Trinidad. It's taken ten years for me to come home."

Milly sighed with relief. "I'm glad you returned." She ran her hand down the center of his chest, eyeing his sex with curiosity.

"You are now, but what happens when you go up for breakfast with your husband?" Hayes stopped her hand.

"I'm a nigger, ma'am, not a *beké*. You touch me too much and you'll just have to open those pretty legs of yours for me again!"

Milly blushed, withdrawing her hand quickly. "How can you say such a thing?"

Hayes opened his eyes wide. "It's the truth."

"You have no modesty?"

"What! Here I am, lying *tutuni* on top of a bed while the most enchanting buckra lady I have ever seen in my life rubs her hand in my short hairs, and you ask me about modesty!"

Milly's color deepened as Hayes spoke. She shook her head. "I . . . er . . . I don't know what to think. You have me confused. You were so tender and loving. Now you seem to be laughing at me."

"You want me to hold you again, Mistress Todd!" Hayes raised his hand to Milly's shoulder, attempting to pull her down toward him. "You want to be reassured, do you? Oh, yes, Milly, I am still Hayes Todd, but remember I am a nigger and because of that I am a feckless rogue. You should have nothing to do with me, for I am no good." He chuckled.

173

"Now lift your skirts and love me again before you go back to that husband of yours!"

"No!" said Milly pulling back, startled. "It's too dangerous now. The slaves are out. Someone might come."

Hayes smiled, nodding his head. "You are right, of course. Wouldn't do for the Bondmaster's wife to be found with a nigger, would it? Mas Carlton would cut off my grain, I'm sure, and banish you to your boudoir with your maid." Hayes laughed but stopped when he saw Milly's shoulder quiver.

"He has done that already," Milly sobbed.

"Now, Milly, don't cry. You'll spoil it." Hayes sat up, swinging his legs over the side of the bed. He put his arm around Milly's shoulder and hugged her.

"I'm a heartless fool, Milly. Tears have me reaching for my breeches and a quick exit through the nearest window. Women can't keep me with tears, Milly. Not even you."

Milly raised her face, peering at him between the blur of her tears. "It's not you I'm crying about, Hayes. It's myself. I feel so useless."

"You can be useful to me, Milly. I thought I would have to mount Mas Carlton's breeding fillies for diversion. I never expected to find my father had added a white wench to his stock. We shall meet here every day, Milly. You'll see how useful you are."

Milly looked aghast at Hayes. "I don't know if you are serious or joking!" she sobbed.

"Don't let that worry you. If my father cannot treat you as he should, then I will." He winked. "I'll wager you'll find my loving more to your taste than his rush to the end."

"I've never heard a man speak like you, Hayes. My brother was a scoundrel, but he never said such things."

174

"To his sister? I should hope not." Hayes stood up and stretched his arms above his head the way he was doing when Milly saw him for the first time an hour earlier. He touched the roof with his outstretched fingers while Milly admired him.

Muscles rippled everywhere on his body. Milly tried to make out the characteristics he had inherited from his Negro mother. His superb physique, his lithe, slender limbs, and his slightly burnished skin. His hair was thicker than a pure-blooded white man would have had, and his ears were smaller. He had Carlton's eyes, even Carlton's way of speaking. Milly was saddened when she thought of Carlton.

"You like what you see, Milly?"

She gasped, unaware that he had been watching.

"Women do," he said conversationally, stepping into his drawers. "It's nothing to be ashamed of. It's all I have, after all."

"What do you mean?" She watched him pick up his trousers, shake them and pull them on over his drawers, tucking himself in and buttoning his waist band. He looked even more attractive dressed than he did naked.

"My body, loving, that's my talent, Milly." He paused and turned on her with a frown. "Dam'me! Why am I telling you this?"

"You seem to enjoy talking about yourself."

"You enjoy it, too," he retorted. "Milly, I want you to know me as I am. I like you. I don't want to hurt you."

"No." Milly sighed, standing up and straightening her gown. "Don't hurt me." She turned to watch Hayes pull on his shirt and tuck it into his waistband. He smoothed it down and reached for his coat, handing it to Milly to hold for him. He slipped his arms into the sleeves and adjusted the coat so it fell to his liking. Deftly, he tied his stock around his neck.

"You have neither washed nor combed your hair," Milly scolded.

Hayes raised his eyebrow. "Do you bully your husband so?" He ran his fingers hopefully through his hair. "And you?"

Milly tossed her head, settling her tresses around her shoulders. "I have been riding around the plantation. Carlton will not notice anything. Do we ride to the house together?"

"Why not!" chuckled Hayes. "In riding around the plantation, you chanced to meet me riding up from the village." He picked up his pack. "My possessions are small, Milly," he smirked, "but my talents are great."

The sun was over the mountain range as they emerged from the cabin and walked to their horses. Birds were chattering in the forest and tiny humming-birds fluttered fussily in the flame-colored flowers of the flamboyant trees. Milly paused beside her horse and gazed fondly at the cabin. She sighed.

"We can come back, Mistress Todd. I'm here to stay." Hayes helped her onto her horse as a fat black woman barged into the glade. The woman stopped in surprise.

"Beggin' excuse, ma'am. Ah does not know yo' was be here." The woman backed away.

Milly glared at her. "What's your name?"

"Ah does be Ivonia, ma'am."

"What are you doing here, Ivonia?" Milly demanded, determined to assert herself.

"Ah does be searchin' fuh firewood, ma'am."

"Why aren't you with your gang, Ivonia?"

"Ah does be cook, ma'am. Ah does be de cook fuh de overseer when he was be here, ma'am. Ah does know where dere does have plenty firewood de oder side de patch, ma'am."

176

"Let her go, Milly, she's done nothing," laughed Hayes.

"Very well, Ivonia. You may go." Milly turned to Hayes. "Why did you say that, Hayes? She could have been spying."

"She could have been my mother!"

"What?" Milly was shocked. She turned in her saddle to stare at Hayes, whose eyes, as usual, seemed to be laughing at her.

"Even that crone was young and attractive twenty years ago."

"Your mother is still a slave here?" Milly pleaded with her eyes for Hayes to say no. It would somehow taint the pleasure she had enjoyed that morning with him.

"No!" Hayes laughed. "She wasn't a field hand, Milly. She was Laura's nanny until Mas Carlton sold her. She escaped."

"Where is she now?" Milly tapped her horse forward through the trees."

"In the heights, Milly." For the first time, Hayes sounded serious. "Tita, that's her name. She is with the runaways, the maroons, Milly, living in the forest like an animal. That's what Mas Carlton did to my mother when he no longer had use for her. He sold her off. He did the same thing with me. Well, I've come back, Milly, to claim what is mine."

"Where the hell have you been? Who's this!" Carlton glanced at Milly, anger blotching his cheeks. He stood on the balcony facing her as she came up the steps followed by Hayes. "Ella said you went out at dawn!"

"Oh, Carlton," murmured Milly condescendingly, "I had no idea I should report to you before taking a ride around the plantation. You allow Laura to do it all the time."

177

"Laura has nothing to do with this!" Carlton stared at Hayes, an uneasy feeling tugging at his stomach. He frowned. "You!" he pointed at Hayes. "What are you doing here?" he snapped.

"Father, is that the welcome you give me?"

"Hayes?" Carlton nodded, stomping over to his chair and throwing himself into it. "I might have known you would turn up." He buried his head in his hands.

"I've come home, Father."

"Shut up, damn you!" Carlton took his hand from his face and scowled. "Milly, what's going on? You had some plan to meet this fellow."

"Oh!" Milly was taken aback. "He's your son, Carlton, not some 'fellow.' You've always wanted a son; now look, you have one. I didn't go to meet him at all. He was coming here when I saw him on the road."

"Hah! I believe you sent for him, Milly!"

"That's ridiculous, Father. I never knew she existed until about ten minutes ago!"

"So you say, so you say." Carlton glowered at Hayes, considering the implications of the youth's arrival. He swallowed as he looked back at Milly.

"I'm his father, Milly, but he ain't no real flesh-and-blood son. That's what I wanted you to give me. This boy can't inherit Roxborough."

"Why not, Carlton, if he's your son?"

"Because he is half black, that's why."

"But he is free. He is not a slave."

"Oh, yes, Milly. But there is the law. No mulatto is equal to a white man."

"The law!" Milly was contemptuous.

"The law could be changed, Father. If you wanted to change it."

"Me!" Carlton raised his hands in exasperation. "I set my own laws for Roxborough, not for the damn

178

island. Looks like I can't even run my own plantation properly. My wife rides off at dawn, and the whelp I think I've set up in Trinidad comes back to haunt me!"

"I ain't here to haunt you, Da'. I've come back to live here."

"By the devil, that's fine!" Carlton growled sarcastically. "I must study that slave ledger to see if I've got any more nigger whelps going to return to Roxborough to live. I ain't even fifty till next year but my offspring are gathering to share the spoils. Look at my crosses!" Carlton put his hand on his brow again.

Milly smiled at Hayes. "I believe he is pleased to see you," she whispered.

Over breakfast, Carlton listened while Hayes spoke about his years in Trinidad. He had been apprenticed by James Macreary, Carlton's agent, to a printer when he was twelve. He liked the work, and his master, with whom he lived, was kind to him. When he had completed his apprenticeship, he stayed on with the printer earning a weekly wage. Hayes explained how he had saved his passage money so he could return home to Roxborough.

"I don't know why you wanted to come back, Hayes. There ain't nothing here for you." Carlton's rage had completely evaporated. It always did. He could never sustain his anger for more than the first few minutes.

Carlton recalled how he had loved Hayes. It was curious seeing him back at Roxborough again, sitting in the same chair where he had sat ten years before.

"You've grown into a fine young man, Hayes." Carlton rested his chin between the thumb and forefinger of his left hand. "You could breed me some whelps, I suppose. Yes!" He took his hand away from his face.

"I've got that girl Miranda!" he exclaimed. "You

179

and she could get me the fanciest whelp you ever did see. I'm the sire of both of you, so the whelp would be almost white. What a dandy house slave he'd make. Those Jamaicans would pay five hundred pounds sterling for such a brat." The coffee cups clattered as Carlton slapped the table in his excitement.

Hayes exchanged a glance with Milly. "I'm a free man, Da'. I don't aim to be a stallion for you."

Carlton stared at Hayes. He raised his eyebrow. "What's wrong, boy? You don't like wenches? Had an overseer like that once. Buggered my best bucks, he did."

"Times are changing, Da'. Slavery is not going to go on forever. You can't keep on breeding whelps to sell, Da'. Soon there will not be anyone to buy them."

Carlton frowned. "Is that what they say in Trinidad?"

"Yes, Da'. That's why I've come back. When slavery is abolished, you will need my help to manage Roxborough. You will have to pay people to work for you instead of beating them. You will not own slaves again, Da'. Everyone will be free."

There was silence while Carlton digested Hayes's remarks. Milly longed to put her arm out to touch Hayes. She admired him for telling Carlton something people had been warning for years.

"It's unthinkable!" snorted Carlton. "The British government would never do such a thing! Emancipation! Why, Dominica would rather go independent than abide by such a law. That's what the planters say. Abolish slavery, and you abolish sugar. That's enough of your Trinidad talk!'

"It will happen, Da'."

"Not in my lifetime, Hayes!" Carlton pushed back his chair and stood up. "Milly, you can tell Pip to

180

clear away. Laura and Brett are down by the mill. Ella has sent their breakfast to them." Carlton turned to Hayes, putting up his hand to clap him on his shoulder.

"I've often thought about you, boy. It was tough for me to send you away. You understand that? I'm pleased you came back." Carlton sighed. "Look around. You'll see a wench you want. Take her. Anyone. I'd like your get, I really would."

"Any wench?" Hayes smiled down at Carlton.

Milly watched, surprised how Carlton, beside Hayes, looked old and pathetic.

Carlton reached up to squeeze Hayes's shoulder affectionately, letting his arm slide down his back. "Sure, son. Any wench you want."

Carlton lowered his head so Hayes would not see the tears in his eyes and shuffled off to his room.

Chapter 20

The waterwheel was idle. Water gushed from the aqueduct falling short of the paddles on the wheel itself and flowing back into the river. A section of the stone aqueduct had been removed so that the wheel would not function. Laura stared at it, astonished by the amount of weeds choking the gullies and gutters. It was difficult to imagine that in the past, the wheel turned for weeks every year, grinding the mill stones together and squeezing juice from the cane.

"A few niggers and a good driver will soon have it cleared," commented Brett.

"You sound like Mas Carlton," smiled Laura. "I know you can get the wheel working again, but what about the slaves? Crop is a testing time for niggers. It's two shifts twelve hours off and twelve hours on until all the cane is ground."

Brett regarded Laura doubtfully. The two of them were inspecting the mill compound, assessing the work to be done to get the mill ready for grinding. The waterwheel, fed by the stone aqueduct channeling water from the river, was to turn the grinding stones. The canes were to be stuffed into the churning jaws to be pulped as juice and trash on the other side. A guttering, overgrown and almost hidden, was to carry the juice to a vat in the boiler house, while the trash was used to fuel the fires under the cauldrons.

Brett and Laura peered into the gloom of the boiler house. Although it had been unused for only one season, the undergrowth from the surrounding bush had begun to invade the building. Lizards scurried for cover under the spreading weeds. Laura wrinkled her nose at the smell that lingered from the time when nine cauldrons had bubbled with cane juice.

This was the process that produced the raw granules carried by a large gutter into a trough or the cooler. From there, Negroes took the sugar in pails to put in the hogsheads. Brett showed Laura where some of the hogsheads built by the cooper remained from last year.

"Each one of them holds sixteen hundredweight of muscovado sugar." Brett aired his knowledge. "Mas Carlton used to say we could get four hogsheads an acre, even with the ratoons; you know, the shoots from the old canes."

Laura grimaced as she looked around the neglected storeroom. "I don't blame my father for giving up sugar. It was such a messy affair. The dust and scum stained his skin for weeks."

"Mas Carlton said he could make four thousand pounds profit in a good year, if he could get the hogsheads shipped to England safely. He only has to sell about thirty slaves to make that much." Brett held back a branch poking through a window in the still room so that Laura could pass.

Neither of them spoke as they mounted their horses and rode away from the deserted mill. Both had been depressed by the visit. Cane grew well at Roxborough when it was nourished with putrescent manures and lime.

When Laura was young, she remembered, a slave with an ox and cart used to be employed daily in gathering manure from cattle fields to spread with the cane trash around the cane holes. One third of the total acreage of Roxborough had been occupied by sugar cane, another third by pasture and provision gardens, and the rest by woodland.

"What about rum?" Laura asked suddenly.

"Rum? We produced some last year." Brett sniffed. They were riding up to the house and Brett's attention had been caught by a strange figure strolling across the balcony.

"Some?" Laura queried. "I was looking at those ledgers Mas Carlton keeps in his bureau. Roxborough used to produce over a hundred puncheons of rum a year. A puncheon holds a hundred and ten gallons, Brett, so that is rum!" She tapped Brett with the handle of her whip to attract his attention.

"Rum is just the coarsest part of the juice, the molasses, drained off and distilled, isn't it? Surely we could go into rum production again?"

"Oh . . . ah . . . yes."

"Brett, what is wrong with you?"

Instead of answering, Brett gestured at the house

with his head. The stranger was leaning over the balcony railing with Miss Milly, watching the two of them riding up the path. Brett was surprised to see the man had his arm around Miss Milly's waist. Perhaps he realized he was being observed, for he withdrew it quickly, leaning forward and whispering something into Milly's ear. Milly laughed.

"I don't believe it!' said Laura, snapping her whip over the rump of her horse. "That's my brother Hayes!"

Brett shrugged his shoulders. He reached the house minutes after Laura had leaped off her horse and run up the front steps. He dismounted and gave the reins to Caliste and strolled across the courtyard to the kitchen. He could hear Laura jabbering away at the stranger, who was himself whooping with delight. Miss Milly was watching the antics with a reserved smile.

"Who is he?" Brett demanded, crashing through the door into the kitchen.

Pip, straining the sangaree into a jug, raised his eyes ceilingwards in an unspoken plea for an end to all the crises that were disrupting his routine. Ella stirred the pot on the fire without looking up.

"He does presage evil, Brett, ah does tell yo' now!" Ella stabbed her wooden spoon into the bubbling soup.

"He does be Mas Carlton's whelp from dat she-cat, Tita!" Ella dropped the spoon with a clatter onto the table, wiping her hands on the checked apron stretched over her gown. She glared at Brett, who was standing with his hands on his hips, his eyes flashing angrily.

"What's he doing here?" Brett shrieked.

"Yo' does understand de ruckus we does have here, boy? He done come back to live in his home. Mas

184

Carlton done welcome he an' tell he take any wench he does want."

Brett grinned despite his jealousy at Hayes's arrival. "He has chosen his wench already," he announced, his eyes glinting.

"Who dat?" Ella demanded eagerly.

"Miss Milly!"

"Oh, lor'!" Pip threw up his hands in amazement. He grabbed the sangaree jug and guzzled quickly from its lip.

"I saw him with his arm around her on the balcony."

"Dat does be de bes' piece of news." Ella sank down on the bench, cackling softly.

There was a pause. Brett scowled and began to pace the kitchen floor. "If he is Mas Carlton's son, maybe Mas Carlton will make him the overseer instead of me."

"An' make him heir to de plantation, too," Ella warned, thumping the table. "But if he does take up wid Miss Milly, Mas Carlton gon' get vex' wid him. "Yo' does be a' right, Brett." She smiled at him reassuringly.

"De buck does be a wench's man. He gon' hang fuh what's in his britches, Brett!"

Milly shut the door as soon as she entered her boudoir. She leaned her back against it, trembling. Her eyes traveled around the chamber without seeing the chaos of the room. Her mind was exclusively occupied with the events of the last few hours since the moment she had set her eyes on Hayes Todd at the overseer's cabin.

She was unwilling to believe that what had happened with Hayes had actually taken place. Yet she was overjoyed that it had. She wanted to hear in her mind every laugh and every cry, to sense every

185

caress and every clasp and to recall his unabashed grin and his resplendent nakedness. She needed to recapture those few hours to confirm to herself that they were really true.

In a daze, she walked over to the unmade bed and threw herself on it. Her long tresses billowed out around her, settling across the pillow as though smothering her. She hugged her arms around her breasts tightly, recalling the firm grasp he had held her in. He had as good as told her that he was a bounder, even scolded her when she breathed "I love you" into his ear. She could not help herself. She was in love.

Milly was astonished by her own behavior. She sought an excuse. He had such an endearing and compelling personality but, Milly reasoned, it was not only that which had made her succumb so quickly. There was the familiarity about his features and manner which made Milly feel that she had belonged to Hayes for years.

That she belonged to him now was certain. She could never face Carlton again. She wondered how he had not discovered what she had done when he looked into her eyes at the breakfast table. Her whole being ached for Hayes; surely her actions must have given her away. Was Carlton too concerned with getting a whelp out of Hayes to see what his son was doing to his own wife?

Milly sighed, rolling her head to one side of the bed. "What's going to happen now?" she asked herself. "Hayes is staying at Roxborough; I will see him every day, even every night. Will he come to me every night?" Milly supposed that she should be shocked at even thinking such a thing. "That must be Hayes's influence on me." She smiled.

Hayes was almost her age, virile, carefree and exciting, the exact opposite of her husband. Fate had brought him her way, she was sure. Fate was kind, perhaps making up for leading her into marriage with Carlton. But Carlton was hers, if she overlooked having to share him occasionally with slave wenches. Hayes was not hers. He had tried to tell her that. Could she capture him, have him for herself alone?

Milly sat up, gazing around the still darkened room. Hayes was somewhere in the house. Hayes, her lover!

Abruptly, Milly wondered why the room was still in darkness.

The shutters should have been wide open to allow the breeze to blow through to chase away the night vapors. The bed should be made, the curtains drawn back and laced around the posts; the boudoir should be neat and ladylike.

She was puzzled. Her wardrobe door hung open. A gown lay on the floor.

"Oh, my God!" Milly jumped up from the bed and rushed over to the dresser. The top drawer had been wrenched open. Her jewelry case lay open on the floor. She gasped and knelt down to pick it up.

"My rings!" she squealed. "My necklaces!" She sifted the remaining jewelry in her fingers, horror crushing the comfort of her thoughts of Hayes.

"Where is Pallis?" she whispered, staring at the chamber again, reluctant to accept the obvious.

The maid was not in the dressing room, and neither were her meager possessions.

"Carlton, Carlton!" she shrieked, throwing open the door and hurrying around the balcony to Carlton's room. He opened the door as she reached it. He put out his arms and folded her into them, clutching her firmly.

She did not see the harried expression on his face give way to relief as he clasped her to him. "Oh, Milly," he murmured while she sobbed, "I need you!"

"I've been robbed, Carlton!" screeched Milly, pull-

187

ing away from his eager lips. "All my jewelry, my gowns!"

Carlton released Milly instantly, bitterness stabbing him. He thought she had answered the prayer he was muttering while he lay in his room. He feared that one day Milly would tire of him and leave him, a lonely and sad old man. He was longing for her to come to him so they could renew their pledge of love for one another.

"Damn you, Milly!" he shouted, shaking her shoulders. "Stop sniveling. What the devil ails you?"

Hayes bounded around the corner of the balcony. He stopped when he saw Carlton and Milly staring at one another. "I say," he drawled nonchalantly, "anything amiss?"

Milly quivered at the sound of his voice. "I've been robbed," she said, facing him. "From my boudoir. My jewels, my gowns."

"Good lord!" exclaimed Hayes. "At Roxborough! I would never have expected it. You have a thieving slave on the plantation, sir?"

"Pah!" said Carlton. "Where's your maid—what's her name? Alice? Pallis!"

Milly lowered her eyes to the floor. "She's gone."

"There is your thief," grunted Carlton. "When did you last see her?"

"This morning," said Milly thoughtfully. "She was in bed when I went out."

"You went out damnably early, Milly." By his tone Carlton seemed to be blaming Milly for what had happened.

"I couldn't sleep. I heard the conch. It was dawn."

"Then she's not gone far." Hayes gave Milly confidence when he spoke. He did not condemn her like Carlton did.

"Do you have any trouble with runaways, Da'?"

Carlton pursed his lips, shaking his head. "There

are some maroons in the heights. We see their smoke sometimes. They are peaceful enough these days. Never troubled Roxborough."

"I'll take a horse and go and bring her in," said Hayes.

"You?" Carlton snorted scornfully. "You don't know the first thing about the bush!"

"I remember!" Hayes was affronted.

"Remember what? All you ever did when you were a boy was chase around beating your nigger playboy. Milly"—Carlton turned to his wife—"do you think she is carrying much?"

Milly pondered. "She has taken only a few of my dresses. The room is in a mess, as though she left in a hurry."

"Then she probably went alone, on the spur of the moment. You give her any cause to be vexed with you, Milly? You treat her all right?"

"Of course!" Milly's cheeks colored slightly, something Hayes noticed with interest.

Carlton pulled his pipe from the deep pocket of his coat. He sucked on it briefly. "Pallis was a good wench. Born and raised in the Paddock. I burst her maid myself." He frowned. "She would not run off out of her own mind. She must have a buck somewhere. But why take jewelry and clothes?"

"If it was me, Da'," Hayes interrupted with a grin, "I'd sell them quick."

"Aha, yes, Hayes. I think you have it. She'll give them to the buck. But slaves don't need money. It can be no ordinary buck who has deceived Pallis. He is someone who needs money. Now where do we look for such a nigger? On a plantation? In the heights?"

"How do you know he is a nigger?" Hayes grinned at Milly to cheer her up.

"Because it is only niggers who are thieves, Hayes. Call Brett. We must have a roll call to see if any

189

bucks are missing. Then Asaph can take a party into the hills to track her."

"I'm going, too," said Hayes. "Be a bit of sport!"

"Oh, yes, it will be that all right, Hayes. A runaway thief! Don't shoot her, that's too good for a nigger. We have to make an example of that wench!" Carlton turned to Milly with a leer.

"What do you think? Five hundred lashes, the gibbet, hang, draw, and quarter her?"

Milly trembled at Carlton's remark. She clutched her breast. Hayes caught her in his arms as she fainted.

Chapter 21

Pallis was panic-stricken. She could hear the shouts of her pursuers and the snuffling of the dogs crashing through the undergrowth after her. Sadly, she dropped the valise she had lugged all the way from the *cou*, so she could make faster progress along the narrow trail leading to the heights. She was distraught when she realized that if she had not tried to carry off Miss Milly's jewels, she could have made the maroon camp before her absence was noticed.

Pallis stumbled. The long dress she wore as a privileged maid was in tatters, ripped by the thorns and bushes that grew across the path. In the cavern of the forest she could not see if she was near her objective. The sun did not penetrate through the tall, heavy trees. Creepers hung down snagging her hair. The forest was damp, echoing with the sound of a stream rushing down a ravine to join the river.

The dogs were almost on her. She knew those animals. Mas Carlton called them his bloodhounds. Brett used them when he hunted manicou or agouti. Pallis screamed as she tripped over a tree root and fell to the ground. Now she was the manicou.

She scrambled to her feet but fell again as she stepped in a hole. She was on her hands and knees, grasping at the roots across the path, trying to pull herself up. It was too late. The dogs were on her, snapping at her heels, barking joyously.

Brett was the first one to find her. He lashed at the dogs with a stick, driving them away. They cowered down, their teeth bared for praise. Pallis lay with her face in the mud, her legs streaked with blood where thorns had torn at her flesh. Her chest was shaking as tears of frustration racked her.

"Pallis!" Brett knelt down and touched her on her shoulder. "Pallis! Are you all right?" It was a silly question, and Brett knew it. "Why did you try to run away?"

Pallis turned her face toward Brett. Mud was caked on her cheek, and her brown eyes were wide with fright. Her shoulders shook.

Brett felt his flesh tingling as he grasped the woman. She was hot; sweat, mud, and blood were smeared across her dark brown skin. The heavy odor of her body hit him as he gripped her under her armpits to raise her to her feet. He frowned, kicking at the dogs with his foot.

"The men are too close," he said. "You cannot get away now."

Pallis paused in her sobbing. "Yo' was be gon' give me dat chance, Brett?"

"It's too late, Pallis," he sighed. "Come on."

For Pallis, the sudden realization that she had a friend in Brett made her capture almost bearable.

Brett stopped Asaph's shackling her with rough iron rings which a slave had carried up for that purpose. The captors, with Pallis scrambling along between them and with a slave carrying the valise, were on their way back down the trail when Hayes, attended by Lambert, met them.

"Aha! So you have the wench!" Hayes leered. "A sprightly filly! Did she give you any trouble?"

"No!" grunted Brett. "That's hardly your affair, is it?" He nodded his head for Asaph and the slaves surrounding Pallis to keep on walking without waiting for Hayes to turn his horse around.

"I say, what's the hurry?" Hayes was puzzled by Brett's manner. "You've got the wench. Why not pause to give a chap a rest. We should question her!" Hayes grinned suggestively, but Brett did not look back.

Hayes turned his horse angrily, urging Lambert to guide the animal down the narrow path after the group already disappearing around the bend. "I command you to halt!" Hayes gasped as he caught up with them.

"Keep going," piped Brett when he saw Asaph falter.

"Look here, boy!" Hayes tapped Brett on his shoulder with the stock of his horsewhip. "You must listen when I speak to you."

Brett snatched the whip out of his hand.

"Hey!" shouted Hayes.

"Hayes!" Brett snarled, his eyes hard and his voice sinister. "I am not your boy, and you are not my master. In fact, I do not know what you are. I don't care. You have no authority to interfere with my duties!" Brett handed the whip to Lambert.

"Here is your whip. Use it on horses, if you like, Hayes, or on niggers. But never touch me again like that, or I'll kill you!"

At first Hayes was speechless at Brett's outburst. Then he chortled loudly, startling Lambert, who released the reins and let the horse move forward. "You threaten me, boy!" Hayes laughed. "A whippersnapper who don't even have no grain yet! Wait till I tell Mas Carlton about this!"

Carlton was waiting as the party proceeded up the trail to the house. The slaves, with Pallis in the center, were on foot, followed by Brett and the dogs. Hayes, on his horse, galloped into the courtyard when he saw Carlton watching. He slid out of his saddle leaving the horse for Lambert to catch and take to the stable. He ran up the steps.

"Good hunting?" Carlton raised his eyebrow and smiled.

"No hunting at all!" Hayes slumped himself into Carlton's chair. "Brett was bringing the wench in when I caught them. The horse delayed me. We had to walk it because the path was so bad. That damn boy of yours wouldn't let me question the wench. He said I had no right to interfere with his duties. He needs a taste of the lash, Da', to teach him respect."

"Indeed!" Carlton glared at Hayes. "And what do you need to teach you respect, Hayes?"

Hayes looked blankly at Carlton.

"You are sitting in my chair, boy. Up!"

Hayes flushed irritably, standing up and stepping over to the balcony railing. "Are you not going to do anything about his tongue, Da'?"

"No more than I am doing about yours, Hayes. You have been here less than a day. I'm pleased to have you back, you know that. But Brett has been well trained to become the overseer for this plantation. I do not think you need to worry about his conduct."

Hayes stifled his retort, vowing to get even with Brett later. He gripped the balcony rail to control his rage as Brett strode up the steps and waited politely for Carlton to question him.

"Well, Brett, our maid seems sorry for herself."

"Yes, sir. She was returning, sir, when we found her. I don't believe she meant real harm, sir."

"Hmm, Brett. But she ran off, didn't she? Where was she bound?"

"For the heights, sir. She was still on Roxborough land when we found her."

"Are you saying she had a change of heart? Not the braying of the hounds, Brett, but a sudden twinge of conscience made her regret her behavior?" Carlton spat in disgust down into the courtyard.

"I took that wench into the bosom of my house and family, Brett. She has even been to Trinidad with me. She had no cause to run off. She must be punished."

"I'll do that!" said Hayes.

"No, Da', give her to me." Laura strode around the corner of the balcony. She was wearing breeches like a man's above her riding boots and a shirt with a stock at her neck. She clasped a supplejack in her hand.

"You, Laura! Whatever for?" Carlton sat in his seat, snapping his fingers for Brett to carry over rum for him.

"I have learned these things in Jamaica from Fletcher, Da'. First, we must find out the information from her. She obviously has contacts with the maroons. And then her punishment."

Milly had been watching Pallis from her boudoir window. She leaned out to call to Carlton. "She has come back, Carlton, do not be hard on her!"

"Hard!" Carlton snorted, grasping the goblet of rum Brett held out for him. He downed the liquor quickly and held out his glass for Brett to fill with water. He gulped the water and stared around him at Hayes, Laura, and Milly.

"Thievery is a capital offense," he began.

"But she has a right to be tried by the authorities in Roseau for that," Milly interrupted.

"Hold your tongue, wife. I am the authority at Roxborough. She could be put to death."

"She was bringing the jewelry back, Carlton!" Milly pleaded.

Carlton scowled. "Neverthless, she is a thief."

"And a runaway," added Laura. "Give her to me, Da'. I'll deal with her appropriately."

"The idea is rather amusing," grinned Carlton. "What do you think, Brett?"

"Why ask him?" Hayes exploded. "I am unable to hold my peace any longer, Da'. The boy is too young. And he is soft. See, the wench is not even shackled. Maybe he is in league with her himself."

"She was returning, so why should I shackle her?" Brett looked at Hayes scornfully.

"She is here, Hayes," said Laura calmly. "You can see that yourself. She did not try to escape."

Carlton pointed to Brett. "Well, boy?"

"Pallis ran off, Mas Carlton, so I believe she must be punished. Because she was returning, I would suggest, sir, that she be spared the death penalty for thieving. She has been a good maid to Miss Milly, sir." Brett took a deep breath.

"Miss Laura is helping me with the plantation, sir. I would like to know what she has learned in Jamaica about punishing disrespectful niggers." Brett flushed and turned away, drained by the effort of speaking.

"Yes, Carlton, yes!" Milly called. "Brett is right."

"Milly, I'll have Constance lash *you* if you do not keep your dainty nose out of this affair!" Carlton looked up at Laura. "Take her, Laura. See what you can discover. Hayes and I will witness your efforts

195

over a glass of sangaree. What do you say, Hayes? Sit here, boy, in the guest chair."

Carlton beckoned Hayes to join him while Laura cantered in her knee-high boots down the steps, following Brett.

Ella was listening in the alcove in the drawing room where she was pretending to polish glasses. She nodded her head with satisfaction. She approved of the bond growing between Brett and Laura. Hayes, it seemed to Ella, could be relied on to aggravate Mas Carlton with his arrogance. That would lessen Mas Carlton's welcome for him.

Ella rubbed the glass in her hand, staring out of the window at the smoke of the maroon fires curling out of the forest far up the valley. From the courtyard, there were shouts as slaves scurried to carry out Miss Laura's orders.

"Strip her, Brett!"

Brett's eyes gleamed. "With pleasure, Miss Laura." He advanced on Pallis, who was held on either side by two slaves recruited from the field gang. He pulled at the torn bodice of her dress, ripping the material down to her waist. He brushed the straps off her shoulders and waved his finger downward so that the slaves holding her allowed the dress to slip to her ankles.

Pallis stood naked, the odor which had so affected Brett in the hills wafting over him again. He sighed, wondering if he would ever have the chance to taste this wench. She owed him something.

"You are not to be put to death," he whispered, leaning forward casually. "You will be all right." He winked.

Brett's obvious concern for her gave Pallis the encouragement to endure the tortune and pain which followed.

196

Laura had a tub of water carried into the courtyard. Pallis was led over to it.

"Make her kneel down with her head poised over the water," Laura ordered Constance, who had been summoned to help with the punishment.

"He doesn't hear, Miss Laura," explained Brett, translating Laura's instruction in sign language.

"Isn't that just like a woman!" protested Hayes. "She's washing the wench's hair!"

"It's curious," agreed Carlton sipping his sangaree. "Laura knows what she's doing."

They watched while Laura spoke to Pallis. The maid refused to answer. Laura questioned her again. Still the sullen glare. Laura nodded at Constance who placed his hand on the back of Pallis's neck and forced her head into the water. He held her under the water level while two field hands prevented Pallis from bucking her body and wriggling away.

Constance kept his eye fastened on Miss Laura's face, while his hands held Pallis firmly. The maid's body stopped wriggling. It seemed that her life was being choked out of her body.

"You ain't supposed to let the wench die!" called Hayes mockingly from the balcony.

Laura nodded, and Constance immediately raised Pallis from the water. She was not breathing. Constance laid her out on the ground while Laura crouched over her, placing her lips on hers and breathing air into her lungs. Constance watched in amazement as Pallis stirred back to life.

Hayes turned to Carlton. "What's the point of that?" he demanded. "You should stop it at once!"

Carlton was fascinated. He watched Laura question Pallis. The girl did not answer, but her eyes stared up in sheer terror. Laura waved her hand quickly; Constance scooped up Pallis, twisted her around, and ducked her head under the water again. He held her there until Laura, counting and watching Pallis's twitching body, signaled for her to be lifted out again.

This time, Constance bent his head over Pallis's lifeless frame and breathed air into the maid's lips the way he had seen Laura do it. He added an extra refinement by letting his hand stray between her thighs, prodding her viciously with his fingers.

Pallis screamed when she opened her eyes and saw the ugly black face of Constance hovering over her. Laura knelt down beside her and hissed into her ear. Almost choking, Pallis began to speak.

Carlton smiled contentedly. "Laura has the information," he said. "Won't you come back to your chair, Hayes, and join me in another glass of sangaree? That was most effective, wasn't it? No scars to mar the wench's skin. Excellent panacea for arrogant niggers, what?"

Hayes sat down, careful not to let Carlton see the resentment in his eyes. He understood Carlton's tone only too well. "It's an honor for me to be here with you, Mas Carlton," he whined. "To hear you talking to me about niggers, I almost forget that I am half one myself."

"Yes," said Carlton, "I suppose you do. I always indulged you when you were a child. I appear to be doing it still."

There was a scream of protest from Pallis. Carlton glanced through the bougainvillea growing around the balcony railing. He raised his eyebrow. "Laura really seems to know her business," he commented.

A hook had been driven into a branch of the saman tree which shaded the courtyard. Pallis had been made to stand under the branch. Laura told her to cross her hands in front of her. She did so reluctantly, whimpering and shrieking for mercy.

Constance tied her hands with a piece of strong rope, deaf to her screams. He prodded her until she stood on a small stool which had been placed directly under the hook. He raised her hands above her head and secured them with the rope to the hook. Her arms were stretched at their full length, and Pallis was forced to stand on the tips of her toes to reach the hook.

Constance pulled off his shirt, revealing the huge biceps on his arms and the knots of muscles across his enormous chest. Even Hayes gasped at the astonishing physique of the giant.

"My executioner," murmured Carlton happily. "He is deaf, so screams cannot fool him. Such a skilled blacksmith. Those enormous hands can forge the most delicate filigree work you ever did see. Amazing, ain't it?"

Constance took the plaited cowskin whip which Asaph handed him. He smiled at Miss Laura.

"How many lashes the law allows you here?" Laura called up to Carlton.

"Law? What law? My law applies at Roxborough!" Carlton grinned. "Since you are so exact, however, Laura, the legal maximum is thirty-nine strokes on any one day."

"Females, too?" Hayes queried.

"Of course. Under the lash of the whip, bucks and wenches are equal!"

Laura kicked the stool from under Pallis's feet. Pallis dangled above the ground, twisting slowly.

Constance commenced to lay the heavy cowskin on Pallis, and soon her warm, red blood, amid her heart-rending shrieks and horrid, unladylike oaths from Laura, fell dripping to the ground.

Chapter 22

Miranda, who was a friend of Pallis and not cowed by the whipping as were the other slaves gathered in the yard, ran forward as Asaph cut her down. Pallis's back and buttocks were streaked with blood, her flesh a pattern of deep incisions. Miranda fell to her knees and cradled the maid's head in her lap. Pallis was moaning, barely conscious. Miranda raised her eyes to look at Laura, whose lips were curled in a cruel smile.

"No, Miranda," snapped Laura, "you may not take her yet. She must be pickled."

Ella brought out hot peppers and limes from the kitchen. She crouched down over Pallis and began to wipe each whip cut with a piece of pepper, squeezing lime juice and smearing it into the stripes. She worked methodically, without speaking.

"Yo' does add to she pain, Ella," Miranda ventured when Laura turned and sauntered off to the steps.

"Aye." Ella continued breaking the fiery peppers in two and rubbing the raw ends into the slices in Pallis's back. "But it does prevent de gangrene!"

"Capital!" exclaimed Carlton as Laura bounced up the steps. "Our niggers are sure to be wary of running away now."

"They will be," said Laura. "I have not finished with her yet. Constance is to fashion a pollock for her."

"What the devil is that?" Hayes watched Laura with distaste.

"It is an iron collar with spikes riveted in it. For her neck. You'll see when Constance has fitted it on her. She'll never run away again with that contraption around her head." Laura strode over to the table and took up the jug of sangaree. She looked around for a glass. Brett, who had been following her, darted into the drawing room and returned with one. He gave it to her, his eyes burning with a doting admiration.

"What confessioin did you extract from the wench?"

"It is curious, Da'." Laura leaned back against the railings of the balcony, her sangaree in her hand, staring at her father. "It seems she is infatuated with the leader of the gang of maroons camped on your very boundary. She was going to meet him."

"He was awaiting her?"

"No. It was a spontaneous decision. She loves him, but I doubt if he is aware of her existence. She took the jewels to impress him."

"Niggers capable of love!" Carlton turned scornfully to Hayes. "What do you make of that, boy?"

Hayes cocked his head. "As I am only half-white, perhaps I am only half capable myself, sir." He grinned mischievously. "Who is this maroon leader who inspires such emotions in a Roxborough wench?"

"This is the curious part, Hayes. He is a Bondmaster breed, too." Laura paused while she waited for her words to sink in.

"What's his name?" Carlton frowned. "I don't recall any capable slaves escaping recently."

"He is not a slave, father. At least, not in law, because his mother was white."

"His mother was white?' Carlton snorted. "His father was a Negro? Not in my breed, never!"

Hayes jumped out of his seat in excitement. "Yes,

Father! Your own wife had a child for a slave!"

Carlton gaped at Hayes, his face reddening rapidly with anger and embarrassment.

"What's the maroon's name?" Brett, listening fascinated from the doorway asked the question.

"Mingoson."

"Mingoson! My old playboy. I was right!" Hayes slapped the balcony in his enthusiasm, staring across the valley and up into the mountain range. The thin stream of smoke marking the maroon camp floated skyward like fire from a beacon.

Hayes turned on Carlton, ignoring the rage coloring the old man's face. "After you sold him in Trinidad to the slave factor, Father, he was bought by a hotel proprietor. He must have escaped and come back here!"

"Trinidad!" Carlton's voice cracked, the anger seeping away as he puzzled over the problem. "Yes, the wench met him there, I suppose, when she came with me and Milly."

Laura nodded her head. "That's right. Pallis said she was allowed to roam Port-of-Spain freely. Mingoson saw you from his hotel and then she met him. Pallis says he returned here a few weeks ago."

Carlton gazed at the mountains. "That damn smoke will be a signal of liberation to the slaves if they get to hear about it."

"That's if they haven't heard already."

"You're right, Hayes. Who knows what may be going on here that we don't even know about? Brett! You searched those slaves cabins recently?"

Brett stuttered. "No, no, sir!"

"Then we will do so, now!"

Hayes declined Carlton's invitation to accompany him on the raid of the slave quarters. He pleaded weariness from the chase of Pallis. Carlton, with a sneering reference to his lack of stamina, left him behind. As soon as Carlton, Laura, and Brett had disappeared down the trail, Hayes tapped on the door to Milly's chamber. She had closed her windows before the punishment of Pallis began.

"Are you all right?" he asked.

"Who is there?" Milly sounded groggy.

"Who but your nigger?"

"Hayes!" Milly unbolted the door and peered around it. Her eyes were shot with streaks of red, sore from crying. Her hair looked listless and dishevelled. "Where's Carlton?"

"He's gone to the quarters to search the slave cabins. May I come in?"

"I look a fright, Hayes. I took a draft of Ella's soursop tea to make me sleep. I couldn't bear it." She opened the door wider for Hayes to slip in. "It is very reckless for me to allow you in here."

"I have come to comfort you, Milly." He wrapped his arms around her, feeling her body flow to him. "You have no resistance to me, have you, Milly?" he marveled.

"Hayes, will you take me away from this horrible place? Let us go to Trinidad! Why, I have money, we could go to England!"

Hayes patted her shoulder. "You are distraught, Milly. I should not have disturbed your sleep." He guided her back to the bed. He bent down and caught her under her knees, lifting her onto the mattress. She clung to his neck.

"No, Milly!" he grinned waggishly. "I may be a nigger, but I ain't foolish. Carlton ain't going to catch me in his wife's chamber. He'll have that bitch Laura chew off my grain. Tell him to let me sleep in the overseer's cabin, instead of here in the house. You shall visit me there."

"Tonight?"

"Tonight." He eased himself out of Milly's lazy

grasp and tiptoed out of the room as she fell asleep, a smile of contentment on her face.

The able-bodied slaves were still in the fields when Carlton, Brett, and Laura rode into the slave compound. An old woman stirring her stewpan over her wood fire dropped her ladle and sank to the ground in a servile crouch. Another woman, pounding roasted breadfruit in a wooden mortar, stared, the pestle poised in her hand, before grovelling in the dirt at the feet of Carlton's horse.

Brett had brought Asaph, the oldest and most trusted of the drivers, with him, together with Lambert and Dale. Carlton instructed them to go into every slave cabin and search for any implement which should not be there.

"Even a simple axe head in the cabin of a slave who is not a woodsman could be a sign of an insurrection!" Carlton bellowed.

The few old slaves in the compound moved closer to each other for comfort. There was no sound. Laura and Carlton watched them suspiciously as Brett led off his gang to the first cabin. The cabins were squalid affairs made of mud and thatched with palm. The furniture inside was minimal, limited to a stool, some earthen jars, and a few calabashes that served as cups. The luckier slaves boasted a board and a blanket for a bed while the others made do with a mat laid on the mud floor.

It soon became clear to Brett as they searched the shanties that all they would find would be the pathetic personal possessions which the slaves had managed to save: buttons, scraps of paper, a piece of candle, clothes kept in boxes, bark ropes, a wicker chair. There was nothing that could be construed as a threat to the plantation.

"It's good to breathe fresh air!" Brett remarked,

after he reported to Carlton. "What a bestial and fetid smell those niggers have!"

"You have it on you, too," laughed Laura. "Go on," she said, driving her horse into the group of ancients who stood watching them silently. "Get back to your work. And tell your menfolk and their fillies that Miss Laura herself is going to string up and lash any nigger that wants to run away."

"It seems as though our amorous Pallis is an exception," Carlton mused as he rode with Laura back up to the house. They had left Brett to conclude the search of the cabins.

"Our slaves are a contented herd, Laura. I often rant at how stupid they are, but if they were not thoughtless and without any power to reason, they would be difficult to hold in check." He guided his horse off the main trail in the direction of the nursery.

"If Mingoson is planning to stir up the Roxborough slaves, he will be disappointed. My niggers are mine, Laura, since birth."

He halted his horse at the nursery fence and pointed to the youngsters romping in the Paddock. "These niggerlings here are being *bred* into slavery, Laura. They feel instinctively that slavery is right. If they are treated well and worked hard, they will remain contented slaves for the rest of their lives. Neither abolitionist, Methodist, nor maroon will convince them otherwise."

It was the custom at Roxborough, after the midafternoon dinner, for the whites to take a nap. Sometimes, Carlton drifted to sleep as he sat in his favorite chair on the balcony. As he grew older, however, and more inclined to trust in Brett's ability to conclude the day's work on the plantation, he retired to his room for an hour or so. Laura, who did not stint herself when it came to eating, also took to her chamber. This arrangement suited Milly and Hayes.

From the morning of his arrival on the plantation, the bond between the two developed at a pace which had Milly breathless. To avoid arousing her husband's suspicions, Milly made for her boudoir as soon as the enormous dinner, where the table groaned with the weight of joints of meat, turtle, fish, and fowl, was over. Hayes, whom Carlton regarded ambivalently because of his Negro heritage, rarely joined Laura, Milly, and Carlton at the table. He took his own meals at the overseer's cabin where Ivonia, the cook, attended him.

The assignment of this cabin to Hayes had been the spur for the sustained animosity Brett held for Hayes. To Brett's mind, the overseer's cabin should have been his. He resented Hayes's intrusion into the plantation routine and resolved that Hayes's days at Roxborough would be limited. Each afternoon, Brett crouched in the cane field adjoining the cabin and awaited Milly's arrival.

Milly, as soon as she was certain that Carlton and Laura had returned to their rooms, scurried down the front steps, across the yard, and down the path. She did not bother to take a horse. Of course, the slaves saw their Mistress scudding through the bush, but Milly did not concern herself with them. They had no truck with the Bondmaster to tell him what she was doing, she reasoned. If Carlton or Laura were to comment on her absence, Milly planned to say that she had merely taken a walk for some fresh air.

"How are you, my precious!" Brett heard Hayes greet Milly as she scurried onto the veranda where he was seated. He did not rise from his chair but held out his hand in greeting.

"Hayes, what a trouble I've had this afternoon!" Milly shook her head, showering her hair around her shoulders to emphasize her disgust. "I thought Carlton would never finish eating. He picked at the pork, stuck his thumb in the stew, and complained that the pigeon was too bitter."

"Pigeon always is bitter. It's the berries the birds eat."

"We had a lecture on Ella's slothfulness and how she is getting too old to cook. But he said she is the only slave he can trust to prepare his food because all the others would poison him!"

Brett, who could hear Milly's shrill voice quite easily from his hiding place, smiled at the remark.

"Finally, after picking at the meats like a cormorant and quaffing his claret like a porpoise, he pronounced his belly full. Up he gets and is about to stumble off to his room when he decides to engage Laura in a discourse about Brett."

"Yes," drawled Hayes, indicating his lack of interest.

"I went to my room praying that he would soon go to his. I have been frantic with wanting to see you, Hayes."

"Really?" Hayes was still stretched out in his chair, his hands clasped behind his head as he gazed up at Milly.

"Hayes! Aren't you pleased to see me?"

"Of course, Milly." Behind his smile, Hayes was wondering if he would have to mount Milly again that afternoon. In the month since his arrival, Milly's insistence on a daily dose of his charms had severely curtailed his activities. There were some choice nigger wenches in the nursery he intended to dally with, and he had women awaiting him in Layou in the evenings.

He rubbed his nose. Milly was his age, and he liked her. She would have to learn that a blade like himself could not be sheathed by one scabbard alone.

"What are you thinking?" Milly demanded.

"About us." Hayes stroked his chin.

"Us?" Milly gasped.

"Yes. What do you think is going to become of this? Do you really relish these clandestine meetings in this cabin every day, Milly?"

"But it was you who asked me to get you this cabin. You could have lived in the house."

"And why, Milly, do you know?" He stood up and put his arm around her waist which, he noticed, had lost its trimness since he first attacked it. "I'll tell you," he continued as she gazed adoringly at him.

"Freedom, Milly. I am a hot-blooded nigger, Mistress Todd. I need to be able to sleep in the morning, saunter in the afternoon, and prowl at night. I cannot be shackled, Milly. To Mas Carlton or, my dear, to you."

His lips quivered above hers. She arched her neck to reach up to kiss him. He drew his head away, released her waist, and walked over to the veranda rail. He gazed at the cane grass, causing Brett to wonder if his hiding place had been discovered. "Do you understand?"

"I know what you are, Hayes. I don't mind," Milly crooned, advancing on him. "Isn't it wonderful? I don't mind!" She stood behind him and entwined her hands around his waist.

"You have such a wonderful body, Hayes. Firm and hard. Not like Carlton's, which is flabby and old with his years of rum and wenching. Hah!" she exclaimed. "Wenching! He could not prod a dead fish compared with you, my love."

"Stop it, Milly," Hayes whined. "Your hands!"

Milly, who knew her man, raised herself on tiptoe as she nibbled his ear and rubbed her breasts and her crotch against his back. He turned his cheek, bending his lips to meet hers.

"You are asking for your punishment, you *naughty* lady!" he murmured.

"Then lash me, Hayes." Milly smiled, holding his hand and pulling him deliberately into the cabin.

"If you can!"

Chapter 23

Milly's affair with Hayes was soon known by all the Roxborough slaves. Even the children in the nursery knew about it. Brett reported daily to Ella, who discussed the affair with Miranda. She passed on the news to Pallis, who now lived in the nursery, and so the children overheard. The older slaves could see for themselves. So could Laura, who was concentrating on revitalizing the plantation with Brett's assistance. The only person who seemed not to know about Milly and Hayes was Carlton.

Carlton was fifty. For a man who had spent a lifetime as a pioneer, building up a great plantation and a famous breed of slaves, fifty was old. Carlton, as he sat on his balcony chair surveying his domain, often recalled how his own father had quit work before he was Carlton's age. It was no surprise, Carlton thought, that he should want to spend his time on the balcony, sipping rum and waited on by Pip and Ella while others attended to the plantation.

Planters who hailed from England were anxious to retire to their home counties at the earliest opportunity. They were afraid that the maroons, a hurricane, or yellow fever would get them before they could spend the fortunes they had made. For Carlton, the island was home.

There was no way Carlton could ever spend the fortune in gold and currency which lay buried under the *balata* tree at the corner of the house. His tastes were simple, his house adequate, his slaves the best breed. He was undoubtedly the wealthiest man in the Leeward Islands.

For what? His wife was pretty, his daughter sensible and hard-working, and his mulatto grandson would become a capable overseer. If only he had a thorough-bred son.

Hayes was no good. He had turned out to be a Negro philanderer whose greatest pleasure was to have the whores of Layou vying for his services. Carlton's contacts in Layou kept him informed of the boy's progress each night through the whorehouses of the waterfront. It would not be many moons, Carlton was sure, before Hayes would be washed up on the black sand of the Layou beach with his throat slit.

"Milly!" Carlton called as his wife entered the balcony. She was dressed in a new gown, her hair sparkling in the afternoon sunlight. "Are you going out?"

"Oh! I did not see you there, Carlton. I thought you were in your room."

"And if I was, would you be going out somewhere?" His voice was weary. Milly still had the power to bedazzle him. He was often amazed at his good luck in having a wife so beautiful. But beauty was of small recompense if she could not breed.

"I like to take a walk after dinner sometimes, Carlton." Milly smiled at him as she would at a child. "I have to keep my figure."

"Ah, yes." Carlton had noticed how Milly had begun

to round out. There was a contentment in her eyes, too, which had replaced the yearning he had seen there when she was younger. "You should be careful, Milly. Do not stray far or be out after nightfall."

"Fie, Carlton!" Milly's laughter trilled through the dead heat of the afternoon. "What could happen to me at Roxborough? Don't you pride yourself in the docility of your slaves? I'm sure none would dare pester me."

"Perhaps not a slave, Milly."

"What do you mean?" Milly's face reddened under Carlton's gaze.

"There are maroons on our borders, Milly," Carlton answered, alerted by his wife's reaction. "Who did you think I meant?"

"Oh, the maroons!" Milly gave a hollow laugh. "Why, I had quite forgotten them. They do not trouble us at all."

"One never knows. Any man, be he maroon or free, were he to meet you wandering abroad quite alone, may decide you are fair game to be molested."

"Carlton! How dare you say such a thing!" Milly flushed. "I am merely taking a stroll to the riverbank, or to the overseer's cabin where I might call on Hayes, or to the nursery to watch the children play."

"Go, Milly, if you wish. I will not stop you."

Milly glanced at Carlton, trying to read a meaning into his remark, if any was there. But Carlton sat hunched in his chair, his head already turned away from her as he gazed into the distance at a schooner negotiating its way through the sandbar into the river mouth.

The schooner brought Keith Lake of St. Kitts to the island. Mr. Lake was driven up to the house by a Layou coachman as night was falling. Carlton watched him descend from the carriage. The man wore the well-cut traveling clothes of a prosperous attorney or merchant. He was tall and clean-shaven with a bald patch on his head and gray locks curling about his ears. Carlton put his age a few years older than himself.

"Ha! Mister Todd, the Bondmaster?" the man greeted Carlton as he began to climb to the top of the steps. Pip was lighting the lanterns on the balcony, softening the sudden descent of darkness. The glow highlighted the stranger's features. They were not the ragged looks of a slave trader, nor the pinched furrows of a revenue collector. Carlton was intrigued. He blocked the entrance to the balcony, his arms akimbo, the full sleeves of his shirt billowing around him in the breeze wafting down the valley.

"Do forgive my arrival at this late hour without notice, Mr. Todd." The man paused on the top step. "The fact is, my schooner is bound for St. Kitts in the morning."

"Oh?" Carlton did not budge from his position.

"I am Keith Lake, Mr. Todd. Of St. Kitts." The man extended his hand, which Carlton shook cautiously. He beckoned the visitor to sit with him on the balcony.

"Are you a planter, Mr. Lake?" Carlton was staring at the freckles on Keith Lake's face and bald patch. He had the feeling that this stranger had a Negro ancestor lurking behind his white ways and manners.

"Not exactly, Todd. I do have a plantation, but my son runs it. No, I am a gentleman of leisure now. I have houses in Barbados and St. Kitts. It was in Barbados that I heard some fascinating tales about the renowned Bondmaster breed of slaves." He spoke in a lowered voice.

"This is why I am here. With all this talk of abolition, I expect you might be selling up your stock soon. I wanted to see what you have."

Carlton frowned. "Selling up? Never thought of it!" He snapped his fingers for Pip to bring out the rum decanter. "You don't look like a slave trader, Lake."

The man shook with a quick gust of laughter. "That's a relief to me to hear, Todd! I'm not. I am interested in purchasing certain . . . ah . . . fancies for myself." He took the glass proffered by Pip and poured a healthy measure into it. He tilted the glass in Carlton's direction before pouring the rum into his mouth. He champed his jaws as though chewing the rum before swallowing it. He beamed appreciatively as Pip poured water into his glass.

"That's a good screw, Todd. How do you do it?"

"Ten years old, sir. Matured in a brandy cask with peppers and beef." Carlton downed his own rum.

"Perhaps you should explain yourself. If you expect me to be selling up because of abolition, why should you want to buy?"

"Your investment, Todd! I understand you have a hundred slaves being reared for sale. If slavery is abolished without compensation, Todd, your loss is tremendous. Obviously, you should try to sell now while there is a chance of your purchasers being able to work their slaves for a few years to get back their money."

Carlton frowned. "You are convinced about emancipation?" The man's skin, under his finery, was white as far as Carlton could see, but he was still doubtful about the bona fides of his visitor.

"It will come, Todd. The abolitionists have been quiet the past few years, but the government's mood is changing. You'll see. They stopped us trading in slaves over twenty years ago. Soon they will prohibit a man owning a slave." He poured himself another rum.

Keith Lake's confident manner convinced Carlton. If the man was some kind of impostor or abolitionist spy, he would not be able to down such a strong rum

213

with obvious relish. It was planter's rum, which only pioneers like himself could stomach.

"If you believe that, then why do you want slaves yourself?" Carlton demanded.

"Not slaves, Carlton. I may call you Carlton, mayn't I? We understand each other so well, you and I. We are of the same generation. Had to fight for our spoils, what? We belong here in these islands. Not for us the fleeing home to England after ten years of reaping profits from the soil."

Carlton warmed to the man. "I still do not see the purpose of your visit."

"Oh, yes. I said I don't want slaves. I seek what the cotton planters of Louisiana call fancies, companionable niggers of a certain age, Carlton. Thirteen or fourteen years old, no more. They will live with me in my house, dance attendance on me, dote on me, Carlton. Care for me."

Carlton grunted. "Emancipation will still free them."

"Yes, yes, Carlton. But not immediately. I should have had their best years, their *virgin* years." His eyes glinted.

"My Negroes are bred for work, Lake. They are reared together in the Paddock, then put to field gangs. They are strong of body and servile by nature. No fancies for you here."

Carlton was disappointed. He liked Lake's spirit but had no use for the man's perversity. "It would be a waste of fine nigger stock, Lake, to sell you my breed."

"They'll be wasted if you cannot sell them at all. Who is going to buy if a planter knows he must set them free in a couple of years? Think of that, Carlton. Your pens will be full of worthless stock, and you'll have to feed them without any prospect of recouping your expenses!"

Carlton placed his glass on the table. "What do you want, Lake?"

"Four female virgins and two males. I'll pay one hundred currency each one. Now."

Brett and Pip were summoned from their quarters in the cellar under the house to carry lanterns. Mr. Lake declined Carlton's invitation to stay the night and insisted that he must return to his schooner that very evening. He followed Carlton eagerly through the darkened plantation to the nursery. Such was the new atmosphere of uncertainty in which planters were obliged to live, Carlton took the precaution of strapping on a brace of pistols before venturing into the night.

Brett roused Miranda in her tiny room at one end of the barnlike building where the whelps had been bedded down.

"Yo' done give me a fright, Mas Carlton. Ah done t'ink yo' does be de jumbie come fuh de children!" Miranda cried, ushering Carlton and the stranger into her chamber.

"What in heaven's name is that?" Mr. Lake's observant eye had picked out Pallis as she crouched in the corner of Miranda's cabin. She was wearing an iron collar which had been forged around her neck by the blacksmith. Protruding from the collar were four iron rods two feet long with double hooks at the end of each rod.

"She does be mah maid, Pallis," announced Miranda proudly.

"The collar is so she cannot escape," explained Carlton. "If she tried to run, the hooks would snag in the bush and trap her."

Miranda led Lake and Carlton through the connecting door into the nursery itself. Most of the children were curled up in bundles of rags on the floor, already asleep. Brett and Miranda were dispatched to

215

rouse a batch of twelve-to-fourteen year-olds for Mr. Lake to inspect.

"I trust you do not allow colts and fillies to sleep together, Carlton," said Lake as he viewed the scene in the dim glow from the lantern. "Negroes are insatiable you know, from such an early age." He sounded wistful.

"No!" chuckled Carlton. "My bucks only rut my fillies when I put them to breed in the barracoon. My wenches are pure, I assure you."

Brett herded eight young girls toward Carlton and Lake. They were rubbing sleep from their eyes, blinking in the lantern light. They wore the osnaburg shifts they had as their day wear, and stared in awe at Carlton and the white man.

Lake clapped his hands in delight. "These black virgins looks so warm and cuddlesome. See their little breasts are like buds ready to burst in the sunlight!" He rubbed his hands together. "Let me finger one, Carlton?"

"Of course." Carlton shrugged his shoulders. A man would not come all this way just to finger a nigger without buying. He motioned to Miranda, who made one of the girls raise her shift to her waist, revealing her soft brown limbs underneath.

"Sit down, girl," Miranda ordered.

The girl got down on the floor and spread her legs wide. Miranda knelt beside her and laid the girl back so that her legs swung up in the air.

Mr. Lake crouched on his knees and bent his head down to peer between the girl's legs, almost stuffing his nose inside her. He touched the girl's pudenda, rubbing his fingers enthusiastically against her until they gained entry. The girl writhed, her shoulders held to the floor by Miranda, who was grinning wildly.

Carlton grunted. "You give a thorough inspection."

"I must know if she suits my taste, Carlton,"

216

wheezed Lake, raising his face from the girl's thighs. "She is rather odorous, but a sluice in the baths at Nevis will tone her up no end!"

Lake inspected the private parts of the other girls with equal care, sniffing and fingering and, apparently unable to restrain himself, prodding the youngest with the tip of his tongue. "The sweetest flower!" he announced. "Freshly bathed in the river, no doubt."

Only after he had given his attention to their intimate areas did he consider the girl's faces and figures. He chose the four who were the most varied. The petite twelve-year-old, a Congo black filly of fourteen, a tough-looking girl with long slender limbs, and a plump child with a skin the color of ripe mango flesh.

The boys Brett brought for him to inspect were given a similar treatment. Each one was made to strip naked in front of Lake. He jiggled balls the size of marbles and pulled soft pricks as though they were rubber. Lake ordered each boy to bend down to touch his toes in front of him, parting the boy's cheeks with his hands. He inserted his fingers roughly, smiling when the boy stumbled forward with a shriek of surprise.

"Quite the best niggerlings I have ever handled, Carlton! The Bondmaster breed should perform as well in bed as in the fields. Would you have these slavelets shackled for me, please, and draw up the bill of sale. I'll take them aboard tonight. We sail with the tide."

"I'm pregnant!" Milly lay beside Hayes on the bed in the overseer's cabin. The heat of the afternoon was unbearable. Even though they had all the shutters and the cabin door open for the breeze to blow through, Milly felt as though she was stifling. The heat brought her out in a rash, her skin reddening angrily. She was irritable.

217

"Really?" Hayes yawned. He was almost asleep. He had spent the night with Suzette, a newly arrived French girl, in her father's home in Layou. Young Suzette knew tricks Milly would not even imagine.

"Is that all you have to say?" Milly pouted.

"No, mah lady. Mas Carlton will be pleased." He rolled over onto his side, drawing his knees up to his chest and sighing comfortably. Milly was forced to retreat against the wall of the cabin as his naked backside pressed against her.

"Mind me!" she exclaimed, thumping his back with her fists.

"Oh! Have a care, Milly. I am so tired. I was gambling in Layou the whole night. Let me sleep now."

"That's why you weren't any good this afternoon!" Milly sulked.

Hayes jerked his head around to face Milly. "No good? You say that! Didn't I pleasure you until you collapsed in raptures?" He grabbed her hand. "See, look, my blood in your fingernails where you clawed at my flesh. I was marvelous and you know it! Now I'm a little tired and would like to sleep."

"And I am pregnant!" Milly cried into his ear.

"You told me so already."

"By you!"

"What nonsense," he drawled.

"It's not nonsense, Hayes Todd. You will be the father of my child."

"You have a husband. He is the father." Hayes covered his head with his hands, then peered through his fingers at the cabin. "Even if he isn't the father, make him believe he is."

"How can I, Hayes? Carlton has not bedded me for months, since before you came to Roxborough. Besides, the child may have your color."

"What!"

"And you are a nigger." Milly smirked complacently. "You know Mas Carlton could hang you if he finds out."

Hayes was sitting up in the bed, scowling furiously. "You trapped me into this, you bitch. I told you I was no good, that I must have my freedom. You are trying to get me into your power with this talk of having my whelp."

"It's true," Milly grunted. "Ask Ella."

"She knows?" Hayes gasped as Milly nodded. "Then everyone knows. She is the obeah queen of the plantation. Are you sure no one else is the father?"

Milly stared at Hayes in amazement. "Hayes, how could you say such a thing?"

Hayes shook his head. "I know," he gasped suddenly with relief. "Ask Ella for one of her dried herb powders. She'll make you a tea to help you lose it. Mas Carlton will never know."

"Oh, no, Hayes." Milly's voice was steady. "This child I am going to have so I can show Mas Carlton I can do it."

"He'll kill me. You are his wife!" Hayes leaped off the bed and padded around the cabin in his anxiety.

"You look so silly like that. Like some nigger on the auction block. Come here and lie down."

"You see, you want to order me. I'll go away!"

"Then I'll come with you. We'll leave here together, Hayes. I have money."

Hayes glared at Milly. "The child, what about that? I don't want you around me with your belly full and sticking out to here." He waved his hand in front of him.

"The child will be ours, Hayes. We'll find somewhere we can settle down. We can open a shop. I am a good seamstress and you can be the shop proprietor.

219

We'll earn enough to bring up our daughter sensibly. Isn't that a lovely idea, Hayes?"

Milly reached out her hand for Hayes to come back to bed with her.

Chapter 24

Hayes shook his head in despair. Night was falling. Milly had left the cabin to return to the house. Hayes had planned to visit Suzette again that night. He was going to climb up the bougainvillea girding her house to escape the notice of his father. But his heart was troubled. He had fled Trinidad when the daughter of the printer for whom he worked had said she was going to have his child. If he had stayed, he could have inherited the printery.

Now it looked as though it was going to happen again. Milly was pregnant by him and wanted him to flee with her so she could set him up in a draper's shop! He spat into the night. He had not returned to Roxborough for that.

In time, Hayes hoped Mas Carlton would accept him as his heir, even though he was half Negro. He was light-skinned, he could pass for white. In Trinidad, a free mulatto like himself was accepted. It was only Mas Carlton who was against him. And Milly.

There was only one thing to do, he decided. Milly would have to lose the whelp before it was born. Ella must give her something in her tea like she had done before, when she made Milly lose the babies she was going to have for Carlton. Hayes cursed. What if Mas Carlton found out? Hayes's life would not be safe! Was there no other solution? Was his fate to be death or a draper?

Hayes raised his head and listened acutely to the night. There was the piping of a lizard nearby, and the caw of the crickets in the plantain leaves. Up the valley, where the river trickled over boulders down the mountain side, he could hear the *crapauds*, gigantic frogs, whistling to each other. A low buzzing as the slaves sat outside their cabins in the quarters and murmured about the day's activities drifted through to him.

He heard the noise again. A crack, like someone stepping on a stick laid across the path. Hayes quickly fell to the floor, out of the splash of light from his lantern latched onto the beam above his head. He crept stealthily on his hands and knees inside the cabin, standing up and reaching for the pistol which lay on his table. He cocked it quickly as another stick snapped.

"Who's there?" he demanded of the night, sheltering behind the doorway.

"Yo' can lay down dat pistol, white boy. Ah done have mah chance to slit yuh t'roat long time!" The voice came from the shadows where the sugar cane brushed the cabin walls. There was something oddly familiar about the voice. Hayes frowned. There was a chuckle from the darkness.

"Ah can see yo', white boy. Ah got eyes dat see in de dark. Yo' sure does be scared, white boy. Now why yo' does be scared of me?"

"Who are you?" Hayes tried to keep the tremor out of his voice. Was it someone from Layou who had come to thrash him for the money he owed them? No, the voice was that of a Negro.

Suddenly the shadow moved. A black face grinned

at Hayes from under the light, making a perfect target. Before Hayes could raise his arm to take aim, the face became a dark blur that rushed him. Hayes fell backwards onto the floor, a Negro astride his chest holding his pistol triumphantly above his head. With his other hand behind his back, the Negro grabbed Hayes's penis through the silk of his trousers.

"White boy, ah jus' have to shoot dis t'ing off an' yo' ain't never gon' go wench-ridin' again!" The Negro's huge chest heaved as he roared with laughter.

"Mingoson!" cried Hayes, suddenly recognizing him. "Mingoson, it's me, Hayes!" he whimpered. "Let go of me, I'm sore down there."

"Ah know who yo' does be, white boy. Why yo' t'ink ah does be here, nuh? Ah bin observin' yo' since yo' done come to Roxbruh." While he spoke, Mingoson tore through the silk and pulled out Hayes's penis, rubbing it casually.

"Get off me, Mingoson! You're hurting. And stop doing that, you'll make me break my water."

"Is dat so, white boy." Mingoson beamed down, tickling Hayes in his ribs with the barrel of the pistol. Hayes squirmed, but he was unable to wriggle out from under the big Negro. Mingoson jerked Hayes with evident relish, shifting down to sit across his stomach.

"Yo' like dat, boy? Yo' feel de quem comin', ready to burst out of yo' like buckshot?" Mingoson grinned as he saw Hayes's eyes contract. He squeezed his bare legs together around Hayes's chest, raising his backside, covered with a rank-smelling loin cloth, and rubbing the tip of Hayes's penis against his buttocks.

Mingoson grinned wildly as Hayes panted, unable to control himself. He leaped off Hayes with a chuckle and sprang to the bed. Hayes rolled over onto his stomach and twitched with the spasms, moaning softly.

"Ah done owe yo' dat, white boy, de time yo' done

222

pull me off when ah was yuh playboy in de *cou*!"

Hayes stared at Mingoson in disbelief. "You remember that?"

"Ah does rem'ber plenty, white boy."

Hayes pulled himself into a sitting position and leaned his back against the table. He stared at the Negro. Mingoson had filled out since Hayes last saw him when they were twelve and were shipped off to Trinidad together. He was tall and strapping, with broad shoulders and chest, a narrow waist and thick thighs. His hair was long and unkempt, the Negro whorls extended into dirt-caked, uncombed locks like rats' tails. He was naked apart from the strip of soiled breech cloth wrapped around his waist.

"If I'm a white boy, you surely are a bush nigger, Mingoson. Are you trying to fool me into believing you are a danda fresh from Africa? You have as much white blood in you as me. You just come out more black looking."

"Ah don' preten' to be white like yo' do, Hayes."

"And I don't pretend to be an African savage like you!" Hayes rubbed his crotch gingerly, wiping his hand on his trousers. "What did you do that for, Mingoson?" He gazed fondly at Mingoson, remembering the days when they had played together as children in the big house.

"Tita done tell me do dat, Hayes. She say dat de onliest way ah gon' get yo' to talk wid me. She say yo' don't t'ink wid not'ing but wid yuh prick."

Hayes grinned ruefully. "Aye. She's right, Mingoson. It sure has got me into trouble this time." As though the years of separation between the two friends had never occurred, Hayes poured out his plight to Mingoson. The Negro listened intelligently.

"Ah gon' tell Tita wha' yo' say, Hayes. She gon' advise us."

"You didn't come here for that, Mingoson." Hayes

223

was sitting on the bed beside the Negro now. He put his arm around his shoulder, winkling his nose. "You smell foul!" he exclaimed, edging away quickly.

Mingoson laughed. "Dat does be de snake grease. We does rub ourself wid grease so de skin does 'come hard."

"Why are you living in the heights, Mingoson, with all this grease and savagery?"

"When ah done escape from Trinidad, Hayes, ah done come back to Roxbruh wid one aim in mind. To liberate de slaves de Bondmaster does breed. We an' de run'ways, we does be bidin' we time to free all de slaves here."

"Huh!" Hayes grunted. "Do you think a bunch of niggers in the bush is going to do that? Even if you managed to massacre Mas Carlton and the whites here, how far are you going to get? The 93rd Regiment is in Roseau. Those soldiers will soon flush you all out of the bush and slaughter you."

Hayes clapped Mingoson on his back. "The maroons are not a menace to the plantations now, which is why the soldiers leave you alone. If you rouse up the maroons to make trouble, Mingoson, you are the one who is going to get the trouble."

"Now yo' done run yuh mout' wid de buckra talk, Hayes, tell me de Negro point of view."

Hayes stared at Mingoson and then laughed. "Boy, you are right! The Negro point of view? The Roxborough slaves are content with what they have got. They don't want no life scrunting in the hills."

"Dat's yo', Hayes. Yo' always was a spoil' nigger."

"It's true. There's the other thing, Mingoson."

"What's dat, Hayes?"

"There is talk everywhere that some day soon slaves are going to be freed by the British government. I even printed pamphlets about it for the people they called abolitionists when I worked in Trinidad.

If slaves are going to be free, anyway, why do you want to fight for it?"

Mingoson stroked his chin, his huge black brow furrowed with worry. "Yo' see how we does take after our sires, Hayes. Yo' is de bright-skin' nigger wid de brain an' ah does be de black-skin nigger wid de strength. Mah da' was be de champion in Dominique when he was be Mas Carlton's fightin' nigger." He clasped Hayes's shoulder in the palm of his enormous hand. Hayes winced.

"Tita does say yo' an' me does be a pair. We raise togeder, we could fight togeder. She does say yo' gon' come to de heights, Hayes."

"Me? Hayes Todd?" Hayes leaped to his feet. He was scornful. "I'm not a runaway slave, Mingoson. I'm a free *mulatre*. One day I want to *own* Roxborough."

"Yo' t'ink of it, dat's all, Hayes." Mingoson eased his bulk off the bed and strode over to the door. "Ah gon' tell Tita all we done talk 'bou', Hayes." He chucked his hand into Hayes's crotch. "She gon' like de way ah done make dat head of yuhs spit! Yassah!"

He stepped off the veranda. "We gon' catch, Hayes." He grinned, loping off into the black of the night, leaving his throaty chuckle hovering on the breeze. Hayes gripped the door jamb and peered after Mingoson, his mind steeped in confusion.

Milly's mind was made up. She was not blind to Hayes's faults, but believed that he was not completely the young spark he pretended to be. She knew he had a genuine feeling for her. She loved him. Every minute when she was alone in her boudoir, she was thinking of him. She wanted to live with him. Now she was going to have his child, she was certain he would agree to running away with her.

Milly was sorry that there was no one she could

talk to about Hayes. Ella knew she was pregnant but thought the child was Carlton's. Laura had never been friendly toward her. In fact, Laura seemed intent on exposing Milly as a useless flibbertigibbet while she showed how she could run the plantation with Brett. In the old days, Milly would have talked to Pallis, but now Pallis was yoked like an ox for trying to run away herself.

Milly raised her eyes from the sampler she was stitching. It was morning. The plantation was droning with activity. Carlton was visiting the mill with Laura and Brett. Cane cropping had begun, and the mill wheel was turning again to grind the cane for rum. There was not an idle slave on the estate. Even the children from the nursery who were old enough to be useful were helping to carry the freshly cut cane to the mill.

Milly wondered what Hayes was doing. Was he still sleeping in his tiny cabin, or had Brett roused him to help with the harvest? She smiled to herself. Hayes would hate having to do anything which he saw as equaling himself with the slaves. What an idle rascal he was! Milly sighed, wincing as she pricked her finger in her carelessness.

She looked out over the acres of waving cane to the Caribbean sea, brilliant with the sun dancing on the gentle waves. Schooners which plied between the islands were anchored in the river mouth. The larger vessels would even be sailing for England as soon as they had been loaded with hogsheads of sugar from the plantation.

Milly turned her head to gaze at the wall of mountains on the other side of the river. Thoughts of England reminded her of her mother. Milly had done what her mother told her, married well. She had gold Carlton had given her, dresses, and jewels galore. She had plenty to set up a new life with Hayes.

Scanning the hills at the height of the valley border-ing the plantation, Milly's eye fell on the spiral of vapor emerging from the thick forest and drifting into the cloudless sky. Poor Pallis had been trying to run away to that smoke. Milly sighed.

"De maroons!" snorted Ella in disgust.

"Oh! You startled me!" Milly twisted her head. Ella was standing in the doorway, a tray in her hand. "I didn't hear you knock."

Ella sniffed. "Ah done bring yo' dis guava juice, Miss Milly. Pip does be at de mill." She placed the glass containing a deep pink liquid on the saman wood table beside Milly's chair.

"De maroons does be cookin' their dinner," she chuckled.

Milly glanced back at the smoke. "What sort of people are the maroons, Ella?" she asked, picking up the glass and raising it to her lips. She sipped slowly. "This is delicious."

"Ah done 'queeze it mahself, Miss Milly. De maroons, dem?" Ella placed her hands on her hips and stood with her arms akimbo, glaring at the distant coil of smoke. "Dey does be de slaves what run from their plantations, ma'am. Dey live in de bush like animals!"

"Have you ever seen them, Ella?"

"Me, ma'am?" Ella looked offended by the ques-tion. "Ah does be a loyal nigger to Mas Carlton an' yo', Miss Milly. Ah don't have no dealin's wid no *negres marron*, ma'am."

"I know that, Ella. I mean what are they like?"

"Dey does be black niggers, ma'am." Ella stared at the smoke. "Some folks say dey does have their own vilage dere in de heights. Dey done build their huts an' plant deir provision gardens. Dey s'pose to have livestock an' fowls. Dey does live in freedom now, ma'am." Ella's voice trailed off.

Milly looked at Ella curiously. "If they are run-away slaves, Ella, why don't the planters go and flush them out?"

Ella frowned. "De maroons ain't no trouble now, Miss Milly. Dey does live quietly. Before dere was be plenty war against dem maroons, but dose days done gone long."

"So if a runaway slave reaches the maroon camp he is safe?"

Ella sniffed. "Ah s'pose so. Ah ain't hear of no rangers an' soldiers search for one little nigger slave." Ella hitched up her bosom. "Ah hear how once over seventy slaves done flee their plantation on de Leeward coast. Den dat Governor Ainslie he done start a war 'gainst de maroons. About fifteen years ago now," Ella cackled.

"All de maroon leaders, dem, dey does be killed. Jacko, he done be de leader fuh forty years, was shot. Five hundred of dem maroons was killed or given back to their masters, Miss Milly. Dat be de end of dat."

"But there are still maroons up there, Ella?"

"Not so many as will trouble no one, Miss Milly. Dey not all run'way slaves now. Some of dem does be free niggers. Dey does live in de heights because all de coast land belong buckra an' dey want land fuh their own gardens."

Milly listened to Ella with growing interest. "Do they ever come down from the heights?" she asked, sipping her juice slowly.

"Oh, yas, ma'am. De free ones do. Dey does carry de coarse food an' such like to sell in de markets on Sunday. Some of dem maroons does go Roseau, *oui?*"

Milly felt excited at an idea beginning to form in her mind. "How do you know who is a maroon, Ella?"

"Ain't no way yo' gon' know, Miss Milly." Ella

smacked her lips with disapproval. "Yo' does be a buckra. Is we niggers does know."

"Tell me something, Ella!" Milly handed Ella her empty glass and looked up into the old slave's eyes. She saw how the whites were yellowed like a fading parchment. The soft flesh around them was wreathed and puckered; lines of age etched down Ella's black cheeks.

"Ella!" Milly turned away and pointed her finger up the valley to the smoke. "How do people get there?"

Ella's tired eyes clouded over with uncertainty.

"De maroons alone does know dat, Miss Milly." Ella shook her head at the foolish questions of her buckra mistress.

She placed the glass on the tray and backed off the balcony, watching Milly as she sat motionless staring up the valley.

Chapter 25

They had argued over the same points every afternoon for five days. "You are just being stubborn!" Milly accused Hayes. "You don't want to accept reality." She was sitting on the edge of the veranda of the overseer's cabin swinging her legs angrily.

Hayes lay stretched out on the floor of the veranda, his shirt open to the waist, his silk trousers dusty and stained. He no longer bothered to dress himself tidily for Milly's visits.

The night before, he had been to Layou again. He longed for Milly to go so he could dream of the little Suzette who had clung to him the whole night. She was begging for more when dawn came and he had to make a hasty exit from her balcony to the road below before her father woke.

"Hayes!" scolded Milly. "You're not listening!"

"Huh?" he said drowsily. "It is so warm this afternoon. The air is still. Why don't you relax, Milly?"

Milly stopped swinging her legs and looked at him in amazement. "Relax! We must do something soon, Hayes. I'm getting fatter already. Carlton will be able to see that I'm pregnant."

Hayes did not move. His eyelids drooped, and his chest began to rise and fall with the pressure of sleep.

Milly clucked in annoyance. She knew how to shake him out of his lethargy. "I think we might just as well run away and join the maroons!" she muttered.

Hayes's lips twitched.

"The maroons please themselves. They even have cabins in the heights. We could build our own little hut and live quietly up there. Nobody would ever know."

Hayes sat up, wide awake now. "What do you know about the maroons?" he demanded sharply.

"Nothing." Milly was pleased she had got his interest at last.

"Why did you mention the maroons, Milly?" Hayes shifted across the floor to sit beside her.

She shrugged her shoulders. "I don't know. I always see their smoke in the forest every day. If you don't want to leave the island, then perhaps we should go and join them."

"You would do that?"

"Hayes, I would do anything to be with you. I am going to have your child. If we go into the heights, I could have the baby there."

"Mas Carlton would look for you." Hayes flopped back against the veranda post.

"Not if he thought I had left the island. He would give me up. He would be pleased." Milly laid her hand on Hayes's thigh. "But you would not want to live with the maroons, Hayes. You are too used to your comforts to leave here."

Hayes pursed his lips together. It could be the solution. If he took Milly into the heights, he could still visit Layou and see Suzette and his other little friends. Milly would be safely out of the way. She wouldn't be able to come down because of Mas Carlton. He beamed, stretching out his legs so Milly's hand could push up to his crotch.

"My mother is in the heights, Milly. She used to nurse Miss Laura and me, of course. She would help you to have the baby."

"You mean you would join the maroons with me?"

"Why not?" Hayes leaned his head against the post, arching his waist toward Milly. "If you can arrange it so Mas Carlton thinks you have left the island, I will contact the maroons."

"Really?" Milly's eyes glowed with excitement. She lifted her hand from Hayes's thigh and brushed her hair back behind her ears. Her profile was outlined against the vivid blue sky as Hayes gazed at her from his position on the floor.

He reached up to trace his finger down her straight nose, over her soft, pouting lips, and down her small dainty chin. He gripped her slender neck in his hand, then dropped his fingers to steal under her bodice to her breasts. With his other hand, he raised the full skirt of her dress and laid it across her thighs. He lowered his head, brushing his chin against the inside of her legs.

Milly's groin quivered while Hayes's lips sought her and his tongue buried into her.

231

The moon swathed the brooding jungle of the upper reaches of the valley in a pall of pale brightness. The air was still, as though the night had caught its breath. Milly shut the door of her dressing room gently so it would not squeak and arouse the household. She padded in her bare feet around the balcony to the grand steps. There was no way she could avoid the probing glow of the moon through the fronds of the palm trees.

She slipped down the steps quickly, clasping the bundle containing her clothes and her jewels in both hands. It was after midnight. Carlton was sleeping. She had placed a note for him in her boudoir. He would not discover it until breakfast. By then she would be in the maroons' camp.

The note explained how she had decided to leave him and sail to Antigua and then to England to start a new life. She pleaded with him not to follow her, as she would never come back. To help in the subterfuge, she had actually booked a passage on a schooner sailing that night for Antigua. She had informed Mr. Gill, the government agent in Layou, of her intention to sail. By the time Carlton checked on her, the schooner would have sailed and he would believe she had left the island.

Milly paused at the bottom of the steps. She did not want to waken the dogs and the slaves asleep in the cellar. She crept stealthily over the cobblestones and plunged down the trail to the river. Hayes had refused to meet her near the house, explaining that if anyone should see them together, he would be suspected.

He was waiting outside his cabin for her. There was a Negro with him. "Oh, Hayes!" she whimpered, collapsing into his arms, her bundle dropping at her feet. "I did it! I did it!"

He embraced her briefly, then held her away from him at arm's length. "Did anyone see you come here?" he hissed.

"No!" she said, frowning. "Why?"

Hayes nodded at the Negro, who glided away soundlessly up the path she had followed. Hayes raised his finger to his lips to caution her not to speak. He relaxed when, after a wait which seemed like minutes but was only a few seconds, the Negro sidled up to his side again. The Negro shook his head.

"This is Mingoson," Hayes said, releasing Milly. "He will guide you to the maroon camp."

"Mingoson! The one Pallis was looking for?"

Hayes nodded his head. "You must depart now. It's a long walk."

Milly felt her heart lurch. "What about you, Hayes? Aren't you coming?"

"How can I come, Milly?" Hayes gestured in exasperation. "If I disappear now, Mas Carlton will know I've gone off with you. I have to stay here, Milly. For a few days, that's all."

"But we planned all that, Hayes!" Milly was close to tears.

"I know, Milly. Don't worry. Mingoson is my brother. We were raised together. And my mother is there. They will both take good care of you. And I can visit you at night, anyway, until I can come and live with you permanently." He pulled her toward him. "Let me kiss away those tears, Milly. Everything is going to be all right."

Mingoson picked up Milly's bundle and placed it on his head. "Come!" he said softly.

"Oh, Hayes!" Milly clasped his hand frantically. "Won't you at least come part of the way?" she pleaded.

"It's too dangerous, Milly. No one must see us together tonight. Mas Carlton will kill me if he thinks I am involved."

Milly felt Mingoson's hand gripping her elbow. She shuddered. In the eerie light from the moon penetrating the glade, she caught sight of his face. She gasped more with surprise than fear. Instead of the squashed negroid features she had expected, she saw Mingoson had a fine nose, with kind, sensitive eyes. He smelled worse than the plantation outhouse, and his body glistened in the moonlight. Milly wondered if he was naked, but modesty prevented her from looking down.

"Come!" Mingoson said again, tugging her arm.

She turned back to Hayes, putting her mouth forward for a farewell kiss. He pecked her quickly on her cheek, slapping her bottom.

"Go, Milly." He smiled to reassure her. "I'll come in a day or two, I promise. As soon as Mas Carlton has quieted down."

Milly gazed back to look at him as Mingoson guided her through the bush. He was watching her, a frown on his face. She held the image in her heart to secure her through the nightlong journey. She did not know that as soon as she was out of sight of the cabin, Hayes bounded off in the opposite direction to Layou to meet Suzette.

The full moon could not penetrate into the tunnel of trees which Mingoson led Milly into after they had forded the river. She clung to the silent Mingoson to stop herself from falling. At times, he clasped her waist to help her over boulders that blocked the trail. At first, she retched at the putrid smell of his body so close to hers, but as she began to weary, she relied more on his help. She was amazed at his strength. Frequently he lifted her bodily in his arms and carried her over a ravine or boulders too difficult for her to climb.

Milly realized that he was not naked, but the brief strip of cloth he wore around his waist barely concealed him. She became fascinated by this taciturn giant, and her repulsion at his odor gave way to a desire for him to hold her in his strong arms while she clung to his neck.

"Are you tired?" he asked, laying her down on the ground after jumping with her across a stream.

"No," she lied. "I didn't know you could speak such good English."

"I can read and write, too, Milly. I used to work in a hotel in Trinidad."

The use of her first name without a title rankled Milly in spite of her tiredness. "You called me Milly."

"That's your name, isn't it?"

"Well, yes."

"You are one of us now, Milly." Mingoson crouched on his haunches beside her. His penis hung down between his huge thighs. "Even though you are white," he added.

Milly frowned, puzzled by his tone. "Yes, Mingoson." she crooned, realizing how completely she was in his control. She laid her head back against her bundle, wondering what he would do to her. "I would like to sleep," she murmured.

"There' be time for that when we reach camp." His voice sounded brusque.

Milly sensed that she must be rousing him. She moved her legs apart and rolled her hips. In the darkness, all she could see was his darker shadow against the night. "I can't see you!" she giggled, putting out her hand to touch his shoulder.

She held her fingers on his shoulder, then slid them, as though by accident, over his collarbone and down onto his chest. She stopped, pressing his flesh.

"I've never seen a slave, I mean a Negro, as big as you," she cooed.

"Dat so, Milly!" He drew away from her grasp and stood up quickly. "We must be going!"

"Couldn't we stay a little longer, Mingoson?" she whimpered. "My feet are so sore."

He did not answer. She peered frantically in the dark engulfing her. "Mingoson!" she cried. "Where are you?"

"Here," he answered suddenly, close to her ear. "Yo' does hear dat?"

She giggled foolishly. "I thought you had left me alone."

"Listen!"

Milly raised her head, trying to make out what the sound was that had disturbed Mingoson. She did not expect to hear anything other than the thumping of her own heart and the night sounds of the forest.

She had discovered that Mingoson, for all his strength, was scared of her.

"Yo' does hear dose drums?"

"No."

"Yas, mon! Listen."

"I don't hear anything, Mingoson. You are imagining it. Come and sit down with me again."

"Yo' ain't Mistress Milly no moh, girl!" Mingoson grunted. "Dat's de drums. We must hurry." He pulled her up by her elbow, hoisting the bundle on his head.

"What drums? Why must we hurry?" Milly's questions went unanswered. She stumbled blindly after Mingoson, listening for the drums. A few minutes later, she heard them.

Mingoson was walking faster now, urging her with his free hand to keep up with him. She was so tired, she longed to flop on the ground so that he would pick her up in his arms and carry her. The rapid pounding of the drums and their insistent rhythm seemed to be coaxing them upwards.

She tripped over a crab hole, fell to the ground, and sighed. Mingoson's strong arms snaked around her body and lifted her up. She hung her head back

236

and closed her eyes as her long red hair trailed behind her. She felt herslf being bounced in Mingoson's arms as he began to run faster and faster, his footsteps following the pattern of the drums. She moaned, feeling her body flow with pleasure at his touch.

The incessant booming of the drums embraced Milly. She abandoned herself to the throbbing rhythm, unaware that Mingoson had lowered her to the ground. She felt as though she was floating on the wave of sound and that if she opened her eyes she would be submerged. It seemed to Milly that the drums echoed her heartbeats, pulsing her blood through her veins. They pitched her beyond fatigue until she believed that if the drumming stopped she would no longer exist.

An old Negress wearing a grimy kerchief tied around her head peered at Milly. She was lying on the ground at the entrance to a cathedral of trees. The only light was from the *flambeaux* that flickered behind two drummers. One of the drummers was an old man whose gnarled hands flew over the goatskin of his hollow tree-trunk drum at a hypnotic pace. His companion was a Negro boy, pounding a small drum formed out of thick bamboo.

The Negress gestured urgently to the old man. With a scuttle of his fingers, the drummer reduced the tempo until the drum was crooning a lullabye. The maroons who were gathered at the far end of the glade began to wail softly. The chanting penetrated Milly's brain and she stirred fitfully, drifting into sleep, exhausted by the climb to the camp.

Tita, bending over her, nodded. "She does be fine, Mingoson. Hayes?"

Mingoson shrugged his naked shoulders, his sweat glistening in the flame-light from the torches. "He done go to Layou," he grunted.

Again, Tita nodded. She stood up and glanced

around. There were some twenty Negroes gathered under the trees. Their eyes were watching her carefully while they gently keened a dirge from the Africa they would never see. Tita stared out of the canopy of trees into the night. Her sharp eye noticed the signs of encroaching dawn over the mountains to the east.

"Yo' done come in time," she said.

Mingoson smiled happily. He backed away from Tita and crouched beside the drummer. He began to moan at a higher pitch than the others. Hearing the note, the maroons stopped chanting. They shuffled forward, scuffling the earth, until they were grouped in front of Tita.

The pounding of the drummers increased in speed. Tita herself began to chant, joined immediately by the others. A weird dance began, gradually becoming delirious in its fervor. Sweat trickled down the face of the old man as his fingers flayed the drum skin. The dancers began to lose control, rolling on the ground and rubbing themselves against the trees.

In the midst of the turmoil Mingoson, now completely naked, held up a small black pig. The pig squealed with fright. The drumming stopped. Tita advanced on Mingoson with a small knife in her hand. He held the pig by its hind legs and snout. Tita shrieked, deftly slitting its throat.

"*Aie bobo!*" shouted the crowd. "*Aie bobo!*"

The drumming resumed its frenetic tempo. A boy, also naked, held a calabash at the pig's throat to catch the blood as it poured out. He poured rum into the blood, swilled it around, and passed the calabash to Tita. She drank from it greedily and passed it to Mingoson. When he had drunk, he returned the calabash to the boy, who offered it to the drummers and then to the dancers.

The drumming began with a new passion. The sky was mellowing after its harsh darkness at the death of the moon. Tita smiled, blood smeared at the corners of her mouth. Her long slave-brown dress raked the damp earth and leaves as she advanced to where Milly lay. Milly's eyes were wide open with terror. Mingoson crouched beside her, gripping her shoulder firmly.

"Mingoson!" Milly whimpered with fear. "What are they doing?"

"It's a sacrifice to the moon and the dawn, Milly."

His cultured voice and his arm around her shoulder lulled her. She smiled wanly. "It's all so scary," she said. "Must we stay?"

"It will be over just now," he said as the drumming rose to a new crescendo.

Milly turned her face away from his and saw that the dancers were advancing slowly toward them with Tita, now naked like the rest of them, at their head. Milly gasped at the grotesque sight of the naked Negroes. She shuddered. Mingoson's hands gripped her firmly.

"What are they going to do?" she whispered.

A surge in the drumming drowned her voice. She turned to ask Mingoson again. His eyes were glazed. He was staring behind her, a beatific grin on his face. Milly frowned, raising her eyes to follow his gaze.

The drumming stopped. Milly shrieked. Mingoson's hands clamped her shoulders.

Tita slashed at Milly's slender white neck. The knife sank into her flesh and tore across her throat.

The naked youth ran forward with the calabash. He held it under Milly's neck to catch the blood as it spurted out.

"*Aie bobo! Aie bobo!*" shouted the Negroes, leaping with joy as the drummers flexed their fingers and the first rays of the sun slipped into the sky.

Chapter 26

Hayes strolled jauntily along the path from Layou. It was daybreak. He carried his long coat hooked in his thumb and slung over his shoulder nonchalantly. His other hand was in his pocket. The birds had begun their morning chorus. He whistled merrily to them, jogging his head from side to side.

A few minutes earlier, he had scrambled down the bougainvillea-encrusted wall from the balcony of Suzette's house. Her father, a French tavernkeeper, slept so soundly, he would not have been disturbed had Hayes played a concertina beneath his window.

Hayes congratulated himself. He had the sweetest fifteen-year-old French girl who adored him, and he had got rid of Milly. He had no intention of joining Milly and Mingoson with the maroons. Why should he? Milly herself had arranged for Carlton to think that she had left Dominica. That subterfuge would keep her in the heights at least until after she had given birth to the child, he thought.

As for Mingoson's wanting help from him to organize an insurrection at Roxborough, the idea was preposterous! Hayes stopped his whistling to laugh aloud. Why should he help the slaves? He would be their Bondmaster himself one day.

The sun began to poke its head over the ridge of mountains above the river. Hayes realized he had cut it a bit fine in leaving Suzette's home so late. However, Milly was not at Roxborough to screech at him for being away from his cabin the whole night. He chuckled again. "What a panic there must be at the *cou*," he thought.

He pulled his hand from his pocket and wiped the sweat from his face. When he reached the mill, the slaves hailed him as they lugged the bundles of cane to the waterwheel. He waved at them cheerily. "Keep it up, good fellows!" he chuckled ignoring the dour face of Asaph, the driver.

He turned off the main path to walk through the undergrowth along the narrow trail to the overseer's cabin. Hayes hoped that Ivonia had prepared coffee. He was thirsty. He burst into the glade in front of the cabin with a shout of greeting.

"Hey there, Ivonia! Coffee ready?"

There was no reply. He strode over to the open *ajoupa* which served as the kitchen. There was no fire, and the grate was cold.

"Damn!" he said aloud. "The bitch is sick or something. I'll have to go up to the house."

It was then he noticed the door of the cabin was wide open. He paused, biting his forefinger nervously. Had he left it open last night when he and Mingoson were waiting for Milly? He clapped his hand to his brow.

"Has the bitch come back?" he exclaimed, running the last few paces to the cabin and leaping onto the veranda. He strode through the doorway angrily.

Milly lay on his bed.

"What the devil are you doing here?" Hayes thundered.

Milly's red hair was flared around the pillow, strands stuck in clots of blood across her throat. Her eyes stared sightlessly in terror.

Hayes faltered, peered at Milly, and then gulped.

241

"No!" he muttered, covering his eyes with his hand. "No!"

He backed out of the room in horror.

"Aye!" He jumped with fright.

A hand grasped his shoulder and slipped around his neck, trapping him in a stranglehold. Hayes struggled to move, but the man holding him was a giant. He raised his eyes. Constance leered down at him.

Hayes was puzzled. Constance swung him around. Standing in the glade watching him were Carlton, Laura, and Brett. Ivonia, his cook, was with them.

"This pistol is primed and pointing at your balls, nigger," spat Carlton. "Brett!"

Brett ran forward with the chains, fastening an iron collar around Hayes's neck. This was linked with a chain to the bracelets Brett snapped on his wrists and to the shackles he clamped onto his ankles. He gave the end of the chain to Constance and ran back to Carlton's side.

Carlton pulled the trigger of his pistol.

There was a loud retort and the ball singed close to Hayes's thigh. He began to urinate down his leg in terror.

"No, Mas Carlton!" Hayes shrieked. "It wasn't me. It wasn't me!"

The crack of Carlton's second shot silenced him. The ball ripped into the floorboard by his foot. Hayes tried to raise his hands to plead with Carlton, but the chain fastening his wrists to his ankles made movement impossible.

Constance tugged on the chain, squawking with delight. Hayes toppled off the veranda into the dust of the yard.

Laura strode over. She kicked Hayes hard in his crotch and clomped onto the veranda and into the cabin. Brett and Carlton followed her.

Carlton poised at the doorway, staring at Milly and at the blood smeared across her throat and gown. Her body was stiff and pallid with death. He spun away and lurched to the veranda rail. He threw up, the vomit gushing over Hayes, who was grovelling in the dust as Constance tugged on his chain.

Hayes was dragged to the *cachot*, a stone-walled cell constructed so that its occupant could neither stand erect nor lie down. He was flung into this bodily, chains and all, by the gigantic Constance, who fastened the tiny door and presented the key to Carlton. Carlton accepted it wordlessly. He marched up to the house, flanked by Laura and Brett, neither daring to speak.

Ella and Pip waited for him. Pip handed Carlton a glass with rum already poured into it. He took the glass and crashed down into his chair, glaring around him. Ella handed him the note she had discovered in Milly's bedroom. He glanced at it, then drained the rum, chasing it down with water. He thrust the note at Laura, who took it and sat in the chair beside him. Carlton heaved a sigh of decision.

"Ella! Anything to say?"

Ella shook her head, pleased that Carlton spoke to her first. It was an acknowledgment of her position. "No, Mas Carlton," she whispered solemnly.

"Go and lay out her body, Ella. Dress her nicely."

"In de cabin, Mas Carlton?"

"Aye, Ella." Carlton choked. "She was happy there." He frowned. "Not in the house. The smell of death . . ." His voice trailed off.

Laura looked up from the letter. "Milly said she was leaving. Maybe she told Hayes that, and that's why he killed her."

Carlton scratched his head. It did not make sense.

"They were doing plenty of talking in the afternoons," said Brett, unable to keep quiet any longer.

"Since Hayes came here, Miss Milly was meeting him in the cabin when you were sleeping after dinner, Mas Carlton."

"I know, Brett." Carlton cuffed Brett's head when he saw how puzzled he looked.

"I knew Miss Milly was meeting Hayes, Brett. No need to be so surprised. The Bondmaster has to know everything." He turned to Laura.

"This may be difficult for you to understand, Laura. I wanted a son, but Milly could not get me one. I thought—" Carlton coughed, reaching for the rum Pip poured out for him. He sipped it.

"I thought perhaps Hayes might somehow make Milly more fertile. That she would return to me and bear my heir." He put his face in his hands.

Laura touched his shoulder compassionately. "What are you going to do?"

Carlton raised his head, frowning. "If he was a slave, I would lynch him myself, Laura, and to hell with it. But Hayes is well known. He's been carousing in the Layou casinos every night. He is a free mulatto."

He paused, staring out over the plantation. The mill was grinding more cane today for their rum production. The slaves would have to be kept occupied. If they had the opportunity to dwell on Milly's murder, they would get restless.

"Brett, ride to Layou and find Gill, the government agent. Report that my wife has been killed and we are holding the murderer. Request him to come with a detachment of soldiers immediately."

"Yes, sir!" Brett replied eagerly, cantering down the steps and shouting to Caliste to saddle a horse for him.

"We will ride to the mill, Laura. The drivers must lash the slaves today. Not just crack the whip so they work in time to the noise, they must flog them at close quarters. Make them prance."

Laura rose from her chair. She lowered her head to Carlton and kissed him on the cheek. "I'm sorry, Father," she murmured. "You won't take it too hard? You have me, and you have Brett. We are your real family."

Ella was on the veranda when Brett rode past the cabin on his way to Layou. She shouted to him to come to her quickly. He reined in his horse with reluctance, aware of the importance of his mission.

"Yo' come an' see dis, Brett." Ella's face was drawn with worry. She was alone on the veranda. "Ivonia done go to de quarters fuh de women to wash Miss Milly," she explained as Brett followed her into the cabin. "Yo' look at Miss Milly, Brett?"

"No more than enough to see she's dead."

"Look again, boy." Ella pushed Brett toward the bed. "What yo' see?"

Ella had removed Milly's gown. The body was stiff and white, a clutch of soft red hair outlining her crotch. Brett licked his lips. There was a gap in Milly's side, a blood-clotted hole where her liver had been cut out.

"Yo' see, boy. Hayes ain't done dat!"

Brett stared at Ella. "You?"

"Me? Someone done eat dat t'ing befoh me."

"Who's that, Ella?" Brett was indignant. "You are the only obeah witch here."

Ella clutched his arm. "Ah does be scare', Brett!"

Brett led her out of the darkened cabin onto the sunlit veranda. Ivonia was coming up the path with the women from the quarters. They were chattering with excitement.

"You know what happened, Ella?"

"Ah does believe Tita in de hills done kill Miss Milly. She vowed vengeance on Mas Carlton long time. Hayes ain't got de spirit fuh dat."

"What are you going to do?"

Ella saw the women crossing the glade. She pulled back her shoulders and thrust out her shrunken bosom. "Ah gon' bathe she an' lay she out nice fuh de burial, Brett."

"Are you not going to tell Mas Carlton?"

"Why dat, Brett? Yo' ain't got no sense in yuh head? Let Mas Carlton see Hayes does be lynch'. Ain't no one gon' stop yo' bein' de Bon'massa one day when Hayes does be dead." Ella spun away from Brett, dismissing for a time the shadow of fear hanging over her from the realization that Tita's powers were equal to hers.

"Hey! Hey!" she called out gaily to the women. "Such a fine *beké* wench we does have to wash. Dere gon' be one big wake, an' we gon' see she spirit does be bury good. We don't want her duppy come haunt buckra!" The women cackled as they trooped into the cabin behind Ella.

Some days later, after Hayes, spluttering his ignorance of the whole affair, had been transported to Roseau for the hearing against him, Carlton had a visitor. The girl sat nervously on the couch in the drawing room. Her blue eyes were fixed on Carlton as he emerged from his chamber in response to Pip's knock.

Carlton faltered under the girl's gaze. He swiftly buttoned his shirt to his collar and ran his hand through what remained of his hair. He was suddenly aware of the effect of his appearance on a complete stranger. With only Laura, Brett, and the slaves seeing him every day, Carlton had lapsed to a state where he no longer cared. But now, seeing the girl's eyes widen as she regarded him, he knew his trousers were creased from sleeping in them and his shirt torn and grimy with mud. He probably smelled as bad as a nigger.

"Forgive me for disturbing you, Mr. Todd!" The girl jumped up from her seat in alarm. "I know you are so distressed by what has happened." The girl spoke English with a slight French accent.

"Yes," he said, pulling at his nose. "But it is you who must forgive me for receiving you in this state, *m'selle*." He gestured at himself apologetically. "I had no idea."

"Do not apologize, Mr. Todd," the girl murmured. "I, too, know grief."

Carlton looked at the girl curiously. She could not have been more than fifteen. Her long straight hair was gathered behind her ears to hang, tied with ribbons, down her back. She wore a black bonnet that framed her pretty face with its delicate nose and bright blue eyes. Her lips were red and sensitive against the carefully protected white of her skin. Her gown was a sober gray with lace trimming the bodice. Carlton wondered whether she was related to a preacher, so somber was her appearance.

"Please sit down, *m'selle*," he uttered quickly. The girl was holding a tiny handkerchief to her face, as though about to cry. "Let me offer you a glass of juice?"

"No thank you, Mr. Todd."

Carlton was relieved when the girl sat down, clasped her handkerchief on her lap and faced him as he sat in a chair opposite her.

"I shall not stay long," she said, nodding her head. "In fact, I should not be here at all. I shall have to bribe my slave so he does not tell anyone. Oh, Mr. Todd!" The girl heaved a sigh laden with sorrow. "I do not know how to begin."

"Come, my dear. Do not be afraid of me! Why, I am only too pleased to help one so young and pretty as yourself. Why are you so distressed, *m'selle*?" Carlton gloated as the girl's bosom rose and fell not two paces from him.

"Who are you, my dear, and what is the reason for this visit?"

"My name is Suzette, Mr. Todd. I cannot tell you more for fear my father may find out." The girl gasped, dabbing her mouth with her handkerchief as though wanting to trap the words inside.

"No one shall know anything from me, my dear." Carlton studied the girl shrewdly. She was petite with the trimmest waist he had ever seen. Her breasts were full, rounded as though ready to burst out of the frills of lace and calico which confined them.

"Please do not be angry with me, Mr. Todd. I know you have lost your wife. It seems I am to lose my lover." She gasped again, terrified at her own boldness.

"You can tell me, Suzette. I am too old and too wise to be angry with beauty, especially beauty distressed."

"You do not know me, Mr. Todd. My father will kill me if he finds out. Hayes was my lover, Mr. Todd!"

Carlton raised his eyebrow. "Indeed." Carlton clenched the arm of his chair, his knuckles turning white as he strained to control himself.

"I'm only telling you this, Mr. Todd, because I know that Hayes did not kill your wife. He could not have done it."

"Why do you say that, my dear?" Carlton croaked.

"Because he was with me the whole of the night she was killed. He did not leave me until daybreak!" The girl lowered her head and sobbed into her handkerchief.

Carlton got up and walked across to the dresser. He poured himself a rum from the decanter and downed it quickly. He looked at the decanter again and frowned. Someone else in the house had a taste for rum, he observed. The level in the decanter had dropped considerably since breakfast.

He was standing behind the girl. Her slim neck quivered. He smiled ironically to himself. Hayes was lucky to have tasted that, he thought. She was loyal, prepared to risk exposure, ruin, and her father's wrath to save a nigger. To lie to save a nigger's life!

He dropped his hand on the girl's shoulder, squeezing her, letting his fingers brush her bosom as though by accident.

"Suzette, you did right to tell me this. It must have been hard for you. Hayes was my son, Suzette, so I appreciate it. Unfortunately, his mother was a Negress. Hayes was not like you and I, he was half black. Half an animal and only half human."

Carlton sat beside Suzette on the couch, catching her hand in his own and pressing it against his thigh. Suzette's eyes, red with weeping, peered into his.

"He was a fine boy in many ways, Suzette, the white ways. But in his black ways, he was evil. You never saw that side of him, Suzette. You do not know what Hayes could do. Did do. No, don't protest, Suzette. I believe you, I really do."

Carlton squeezed her hand. "Tell no one what you told me. It will only make it worse for Hayes. And for you. I shall tell no one, either." He smiled, putting his face close to the girl's and pursing his lips to kiss her on her cheek.

Suzette gasped. She pulled herself away from him in horror. She jumped off the couch and scampered quickly down the stairs to her waiting coachman.

"Damn, damn, damn!" muttered Carlton, picking up the girl's handkerchief from where it had fallen on the floor. It was damp with her tears. He wiped it sorrowfully across his brow. "Damn!"

"Hayes Todd, aged 23, the son of Mr. Carlton Todd, Bondmaster of Roxborough, and a slave wench, was found guilty of the murder of Millicent Todd, aged 24, wife of Mr. Carlton Todd, on February 10, 1830, and sentenced to be hanged, drawn and quartered.

"The sentence was carried out in the Roseau market square in the presence of the bench of magistrates, the new Rector of Roseau, the Reverend George Clarke, officers and soldiers of the 93rd Regiment, and several hundred white citizens, free persons of color, and slaves."

The Dominica Colonist.

BOOK THREE

The Mulatto Ascendancy

1830—1832

Chapter 27

Carlton accepted the plate of stewed iguana handed to him by Laura. The green skin of the lizard was shriveled by the cooking process, its brown flesh firm around its spine. Carlton poked his fork at the soft white eggs floating in the soup. He beamed at Laura.

"Our English neighbors would turn up their refined noses at such local fare!" he chuckled.

"I was not aware we had neighbors." Laura heaped yams on her dish before passing the tureen to Carlton. "I never see them."

"Pah!" Carlton slipped an iguana egg into his mouth, munching it with relish as yolk trickled down his chin. "Of course we have neighors. There are the St. Joseph planters to the north and those English-owned plantations all the way down the coast to Roseau." He quaffed the tumbler of claret at his elbow.

"You spend all your time riding around the plantation," Carlton continued, "instead of going out and enjoying yourself. I'm sure other women give tea parties and *tête-à-têtes* for the estate ladies."

"Is that my father talking?" asked Laura with a twinkle in her eye. "I thought you could not stand the company of white society."

"You are right, Laura." Carlton scratched his bald head, a scab falling down into his soup. "But sometimes I feel I am neglecting my social life unnecessarily. You saw the crowds when they hung Hayes. We were quite celebrities. I had no idea so many people knew me."

"You are famous throughout the West Indies because of your slave breeding, Father, and you know it. You just don't like the white people here, that's all. You've never had the time to bother with them."

"I'm a Creole myself, you see, Laura. Born here like the slaves, with all my uncouth ways. The Governor, the Rector, the officers, most of the planters come from England. They look down on us creoles."

"No one looks down on you, Father."

"Hah! I know the English. They have to preserve their own traditions and identity. You would never find an Englishman eating iguana and wild pigeon and agouti and *crapaud*. He wants his imported viands." Carlton forked a whole plantain into his mouth and chewed thoughtfully.

Laura glanced at her father. She had studied his behavior carefully in the six weeks since Milly's murder. He had changed. He was taking a greater interest in the plantation, discussing with Laura even the routine affairs like the ordering of slaves' clothing for the next year. The revival of the rum production had been a success, and the hogsheads were maturing in the still ready for distribution throughout Layou. There was enough work for Laura and Brett to supervise together, and for the slaves.

Laura was relieved that Carlton was concerned once again with the plantation's future.

"I had a good time when I was in England," Carlton mused, squashing the yam in his soup. "I am not denying that. Oh, the balls, Laura! The dancing at Almack's in my fine clothes like Beau Brummell. Ladies of quality begged me for my favors!"

"You must have been very dashing then," smiled Laura. "I'm sure you broke a score of hearts."

Carlton leaned forward across the table. "That was the cream of society, Laura. People like Lady Cowper and Madame de Lieven herself. It is said they wielded more power in that hothouse of scandal and gossip than the government of the nation. Everyone wanted to be seen at Almack's. I was on the list for years!"

He returned his attention to the iguana before leaning across to Laura again, the sleeve from his shirt settling in the soup. "What do these English popinjays know about being among the elite of England at Almack's, eh?" he grunted. "Was it not at Almack's that Madame de Lieven and Viscount Palmerston—we called him Cupid—introduced the waltz? It was a sensation."

"The waltz, Father?" Laura dropped her fork in surprise. "Can you dance the waltz?"

"Why, yes. I have danced it with Countess de Lieven herself."

Laura giggled, stamping her feet under the table with excitement. "I never knew such a staid and stern slave breeder like you, Father, had his romantic side."

"Fie! You think you can mock me, Laura." Carlton shook his sleeve free of the soup and pushed his plate away. "Slice me some pork! Pip, my glass is empty!"

Laura cut thick slices from the back of the roast suckling pig which lay staring at them from the end of the table. Pip shuffled over and filled his master's glass, removing the decanter.

"You like good wine, Pip?"

"Sah?" The slave lowered his eyes to the floor.

"I see you want to drain my decanter. Very well, Pip. You may sip before me, boy, but only drink after me."

Carlton took the plate from Laura, winking at her. "The boy has a fine palate. He tastes all the wines

254

and rum. I declare the ones he considers unfit for my gullet, he drains down his own!"

"Could you still dance the waltz, Father?"

"If you have the musicians. Here." Carlton pushed back his chair and stood up. "Come, Laura!" He bowed to her, extending his hand.

"But I cannot dance!" She laughed.

"Who's to know? I will show you." He pulled her to her feet, placed his right hand on her waist, and lifted her right hand high with his left. He moved his feet in a pattern, explained to Laura how to follow.

"My, you are completely wooden!" he exclaimed. "With you wearing your boots and britches I fancy I am dancing with a man!" He twirled away from Laura with a shout, waltzing into the drawing room. "One, two, three," he sang, his face perfectly serious. "One, two, three."

Ella rushed up the back stairs and peered with alarm into the dining room.

"Its all right, Ella," laughed Laura, slapping her thighs with delight. "Mas Carlton is dancing!"

"Dancing, Miss Laura?" Ella sniffed. "Dere ain't never been no dancing in dis house, ma'am."

"Well, there should be!" Laura giggled again. "Why don't we have a ball, Father? We could invite all the neighbors you say we have. Let us meet them socially. You can introduce them to the waltz. They'll not think of you as an uncouth Creole nigger breeder then!"

Carlton spun back to the dining room, resting his bottom on the table with relief. He was panting. Ella quickly moved the suckling pig out of his way as he hitched himself up. He picked up a piece of meat and stuffed it into his mouth, looking at Laura quizzically.

"By the devil," he gulped. "Why not!"

"Oh, Father!" Laura embraced him happily, kissing him on both cheeks, smudging the yolk stain on his chin. "It will be wonderful."

255

"You must do the arrangements, Laura. I know nothing about these things. A ball, yes. Ella can do the catering. What about the music? We'll have to have an orchestra from Roseau. We must get the young bucks trained to wait on the guests. Each one can have a special livery and white gloves!" He jumped down from the table, grasping Laura's hand with excitement.

"Come, Laura," he said, pulling her into the drawing room. He opened his bureau and sat in front of it. "We must make a list of everything we need."

Laura looked back into the dining room. Ella's wizened face was a study of puritanical disapproval.

"Hah!" Laura sneered defiantly at her. "Now we shall see how the Bondmaster can be the master in his own house. You want a ball, Father? You shall have one!"

The weeks preceding the ball breathed new life into Roxborough. No one on the plantation could remember a time when they had worked so hard. The unskilled slaves were recruited to clean, clear, and landscape all the roads and fields adjoining the house. Even the forest had to be trimmed and tidied. The slaves with any skills at all were brought up to help transform the old house into a mansion. Coopers became carpenters, boilermen tried masonry, and wheelwrights took to roofing.

Under Carlton's direction, a change came over the estate. Forty years of benign neglect were swept away to reveal a home any Englishman would feel honored to visit. Timber in the house was renewed, the floors of the rooms and the balconies were strengthened, new shingles were laid on the roof, tiles were scraped, steps chipped, gardens laid out, flowers planted. The furniture in the house was dusted, polished, polished and dusted.

Laura and Ella drilled a platoon of slaves for house duties. A sisterhood of seamstresses sat each day to sew new breeches and shirts for the bucks and gingham shifts for the wenches. Pip was put in charge of the wines and the rums and passed each day in a blur of apprehension, testing and tasting the hogsheads to find the finest rum for the night. Ella commanded a troop of cooks and scullery maids, training them for the day itself when pigs were to be barbecued, an ox roasted, chickens stuffed, pigeons baked, and goats stewed.

Brett was detailed to be the butler. His would be the task of greeting the guests upon arrival, escorting them up the steps, and seeing that the entire operation functioned with precison and efficiency. A splendid livery was designed for him by Laura. He was to wear brocade breeches with white stockings, black shoes with silver buckles, a full-dress coat with two long tapering skirts at the back made out of material the deep purple color of sorrel, and a gold stock with a shirt of pale blue.

Excitement among the slaves mounted. Everyone wanted to be involved. Carlton, bemused by the enthusiastic response of his Negroes, which seemed so alien to their usual chacacter, felt benevolent toward them. He instructed Constance to free Pallis from her iron yoke, a gesture which won him huzzahs from the slaves.

The house and outfields were filled with singing from dawn to dusk, not the mesmeric chants of the slave gangs, but the bright refrains and responses of Negroes pleased with their work.

Mingoson, who slipped into the slave quarters at night to prowl and listen outside the *ajoupas*, was baffled. He had to carry back reports to Tita of a slave population at Roxborough who were well content with their lot. There was no one with whom he could discuss the maroon plan for an insurrection. Even the breeding bucks shunned him, longing for the day when they could strut and preen themselves in their new livery in front of the white guests.

Laura made several trips to Roseau, sailing south in the drogher from Layou, The ocean was the highway to Roseau because of the deterioration of the roads, which made travel, except on horseback or mule, impossible. For this reason, accommodation in Layou was arranged for the guests from the capital who did not wish to sail back to Roseau at night after the ball.

"Roseau is agog with the news of our fete," reported Laura when she returned from her third trip.

"How do people know?" asked Brett. He was sitting on the top step listening to Carlton and Laura discussing plans. The impertinence of his interruption was ignored.

"Oh, the seamstresses, the merchants, the tailors, everybody gossips." Laura told him. "People are dying to know if they are to be invited!"

Brett listened with fascination to Laura's descriptions of the glasses she had rented, the printing being done for the invitations, and the negotiations for the orchestra.

"Will I be able to dance to the orchestra?" he demanded.

Ella, eavesdropping from her usual place in the alcove of the drawing room, bit her tongue. Brett had become so bold of late. Since he had moved into the overseer's cabin and been taken up by Miss Laura, he declined to be intimidated by anyone. Mas Carlton, to Ella's surprise, seemed to encourage him.

"I shall have to give you lessons, Brett. We shall show the ladies how to waltz!"

"The invitations are nearly ready," Laura reported. "We only have to determine the names on the list."

She had been over the list several times with Carlton. All the neighboring planters were included, as well as the prominent citizens of Roseau, including the Governor. Carlton took Laura's list from her hand and glanced at it. He was about to hand it back when a name caught his eye. He frowned.

"This name which you have added here," he said, pointing to the end of the list. "James Garraway. You must have made a mistake. He is some kind of mulatto. Mixed blood. And this fellow, too, Michael Boland. Can't have them here."

"Why not, Father?"

"They've got Negro blood in them. Descended from slaves, what!"

"But, Father, they are perfectly respectable members of the community. Everyone speaks very highly of them."

"I'm sure they do. They look niggery, Laura. They would be out of place."

Brett stroked his cheek and frowned.

"It's you who is out of place, Father. You are worse than the English residents! There are only a few white Creoles in society, Father, the rest are mulattoes like Mr. Garraway and Mr. Boland. General Nicolay has entertained them at Government House."

"No, Laura. It wouldn't be right. If we start by asking them, we may even have descendants of my own slaves dancing and dining with us in this very house. It's unthinkable."

Brett slipped down the steps without being noticed by Carlton or Laura. The ball promised to be a wonderful affair, he thought, but for the whites alone. What about him, Brett? He was not allowed to eat with Mas Carlton and Miss Laura. Would he be allowed to dance with the guests? Would Mas Carlton introduce him as Brett Todd, heir to the Bondmaster?

Or would he have to scrape and bow and scurry away to sip his punch and eat his pork in the kitchen with the slaves?

Brett shrugged. What was he, anyway?

Chapter 28

The strains of the string ensemble, the reduced orchestra which Laura had hired, lilted across the plantation. The slaves who were not employed as foot boys, scullery girls, and waiters gathered under the coconut oil lamps strung around the edge of the courtyard. Their black and brown faces beamed broadly at the magnificence of each new arrival.

Their eager eyes followed the progress of the guests up the garland-strewn grand steps as they were escorted by Brett. The slaves were proud of Brett. The boy they had watched grow up and were accustomed to see near-naked every day in the fields with them was a real gentleman in his buckled shoes and colorful livery.

Mas Carlton himself was the surprise. "Where de buckra?" cried Norah, an old slave with tufts of gray hair sticking out under her madras head tie. She prodded her companion in the ribs.

Hannibal, who used to be a groom before he got too old to run after the horses, peered up to the top of the steps. "He dere!" he wheezed.

"No, he ain't!" Norah was adamant. "De *beké* dere ain't de buckra. Mas Carlton don't look like dat."

"Is he self!" Hannibal thumped his stick on the ground impatiently. "Yo' don't see Mas Brett done present de guests to him? Look, Mas Carlton done kiss de lady hand an' shake de hand of de nex' *beké*. See how he does interduce Miss Laura. Is de way de buckras does do it."

"Ah does be vex'!" cackled Norah. "Mas Carlton does be one pretty buckra tonight. Ah done swear he ain't de same buckra what lash me in de mill at crop time. Look he, see de gold trowsers, de coat of blue. De man does look so pretty!"

"Ech!" grunted Hannibal. "It does be sweet to see Miss Laura in a robe like a lady. She done do she hair so nice on top she head like dat. See she neck so dainty."

Norah prodded the old man in the ribs again. "Hey, hey, Hannibal! Ah declare dere ain't no slaves does have buckras so fine as we!"

Norah's sentiment was shared by all the slaves as they gazed at the whites arriving for the ball. As each carriage drew up, a footboy ran forward and opened the door. He helped the guests descend, and then Brett bowed deeply and escorted them up the steps. At first Brett was nervous, but finding the white gentlemen and their ladies were well disposed toward him, he ventured to converse.

"Your journey was not irksome, I hope, sir," he uttered grandly to a fine gentleman in a well-cut dark blue coat. The man was accompanied by a lady in a sensible gown and a girl.

"Very pleasant, thank you, young man. And who might you be? Todd's son?"

Brett flushed with pride. "His grandson, sir."

"Indeed! You must ask my daughter Davril, here, for a dance! She will be bored dancing with us old fogeys all the evening."

Brett glanced backwards at the girl. She lowered

her eyes modestly. "It will be my pleasure, sir." He had reached the top of the step and stood aside as Carlton extended his hand to the gentleman.

"Warren! I'm so pleased you could come!" Carlton's smile was bright and relaxed. He showed none of the strain of the events of the past few months.

Brett scuttled down the steps to meet another carriage which had just drawn up. He glanced at Davril as he dashed by. She was eyeing him shyly. There was a flicker of a smile on her lips. His spirits soared, but he forgot about Davril the next instant when he saw the new arrivals clambering out of their carriage.

The man, dressed soberly in bible black, was unmistakably a half-breed. His skin was the color of cinnamon bark, his nose spread wide across his face with large nostrils through which he snorted as Brett bowed to him. In the glow of the lights which lined the steps, Brett saw the man's eyes were gray and kind. His hair was white and crinkly, falling down his neck in a shaggy mane.

"Good night, sir!" said Brett, hoping to conceal his surprise.

"Good night," grunted the man, turning to help his lady onto the steps.

She was ighter in complexion than he was and wore the creole dress normally sported by free women and slaves on Sundays and feast days. Her floor-length skirt was a bright yellow with a blue foulard draped over her bosom and a chemise of white cotton. Ribbons were threaded through the lace of the sleeves and neck of the chemise. To Brett's consternation, as she ascended the step the lady followed the thoroughly West African custom of lifting her skirt and flinging it carelessly over her arm, allowing a partial view of her heavily starched and beribboned petticoat.

Brett escorted this distinguished-looking pair up the steps with trepidation. He could hear the rustling of disapproval from the slaves watching in the court-yard.

"Who dat fresh nigger!" demanded Norah angrily. Hannibal shook his head in silent censure. "What he does be doin' in mah buckra's house?"

Brett paused before Carlton, watching the gleam of consternation enter his eye. It was Laura who stepped forward and held out her hand.

"I'm so pleased you could come, Mr. Boland," she smiled. "I don't believe you have met my father, Mr. Todd."

Carlton recovered his composure and bowed curtly to Mr. and Mrs. Boland. Lambert glided up with a tray of punch, and the Bolands were swallowed up inside the house by the pressure of the other guests. The strings rose to a crescendo, drowning Carlton's voice.

"I thought I told you not to invite them!" he hissed at Laura. "See how they'll feel out of place."

"I don't think so, Father. I've asked the Garraways and Lionnés, too. The invitations must have been delivered by mistake." Laura smiled graciously at Carlton. "You'll see, Father. People will think you are very progressive!"

Carlton was forced to cut off his angry growl of protest as Brett escorted another pair of guests, two officers from the 93rd Regiment, up the steps.

When Carlton and Laura had finished greeting their guests, they eased their way into the crowded drawing room to find that the ball was underway successfully. Pip's rum punches were being circulated by the waiters at a lively rate and were obviously much appreciated. Several couples had already joined formations to dance quadrilles to the rousing music of the ensemble playing on the balcony.

Chairs had been placed around both the drawing room and the dining room for the older folk, and the two guest chambers had been opened up as additional reception rooms. As most of the guests already knew each other, an easy feeling of camaraderie had already sprung up.

"An excellent entertainment, Todd!" exclaimed General Nicolay, ogling Laura and exchanging his half-filled punch glass for a full one. "Plenty to drink, good company, obliging niggers, sprightly music, what more can a man want?"

Carlton smiled happily at the Governor's compliment.

"A woman, Todd, that's what. May I have the honor?" The general sipped quickly at his glass and thrust it at Carlton. He extended his arm for Laura, and together they stepped onto the floor as a quadrille began.

Carlton beamed as he realized that in spite of his concern about the presence of the mulattoes, the ball was going to be a great success. He abandoned himself to the spirit of the evening. He danced the waltz with a lady recently arrived from England, much to the admiration of General Nicolay and the army officers who set about instructing those who professed themselves unfamiliar with the new dance. Soon, the notes of the waltz were echoing over the plantation while the slaves below watched in disbelief at the white man's antics.

"Damn good fete, Carlton!" Warren Gordon clutched Carlton's elbow and led him toward the balcony. "You should have done this long ago!"

"That's what I see now!" laughed Carlton. "Why, I feel years younger." He panted. "I haven't danced the waltz since I was in England nearly twenty years ago."

"I don't mean the dancing, Carlton." The two men had reached the balcony. Warren Gordon leaned over the railing and gazed down at the brightly lit courtyard.

The slaves were still gathered below. Some of them were trying to imitate the guests, twirling their partners in an exaggerated display of dancing. The footboys were chatting to the carriagemen whose conveyances were drawn up around the stable. As the two men watched, a team of wenches climbed the back steps laden with trays containing the food prepared by Ella and her kitchen girls.

"It's not wise for us whites to remain isolated from each other, Carlton." Warren Gordon nodded his head emphatically, staring at Carlton. "You know what I mean?"

Carlton liked Warren Gordon. He had an estate four miles up the coast to the north, at Batalie. Like Carlton, he ran his own plantation. He had come to Dominica from England twenty years before and took an active part in the affairs of the island.

"Why, Carlton. I scarcely see you unless we meet at slave auctions."

"I've never been one for socializing, Warren. You know that," said Carlton gruffly. "I've always been too involved in Roxborough."

"I know. That's why I'm glad to see you are accepting reality now. Giving a lead to some of the Roseau set."

"What do you mean? Having a ball is accepting reality?" Carlton smiled, turning away from the railing to look inside at the guests gathering around the buffet being laid out under Laura's supervision.

"The ball might not be, but your guest list is. What a splendid idea to invite the leaders of the mulatto clique. I must say I did not know you were on our side. It's such an assurance to have your support." Warren clapped his arm around Carlton's shoulder.

"You'll find you've done the right thing for Dominica. We must get together to discuss this in greater detail, Carlton! Now you have the time, perhaps you would consider using your influence to help us. Maybe in the Legislative Assembly itself."

Carlton faced Warren, frowning slightly. He was not sure what he should say without exposing himself to ridicule. "I'll discuss it with my daughter," he muttered to hide his confusion.

"Splendid, Carlton!" Warren hugged him enthusiastically. "You've reminded me. I don't see that grandson of yours in the frolics. My daughter would be overjoyed if he would ask her for a piece of dance. Young people enjoy these things more together."

"My grandson?" Carlton was bemused. "But he . . ." Carlton's voice trailed away as, through the doorway, he saw Michael Boland dancing sedately with the Governor's wife.

"Don't make him a slave to work, Carlton," grinned Warren. "Let the lad enjoy himself, too."

Brett was sulking in the kitchen when Pip told him that Mas Carlton wanted to see him.

"You think he wants me to strip down like a nigger, Ella, so the buckras can finger me?" Brett pouted.

"Oh, mah gawd, Brett! What does be de matter wid yo'?" Ella bustled around the kitchen loading the trays with more meat for the maids to carry upstairs. "Why ain't yo' up dere wid all de buckras, dem?"

"Mas Carlton has not told me I am invited." Brett shrugged his shoulder.

"Whoo!" Ella turned her attention away from the meats and fussed her way through the crowded kitchen to where Brett sat by the water cooler. "Yo' is down in yuh spirit, Brett?" She patted his shoulder, frowning as Brett moved away from her.

"It's nothing!"

"Yo' right. When yo' is yuh age, boy, de melancholy does get yo' sometimes."

266

"I ain't sick, Ella!" he snapped.

"Ah know, Brett. Yo' does be worried if yo' good enough fuh all dem buckras an' their ladies, not so?"

Brett did not answer. He was thinking of Davril's shy smile and her pale blue eyes.

"Ah does know it. Yo' be best of all of dem, Brett. Yo' have Royal Watutsi blood in yuh veins, Brett. De best in Afrique. An' yo' does be de onlyest gran'son of de Bon'massa, heself. Dere ain't none of dem buckras up dere, not even de King's Governor heself, dat be better breed dan yo'."

Brett lifted his head and grinned ruefully at Ella. The old woman's face creased happily.

"Yas, mam!" He stood up. "Yo' does check mah ped'gree like ah does be a breedin' buck, Ella." His face was serious again as he dropped the slave talk. "I'm going to see what Mas Carlton wants," he sighed.

Davril sat morosely on a chair by the door. She had sat there for the whole evening, watching eagerly for a sight of Brett. As the evening wore on, she grew saddened by his nonappearance. She had declined every dance in the hope that he would come to her. Now nobody was asking her to dance at all. She gazed through the doorway at the slaves prancing at the edge of the courtyard. Even the blacks were having more fun than she was, she thought.

"Oh, no, thank you," she said as someone tapped her on the shoulder. "I don't dance." She raised her eyes slowly so the person would go away.

"This is my grandson, Brett!" Carlton Todd was beaming down at her as her father stood behind him. "Your father thinks you might enjoy Brett's company more than that of my ancient guests."

Davril blushed, speechless. Her father smiled kindly, and in a trice the two men were gone, leaving Brett standing alone in front of her. The strings swelled into the haunting strains of another waltz.

267

"I've never danced before," said Brett. "Do you think we should try?"

"Oh, yes," Davril stood up quickly. "I do."

Lambert, standing in the corner of the room with a tray of drinks in his hand, nudged Dale with his elbow. They both stared at Brett and the white girl waltzing around the room with apparent ease.

Dale smirked. "Dat white boy does be Brett?"

"Brett, de slave overseer?" Lambert replied. "No, yo' does be mistaken. Dat Brett does be a young buckra wid his *beké* wench!" The two boys chortled with delight, placing their trays on the bar table and scampering down the back stairs to tell the slaves in the kitchen what they had seen.

Brett's nervousness at trying to dance evaporated at Davril's closeness to him. He had practiced waltz steps alone in his cabin, and Davril followed the movement of his feet as though they had danced together for hours. They were oblivious of the other dancers and glided around the drawing room with their eyes on each other.

Brett longed to speak to Davril, but he could think of nothing to say. He clasped her lightly and, when the music finished, stayed with her on the floor awaiting the next tune.

"That was heavenly," murmured Davril.

"You dance very well." Brett blushed.

"So do you." Davril lowered her gaze. She found Brett's eyes were hypnotic in their intensity. She longed for the music to start again. The guests pushed around them, chattering and eating and shouting and drinking. It was so noisy. She stole a glance at Brett. He was the most handsome young man she had ever seen. She wanted to touch the smooth tanned skin of his face and run her fingers through the soft ringlets of his hair. She would remember this night forever.

Gay clapping greeted the first bars of a new waltz,

and the couples moved together. Brett wondered if it was the crush of the other dancers which made it necessary for Davril to dance so close to him. He swirled her around the dance floor to the delight of the middle-aged matrons who sat on chairs at the edge of the room exchanging the latest gossip.

Davril's mother was speaking to the mulattress who was Michael Boland's wife. "There's my daughter!" Mrs. Gordon said proudly, touching up her bun of hair.

"She looked so pretty," encouraged Mrs. Boland. "Who is the young man? Is he her intended? They make such a perfect couple."

Mrs. Gordon peered at her daughter in a new light. "Yes, they do, don't they?" She patted Mrs. Boland's hand excitedly. "The young man is our host's grandson! They have only just met."

"Really?" Mrs. Boland regarded Brett curiously. She saw a strapping upright youth. He was colored, of course. She wondered whether Mrs. Gordon was aware of that. He would make an ideal husband for her own Charlotte. Mrs. Boland gazed around. She sniffed.

"Our host has plenty of slaves," she commented to Mrs. Gordon. "But his house seems short on pieces of furniture. Do you think he is as wealthy as they say?"

"Oh, he is!" Mrs. Gordon leaned over in her seat. "My husband tells me that Carlton Todd is the only planter in Dominica who has no mortgage on his slaves or property, not even a *first* mortgage, my dear. And Colquhorn, the planters' agent in London, controls more credit for Todd than the rest of the planters have debits, and you know how bad things are with sugar for absolutely every one."

"Oh, yes," sneered Mrs. Boland, wanting to shock the white woman. "Of course, the boy dancing with your daughter is a mulatto like myself. The law would not let him inherit, so all Todd's money will go to his daughter, Laura."

"Colored *class*, my dear, and isn't he handsome?" retaliated Mrs. Gordon. "If equal rights are ever allowed to people of your color, he will surely have his share of the inheritance. The daughter is quite charming, I declare, but there is talk of some . . . eh . . . indiscretions?"

The two women put their heads close together as Brett and Davril danced past them again. Davril returned her mother's smile of evident approval.

"My mother likes you," Davril said when the music finished and she strolled outside onto the balcony with Brett.

"And you?" Brett remembered Ella's words that he was better than any of the guests there. Did that include Davril?

Davril laughed. "What a funny question. I would not dance with you if I did not like you, would I?"

They stared together at the moon, high and clear in a cloudless sky shattered with innumerable stars.

Time seemed to stop still for Brett. He and Davril talked, they danced, they talked again. And they watched the moon, first over the coconut trees, and then over the cane, and, much later, poised over the sea.

Carriages drew up to carry away the guests, every one of them laughing and shrieking, the ladies clutching their men and the men reddened with rum and dancing, chuffing and snorting.

The moment came for Davril to leave. She clasped Brett's hand warmly as she stood at the bottom of the steps.

"It has been a wonderful night, Brett," she whispered.

"Hope to see you at home sometime soon, young

man," boomed Mr. Gordon. "Your grandfather and I have some business to discuss."

Brett watched the carriage drive from the house as the dawn conch shell blew plaintively in the slave quarters. He turned away, suddenly seized with an inexplicable sadness.

Chapter 29

"Did you ever see such a change in your slaves!" Laura exclaimed. She and Brett were walking with Carlton through the cane-piece toward the house. A dozen slaves were working their way over the soil under the watchful eye of Tency, the female driver. They were clearing around the ratoons, the stumps of cane which remained in the ground after cropping. It was a blazing hot day and sweat showered from the slaves' bodies as they inched their way across the field.

"They seem to be *proud* of us now."

"Aye!" chuckled Carlton, waving his hand nonchalantly at the slaves who greeted him. "They've got something to gossip about when they go to the market on Sunday. Everybody on the island has heard about our ball, because of the waltzing. After the quadrilles the guests were accustomed to, the waltz seemed very bold. It was the same in England, I remember."

Brett detached himself from Carlton and Laura to walk over to Tency as she stood in the shade of a young mango tree. Carlton watched him speak with her. He shook his head in amusement.

"See Brett now, Laura. The boy is so solemn since the fete. I'll wager that girl Davril Gordon is in his thoughts day and night."

"She is very pretty. They make a good pair."

Carlton turned on his daughter irritably. "Surely you are not forgetting who Brett is, Laura. His father was half Negro and a slave. Brett is my slave; his mother sold him to me. You say he and an Englishman's daughter make a good pair?"

"His father was a mulatto, and his mother was white, Father!" Laura sounded exasperated. "You could call him a quadroon. Those differences don't matter so much any more, Father. He and the Gordon girl looked good together, everyone said so."

"Laura, I raise the most perfect breed of slaves ever seen." Carlton slapped his whip against his thigh. "I cross the purest African stock for field niggers. I lighten it up a bit for house slaves. But I ain't breeding no quadroon to pass as white and slip his prick inside an English virgin's drawers." Carlton quickened his pace.

"Brett has black wenches here to mount and get a yellow whelp. It's the system, Laura, and the law. A mulatto just ain't equal to whites, that's all."

"Law!" snapped Laura. "Who makes the law? A group of ossified Roseau Englishmen. They are the very people you say you despise! You say Brett is a slave. You could free him if you wanted to. And you could change the law. With your influence as the Bondmaster, Father, you could achieve what you want."

Carlton's boots clattered on the cobblestones of the courtyard. He strode toward the grand steps without speaking. Lambert, crossing from the kitchen, stopped to let them pass. He saluted Carlton and grinned broadly at Laura. Laura returned his greeting cheerily, her eyes quickly taking in his superb physique. Lambèrt nodded his head and trotted off down the path as Laura watched.

"Is that why you invited those Negroes to the ball, Laura?" Carlton slumped in his chair, seizing the punch from the tray which Pip hurriedly placed in front of him. Laura took her punch, smiling her thanks.

"They are not Negroes, and you know it," Laura retorted. "The change in views is coming, Father. So many whites have colored children. Those children are brown people, not Negroes."

"That's enough, Laura!" Carlton snapped. "Anyone with nigger blood in him has got the devil in him, too. He ain't wholly human."

Laura bit her lower lip to prevent what she wanted to say. She did not want to provoke Carlton any more. In time, she hoped, his beliefs would change.

Brett was ambling across the courtyard, his youthful face dour. He went to the kitchen without looking up at the balcony.

Since the night of the ball, Laura had noticed a difference in Brett's attitude toward her. They had grown close, or so she thought. Brett valued her advice on plantation matters. He listened to her carefully and took quickly to her attempts to teach him to read and write. He spoke openly with her, a bond of mutual respect and trust springing up between them, to Laura's delight.

She found Brett extremely attractive. He moved with a lithe grace and exuded an unmistakable sensuality. Laura understood immediately how the young Davril Gordon must have been captivated by him. Carlton was right, Laura grinned ruefully to herself. Brett's gloom since the ball must be due to his feelings for Davril. Laura, remembering the uncertainties of

273

her own youth, resolved to help him. Whatever Carlton thought, she *knew* Brett had emotions just like whites.

It was mid-morning. Laura had promised she would visit Miranda in the nursery to help her choose the next crop of young wenches to be billeted in the slave quarters for breeding.

Carlton changed his breeders every six months. If a buck had not got his assigned wench pregnant in that time, the wench was paired with another buck. After three unsuccessful pairings both buck and wench were sold off as nonproductive. Carlton expected his whelps to start breeding at fifteen.

A new breeding cycle was due to begin the following month. Carlton had asked Miranda to select the fillies she thought were ready. The colts were to be sent to the barracoon to live by themselves for three weeks. Although Carlton did not know it, this isolation of the males was similar to the manhood initiation period of the slaves' African forebears. His slaves knew that the nights alone in the barracoon marked the beginning of their adult life.

The girls who were chosen for mating were each billeted with an old wench in the slave quarters. It was the crone's task to prepare the girl for her buck and to supervise the breeding process. After their three weeks of abstinence, each buck was housed with his assigned wench.

The process intrigued Laura. In the Paddock, she viewed the eight wenches whom Miranda had chosen for Carlton's approval. "They seem fine to me, Miranda. What about the bucks?"

Miranda shot her a knowing glance. "Brett does pick dose. Ah ain't s'posed to know about dem."

They were standing together outside the nursery building with the eight girls lined up in front of them. Laura's eyes roved over the heads of the girls to where the boys were wrestling among themselves under the flamboyant trees.

"Do you like this system, Miranda? I mean, not having to worry about anything. You just let Mas Carlton assign you a man."

Miranda shrugged her shoulders. She knew what Miss Laura was missing. "Ah does take mah own buck now Mas Carlton done finish wid me, Miss Laura."

As the breeze tugged at her hair, Laura smoothed the tresses back from her eyes. "Slaves lead such uncomplicated lives, Miranda. I sometimes wish I could take a buck just like you." She sighed.

Miranda said nothing. Laura was like Carlton, she thought. She wanted to use a slave's body and then cast him aside when she was finished.

"Which buck do you have now, Miranda?" Laura tried to make the question sound inconsequential.

"Me, Miss Laura?" Miranda regretted having spoken the way she had. Laura would tell Mas Carlton, and it was impossible to know what he might do.

"Yes, you, Miranda." Laura's lips were parted in a false smile. She tapped her knee with the short riding whip she always carried.

"Ah does not have no buck, Miss Laura."

"Indeed?" Laura looked around the nursery again. Her thirst was for more than she would find there, she decided. She left Miranda abruptly and strolled back to the house. There were two hours to wait for dinner. There was nothing for her to do. She decided she would relax in the boudoir she had inherited from Milly.

Lambert was lolloping down the trail toward her, his face bright with joy. Laura wondered if it was coincidence that she should be meeting him for a second time that day. Laura stared at his massive thighs, swinging easily under his breech cloth. She could not remember when she first became aware of Lambert. At the ball, when he had been wearing the livery she had designed for the waiters, it had occurred to her how handsome he looked.

He was light-skinned, with a casual arrogance which marked him as an exception to the other slaves. Laura had looked him up in Carlton' stock book. He had sired a whelp by a filly called Melia. He was due to be assigned a new wench next month.

"How de day, Miss Laura?" Lambert's sudden question caught Laura by surprise. He stood in front of her, blocking the path, his naked chest glistening with sweat.

Laura hesitated, then breathed in deeply. Lambert's odor was manly, making her senses twitch with anticipation. "The day is fine, boy. Why are you blocking my path?"

"Ah does be sorry, ma'am!" Lambert bowed with an exaggerated flourish and stepped to the side of the path.

"I'm always seeing you these days, boy. What work are you supposed to be doing?"

"Well, Miss Laura. Sometimes ah does be in de field gang an' sometimes ah does be cutlassin' de road. Ah does go where Brett, Mas Brett, ma'am, does send me."

"Hmm." Laura let her eyes fall down the full length of his body. He was her height, with a physique developed by hard work. He stood before her unabashed by his near nakedness, his breech cloth bulging suspiciously.

"I believe I have need of a slave to assist me in my boudoir," Laura muttered softly. "To move furniture. Pip is too old for that." Laura wondered why she was trying to justify herself to the slave. "Come to my chamber after dinner."

"Yas, Miss Laura."

276

It seemed that Lambert had a knowing twinkle in his eye. Laura frowned. "You shall come up the back stairs and pass around the balcony. You must not disturb Mas Carlton because he will be sleeping," she said pointedly. "Knock on my dressing room door on the balcony."

"Ah gon' do dat, Miss Laura. Ah gon' move anyt'in' yo' does tell me move!"

The letter arrived while Carlton and Laura were having dinner. Brett clattered up the back stairs and dropped it in front of Carlton with a flourish. Carlton looked quizzically at Brett, observing his sullenness had vanished.

"It's from Mr. Gordon. His messenger is waiting in the kitchen." Brett pouted. Laura smiled at him encouragingly.

"I'll read it after dinner."

"But, Mas Carlton, the messenger needs the reply. He is supposed to get back to Batalie before dark!"

"Brett!" Carlton looked up from his plate. "Does your excitement make you query my decision? What has become of the woebegone youth we've had moping around the house these past few days?"

"Sir?" Brett pursed his lips.

"Oh, Father, stop teasing the boy!" Laura reached for the letter. "If you won't open it, I will."

Carlton dug into his chicken, avoiding Brett's eye.

Laura scanned the letter and passed it over to Carlton, who ignored it. Anguish clouded Brett's face.

"It says," announced Laura deliberately, "that the three of us are invited to take dinner with the Gordons on Saturday. You see, Father, now people are beginning to take notice of us. We must be on everybody's list after our ball!"

"Three of us?" snorted Carlton, grabbing his glass and drinking his claret quickly to prevent his choking. "Who are the three of us?"

"Mr. Carlton Todd, his daughter Laura, and his grandson Brett."

"Pah!" Carlton banged down the glass. "Who do they think Brett is, your child?"

"I'm sure that Mistress Gordon is as well acquainted with the scandals of Roxborough as any of our own house slaves. Don't you see, Father, progressive people like the Gordons don't have your old-fashioned standards."

"Laura, don't start at me again. I'm going to accept the invitation because I want to look at Gordon's plantation. Not for any other reason. Brett"—he patted the back of the boy's knee as he stood beside him—"you can tell the messenger to wait while Laura writes out a letter for him to take back."

Laura wrote the letter as instructed and hurried to her boudoir as soon as Carlton had gone to his own chamber. She sat down on her couch to wait for Lambert's knock on her door. After ten minutes, she wondered if he was going to come. After another ten she was distraught, plotting what she could do to punish him. It made her feel foolish, sitting in her boudoir waiting for a slave.

The rap on the dressing room door surprised her. She sped across the floor into the dressing room. Before dinner, she had changed into a golden floor-length gown that matched the color of her hair. It had a low-cut neck with a fringe of lace around the bodice and full-length sleeves. She threw open the door and stood, breathless, in front of Lambert.

The slave scratched himself nervously on his crotch. He removed his hand as he looked at Laura. "Ah does be here, Miss Laura." He rubbed one ankle against the other.

"Lambert!" she said softly, poking her head out of the door and glancing up and down the balcony.

278

"Did anyone see you come here?" she asked, ushering him into the room.

"Oh, yes, Miss Laura." His voice was proud. "Miss Ella an' Brett. Ah done tell dey yo' done send fuh me move de furnitures."

"You shouldn't have said anything!" snapped Laura. "Ella just cannot mind her own business. Come." She walked into the bedroom and sat immediately on her bed.

Lambert paused in front of her, gazing around the room in awe. "What yo' does want me to move fuh yo', Miss Laura?"

"I've changed my mind, Lambert." Laura spoke quickly.

"Yas, Miss Laura." Lambert no longer had that mischievous twinkle in his eye.

"Surely you are not scared being alone with me in my boudoir, are you, Lambert?"

"Ah ain't bin in dis chamber befoh, Miss Laura. Yo' have plenty lovely things."

She was making progress. Laura decided to plunge ahead. "Lambert, Mas Carlton says you are to be put to a new breeding wench next month."

"Yas, Miss Laura." Lambert rubbed his nose with the back of his hand.

"I was inspecting the new wenches today, Lambert. I was wondering whom I should ask Mas Carlton to give you."

"Any one does be a' right, Miss." Lambert scraped his hand across his stomach. The gesture intrigued Laura.

"I really don't know who would be all right for you, Lambert. I think I should inspect you myself."

"Yas, Miss Laura." Lambert's expression did not change.

"Do you understand, Lambert? I want to see what you are like." She bit her lip, saliva draining out of

279

her mouth. She swallowed quickly. "Remove your breeches, if you please."

"Yas, Miss Laura." Lambert stood as though he had not heard.

"Go on, Lambert!" Laura stared at him nervously. "Step out of your breech cloth!"

"Beg pardon, Miss Laura." Lambert brought his hands together and clasped them across his crotch. "Ah does not want to disobey yo', Miss Laura. But yo' does be a lady, Miss Laura."

"Good gracious, do slaves have scruples, Lambert?"

"It does not be scruples ah does have, Miss Laura. Mah *tuli* does get wicious wid ladies, Miss Laura!"

"Ah!" Laura lunged at Lambert and parted his hands. She pulled at the piece of rope holding the torn breeches around his waist. The cloth slipped down, hanging on his penis which pulsed grotesquely in front of him.

"Lambert!" said Laura, grasping him quickly. "Yours is neither the first black prick I've seen nor the first I've tasted. Now come here. Let me see what you can do for a wench." She yanked him by his penis so he stood facing her at the side of the bed. Hitching up her skirt until it reached her thighs, she pushed herself forward to meet him, sliding her feet up the back of his legs, easing him into her.

"Lambert!" she exclaimed. "I order you! Do it, do it!"

"Yas, Miss Laura." He stood firmly on his feet while Laura bounced herself against him.

In the kitchen below the bedroom, Ella and Brett raised their eyes to the ceiling. There was a loud scrape on the floor as the bed moved and Lambert stumbled across Laura.

Pip held his glass aloft. "De devil help de bucks." he muttered, gulping the brandy down quickly.

"He does be movin' furniture in trut'," cackled Ella.

Chapter 30

"Brett, you don't talk very much, do you?" Davril's blue eyes sparkled with happiness as she walked beside Brett. They were approaching the bench at the end of the flower garden behind the Gordon plantation house.

"Let's sit here," Davril suggested without giving Brett a chance to reply. "It is cool here, even in the height of the sun."

Brett waited while Davril sat on the bench. It was made out of a saman board which had been rubbed to a smooth surface and erected on the sawn-off trunks of two trees. Shade came from the passion fruit bower above it, with the dark green leaves and white and purple flowers of the plant growing profusely. A gigantic saman tree with its heavy boughs parasoling the entire garden grew behind the arbor.

The view was idyllic. First the rolling lands of the cane-pieces running down the hillside to the coast, and the sea itself with the sun frolicking on its waves. The house, with its stone cloister around its squat single story, was hidden by the lushness of the foliage that concealed the bench from the rest of the garden.

"Sit down, Brett, don't be shy." Davril patted a spot on the bench close beside her. "We are completely private here."

Brett was staring at the cane fields stretching below

him. Davril's voice interrupted his thoughts. He smiled ruefully and sat down beside her.

"A bitt for your thoughts, Brett," she teased.

"I don't see any slaves." Brett gestured at the cane. "There are none in the fields, nor on the trail. Even at your house I saw only your father's houseman, no footboys or grooms."

Davril pulled a face to show her disappointment. "Do you only think of slavery, Brett?"

"No!" He shifted an inch or two away from her, feeling uneasy beside the white girl. "I am curious how a plantation can look so well-managed without niggers."

Davril sighed. "Because it is well-managed, Brett." She loathed plantation talk. "Daddy looks after everything himself."

"But where are the slaves? He doesn't hole the cane himself, does he?"

Davril smiled. Brett had come to life. "Of course not. The slaves are in their gardens today. Daddy gives them two days each week to work their own provision grounds, and four days for us. Sunday is their own."

"I've never heard of anything like that!" Brett sounded offended. "The slaves are almost free!"

"That's why Daddy does it. He says emancipation must come some day, and he wants to prepare his slaves for it. It's called the *meteyer* system, I think. Daddy gives the slaves the land and the capital, and they do the work and share the income with him. Isn't it clever?"

Brett stroked his chin, his eyes serious. There was so much he did not know. Mas Carlton, Miss Laura, and Ella had not prepared him for the questions this young white girl was planting in his mind. What was emancipation? How could a slave *share* something with his master? Wasn't it his master's all the time?

"Oh, Brett!" Davril touched him lightly on his shoulder. He was dressed like an English gentleman in his bright blue coat and fashionable wasp-waisted trousers. His ringlets stirred in the breeze. "Why are you always so thoughtful? I was looking forward to this afternoon. You hardly said a word during dinner, and now you are serious again."

It was true. Dinner had been a strain for Brett. He had never eaten at table with Mas Carlton and Miss Laura before. Sometimes he had waited on them, but he always took his own meals with the slaves in the kitchen. The Gordon family, however, seemed to treat him as an equal, engaging him in small talk and seating him beside Davril at the dinner table. Brett had seen Carlton's brow darken with indignation. It was Laura who had patted Carlton's arm and whispered in his ear and kept him from saying anything.

Throughout dinner, Brett had been conscious of Carlton watching him. He had scowled at first but then lost interest as Mr. Gordon engaged him in conversation. Brett knew how to behave. He was certain he had not disgraced his master.

Mr. Gordon had told Brett to join Davril for a walk in the garden after dinner. It amazed Brett that he should be allowed to walk in the garden with Davril without a chaperone being present.

"Your father . . ." Brett began.

"Yes?" Davril looked at him eagerly.

"He seems a very unusual man."

"Not really." Davril placed her hands daintily in her lap as though preparing to address a child. "He is English. He's always tried to be fair with people. Governor Nicolay regards him as his chief adviser."

"On what?" Brett's brusqueness surprised her.

"Why, on the slave question, of course. On amelioration. On helping mulattoes gain their rightful place in society."

283

Brett stood up quickly. "I shouldn't be here!"

Davril gasped. "Whatever is it?" She put out her hand to catch Brett's and guide him back to the seat.

Brett pulled his hand away and glared at her. He ignored the blush rising into her cheeks and the agitated opening of her lips. "I don't belong here!" he snapped. "Here with all you whites, listening to you speak to me about niggers and mulattoes! I'm one, Davril. I'm a mulatto, and I'm a slave!"

He buried his face in his hands. Davril put her arm gently around his shoulders and eased him back onto the seat. She touched his hair hurriedly, then withdrew her hand and sat demurely beside him. She said nothing.

When he realized no response was forthcoming, Brett opened his eyes and peeked quickly through his fingers. Davril was waiting patiently. He unlaced his fingers, sliding them slowly down his cheeks. He glanced at her with a frown.

"You are not shocked?"

"Why should I be?"

"You knew?" Brett was puzzled.

"Oh, yes! I mean, you look white, don't you, but Mummy and Daddy told me the night of the ball. What difference does it make?"

"It makes a difference to me!"

"Well, it should not! You are lucky. Your grandfather can free you at any time. Soon mulattoes will have equal rights with whites, if people like Daddy get their way."

Brett slapped his brow with his hand. "Glory be! Tell that to Mas Carlton, and he'll call for Constance to lash me. He ain't got those ideas at all."

"Yes, he has, Daddy says." Again Davril touched Brett's shoulder. "You are so handsome, Brett."

Brett stared into Davril's eyes. "I haven't dared to think of you, Davril. I've been scared out of my wits

284

about what you would do when you found out about me."

"I've thought of you all the time, Brett."

"You have?"

"Oh, yes. Daddy says we can meet whenever we want. He approves of you."

Brett's lip curled cynically. "Because I'm one of the Bondmaster's breed?"

"Oh, Brett, why do you torture yourself? He thinks you are a gentleman. And so do I." She squeezed his arm.

"Come on!" Brett stood up and reached out his hand. I'll race you up to the house."

"What?" Davril rose to her feet in surprise as Brett pulled her out of the bower and onto the lawn. She giggled in protest when Brett set off, holding her hand. He released her hand and raced away from her. Picking up her skirt, she ran after him, laughing gaily.

Carlton belched. He caught a glimpse of Brett running toward the house weaving through the crotan bushes and around the travelers palm trees. Davril chased after him, shrieking joyfully. They were playing like children, with a happy innocence that irked Carlton.

"I understand your arguments about the mulattoes, Warren." Carlton took out his pipe from his pocket and stuck it in his mouth. He hesitated, removing it quickly.

"It's quite all right, Carlton, please go ahead," Mrs. Gordon smiled. The houseman sidled up with fire while Carlton stuffed the tobacco into the bowl and puffed it into life.

He watched the smoke curl up and continued. "I must confess it was my daughter's idea to invite that brown clique to our ball. My views have always been against giving a nigger too much rope—he'll hang us before he hangs himself."

Warren Gordon smiled. Brett and Davril were standing in front of a thicket of tropical blooms which his wife had cultivated with zealous care. Davril appeared to be explaining the flowers to Brett while he watched her with admiration. They were a perfect pair.

"I have been happily married to my wife for eighteen years, Carlton." Warren leaned forward. "Davril is my only child. I have no outside offspring at all. But I am human. I know how a hot-blooded white man behaves in these islands, especially when he has no wife."

Carlton continued to puff at his pipe, listening to his host with interest.

"Moralists can condemn all they like. The fact is, Carlton, there are hundreds of brown and colored people in Dominica who are not slaves. They are children of white men such as ourselves. They are free, Carlton, so why should they be denied the same rights as white people? That's what Boland and Garraway are campaigning for, and they have my support."

Carlton removed his pipe from his mouth. Before he could speak, Mrs. Warren leaned forward.

"If mulattoes have their rights, Carlton, children like Brett can legally inherit the estates of their parents."

"Or grandparents." Warren tapped Carlton on the knee. "And they can marry whites, too."

Carlton was shocked. He clenched his pipe in his hand, following Warren's gaze to where Brett and Davril stood together, locked in their own conversation in the garden.

"Are you telling me you would let your daughter marry a nigger? It's preposterous!"

"No, Carlton. Not a Negro, as you say. A mulatto is a different being, one that we whites have created ourselves. I maintain that as we have created him in

286

the flesh, we must give him the dignity to make himself a citizen equal to us in spirit, too."

Carlton sucked at his pipe for support. It was dry. Laura was smiling at him. He saw Brett slip his arm around Davril's waist as the two strolled toward the house. Carlton realized he had never seen Brett so relaxed. Perhaps it was because, as Warren had said, he had found himself an equal.

"If this campaign you have mentioned changes the law, what will it do?"

"It will allow equal political and social rights to free nonwhites."

"And someone like Brett, for instance, could become my heir, legally?"

"Yes."

"What do you want me to do?" Carlton laid down his pipe on the table. He avoided Laura's beam of pleasure.

"Support us." Warren sat back in his chair and crossed his legs. "You are a respected man in this island, Carlton. Every planter has slaves he has bought from you. He swears by them.

"Planters trust your views. If you can speak with the members of the Legislative Assembly, they will listen to you. My voice alone is not enough. I will try to get the Governor to nominate you."

He uncrossed his legs and leaned forward. "With your support inside the white hierarchy, Carlton, we can achieve a step toward the amelioration the Colonial Office wants.

"I tell you in confidence that if the plantocracy here defies the Colonial Office much more on this matter, the imperial parliament could nullify the island's autonomy altogether.

"Help us and you'll be helping Dominica. Help us and the King is sure to know."

Warren's conspiratorial wink made Carlton feel

ashamed. It was the first time he had considered that his personal feelings could have an effect on the government not only of Dominica, but of England, too.

Davril joined them as they sat in the cool shade of the cloister. She was a very pretty girl, Brett's height and age, with the same concerned smile her father had.

"I hope that Brett's work at Roxborough will not make him a stranger here, Mr. Todd," she said boldly.

Mrs. Warren smiled with embarrassment. "Children today are so forward, Carlton. I don't know what is to become of them."

"She has your husband's crusading spirit, Mistress Warren!" Carlton studied Brett. The boy hung his head sheepishly.

"Do not be ashamed, Brett!" Carlton exclaimed with exasperation at Brett's shyness. "If our hosts welcome your visits, then who am I to deny them?"

"Thank you, sir. Thank you!" cried Brett as Davril gripped his hand and pulled him away before he could say more. He glanced back and winked at Laura, then walked away happily with his hand clasped in Davril's to view the sunset.

Chapter 31

Laura let her hair flow freely behind her as she rode her horse through the forest. In the moonlight, she resembled a white witch as she plunged down the trail to the overseer's cabin. The blouse she wore tucked into her breeches was unbuttoned, revealing the whiteness of her breasts. Her long leather riding boots pounded her horse's flanks as she hurtled through the glade in front of the cabin. Her destination was the barracoon on the eastern side of the plantation.

The old watchman crouching inside the door of the barracoon heard the crashing of the horse's hooves. He shuddered. He glanced at the bucks who had been placed under his control. They were curled up on their mats on the hard mud floor deep in sleep. Hannibal huddled closer to the meager flame from his candle, his lips moving slowly.

The horse snorted suddenly at the other side of the door. Hannibal felt his skin prickle as he heard Laura demand that the door be opened.

Hannibal gazed at the bucks on the floor. There were eight of them. They were assigned to the barracoon by Mas Carlton to be mated with the wenches who had been sent to the quarters. Hannibal crawled over to the nearest buck and tugged him on the ankle to wake him. The boy stirred slowly while the knocking on the door increased.

"Open up, I say! Are you sleeping in there?"

"What, what, what! Loose me, yuh ol' nigger!" Dale angrily shook his ankle free of the old man's fingers.

"Help me, boy. Dere does be a *soucoyant* a' de door!"

Dale scratched his crotch thoughtfully as the door shivered under the blows of Laura's assault. He listened carefully. "Who dat?" he called.

"Miss Laura, damn you! Open up."

Dale cursed Hannibal and hastened to raise the bar across the door. "Ah does be sorry, Miss Laura." He grinned broadly. "Dis ol' nigger's grain shrivel so he scared his own prick! He done t'ink yo' does be a jumbie witch."

Laura lowered her head close to her horse's neck to peer into the gloomy interior of the barracoon. Her eyes swept over the naked figures stretched out on the floor. She scrutinized Dale eagerly.

"Ah does be Dale, Miss Laura. Yo' does need me? Ah does be de pardner to Lambert."

"Yo' too damn black an' ugly, boy!" Laura leaned over to prod him in his stomach. She flicked his penis up with the handle of her whip, letting it flop down against his thigh. She snickered. "Where's Lambert?"

"He here, Miss Laura," wheezed Hannibal, anxious to redeem himself.

"Get him!"

"Ah does be ready fuh yo', Miss Laura." Dale leered. "Anytime!" He ducked as Laura's horsewhip slashed across his shoulder.

"Boy, that tongue of yours is good to cut out!"

"Yas, Miss Laura?" Lambert stood beside Dale rubbing sleep out of his eyes.

Laura looked from Lambert to Dale and back. Both were naked. Dale, she realized, was not only blacker than Lambert, he was bigger, too. They made an interesting pair. A lascivious gleam entered her eyes.

"Lambert, pull on your breeches and come with me. You, boy, you can come, too."

"Yas, Miss Laura. Mas Carlton done say we not to leave de barracoon at night."

"Shut yuh mout', Lambert!" Dale punched him in his ribs. "Is Miss Laura does say come, so we come. He too *sot*, Miss Laura! A stupid nigger!"

Dale wriggled into his breeches quickly while Lambert disappeared into the gloom and emerged wearing his own. Laura beckoned them. They left the barracoon and trotted after her.

"Where we gon', Miss Laura?" demanded Dale.

"Is yo' to shut yuh mout' now, boy!" warned Lambert.

Laura led them into the clearing in front of the overseer's cabin. She knew Brett was not there that night.

Lambert steadied her horse while Laura dismounted. He fastened the reins to the veranda railing. He and Dale scampered after Laura as she strode onto the veranda and flung open the door to the cabin.

It was dark inside, and she had no fire for the lantern. She paused abruptly, causing Dale to bump into her. Laura lashed out angrily with her horsewhip, cutting Dale across his chest.

"Listen, boy," she hissed, eyeing him doubtfully in the moonlight. "You are not to touch me, you hear?"

"Yas, Miss Laura." Dale rubbed the whip-sting on his chest, throwing a puzzled glance at Lambert.

Laura looked behind him. The light from the moon was barely adequate. The two boys were shadows. "Right," she decided. "Strip off your britches. I want to inspect you."

Dale complied immediately, prancing proudly up and down the veranda. Lambert scowled into the night so Laura could not see, then removed his own short piece of clothing. He stood with his hands clasped in front of him.

"Come on, boy, move!" Laura flicked her whip around Lambert's waist. "Dance like that nigger!"

Laura sneered with contempt as the two boys jumped up and down on the veranda, the moonlight pitching on their private parts bouncing in front of them. She knew what she was going to do and she hated herself for it.

"Keep dancing!" she warned, moving into the darkness of the cabin. At the bed, she sighed, sitting down on the edge of it to pull off her long riding boots.

"Boy!" she called suddenly. The two stopped prancing.

"Both of you, come here!" She saw the black shapes standing in front of her, silhouetted against the light of the night through the doorway. "Remove my boots!"

Carlton enjoyed his new status as politician. His visits to Roseau became frequent. Because the trail for the twelve miles from Layou to the capital was so bad, he traveled by canoe, rowed by his Wagenie slaves. The Negroes were strong and completed the journey in two hours.

Carlton's task was to lobby the Legislative Assembly members who were known to oppose the measures for the advancement of the mulattoes. Warren Gordon had been right. When the die-hards among the whites discovered that Carlton Todd favored the move, they agreed to support it. As a result, the Brown Privilege Act giving equal political and social rights to free nonwhites was passed in April of that year, 1831.

Laura was overjoyed when Carlton brought the news from Roseau. She kissed Carlton firmly on both cheeks, hugging him fondly.

"Now you've really done something for the country!" she exclaimed.

"Pah!" Carlton slumped into his chair as Pip ambled onto the balcony with the rum decanter. "I think I was more inclined to do something for myself, Laura, I can make Brett my heir now. Roxborough won't die when I do."

He poured the rum out for himself, raising an eyebrow when Pip served Laura as well.

"You drinking your grog like a man as well as dressing like one, Laura?"

"Daddy, you know with all these slaves here, it's

practical for me to dress so. Every day I ride around the plantation. I'm helping to train Brett." She gulped her rum and held her glass out for Pip to fill with water. She swallowed the water slowly.

"Brett doesn't need much training, Laura. He knows as much about the slaves and the other livestock and cane and gardening as I do. What he needs now is a bed wench."

"Why not a wife?"

Carlton grunted. "The Gordon girl, you mean?"

"Brett spends every Sunday with her and pines for her the rest of the week."

"Huh! That's youthful infatuation. I gave him Empress, but he doesn't seem to be doing anything with her. By the devil!" Carlton gripped his glass. "He's not mounting Davril, is he?"

"Your precious Brett is too honorable for that, Father, so don't worry. Davril is a virgin, I'm sure, unless she has been dallying with her darling blacks." Laura sneered.

"How can you say such a thing, Laura? Not all women are like you, praise be!"

"There is nothing wrong in lying with a Negro, Father. Now you've got that law passed, nobody can stop me."

The blood drained from Carlton's face. "Explain yourself!" he croaked.

"Gladly, Father." Laura snickered. "As I happen to be free, any child of mine would be free, too, no matter if his father is a black slave. The child would be brown, to be sure. Thanks to your law, he will be as privileged as you or I."

"The devil take you, Laura! That law is for the offspring of white men and their black wenches, not to enable white ladies to lie with niggers!"

"Is it, Daddy?" she simpered.

"Is this why you've been encouraging me to speak

up for the mulattoes, Laura? So you could frolic freely with my niggers?" Carlton beat his brow with the palm of his hand.

"Who knows, Daddy?" Laura stood up. "I may be able to give you a brown heir for Roxborough myself. Pick out a prize nigger and I'll see what I can do!" She stomped off the balcony, banging the boudoir door behind her.

"Brett!" Carlton bellowed quickly. He had seen Brett ducking into the kitchen when he rode up. He was puzzled why the boy had not joined him as he usually did.

"Yes, sir?"

Brett stood by Carlton's side. He had filled out in the past year. His keen features were harder, the softness of his boyhood completely gone. He had discarded the breech cloth he used to wear and now dressed in shirt and smart breeches with polished leather boots; just like a young attorney, thought Carlton idly.

Brett's black ringets had been chopped off by Ella, leaving his hair a thick crown of soft black curls. His face and arms were heavily tanned, and his muscles rippled under his clothes. His countenance was always serious.

"Sit down, Brett."

Brett sat quietly in the chair Laura had vacated. He waited patiently for Carlton to speak.

"What's your age, Brett?"

"I'm going on for eighteen now, sir."

"Are you, be damned." Carlton squinted at him.

"Aye, you look like a man, boy. Even your voice is hard now. But no whelps, eh? When I was your age, I don't know how many wenches I had with full bellies for me, and gets crying in the nursery, too!"

"Yes, sir." Brett bit his lip. He was thinking of

Davril. "I am sure I will father children someday, sir. Perhaps when I am married."

Carlton heaved a deep sigh. Maybe he was the one to blame. He wanted his grandson to be white, yet when the boy spoke about marriage, just like a white man would, it rankled him.

"Brett. The law was passed this month. In law, you are equal to any white man in Dominica!"

Brett gazed at Carlton without speaking. His finger idly traced the scar across his throat, slashed into his flesh by a white man when he was five. As his hand slipped away down his chest, he touched the obeah charm given to him by his Negro grandmother, Ella. He hastily closed his shirt and nodded his head at Carlton to show he understood.

"Your mother sold you to me, Brett, to raise you. You were to be one of my whelps, to be sold at the auction to the highest bidder. A planter has to get the Governor's permission to manumit a slave, Brett. I have the Governor's authority. Your freedom paper is here." Carlton held out a vellum document folded small like a purse. It had a red seal attached to it.

"Go on, boy, take it!"

Carlton's voice was gruff. Brett raised his hand to take the paper. As his fingers touched Carlton's, the paper dropped to the floor. Brett sank to his knees, burying his head in Carlton's lap.

Carlton patted Brett's shoulders, ashamed at the tear pricking his own eyes. "Get up off your knees, boy!" he scolded. "You keep that paper safe, now."

"Yes, sir!" Brett's face was still serious as he withdrew from Carlton's embrace. He scooped the paper up in his hand and clutched it to his chest, sitting back on the edge of the chair.

"When I'm ready, boy, I'm going to present you to the slaves as the new Bondmaster. That's what my father did, and that's what I'll do for you. You'll have to make this plantation pay its way, Brett. I have gold buried here from the sale of slaves over the past thirty years. When I die, it will be for you and," he paused, "Laura."

Brett nodded his head solemnly.

Carlton was regarding Brett thoughtfully. He pulled his nose. "You have to help me lick the problems of running Roxborough, Brett."

"Of course, sir!"

Carlton fumbled in his pocket for his pipe. When he found it, he began to pack it with tobacco from the wooden box on the table by the chair. Brett watched this performance and got up to call for Pip to bring fire. When Carlton had got the pipe smoking ·to his satisfaction, he leaned forward and tapped Brett on his knee.

"Laura is a problem, boy."

"Yes, sir?"

"Dam'me, Brett. Is that all you say? You were bolder with your tongue when you were a young tyke. Speak! Tell me, what do you know of Laura?"

"She is troubling the bucks, sir!" Brett blushed.

"Precisely!" Carlton wafted a cloud of smoke over Brett. "Draining my colts when they should be mounting the fillies I've given them. But there's something else, Brett." Carlton's eyes narrowed. "What happens if she has a child by one of my niggers? You know?"

"He'll be your grandson, sir."

"By the devil, you're right! And he'll be free and under the same law which gives you equality, he'll have it, too."

Carlton sucked angrily on his pipe waiting for Brett's reaction.

"Sir?"

"Yes?"

"May I get married, sir?"

296

The pipe clattered to the floor. Carlton stared at Brett. "Dam'me, boy, you haven't been listening to me!"

"Yes, I have, sir. I would like permission to marry Davril Gordon, now I'm free and equal."

"She full, boy? You pester that white girl already?"

"Oh, no, sir!" Brett stood up and eyed Carlton reproachfully.

"Hah! Don't know how I could keep my pecker away from that one if I were in your position! Why do you want to marry her?"

"I love her, sir!" Brett's voice was soft and calm.

Carlton exploded. "Love! How do you know what love is?" He picked his pipe up from the floor. "You asked her yet?"

"No, sir. I wouldn't do that without your consent."

"Hurrumph!"

Carlton's scowl cleared. "It might not be a bad idea, actually. The Gordon plantation is not far. It's well run. It would be a fair match." He looked thoughtfully at Brett.

"You consent, sir?" Brett sucked his lower lip anxiously.

"I'll discuss it with Warren Gordon, Brett. He owes me plenty, now I got his pesky law passed for him." Carlton's brow furrowed as he thought of that law and what Laura had threatened to do.

"There's one condition, Brett. You are a man now. You can handle women. You could keep a woman happy, right? I mean here, where it counts." He jabbed the stem of his pipe into Brett's crotch.

Brett blushed, shuffling backwards out of Carlton's reach.

"I want you to service Laura, Brett. Stop her draining my bucks. Give her a whelp. If she has your get, he will be our breed. He'll be white. I'll have no fear of another nigger grandson sitting at my dining table demanding equal rights!"

Carlton grunted, sitting back in his chair with a smile on his face. "Do that for me, Brett, and you shall marry Davril Gordon."

BOOK FOUR

The Maroon Menace

1832—1833

Chapter 32

Mingoson sat with a stick in his hand, whittling it carelessly. He had scrambed to the top of the boulder the size of a slave cabin and was poised at its summit glaring at the thickly forested plateau far below him. The boulder was balanced atop a precipice whose sheer drop was an almost vertical cliff face. Where the precipice ended, the hills began, lurching off into the distance to the valley floor and eventually to the sea.

Like pox scars, cabins were dotted on the distant landscape, huddled around the coastline and the slash of the river where it burst through the forest and drained into the sea. Mingoson could see where trees had been rippd away to make space for the cane-pieces that covered the valley floor.

The pale green cane was a blur against the wild darkness of the glowering trees and rain forest ferns. In the midst of its kingdom of cane Roxborough Hall was perched on an insignificant hill. Mingoson, viewing the valley like a hirsute ogre considering his domain, need only reach out his finger to topple the house from its hillside.

He snorted. To the south of the hill, clustered together under shade trees where he could barely see them, were the *ajoupas* and cabins of the Bond-master's slaves. The drab colors of their thatched roofs blended into the landscape. Mingoson was too far away to see the movement of the slaves who lived there. He pared chips off his stick automatically, his brain aswarm with worry about those slaves.

To Mingoson, it was inconceivable that a slave should actually enjoy the status of enslavement. He had escaped from Trinidad to liberate the slaves of Roxborough, whom he regarded as his people. He vowed to give them freedom from the oppressive whims of the Bondmaster and his family. But the Roxborough slaves spurned him when he slipped into the compound at night to encourage them to rise up. Why? He slashed at his stick in anger, cutting off the spear end he had fashioned unconsciously.

"Chupes!" He sucked his lips in a loud sound of annoyance. He flung the stick from him high into the air so it slipped over the precipice and twisted down to the forest below. He stared at the plantation. Those slaves were such stupid niggers, he thought. They were proud of being the Bondmaster's breed, blind to the benefits of being free men like the small group of maroons Mingoson led.

In spite of his exasperation, Mingoson smiled cynically to himself. He knew it was Tita who was the leader of their group, not he. By the force of her personality and a rudimentary knowledge of herbs and their poisonous properties, Tita had parlayed her understanding of a Negro's fears into a position of supreme influence.

Mingoson, who had been raised by Tita when she was a nanny at Roxborough, was the only one who knew that Tita was not a real obeah woman. She appeared adept at sorcery because of her guile. It had led to her being acclaimed the Queen of the Maroons, feared and obeyed by all the runaways in the mountaintop camps throughout the island.

Tita claimed that the sacrifice of the Bondmaster's wife was her greatest triumph. Mingoson was doubtful. If he had known that Tita intended to slaughter

Milly, he would never have brought her to the camp. He remembered that night clearly. When he saw the blood spurting from Milly's neck, he had retched in horror.

"Yo' cut her!" he had screamed.

Tita's eyes were glazed, her back erect and her head stiff as she faced the pale sun glare stripping the darkness from the sky.

He had let Milly slip from his grasp as life gurgled out of her. He felt wretched. "Why yo' cut her, Tita?"

The frenetic pounding of the drums and the shrieking of the maroons as they pranced around Milly's body in a frenzy, silenced him. He was powerless to intervene as Tita sliced into Milly's side and dug out her liver. It was placed in the calabash dish together with the blood from her throat and passed among the maroons to be devoured.

When Tita collapsed exhausted, Mingoson had removed Milly's body from the arena glade, slung it over his massive shoulder, and stumbled down the mountainside with it. Mingoson saw this as his way of telling Hayes that it was not his fault. Milly had been returned, in death, to Hayes and Mas Carlton.

Later, Tita had denied all knowledge of the sacrifice. "Dat does be de spirits, Mingoson," she railed. "Don't yo' dare to question de will of de spirits!"

"Tita!" Mingoson snapped angrily. "Yo' ain't no obeah woman. Ah does know dat an' so does yo'. Yo' done say yo' gon' scare de *beké* so she don't tell on all of us. Why yo' cut her?"

"Ah done do nothin', Mingoson. Is de spirit!"

"Tita!" Mingoson slipped into English. "I don't believe in obeah and spirits. It's all in the mind. You know that, too. You killed the Bondmaster's wife, Tita! For what? She was Hayes's woman!"

Tita eyed Mingoson under her heavy lids. "De drums does seize a body! Wha' happens, happens!"

She spat on the ground where the two of them crouched, talking privately away from the maroons.

"Hayes does be a foolish buck. He does want to be white. He ain't gon' come an' join us, no way."

Days later, when the news that Hayes had been executed for Milly's death reached them, Tita had only shrugged her shrunken shoulders and cackled.

Mingoson stood up from his cramped position on the boulder. He stretched his legs, flinging his arms above his head and yawning, expelling the stale air from his gigantic body. He slid down from the boulder. It was his habit to come to that spot when he wanted to think. He was exasperated by his failure to incite the Roxborough slaves to join him in the hills. A few more hard workers would give him the chance to establish a vigorous community.

Mingoson ambled through the bush toward the camp. He had been with the maroons for twenty months. During that time he had helped the gaggle of runaways who remained, after the extermination of the original maroons years before, to grow into a formidable group. A few of the maroons, like Tita, had been born in Africa. They had been ripped from their native villages and shipped across the Atlantic eventually landing in Roseau where, emaciated and confused, they were sold on arrival to the highest bidders. Some had escaped immediately and had lived in the Dominica forest for as many as thirty years.

These bush Negroes knew no other kind of life. Their existence was not very much different from existence in their tribal homelands in Africa. They preserved their traditional beliefs although, coming from so many different parts of Africa, they shared no common language. They communicated with each other and with the runaway slaves who joined them in the hills by absorbing the *lingua franca* of the slaves, the Creole patois.

The Creole or island-born slaves among the maroons were scornful of the bush-living habits of the Africans. They had escaped from their plantations not to preserve African mores but to avoid the demands of their masters. They wanted the comforts they were accustomed to and soon built *ajoupas* for shelter and laid out provision gardens for food, instead of the itinerant existence of the Africans. Frequently, a male slave joined the maroons together with his wench to avoid separation by their master. This helped to balance the community until, when Mingoson arrived, there were fifteen families with their children and at least a score of males as well as the older Africans such as Tita.

With his wider experience, through having worked in Trinidad, Mingoson had tried to cause the maroons to be more effective. He encouraged the maroon youths to infiltrate into the free Negro community, to sell their produce in the Sunday markets, and to barter for the items they needed. He urged them to work together instead of individually, so that they could create a viable community for themselves.

Mingoson sauntered into the tableland which had been cleared for the maroon encampment. It was quiet. The able-bodied men and women were still in their gardens, the ancients were mumbling to themselves or sleeping in the shade. Even the children who were too young to accompany their parents to the provision grounds were silent. The heat thrown down by the sun at its peak was not tempered by the breeze that stirred fitfully.

The stillness of the camp was a symptom of all that was worrying Mingoson.

He sought out Tita in her *ajoupa*. It was the most substantial in the community, built of watling lined on the inside with a plaster of clay and roofed with a thatchwork of coconut branches. Mingoson rapped on the door and waited until he heard Tita's moan from within.

"Who dat?" Tita rasped irritably.

"Who yo' t'ink. Only Mingoson gon' come visit yo', Tita," he joked.

She bid him enter. The door, made out of boards the maroons had sawn for themselves, was hinged to the frame of round wood posts by undressed leather straps. Mingoson stooped until he was almost crawling through the entrance. The interior was dreadfully gloomy. He knew Tita would be lying on her board laid on the mud against the back wall, so he let the door shut and crouched opposite her. He waited for his eyes to grow accustomed to the darkness.

Tita was the color of dried plantain leaves, withered and shriveled with age. She was draped with a drab osnaburg robe, her long gray hair bunched in straggling plaits under her faded madras *mouchoir* head tie. Mingoson could remember how she had been a fine dusky beauty in her youth with fiery eyes and inviting lips.

In her twenty years at Roxborough Tita led a pampered life as a favored house slave. Her beauty and body were broken from the day she was cast out by Mas Carlton. In the eight years she had lived in the heights, she had crumpled into an obscene scab-ridden crone.

"Where yo' been, Mingoson? Ah don't see yo' fuh some days!" Tita's voice was harsh and bitter. In Tita's world, everything seemed to be a personal affront to her.

"Ah was be down a' Roxbruh, Tita." Mingoson knew that Tita's only power over the maroons was through fear. He himself refused to be intimidated by her.

Tita sneered at him. "Heh! Heh! Yo' tryin' to mount dat Laura wench along wid de slaves dem?"

305

"If she gets me, Tita, she won't want no other!" Mingoson shifted on his haunches. "Ah was be speakin' to de slaves, Tita. Dey ain't bursting to come join us 'tall."

Tita grunted contemptuously. "Well, leave dem be!"

"Tita, yo' don't understan'. We does be a dyin' race here in de hills." Mingoson spread out his hands, peering at Tita lying on the board with her head turned toward him. "If we does have moh blood, moh bucks an' wenches here wid us, we can build a good life. But widout new people, Tita, we ain't gon' survive."

Tita sucked wheezily on her toothless gums. "De Africans done live a' right afore we come join dem." She spat in the mud.

"No, Tita. Dey done live wretched. An' de Africans does be ol'. Dey need people care fuh dem. We need bucks to grow de provision fuh de market. We need hunters to shoot de ramier an' de agouti to feed. We does need moh people, Tita, uh we gon' hab to go back to de plantations to live."

"No!" Tita pulled herself upright and stared at Mingoson. "Yo' mam was be white, Mingoson, but yo' does be foolish like yuh nigger sire. Ain't no one gon' go back to dose slave days! Ah gon' curse yo' fuh sayin' dat, *oui?*"

"Yuh curses don't catch *crapaud!*" Mingoson placed his hands on his knees to emphasize his point.

"Tita, de maroons, dem does be under yuh control now. Yo' done give dem Miss Milly blood. Dey does be workin' in de provision groun' an' a' night we does have de rum we does steal from de still." He glared at her to make her understand.

"It ain't gon' be like so fuh ever, Tita. De bucks an' their wenches gon' go if we don't have moh run'- ways wid us."

"Den gon' get moh run'ways, Mingoson!" Tita

shrieked, falling back on her board with the shock of her shout.

"Dere ain't none, Tita. De slaves like de slavery too much. De buckras does be smart. Dey does have one policy of amelioration. Dey does make de slave feel he doin' good wid slavery, Tita. Ain't no slave dat does want to come to de hills now."

"Dat *sot* talk, Mingoson. Yo' sure does be stupid. Mas Carlton ain't no soft-head. He bound to lash he niggers. When he lash, dey run." Tita turned her back on him, grumpily indicating that the audience was at an end.

"He don't lash no more, Tita," whined Mingoson. "Is Brett does be de overseer. Brett some kind of *maco*. He ain't punish no slave, but dey does do what he does ax dem."

Tita sighed. "Mingoson! If yo' does want moh run'ways fuh our camp, den get dem! Ah gon' chop yuh *tuli* one day an' t'row yuh grain to de parrots. Yuh ax me what yo' know!"

Mingoson scowled. "Yo' does say dat cuz yo' does be a dried-up ol' *beké* whore! Yo' don't have no obeah in yo' at all!"

Mingoson saw Tita's hand move. He threw himself to the floor of the *ajoupa* as the cutlass slammed into the post where he had been leaning. The blade quivered, then fell to the ground with a clatter. Mingoson leaped for it, clasping the worn wooden handle. He kept his eyes on Tita as he fingered the blade, honed down to a fine lethal sharpness.

"What fuh ol' *bagasse* like yo' does have a cutlass, Tita? Yo' scared *soucouyant* gon' hol' yo' in de night?"

"Give me dat!" Tita's shrunken body shook with impotent fury.

"Oh yas, Tita. Ah gon' give yo' de t'ing. Sure. Yo' does want me dead, Tita, is dat why yo' throw de cutlash at me? Heh?"

"Yo' too damn fresh in yuh arse!"

"Tut, tut, Tita. Where yuh obeah now, eh? Yo' know ah does have yuh cutlash. Ain't no problem to slice yuh ugly head from yuh carcass at all!" Mingoson was crouched as though ready to leap, his lips stretched tautly over his gleaming teeth in a sinister snarl.

"Mingoson, hear me!" Tita panicked. She gathered her skinny limbs together on the board, trying to coordinate herself while eyeing his huge body blocking the doorway.

"Ah was be yuh nanny, Mingoson!" The harshness in Tita's voice faded to a gasping whisper. "Ah does be ol' an' frail, Mingoson, but de times we does have. Yo' fuhgit dat?"

"No!" Mingoson sat back, still with the cutlass in his hand poised at Tita's throat. He was undecided what he should do. "Yo' done fuhgit dat! Not me. Yo' done throw de blade at me, Tita."

"Ah was be vex', Mingoson. Ah ain't mean nothin'."

"Like yo' ain't mean to cut Miss Milly's throat?"

"De drums, Mingoson. Dey does touch me here." She patted her sagging chest over her heart under the loose folds of her shift.

Mingoson hissed like a snake. Tita glanced at him in alarm.

He raised his arm above her head. Before she could scramble away, he sliced the cutlass down through the air and into her bed board, splitting it in two.

"Yo' does be one schemin' ol' evil-hearted nigger toad, Tita. Ah does be warnin' yo'. Yo' ain't gon' fool de maroons no moh! Dem gon' leave yo' to die in de bush alone, Tita, if we don't get moh men wid us. Den yo' gon' be sorry ah ain't chop yo' mahself."

Mingoson rose to his feet, his back bent low to pass

through the doorway. He kept his eyes on her as he reached for the door.

"Mingoson!" Tita's voice was soft, half pleading like a child who has been reprimanded. "Yo' ain't gon' tell de maroons?"

Mingoson sniffed.

"Yo' ain't never turn dem against me befoh!"

He nodded his head, waiting.

"Ah gon' tell yo' how to get moh run'ways, Mingoson."

Chapter 33

Ella was getting stout. She knew it, and she was content. She linked her hands over her fat stomach as she sat in her chair watching Brett sip his coffee. She was proud of Brett. Her happy, jowly face quivered. He looked such a man!

"When Mas Carlton say he gon' make yo' de Bon'massa?" Ella's question was the same she asked every day. She liked to gloat on Brett's answer.

Brett raised his hand from the coffee dish. His leather jerkin fitted his body snugly, the full sleeves of his shirt billowing out and concealing his sinewy arms. His earnest face met Ella's. "When he is ready, Ella."

Ella's whole body shook as she grunted with satisfaction.

"Ella?" Brett placed the dish on the table, pushing it away from him. He and his grandmother were alone in the kitchen. Outside, it was starless, charcoal black, with the tweet and chirr of the night insects throbbing as they waited for the dawn.

Ella beamed at Brett.

"Mas Carlton told me he has gold to give me and Laura when he dies. Where's the gold, Ella?"

"Whoooo!" Ella's hands fled to her forehead, and she clutched her temple as though shocked. "Oh, mah gawd!" The flesh on her arms trembled. "De gold, Brett?" She lowered her hands and considered him. He was watching her thoughtfully.

"Yo' does be a good boy, Brett. Yo' does not trifle." She paused. "De gold is not fifty paces from here. By de *balata* tree dat does stand near de corner of de house. Ah done bury it mahself wid Mas Carlton an' yuh pa. He right. De gold does be yuh'n." She sniffed, tugging her ear. "Don't know about Miss Laura, though."

Brett frowned. "Mas Carlton told me he wants me and Laura to get together. You know . . . for me to give her a child. He says she has a thirst for bucks and I can quench that."

"Heh, heh, heh!" Ella rocked forward in her chair. "Mas Carlton real smart, Brett. If she does be yuh wench, yo' does have everyt'ing!"

Brett looked gloomy. "I don't feel like that to Miss Laura, Ella! Not now."

"Lor'! Yo' does be Miss Ella's boy uh no? Bon'massa breed ain't a shy little pussy!" Ella threw her pudgy hands into the air with delight. "Yo' jus' go fuh dat t'ing, an' Miss Laura sure gon' love yo'."

"Ella!" Brett's glare was serious. "I'm not a rutting nigger from the barracoon. I'm me, Brett Todd. I'm a human being with my private feelings. I haven't got taste for Laura, Ella. You know that. It's Davril I love."

"Love!" Ella shrieked with mockery but when she

310

saw the defiant look in Brett's eye, she decided to change her tone. "Dere ain't many bucks does know dat love yo' speak of, Brett. Least, not *beké* bucks like yo' does be."

She champed her jaw reflectively. "Ah s'pose dat does be de Negro heart yo' does have underneath yuh white skin!" She smiled as Brett unconsciously pulled back his shoulders and sat up straighter.

"Brett." Ella's voice assumed the tones of wisdom. "Dere ain't no reason why yo' can't love yuh Davril an' mount wid Laura. De two thing ain't de same." Brett's face was still doubtful, so she rose to her feet and, with her arms akimbo, said proudly, "We Negroes does do dat all de time."

Brett nodded his head somberly.

Ella waddled across the floor, her gray gown dragging on the flagstones. She placed her hands on Brett's shoulders and clasped him to her enormous bosom. "Don't fret about de t'ing, Brett. When yuh *tuli* does see dat white pussy, de mister gon' leap fuh joy and spit out he juice fuh her. Yo' does be one lucky buck nigger, Brett!"

The doleful braying of the conch shell being blown to rouse the slaves cleaved the silence of the dawn. Brett pulled himself away from Ella. He regarded her without speaking, digesting her remark. His lips twitched.

Suddenly he sighed, shaking his head. "Am I always going to be like this, Ella? *Beké* one minute, *neg* the next?"

Ella swooped down and boxed his ears playfully. "Yo' don't need dwell on dat no moh, Brett! Ella gon' fix de thing."

Brett scowled, rising to his feet. "I'm going to set the slaves to work, Ella. You don't understand. I guess no one will. I'll do what is necessary to make you and Mas Carlton happy."

311

His face was serious. He hitched up his breeches, tucking his shirt under his belt, picked up his cowskin whip, and strode out of the kitchen.

Ella stared after him. "Oh lor'!" she exclaimed happily. "Ah does have so much to do!" She bustled over to her cupboard of dried herbs and leaves, muttering to herself as she sought the leaf to slip in Laura's coffee. She would brew one in Brett's own tea and then . . . Ella clapped her pudgy hands together with excitement.

Brett had idled too long in the kitchen. It was his habit to be in the quarters when the conch blew so he could exhort the slaves to work. He did not expect any slave to do something he was not prepared to do himself. Caliste had saddled his horse for him and stood waiting with it outside the stable. He nodded at the slave, mounted quickly, took the reins and galloped down to the compound.

The slaves were already forming into gangs under their drivers. The loud peals of Tency's whip ringing through the air helped dash the sleep from their eyes. Tency had trained her gang to respond to the sound of the whip instead of its lash. She signaled to them to march forward.

The slaves waved cheerily to Brett, laughing among themselves as they set off. They had an unspoken bargain. If the slaves completed the required amount of work, neither Tency nor Brett would seek to harass them unnecessarily. It suited the slaves, who wanted an easy life, and it suited Tency and Brett, as the tasks got done and there was no confrontation.

There were the usual good-humored moans from the slaves as they milled around. They shuffled to collect their tools from the storekeeper and urged their cooks not to be late in bringing breakfast to the fields. The few who were still sipping coffee when Brett arrived drained their calabashes quickly and fell into line with their gangs.

Brett had organized the slaves into efficient working units based on what he had gleaned from his visits to the Gordon plantation. Under Carlton, work had happened in a haphazard way, with slaves feigning sickness when they were weary of labor. Brett contrived to make the work interesting so he got greater production and a more willing attitude. Slavery was not cheap, he had learned. For every slave who was working productively, there were two others to be maintained. His efforts had reduced malingering, and his benevolence had removed the reliance on punishment to achieve results.

Brett accepted what slave overseers forgot. He knew that however authoritarian he was and however impressive his punishments, his success at Roxborough was limited by the will of his slaves. They had the complete power to disobey, sabotage, rebel, or work. The slave system had begun as a coercive one, but Brett recognized that it had developed into one of consent.

There were no new Negroes at Roxborough to stir up disrespect for Brett's system, and every slave under his control was Roxborough born and bred. They were superb specimens. Those in their prime had physiques of such stature that strangers gaped to see them. The women were tall and handsome, with strong and supple bodies. The men had a prestige of their own, lusty and dutiful.

"Yer niggers like ye."

Brett glared at the white man who emerged from the store. He had a book under his arm in which he had been entering the tools taken by each slave. He was Ward Scrivener, a new bookkeeper hired by Carlton.

"That's because I like them, Ward!"

313

The bookkeeper watched Brett's face for a moment, trying to discern a twinkle in his mask of seriousness. "Aye!" He wagged his head disapprovingly. "Have ye read Mr. Collins's manual?"

"No." Brett's tone was expressionless. He himself had asked Carlton to hire a bookkeeper to take over the ledgers and check the hogsheads, the rations, the stores, and all the routine estate chores which had been neglected in the past. Carlton had demurred at first. Brett explained that a bookkeeper, at no more than two hundred pounds a year, would be cheaper than the sum lost through ill-kept records and pilferage. Brett argued that he would need the skilled help of a bookkeeper to make the estate profitable.

Ward Scrivener was referred to Carlton by Warren Gordon. After he had interviewed him, Carlton agreed to the man being hired for the three years. Ward impressed him. He was middle-aged, Creole born, and had worked on plantations for the whole of his life. He limped from a cutlass wound sustained when a slave went berserk and chopped his leg. He was a disciplinarian, Carlton could see by his eyes.

"In his manual," Ward stated pedantically, "Mr. Collins says Negroes are brought to action by the greatest operation of fear or the dread of punishment. He says that love does little and shame less to produce that effect."

"Indeed, Ward? I am grateful for your observation. How are your books?"

"The books are in order!" Ward limped away sorrowfully.

Brett heeled his horse to follow Ward. He did not wish to offend the man; there was much he could learn from him. But the bookkeeper was a slave to the system, too. In the first year, his wages would be consumed by the purchase of a horse (for no white man worth his color walked). The second year his money would go on doctor's bills, and the third year he would pay out the merchants and his tailor.

By his very profession, Ward Scrivener had been failing before he began. The rewards for a bookkeeper were the choleric temper of the plantation owner and the insufferable manners of the overseer.

"Ward!"

The bookkeeper raised his eyes at Brett towering over him astride his horse.

"Where are you going?"

"To the still. I'm making an inventory of the hogsheads yer niggers have left for ye."

"Do you read many books, Ward?"

It was a curious question, and Ward thought carefully before he replied. Had Brett been an older man or one with a trace of malice about him, Ward would have been cautious about laying himself open to ridicule. He gazed up at Brett, who was regarding him earnestly.

"I do."

"Where do you obtain your books, Ward?"

"Why, from the booksellers. Arnold Chase in Roseau has such a store."

"A store selling books?"

Ward caught the puzzled frown which crossed Brett's brow. He smiled to himself. "Do ye read much?" he ventured.

"No!" Brett touched his chin. "I don't have time."

"You young people are all the same," Ward chuckled. "It's a shame. I could help ye if ye wants." He began to limp away, turning suddenly. "When ye have the time!" he added quietly.

"Aye!" said Brett. "I would appreciate that." He sighed. Laura had explained a little about reading, but his relationship with Laura was strained since he had met Davril. The bookkeeper could help him, pro-

315

vided he kept his long English nose out of how Brett governed his slaves.

"I'm clearing a new garden on the eastern boundary, Ward," Brett shouted. "You can find me there if I'm needed!" He galloped up the main drive along the avenue of royal palm trees to the house. He waved to Ella climbing the back stairs with a dish of coffee, and spurred on his horse until he caught up with Tency and her gang climbing the hill path to the provision grounds.

Ella watched him disappearing into the thickets growing beyond the cane-pieces. With Brett on the plantation, she felt they had nothing to fear. With the slaves docile and unharassed, Tita and her group of maroons would get short shrift if they tried to interfere.

Mas Carlton, Ella knew, was growing weary. Sometimes he did not emerge from his bedroom until breakfast time. So the safety of Roxborough was entirely in Brett's hands.

Ella waddled through the dining room where Pip was setting the table for breakfast. A girl was sweeping the drawing room floor. Ella shielded the coffee she was carrying for Laura with her hand. She banged on Laura's door before entering.

Laura's room was in darkness. Ella had heard her come back to the house in the early hours of the morning. She placed the tray on the table beside the bed and moved to open the jalousies.

"No!" murmured Laura. "It's not daybreak already?"

"Lor', Miss Laura, sun-up done pass dese four hours. Pip does be settin' de table fuh breakfast."

"Mas Carlton up yet?"

"He ain't show heself yet, Miss Laura." Ella jerked the jalousie so the light filtered in between the slats. The curtains of Laura's four-poster bed were closed.

316

"Yuh coffee dose be gettin' cold, Miss Laura."

"Damn the coffee!"

"Miss Laura?' Ella clucked with disapproval. "Yo' does ride again last night?"

The curtain flicked open, and Laura stared out. Her hair hung limply around her face, which was lined with the lack of sleep. "Who told you that, Ella? I'll beat that maid of mine!"

"Ah does not need no maid to tell me who does be clumping on de floor what does be ceiling of mah chamber in de young hour."

Laura snorted contemptuously. "Sorry I disturbed you!" She reached over for her coffee. Ella settled herself in the armchair, fixing Laura with a stare. Laura sipped at the dish, too tired to reprimand Ella for her familiarity. It would not make any difference. Ella was so much a part of Roxborough that she pleased herself.

"Yo' does ride in de night like yo' searchin' fuh somethin'!" Ella wrapped her plump arms around her belly and shook her head profoundly.

"What if I am?"

"Mayhap yo' does be lookin' too far, Miss Laura?" Ella tapped her nose with her left finger to indicate the wisdom of her remark. "Mayhap what yo' does be searchin' does be closer to de home."

"You silly old cow, Ella. What are you talking about?"

To Laura, Ella did resemble a cow. She had the same color. Her face was long and wrinkled, and tufts of hair grew on her upper lip and chin. She had blown up in size during the past few months, so she was quite like a bloated bovine. When she wailed it was like a cow's blart.

"Moo! Miss Laura!" Ella sniggered. "Is dose at home what admire yo' what does miss yo'. De coffee good?"

317

Laura sniffed suspiciously. "Yes. Ella! I'm in no mood for your stupid riddles this morning. Explain yourself properly, for heaven's sake."

"Fuh yuh sake, Miss Laura. Ah does know a buck so handsome an' fine, it does only be cuz he scare' to speak dat yo' ain't found him yet!" She winked suggestively, causing Laura to shudder.

Laura sipped the coffee thoughtfully. "Who is the one?" she snapped to show her displeasure.

"Eh, eh, eh! Miss Laura. Yo' old cow does give yo' milk dat taste so sweet?"

"Ella, shut up! If you haven't got anything sensible to say, then get out and send in the girl to help me dress." Laura banged the coffee dish on the table and threw back the covers of her bed.

The smell of her unwashed body wafted over to Ella, who wrinkled her nose. Laura's skin was loose under her chin, showing the signs of age. Her breasts were no longer firm, and her ankles, poking out from her nightgown, were swollen.

"Ah gon' sen' de buck meet yo' tonight," Ella said, heaving herself out of the chair. "Yuh searchin' does be done, Miss Laura!"

Cackling, she waddled out of the room, swinging her hips obscenely.

Chapter 34

The day was an agonizing one for Laura. After breakfast, she strolled down to the nursery to spend time with Miranda and Pallis, gossiping about the whelps and the plantation slaves. Since the hiring of Ward Scrivener and Brett's newfound self-assurance as the overseer, Laura's days were empty. She had tried to help Ella as the housekeeper, but it was obvious that Ella and the house slaves would not brook interference from her.

From the nursery, Laura took a lonely walk down to the river where the women were washing. She chatted with them while they beat the clothes on the stones to get them clean. Afterwards, she ambled back to the house to wait for dinner. Carlton was in a morose mood and spoke only irritably to her. She fled to her chamber after dinner to sleep and in the evening ventured on the balcony to read by the vague light from the lamp while Carlton sipped his rum and ground his teeth. At eight o'clock, Laura bade him good night and retired to her room.

She threw herself fully clothed across the bed, beating the pillow with her fists until the feathers began to fly.

She gasped for breath, twisting her body around. The jalousies were open, but the night was airless. Insects, like large flying ants, swarmed around the lantern and flopped to the floor in dozens. Laura groaned.

She got to her feet, smacking her lips together in a kiss of frustration. In the center of the room she paused, wondering what to do. She glared at the walls, at the wardrobe containing her gowns which never had the chance of being worn, and at the door to the drawing room which she had locked. She scuffed off her shoes, angry at herself for her dejection.

Reaching behind her neck, she unlaced her gown, peeling it off until it dropped around her ankles. She stepped from it irritably, walking in her petticoat toward the mirror of the dressing table. She pulled out her stool from under the table. She plonked herself down on the stool and stared into the glass.

Laura marveled how none of the anguish she felt showed in her eyes. She craned her neck closer to the mirror, peering into the depths of the dark blue irises. She saw only the heavy red rim of the lower eyelids as evidence of her torment. Below the eyes, her flesh was dark and puffy, testimony of her midnight rides through the plantation to the barracoon for bucks. She noticed how tiny wrinkles fanned out from the outer corners of her eyes.

Laura touched her cheek thoughtfully. The luster of her complexion had dulled. The sun had scorched the life out of her skin, once the color of a new pearl but now the sallow shade of faded parchment. Her blond hair no longer glistened; instead it hung dryly over her ears, flecked with skin flaked from her scalp.

She pressed her breasts under her petticoat, cupping them so they flopped out. The nipples drooped wearily. Laura was conscious of her sagging waistline and the fattening of her hips. She squeezed the lobe of her ear with her fingers until the pain caused her to stop. She wanted to scare away the depression settling on her. She would have to ride to the barracoon again that night. She was desperate for satisfaction, but knew that every time she found what she sought, the satisfaction eluded her.

She raised her handbrush from the dressing table and beat the mirror with it, trying to smash her reflection. The glass resisted her. She thumped it again. There was an echo of a knock answering her own. She let the brush fall amidst a cluster of bottles and makeup jars.

"Who's that?" she asked her reflection. Her eyebrows quivered. She lifted her head and listened. Someone was knocking on the door of the dressing room. "My God! It's Ella's nigger!"

Laura leaped up. She dashed to the wardrobe and removed the nightgown which hung there. She pulled it around her and laced it up with a bow at the front. She frowned at her bedraggled appearance, then laughed coarsely. Why should she worry about what she looked like? It was only a slave.

She was puzzled as to who the creature would be whom Ella had recommended so highly. She stepped through to the dressing room and unbolted the door, flinging it open with a flourish to hide her nervousness.

"You!"

"Ella sent me." Brett sauntered into the room, glancing disdainfully at Laura.

"Ella sent you!" Laura clutched the door for support, letting it close gently. She leaned back against it. Brett strolled into the boudoir, sitting on the couch and stretching his long legs out in front of him. His tight trousers, molded to his thighs like a second skin, were deep maroon, a splash of violent color against the pale shades of her room.

"I didn't know. . . ." Laura gasped, sweeping unsteadily into the boudoir. She hovered at his side.

"Huh!" Brett looked up at her, his bright eyes expressionless.

"Of course!" Laura believed she understood. "Why didn't you come before tonight? Did you have to wait for Ella to tell you?" Laura settled herself on the couch next to Brett, running her hand up his arm to his shoulder.

"You don't have to be shy with me, Brett." Laura twisted her fingers in the curls at the back of his head, massaging his neck. "Look at the opportunities we have missed!" She sighed, parting her lips and thrusting her face close to Brett's.

He turned his head aside, his fists clenched on his thighs.

"Brett," she fawned, "you don't have to hold anything back with me. I'm not one of Mas Carlton's Negresses. You can kiss me. You won't get diseased!"

Laura's fingers curled around his neck, clasping his head as she pushed herself close to him. She puckered her lips, closed her eyes, and waited for him to respond.

She opened her eyes in alarm as she felt him tear himself away from her grasp.

He stood up.

"Brett!" Laura was disappointed. She reached out to touch him, but he began to pace the floor. Laura watched him turn at the door and stride back across the room to the far corner. He spun around again and walked back. Laura recalled how she had seen an agouti trapped in a cage behave the same way.

"I understand, Brett," she soothed. "Some men are like that." She rose from the couch and walked to the bed, catching Brett's hand as he prowled past her. "Come sit here with me then, on the bed." She gazed up at him as he stood, poised, in front of her. She smiled brazenly.

Brett flopped himself down on the bed. He lay with his head back and his hands locked behind his neck. His long legs dangled over the edge of the bed, the heels of his boots scraping the floor. He closed his eyes.

A flutter of excitement beat against Laura's chest. She contemplated the man stretched out in front of her. Brett was sensous and handsome. His lithe body was tanned and muscular. His cotton shirt was open at the throat. He wore no stock. His chin and upper lip, Laura realized, were coated with soft hairs, bleached by the sun, which one day would mature into a beard. She touched his chin with her finger. His eyes remained closed.

Slowly she ran her fingers down his chin to the scar on his throat. She knew how proud Brett was of that scar. She traced her fingers along the welt from his right ear across his larynx to the left ear. He still did not stir.

Laura smiled to herself. "He is just like a nigger," she thought. "He wants me to do all the work!"

She slipped her hand under his shirt, unfastening it quickly. She could feel excitement rising through her. When his shirt was open to the waistband of his trousers, she parted it so it lay on either side of his body like wings. She gazed adoringly on his sun-brown torso.

Laura bent her head low, her hair brushing across Brett's chest. She stabbed his nipple with her tongue, deftly licking it until the teat hardened. She closed her teeth over it and gently bit him.

Brett brushed her face away brusquely. Laura looked up. He still lay across the bed, his head nestling in his hands and his legs wide apart stretched out onto the floor. Laura smiled again. His attitude already said that he was hers. She would soon have him roused and pleading with her for more!

Her lips slipped down his chest and into the trail of soft hairs growing over the taut muscles of his abdomen. She knelt down on the floor beside him and began to massage the inside of his thighs while her lips strayed down to the waistband of his trousers. She paused and lifted her head. She was only inches away from his sex. Unable to restrain herself, Laura let her hand slip gently onto him.

She frowned. Brett was soft and lifeless. She pummeled him with her fingers and began to knead him as though he was a wad of dough. She glanced at him, consternation creasing her face.

Brett scowled, raising himself to a sitting position. Laura buried her head in his lap, gnawing with her teeth through the fabric of his trousers in an effort to rouse him.

Brett grasped her by her hair and yanked her head up. Her eyes stared at his own in complete surprise. She opened her mouth to order him to let her go. As she was about to speak, the back of Brett's fist smashed into her face, pounding her cheek and sending her hurtling backwards to the floor.

Brett got to his feet. He stood over Laura, his upper lip curling in a sneer of contempt. Deliberately, he placed his feet on either side of her body, glaring down at her.

She was sniveling. She had rolled herself into a fetal position to ward off the blows she was expecting.

"Laura!" Brett's voice was stern. "Look at me!"

Laura stopped sniveling immediately. The forcefulness of Brett's voice was irresistible. Slowly she turned her head, peering up at him. She shifted her body so she was on her back on the hard floor and could see him better. Frantically, she tried to assess his mood.

"Laura!" he commanded. "See this!" Brett's hand tugged at his belt, flicking it open. He ripped the front of his pants apart and pulled himself out. His penis hung down lazily.

"You want that, Laura?" Brett snapped. "That's for the girl I love, not you! Look at it now. It's the last time you're ever going to see it." Brett's voice hung in the air with unspoken curses as he stuffed himself back into his pants. Instead of fastening his strap, he pulled the leather belt out and let it dangle in his hand.

"What are you doing?" Laura found her voice at last. "Let me go!"

"Yes, Laura. When I've finished."

"What do you mean? You've no right to do this to me!"

"I have as much right as you have trying to get

every nigger on this plantation to mount you. What's wrong with you, Laura?"

"There ain't nothing wrong in a woman wanting a man, Brett!" Laura whined. "There ain't no white men here, so I got to take niggers."

Brett snapped his strap through the air above Laura's face. The heavy brass buckles clanked together ominously.

Laura's eyes widened. "What are you doing with that strap!"

"I'm going to thrash you, Laura." Brett's voice was cool. "I'm going to thrash you now, and I'm going to thrash you every time you molest one of my Negroes. You've just got to stop it, Laura! Do you hear?"

Brett slashed the strap down onto Laura. She twisted. The belt landed with a thwack on her rump. Brett gritted his teeth and flayed her again. This time the strap cut into the loose flesh of her thigh. Laura winced.

"Stop it, Brett!"

"Stop?" He lifted his hand for another swipe. "I haven't begun to hurt you yet." He rained the blows down on Laura's hips while she twisted to escape him. She dragged herself across the floor, cowering beside the bed.

"Oh, please, Brett!" she sniffed. "Stop it!"

"And you?" asked Brett, pausing with his hand poised to strike her again. "Are you going to stop?"

"Yes! Yes!" whispered Laura. "Anything you say."

"Huh!" He watched her menacingly. "I don't believe you."

"You can believe me, Brett!" Laura's voice was husky. She gazed up at Brett towering over her. She was smarting from his blows. She saw Brett's chest was heaving like her own. Instead of feeling outraged

325

at his behavior, Laura felt strangely humbled. She felt herself melting inside.

"I'm yours, Brett," she breathed with relief. "I'm yours."

Brett raised his eyebrow arrogantly. "Get up!"

Laura scrambled to her feet, mesmerized by Brett's voice. She sat on the edge of the bed, staring at him adoringly.

He fastened the broad leather belt around his waist and sprawled out on the couch. He ran his hand through his hair, ruffling his black locks as he eyed Laura. His legs were stretched out in front of him, his crotch swollen. Laura lowered her eyes to the floor.

"You're a damn bitch, Laura!"

Laura's lips twitched. "Brett, it's not my fault. You don't know the anguish I go through at night lying here alone. I'm a woman, Brett!"

"I know, Laura." Brett seemed to snarl. "And I'm a man, not a prize stallion. Mas Carlton told me to mount you to keep you out of the niggers' britches. Ella told me to take you. She even gave you a powder to make you want me." Brett tucked his legs under the couch and leaned forward.

"And you want me, don't you?"

"Yes," breathed Laura, her lips parted as she gazed at Brett. "I do. Come, Brett. Take me, take me!"

"By the devil, Laura!" Brett leaped to his feet. "Don't you understand? I'm not a rutting nigger!" His nostrils flared as he faced her.

"Yes, Brett." Laura raised her hand and laid it on Brett's chest. She could feel his heart pounding. "You are right, Brett. You are a real man. I need you, Brett!"

"Damn you, Laura!" Brett pulled away and threw himself down on the couch again. "You need another thrashing, not a man."

"There's only one man who's ever treated me like you did, Brett."

"Who was that?" Brett asked curtly.

"Fletcher."

Brett's brow wrinkled with interest. He leaned forward, an idea flashing into his mind. "You miss him, Laura?"

"Yes, Brett." Laura sensed that the tension had passed. She eased herself up to sit on the bed. She realized she could not hope to have Brett now.

"He knew how to handle me, Brett. He was more of a man than any Negro, in every way. You remind me of him, Brett. You have the same air of wild determination that he had."

"Huh!" Brett scowled. Fletcher was the man who had ordered his father's murder. "Why don't you send for him?" he asked casually.

"What? Fletcher?"

"Why not? Mas Carlton won't mind. With Fletcher here, you'll have the man you want around you all the time."

"Fletcher is not the kind of man you think he is. You've never seen him, Brett. He'd never come!" Laura sighed.

"He would come, Laura." Brett's eyes glinted evilly. "Write to him. Tell him you know where Mas Carlton's gold is buried. He'll be yours then."

Laura stared at Brett incredulously

"I mean it. If he thinks he has a chance of getting at the gold, he'll take the first vessel here. You'll have him under your thumb all the time."

Laura sucked her lower lip nervously. "You know him?" she uttered breathlessly.

"No." Brett shrugged his shoulders. "It's a natural reaction."

"But I don't know where Mas Carlton has his gold

hidden," pouted Laura. "And if I did, I would not tell Fletcher!"

"Exactly. But he doesn't know that, does he? You'll have him here under your control." Brett smirked.

Laura studied Brett. There was no humor in his eyes. His body was tense, his fists clenched on his thighs as though he was trying to contain some private excitement of his own. Laura longed for him.

"You want me to write to him, Brett?"

"Yes. Get him here!" Brett's voice squealed. "For you!" he added as an afterthought.

Laura stood up. She paused, letting her nightgown fall open. She thrust her breasts out as she walked over to Brett, letting the white half-moons soar tantalizingly above the lace top of her petticoat. She patted her hair coquettishly.

"Brett," she whispered.

He looked up at her, shaking his head to clear his thoughts.

She extended her hands to him. He hesitated before taking Laura's hands in his own. She bent down to plant an aunt's kiss on his cheek.

He moved, tilting back his head so that his lips met hers.

Chapter 35

Mingoson crouched under the *balata* tree. The glow of the lantern edged in stripes across the courtyard through the open jalousies of Laura's bedroom. Mingoson saw the movement of two shadows dancing toward each other, merging into one. The shadowy mass dipped out of his vision below the jalousies, leaving only the dim light flickering in the black hulk of the house.

Mingoson had observed Pip extinguish the lights on the balcony after Mas Carlton had stumbled off to his chamber, carying the decanter of rum with him. Pip had closed the doors of the house, then shuffled down the back steps and into the kitchen. Mingoson had seen Ella's tired old head peer out into the coal-black night before she closed the shutters of the kitchen, blending the house into the engulfing darkness.

He fastened his eyes on the light in Laura's boudoir, seeing it as a beacon for his desire.

Mingoson had thought a lot about Laura. He had glimpsed her occasionally through screens of dense foliage when he ventured down from the heights to spy on the plantation. He had been entranced by her, never believing that he might one day have her for himself. Since then, Mingoson had learned from the bucks in the barracoon about Laura's nightly rides. Tonight, he vowed, she would not have to ride to the barracoon. Mingoson intended to intercept her before she even reached the stables.

He eyed the glow in her room curiously. Mingoson knew someone was with Laura. He squatted on a thick root trailing away from the trunk of the *balata* tree to wait. The door onto the balcony from Laura's room opened. Mingoson started up in surprise as Brett stepped from it. He stood quietly beside the *balata* as Brett glided along the balcony and down the front steps of the house.

Brett paused. He frowned, tilting his head and sniffing the air. Mingoson wondered what had caught Brett's attention. Brett turned and peered into the darkness in the direction of the *balata* tree. Mingoson could hear him inhaling deeply. He froze, gripping his cutlass tightly in case Brett decided to walk over to the tree.

Brett pulled his nose suspiciously, unable to identify the aroma wafting toward him on the night air. Although there was no moon and the night was pitch-black, he dived off the steps to head unerringly for the trail to his cabin. He would investigate the source of the foul stink in the morning.

Mingoson listened cautiously. Brett moved with the stealth of a night animal and, once he had disappeared out of the halo of dim light from Laura's room, it was impossible to judge his whereabouts. Mingoson's senses tingled and he lowered himself to the ground, ready to dive into the bush or leap at Brett's throat if he came near. He let five minutes pass before he began to relax. Laura, meanwhile, had extinguished the lantern in her room so that the whole house abruptly became part of the sullen night.

Mingoson rose to his feet, his cutlass clutched eagerly in his hand. He stole across the courtyard and paused at the foot of the grand steps. The memory of the days when he had lived in that house and been forbidden to use the front steps triggered a smile on his rugged face. He gripped the wrought-iron railing and hauled himself quietly up the steps to the balcony.

The floorboards creaked under his weight as he crept around the balcony and paused outside Laura's room. He cocked his ear to the night but heard no answering creak of a door opening or a bark from a suspicious dog. He wondered if Laura was sleeping. He tapped lightly on the door.

"Brett?" Laura's voice replied immediately. "Oh, I hoped you would come back."

Mingoson heard Laura fumbling with the key. The door opened, and he put his foot against it to keep Laura from closing it again.

"I have no lantern, Brett, I can't see you." Laura peered out.

"It matters not!" Mingoson swiftly clapped his hand over Laura's mouth, twisting her around so that her back was facing him. He held her tightly across her chest with his other arm, the cutlass dangling in his hand.

"Walk into the room, Laura. Don't worry, I'm not going to harm you!" Mingoson pushed Laura forward with his body, feeling himself beginning to swell at her closeness.

Laura was panting for breath, choking from the smell of Mingoson as much as from his hand blocking her mouth. She wriggled frantically against his body to indicate her distress.

"Stay still, Laura," pleaded Mingoson. "I ain't going to harm you, I say. I'll take my hand from your mouth, but don't scream. If you do, I'll have to use my cutlass. Laura, nod your head if you agree."

Mingoson felt Laura's head bob quickly, and he released his hand from her mouth. Laura heaved, bending her body forward. Mingoson closed the door quietly behind him and propelled Laura into the boudoir. She squinted at him.

"Who are you?" she whispered.

"Mingoson."

"Mingoson!" Laura snorted, extracting herself from his grasp. "You smell awful. What have you got on your skin. It's slippery!"

"Snake grease."

Laura touched his hair. "I can't see you in the dark. You probably look like an animal. Are you naked?"

In answer, Mingoson took Laura's hand and placed it on his breech cloth by his hip. Laura pulled her hand back quickly.

"What are you doing here? Mas Carlton will shoot you. You're a maroon, aren't you?"

"I came for my share."

"Your share of what?" Laura stood nervously at the edge of the bed. A firefly broke through the jalousies illuminating the room with a bright green glow. Laura gasped.

Mingoson's face was close to hers, his fine black nose almost touching her cheek. His eyes, she saw with sudden relief, were kind and sensitive, not brittle like Brett's piercing glare.

"Mingoson, why have you come here?" She let herself slip down onto the bed. Mingoson loomed over her.

"For you, Laura." His lips hovered above hers as the firefly darted between the posts of the bed. Laura protested weakly, falling back across the mattress and shaking her head from side to side. He closed in, fastening his mouth on hers, sliding his sticky body on top of her.

The whip flayed through the air and sank into Mingoson's flesh a second after the bedroom door crashed open. Mingoson felt the blade of the whip's tongue slice across his shoulders and cut down on his buttocks. He yelled, rolling off Laura and hitting the floor, fumbling for his cutlass.

"Damn niggers, Laura! I warned you!" Carlton spat out viciously in the darkness. The whip slashed down again, cutting Laura across her thighs. She screamed, diving off the bed for cover.

"I'm going to string up the nigger you have here!" Carlton's whip snapped down again, failing to contact. "Phew!" He gasped. "That buck's more ranky than nigger shit."

Mingoson groped frantically under the bed for the cutlass.

"I see you, boy!" bellowed Carlton, slashing at the darker shadow grovelling on the floor. He grunted as

332

the whip made contact. "You are sure going to swing by your balls for this!"

The whip wrapped around Mingoson's waist. He cursed himself for losing his cutlass. The whip lashed his ankles as he cringed against the wall, trying to merge into the blackness. He knew it would not be long before someone came running with a lantern.

Edging along the wall, Mingoson found the opening to the dressing room. He dodged the lash of the Bondmaster's whip and dived into the room. He wrenched open the door and hurtled along the balcony.

Carlton dashed for the door, throwing the whip aside and brandishing his pistol, which he held in his other hand.

He peered along the balcony, listening as Mingoson scuttled down the steps. He aimed into the night and fired. The flash of flame from the pistol lit up the courtyard.

"Who the devil is that?" Carlton frowned. He had glimpsed Mingoson with his plaited hair caked with cow dung racing for the cover of the bush. "Looks like a bloody African."

Ella waddled in with a lantern. Her face was drawn. She had recognized the figure fleeing into the bush.

"Hold your light here, Ella!" Carlton gripped her wrist, forcing it upwards. He peered over the balcony rail. "Damn nigger's gone now!" He hawked, sending a glob of phlem spiraling into the night.

He spun around to face Laura watching from her doorway. "Don't tell me," he sneered. "He forced his way into your room. He was raping you at cutlass point so you couldn't scream for help! Isn't that always the way?"

Laura stared at Carlton. She was beyond weeping. "Look," she said, holding out Mingoson's cutlass.

"Huh! He really did have a weapon!"

Laura shook her head sadly. "I know you won't

believe me. He was a maroon, not one of your slaves."

Carlton frowned. "You are making it up. The maroons would not dare to come here."

"This one did."

"She does be right, Mas Carlton." Ella's voice quavered. She eyed Laura. "I done recognize him."

"By the devil, Ella. Who was he?"

Ella glanced at Laura.

"Mingoson!" Laura answered quickly, flinging the cutlass over the balcony railing into the night.

"You asked him to come here, Laura?"

Laura looked at Carlton with a mixture of contempt and amazement. "No!" she uttered loudly, shuddering. "He's a savage."

"What yo' gon' do, Mas Carlton?" Ella knew that there could be trouble for all of them if Carlton reported this to the authorities. The uneasy truce which had lasted for years would be shattered.

Carlton scratched the back of his head. He was loath to stir up any confrontation with the maroons. Although he knew their camp was on the plantation boundary, it would take time flushing them out of the bush. Apart from this incident, they had been quiet during the years, leaving him and the other planters alone.

"Now, Ella, I'm going to my bed. You sleep here with Laura. She got to have a maid with her from tomorrow on. There ain't no one got to come in this chamber at all, do you hear, Laura?"

Laura scowled, flouncing back into her room.

Mingoson slipped out of his hiding place behind the *balata* tree as Carlton and Ella went back into the house. He located his cutlass where Laura had thrown it, picking it up fondly. He raised his eyes to the balcony and nodded his head. One day, he vowed, Laura would be his.

* * *

Brett and Ward Scrivener sat grim-faced in the drawing room of Roxborough Hall as they listened to Carlton.

"The situation is clear," Carlton drawled. "A maroon was here at Roxborough. What do we do?"

Silence greeted his question. Carlton stared at Brett, whose thin lips were closed tightly in a straight line of frustration. Carlton glanced at Ward, raising his eyebrows.

Ward was fidgeting. He was stymied by Brett's silence. He knew it would not be correct for him to speak before his young master.

"Come on, man! Out with it!" Carlton glowered.

Ward inclined his head toward Brett. "Ain't no doubt in me mind, Mr. Todd. The maroons is a menace. Got to be wiped out. I say ye should send for the rangers and hunt those varmints until they all are killed off, every one of them."

Brett turned on Ward. "You're the one who reads all the books! Ain't you heard about the liberation that is supposed to be coming? If we started to hunt maroons, the slaves on all the plantations for miles around would get jittery. There would be uprisings for sure."

Brett rested his head in the palm of his hand. He was trying to wipe out the thought of Mingoson following him into Laura's room. Somehow, he blamed himself.

"You are half right," muttered Carlton. "The British Government is all for amelioration. The abolitionists have a powerful voice now. I don't think Governor Nicolay would agree to a campaign against the maroons. Why, we've just granted those yellow serpents, the mulattoes, equal rights!"

Ward coughed to conceal his impatience with his two masters. "I get a twinge in me pins right here, Master Brett," he said, tapping his game leg, "when-

335

ever I hear of softness to niggers. Blacks take kindness as a sign of weakness, I tell you. Ain't no one going to thank ye for it." Blood shot to his cheeks in his rage.

"Dam'me, sirs, if ye'll pardon me expression. Ye ain't advocating that we do nothing! Miss Laura bloody near raped by a stinking savage! And here in the house, too. Them maroons going to slaughter all of us whites if we don't do something about it!"

Ward wiped his mouth with the back of his hand, glaring at Brett. Carlton shook his head in confusion.

"I agree with you, Ward," Carlton murmured, wearied by the argument. "But perhaps there are things you don't know. The maroons have never troubled us before. Mingoson used to live here. Legally he is a free man, a mulatto. His mother was white; she was my first wife. That makes him Laura's half-brother. Now, did he come here as one of the maroons or as a hot-blooded nigger after a piece of tail every buck in the barracoon has had already?"

Ward sat back and stared at Carlton with astonishment. "Sir!" he protested. "Miss Laura, sir!" Ward looked across at Brett for support. He saw Brett's face was stern, coloring rapidly with embarrassment at Carlton's remark.

"I don't know what abominations have occurred here, sir," Ward added, forgetting discretion at the shock of what he had heard. "To me Miss Laura is a lady, and the nigger who jumped her last night should have his guts torn out." He wiped the sweat off his forehead with the palm of his hand.

"I've heard about ye for years, sir. I always respected the Bondmaster for his dealings with his slaves. Men like yerself, sir, is what has kept these islands prosperous. Yer breed of niggers are strong and tractable."

Ward's face was a bright red as he continued. "I

can't understand why ye let a black molest yer daughter, sir, without hunting him down!"

Carlton sighed, gazing at the bookkeeper from the depths of his heavily hooded eyes. "A man changes, sir!" he spat out. "Laura and Mingoson, they both come from the same womb." He waved his hand sadly. "I'm not trying to spare Mingoson because he was my first wife's son. Didn't I send my own get, Hayes, to the gallows?"

Carlton frowned, reaching for the decanter of rum on the table between them. He concentrated on the amber liquid splashing into his glass. He stopped and raised his head. Ward and Brett were watching him closely.

"Is it Mingoson alone who should be punished?" he croaked, as though pleading for help. "Or is it Laura who should suffer, too?"

Ward rose to his feet unsteadily. "Begging ye pardon, masters, both!" he stammered. "I have me checking to do."

Brett nodded Ward's dismissal. He studied the back of the man as he limped from the room. Outrage at what he had heard seemed to be reflected in the insolent hunch of the man's shoulders.

"You upset our bookkeeper!" he observed to Carlton.

"Dam'me, Brett! That's the least of my problems."

"I suppose he'll leave now. That's unfortunate. He is mighty useful."

"A bookkeeper ain't got no cause to have principles, Brett. He's a jumped-up slave, that's all. I pay him instead of whipping him."

"He came here because he believed in the Bondmaster. Now he thinks you are conniving with the maroons."

"And you, Brett? What do you think?"

Brett shook his head. "Is it revenge Mingoson wants, Mas Carlton? Or is it Laura?"

Ward, pausing at the top of the stone steps, clutched the wrought-iron railing for support. He was blind to the prettiness of the flowering creeper which twined around the railing. In his rage, he could not appreciate the serene beauty of the plantation rolling down the valley to the meandering river below. The tranquillity of Roxorough had no effect on the thoughts tumbling through his angered brain.

He, Ward Scrivener, vowed to show those lily-livered planters who had bossed him around all his life that he still knew right from wrong. Even if he had to do it alone, he would hunt down that half-breed varmint Mingoson. He would expunge that evil from Roxborough so that the Bondmaster and his grandson could hold up their heads with pride again.

He, Ward, would be a hero at last, instead of a bootlicking slave bookkeeper!

Chapter 36

Ward admired Tency. She was a fine-looking, mature wench. True, he considered, her face was black and blubbery and she had the foul niggery smell of decayed biscuits when she came in from the fields. Yet she was well-built with full burnt-coffee-bean breasts and ample, hard-working thighs. Her hips, when she stalked proudly behind her gang, her whip swinging in her hand, rolled aggressively.

Ward eyed her intensely as she herded her gang to the store and he checked the hoes and cutlasses the slaves presented to him. The arrogant toss of her head as she cracked her whip to dismiss the slaves assured Ward that she was aware of his appraisal. He smirked as she hitched down the hem of her short dull brown osnaburg shift.

Ward was not especially partial to black wenches, but on his annual salary he could not afford the white whores in Layou, and no other kind of white woman would care to look at an impoverished bookkeeper. Roxborough had no white house servants, so he had no scope there. A slave wench was all he could aspire to. Tency, with her exalted status as a driver, seemed the best.

"Yer gang serve ye well today, Tency?" he demanded when she swaggered toward him as the slaves ambled off to their shacks.

"Aye, Massa Ward. Mah niggers don't give no trouble. Dey knows ah does lash dem hard as any buck if dey does." She leered at him.

Ward sniffed, grimacing at the odor. "What are ye going to do now, Tency?"

"Me, massa?" Tency's pink tongue darted out swiftly, wiping saliva over her thick brown lips.

"Yes, Tency," Ward muttered, knowing slaves were reluctant to answer a straightforward question in case it incriminated them in some way. "Where are ye going now?"

"Ah does be goin' dis way, sah!" Tency pointed in the direction being taken by the other slaves, hoping it was the answer the buckra wanted to hear.

Ward wiped his face with the palm of his hand. He always got exasperated when he tried to talk to slaves. "Tency!" He thought of the way Mas Carlton would deal with this situation. "I want ye to bathe yerself in the river and come to me cabin, ye hear?"

Tency's dark eyes seemed to glow, her face splitting into a wide grin. Ward winced as her foul breath wafted over him. "Ah does be joyful, sah! As does be de one fuh yo,' buckra, sah!"

Ward stepped back, fearful that Tency was going to hug him. "I want to discuss some business concerning the slaves with ye, ye understand?"

"Ah, de buckra choose right, sah! Tency de one fuh de business!" She gave a shriek of laughter and scampered off after her gang.

Ward's heart sank. Now every slave in the plantation would know that he had chosen Tency as his mistress. "Damn!" he muttered to himself, walking slowly up the path to his cabin near the nursery.

His game leg was aching by the time he reached the cabin. It was dusk and with the short twilights of the tropics would soon be completely dark. His cook had placed his meager supper on the table for him, and the lantern had been lit. He washed his hands in the basin of water, splashing his face to wipe the grime away. His shirt was soiled with a week's work, and his breeches were mud-stained and threadbare.

Ward shrugged his shoulders. It was a month since he had bathed himself all over, he calculated. Well, he thought, he was not going to go through that again just because a slave wench was coming to his cabin. He threw the soapy water out of the cabin window and wiped his face and hands with a heavily stained towel.

He scratched himself under his armpit and settled down to eat the cold ham on his plate, sipping the lukewarm cocoa tea unenthusiastically. He had a book propped open against the jar of pickled hot peppers and read slowly as he shoveled the ham into his mouth.

The knock on the door startled him. He rose wearily from his chair and staggered to the door, rubbing his thigh vigorously to restore life to it.

"Tency!" He peered at the black face beaming at him out of the darkness.

"Yas, massa!"

"Eh, come in!" He was surprised. Tency had dressed herself in her Sunday finery, an old collection of assorted kerchiefs and petticoats assembled without thought for their overall effect. Poor Tency was grotesque in her emulation of white fashion.

Ward limped back to his chair and gestured apologetically at the bed. "There ain't no other chair," he said, lowering himself back into his seat. He carefully marked his page in the book with a strip of dried grass from the thatched roof. Tency was staring around the cabin.

"Why, yo' ain't got no moh in yuh shack dan me!" She sounded shocked. "Ah does have a mattress an' a pallet so! An' ah does have chairs, too." Her voice had now taken on a note of disapproval.

"But ye don't have a lantern and books, I'm sure, Tency."

Ward was rewarded with a stare of contempt. "A slave ain't got no business wid books, Mas Ward, sah." Tency pouted. As though remembering what she had been summoned for, Tency arranged her petticoats around her ankles and clasped her hands over her crotch.

Ward's nose wrinkled with distaste as he observed her mud-caked bare feet with thick skin like a horse's hoof. In the clothes with which she had wrapped herself, it was hard for Ward to imagine the body which had vaguely attracted him. He knew it was abstinence rather than desire which made his need for Tency so pressing.

The way with Negroes, Ward had learned as a youth, was to tell them what to do.

"Hoick up yer skirts, Tency." Ward stood up and hobbled over to the bed, rubbing his crotch to stir

341

himself to life. "Git yer head back there on the bolster."

He paused as he stood beside the bed. Tency was hauling her body up the length of the bed, her skirts already rumpled around her waist. Her huge dark thighs were shaking with anticipation. "Ye did bathe, girl?"

"Oh yas, Mas Ward. Ah done wash de pussy, too!" She cackled, fingering herself proudly. "Yo' gon' like what Tency does have here!"

Ward contemplated Tency's open thighs dourly. He liked a tough wench he could dominate until she was screaming underneath him. He unbuckled his strap and opened the front of his breeches. He fumbled to get himself rigid.

"Give that here!" Tency laughed, raising her head to his thighs as he stood beside the bed. She poked him inside her mouth and sucked him as though she was a child with a mango pip. Ward moaned, pushed her back, and clambered on top of her.

He stretched down to the floor with his hand for his short horsewhip, a strip of finely polished leather with a small handle. Tency's bulky legs locked behind his back as he bucked and barged into her. With the whip gripped in his right hand, he reached back and flayed his buttocks, slashing wildly at his own flesh.

Tency cupped her hand around his.

"No!" he yelled in panic. "No! Don't stop me!"

"Ah does be de driver, Massa Ward!" Tency yawped, wresting the whip from his grasp.

She scythed the whip down on Ward's naked butt with a cruel accuracy, torturing his tight scrotum and tender flesh until he thrust and drained himself into her with a shriek of submission.

Tency lay beneath him waiting for Ward to roll off. She retched at the fetid odor of the old white man as he finally moved and lay beside her. He was whimpering softly like a child. Tency put her arm out and patted his chest.

"Ah does be good, massa?"

Ward was swallowing, trying to get his breath back. Now he felt like a man who could accomplish anything. Such a warm glow enveloped him. His body was stinging from her lashes. He forgot about his lameness in the pain soaring through his thighs and groin.

"Yes!" he gasped, "Bloody good!"

Tency smiled. No nigger had ever told her that. Her hand slipped down to her crotch and she fingered herself absent-mindedly while the buckra spoke.

"I'm going to show all ye slaves here," Ward panted, "how right is right. Ye can help me, Tency."

"Yas, massa," she murmured drowsily.

"The maroons, Tency, what do ye make of them?" Ward recovered his breath and laid his head back on the bolster, staring at the ceiling.

Tency abruptly stopped rubbing herself. This was dangerous talk. "What maroons?" she ventured.

"Those in the hills, Tency. Do they ever come down here and ask the slaves to run away?"

"Oh no, sah!"

"If they did come, do ye think the slaves would join them?"

Tency saw this was all a trick. The buckra had lured her to his cabin just to question her. "Ah don't know about no maroons, sah."

"Nonsense, Tency!" Ward turned his head to look at her. "Ye are a driver. Ye must have heard the slaves talking."

"Mah slaves does not talk, sah!"

Ward sighed. "At night, Tency. Have ye never heard talk of the maroons at night?"

Tency decided a bold reply was necessary to make the buckra drop the subject. "Ain't no Roxbruh slave gon' run 'way join de maroons, dem." she answered him vehemently.

"Ain't no Roxbruh slave gon' lose his home, he clothes, his meat, all he does have fuh to join de maroons. When we sick, de massa doctor does physic us. When we does birth a whelp, de massa does give us cloth for clothes an' de buck does get a gold piece. No maroon gon' mek no mischief at Roxbruh, sah!"

Tency was exhausted by her speech. She twisted her hair nervously, wondering if she had made the buckra understand her properly. His reply surprised her.

"I'm going to hunt down the leader of the maroons and kill him, Tency!"

"Yo', sah!" She spoke without thinking.

"Why not me, Tency?" He was hurt.

"Ain't no reason why not, sah. Is yo', sah, if yo' does want!"

Ward sat up, staring intently at the lantern. "It's to save Roxborough, Tency. The plantation has a great name, but Mas Carlton is old now. Brett does not have the same values. The maroons must be wiped out before they destroy Roxborough and all it stands for!"

Tency was appalled. "Yo t'ink dey gon' destroy us, sah?" Mingoson had never said anything like that when he came to the quarters at night, she thought.

"Yes, Tency. Unless I stop it. I can, ye know, with yer help, Tency." Ward's bottom tingled as he wriggled on the edge of the bed.

"Mah help, sah?" Tency was unhappy.

"Yes, Tency. I'm going to find the maroon camp. I'm certain some of the slaves here know where it is. So many of the slaves look alike, the maroons could be passing freely through the plantation and Mas Carlton and Brett don't even know it." He jabbed the whip handle into Tency's waist.

344

"Some of the slaves here know the maroons and their camp, don't they?"

"Ah don' know, sah!"

"Ye needn't lie to me, Tency. I'm not going to do anything to ye." He grinned. "Only what I just did!" He stood up, pulling his breeches up to his waist, wincing with pleasure at the agony of Tency's beating.

"I want ye to send me some slaves who know where the camp is, Tency. I want about two strong niggers to help me hunt that Mingoson." He turned to face Tency.

"Ye know yer niggers, Tency. I'm going to see that ye get fine things for yer cabin if ye find me the slaves I want. Not bucks who are scared to fight, Tency. I want loyal Roxborough niggers who are going to be proud to flush out them maroons."

Tency nodded her head. She was confused. She sat up slowly, brushing her petticoat down. She raised her eyes to the buckra, who was rubbing his backside, a smile of contentment on his lips.

"Yas, massa!" she whispered. "Ah does do what yo' does say. May ah go now, sah?"

Ward opened his eyes and looked at Tency with a frown. It was always the same, he thought. Once you started to have something with a slave, she thought she could do what she liked. "Go?" he queried.

"Yas, sah. Ah does go look fuh de bucks fuh yo', sah. Ah gon' tell yo' tomorrow, sah."

"Yes, all right." Ward stroked his chin. His plan was going to work, he thought gleefully. He walked over to the table, dismissing Tency from his mind as she rustled out of the cabin and into the night.

When Mingoson heard what the bookkeeper had told Tency, he snorted with laughter. He was sitting on a boulder in the middle of the Layou River. He was stark naked, his legs dangling down the side of the boulder into the water as it rushed in bubbling rapids at his feet.

Lambert, who had carried Tency's message to him, crouched on a smaller stone watching the river swirl around thcm. Mingoson had been looking for crayfish under the rocks when Lambert had found him. They were in the upper reaches of the Layou Valley, close to the plantation boundary. The crayfish Mingoson had caught were hooked on a vine-string and lay on the boulder beside him.

"Tita gon' love dis!" Mingoson guffawed.

"Yo' not scared, Mingoson?" Lambert had the inbuilt respect of a slave for the superiority of a white man.

Mingoson beamed at Lambert, reaching down to scoop up water in his hand. He splashed it over Lambert with a chuckle. "Wash dat slave thought out yuh mind, Lambi! What ah does have to be scared fuh! He gon' shoot me? Me, Mingoson?"

"He does have his pistol, Mingoson!"

"So have I!" Mingoson pulled his penis and shook it vigorously.

Lambert grinned. "What yo' gon' do?"

"Yo'll see, boy." Mingoson dabbled his feet in the river. Slowly, he slid off the boulder. The sunlight darted through the heavy branches of the trees bending over the river. Mingoson lowered his head cautiously, eyeing the surface of the gurgling water.

Stealthily, he slipped into the river, plunging his head down so only his backside showed above the water like a creased brown stone. Then that too disappeared. Lambert watched, waiting patiently.

Mingoson emerged triumphantly, showering drops of water around him and clutching an enormous crayfish in his hand. He beamed happily at Lambert,

346

punching a hole in the soft flesh and threading the crayfish onto the vine with the others.

"Here, Lambi!" he said. "Take dis fuh Tency. Tell she send de buckra hunt me when de moon does be full." He paused thoughtfully. "Dat does be two nights time." He cuffed Lambert behind his head, squeezing his bottom under his breech cloth with his other hand.

"Yo' an' dat pardner of yuhs, Dale. Yo' lead de buckra here. Tell he is here ah does come to mek me sacrifice to de moon!"

Mingoson's chuckle swelled in the morning breeze as Lambert started back down the trail. His laughter was echoed by the whistle of a startled sisserou parrot which swooped down from a tall gomier tree.

Mingoson snatched up his bow and arrow and carefully took aim.

Chapter 37

Brett accepted the glass of lime juice which Davril was holding out for him. Mrs. Gordon smiled happily. The sun seeping through the vast boughs of the saman tree dappled Brett's face with leaf-shadows and caused his hair to glitter like onyx. Mrs. Gordon leaned forward, grasping her own glass daintily in her hand with her little finger protruding coquettishly.

"I'm so glad you could come to stay, Brett. Davril talks of no one but you the whole day." Mrs. Gordon's shoulders twitched under her high-necked gown.

"Oh, Mother!" Davril patted her lips with her

handkerchief, hoping to hide her blush. "I declare you are as pleased to see Brett as I!"

"Indeed I am." Mrs. Gordon's smile was carefree. She sat back against the cushion in her cane chair and gazed around the flower garden.

They made such a perfect couple, she thought. Brett was handsome and strong and, according to her husband, who knew about such matters, was intelligent and capable. Mr. Gordon had said he expected Brett to be a leader of his people one day. And Davril, her sweet and only daughter, was so in love with him.

"Brett is such a gentleman, Davril," Mrs. Gordon murmured, letting her thoughts spill out in conversation. "Those Roseau dandies who want to court you are uncouth fortune-hunters with neither respect for your virtues nor manners for your vanity!"

Davril giggled, again seeking refuge behind her kerchief. "Are you saying Brett is here to court me?" She blushed. "I believe Daddy invited him to study the way he runs the plantation."

"I am here to learn, Davril," Brett stammered, feeling the sweat trickle down his back under his silk shirt and long jacket. He patted his thighs nervously with his hands. "Of course, were there not two charming ladies with whom to discourse, the learning could be a mite tedious."

Mrs. Gordon placed her glass on the small table between them and threw up her hands with a squeak of delight. "Did I not tell you, Davril!" she exclaimed. "Brett, my dear boy! My husband believes you to have a great future ahead of you. I am not one for politics, but I follow events. I have to, with Mr. Gordon being so close to the Governor."

Davril placed her hand over Brett's as it lay on his thigh. She squeezed. "Mother is about to give you her Patriot's Speech," she giggled.

"Davril, what I have to say is the truth, and you

348

know it as well as your father and I. If he puts his mind to it, Brett could be a legislator looking after the interests of his people far better than the ex-white patriates who seek to control the free natives."

"You mean white expatriates, Mother." Davril giggled.

"The way some of them behave with their wenching and maltreatment of their slaves, they have lost all right to be called white. They are worse than Satan himself!" Mrs. Gordon gestured at Brett.

"Davril is right, Brett. I do get carried away. It hurts me and my husband to see what some of our countrymen do to *your* countrymen in the name of justice. Tyranny and terror is more like it!"

"My countrymen, ma'am?" Brett bridled.

"Mother means people born here, Brett," soothed Davril, squeezing his hand again. "Not slaves, but free mulattoes and whites. Like you and I."

"Of course, dear. Why, Brett, since that law which your grandfather helped to get passed last year, do you know what has happened?"

Brett shook his head politely. The effect of Davril's fingers curling around his own was beginning to disturb him.

"Michael Boland, James Garraway, and even Lawrence Lionné, who only a few years ago was a slave stripped naked to his waist cutting cane—they have all been elected to the House of Assembly. Is it not wonderful!"

Brett inclined his head respectfully to show his agreement.

"How serious you always are, Brett!" Mrs. Gordon remarked. "Such a young man to wear such an earnest frown."

"It seems a serious achievement of which you are speaking."

"There! I knew you would be impressed. Davril,

you must make Brett relax while he is with us. Even a politician must enjoy the lighter side of life."

Brett allowed his lips to spread shyly in an apologetic grin. "I scarcely think I am cut out for politics, Mistress Gordon. Management of Roxborough Plantation consumes all my energies."

"Nonsense, Brett. You are still young, but you have the aura of leadership about you. My daughter has it, too," she added smugly.

"Mother, you are embarrassing us. I would like to take Brett for a walk before the sun sets. He has yet to see my new horse which Daddy gave me at Christmas."

"Of course, of course, my dears. Do not let me detain you. But remember my words, Brett. You are destined to do a lot for your country. You must have confidence in your ability."

"I have, ma'am!" Brett bowed. He raised his head and, to Mrs. Gordon's astonishment, smiled boldly into her eyes.

Mrs. Gordon leaned back in the cushions staring after Brett as he escorted Davril across the lawn, his arm correctly crooked for her to clutch precisely. In Mrs. Gordon's memories, a long-forgotten thrust of desire stirred at the sight. Brett's agile body and slender limbs recalled for her the time when, at Davril's age, she too had worshipped at the altar of youth. Brett was far more handsome and masculine than any young man she had ever met. Her husband, Warren, she mused sadly, was good to her. But where was the excitement which a man like Brett could surely bring to a woman?

The slave startled her. She gasped, clapping her hands together and clasping them in front of her bosom. She wondered how long he had been standing beside her. Had she spoken her thoughts aloud?

"What do you want, Isaiah?" Mrs. Gordon suddenly felt hot.

"Ah come to clear de table, ma'am, 'less yo' does need moh squash?"

"Yes, Isaiah. Pray proceed." Mrs. Gordon rose from her chair and stepped from the shadow of the huge tree. She unfurled her parasol above her bonnet to keep the sun from reddening her harsh white complexion. She cast a last, longing glance at Brett as he passed out of view behind the fan-like travelers palm at the edge of the lawn. She glided across the lawn in the opposite direction toward the cloisters of the house, not seeing the respectful bobbing of her slave as she passed.

Davril laughed. "My mother's jealous. She wants to mold you into patriotic works the same way she influences Daddy. She left England because of some scandal, you see. She can never return, so she has no country of her own, except here. She's always been fierce on loyalty to one's birthplace since then."

"Really?" Brett enjoyed Davril's chatter. It was so different from the narrow world of the house slaves at Roxborough. "Where are we going?"

"Oh, I don't know. Isn't it nice to be alone for a while?" Davril withdrew her arm from the formal grasp of Brett's elbow and caught up his hand in hers.

"Brett," she whispered. "I've been longing to see you."

"Me, too." Brett raised her hand to his mouth, kissing her fingers softly.

Davril drew her head back, entwining her arms around his waist as he stepped close to her. His lips hovered over hers, then caressed her long, elegantly white neck. She shivered.

"What's wrong?"

"Nothing, Brett, nothing. Don't stop."

He placed his hands firmly on her hips, waiting

while she lowered her head so that her eyes met his. Birds swooped and shrilled in the glade and a tiny stream gurgled over moss-covered stones beside the path.

"Why are you looking at me like that?" Davril twisted nervously in his grasp. Brett's bright eyes seared into hers, his expression changing from one of doubt to desire.

"I want you!" Brett held Davril's body tightly, pressing himself against her, crushing her mouth with his lips.

She hesitated, confused by the sensations sweeping over her. His hands at her waist made her feel weak, but protected. His burning eyes ravaged her mind, setting new emotions ablaze. His words both terrified and excited her. His lips demanding her kisses encouraged her own unfulfilled passion.

She opened her mouth to protest and placed her hands on his chest to ward him off. Instead, she found herself accepting his tongue eagerly as it probed her mouth. Her hands, wide open, clawed at his chest.

"I love you!" she breathed as he paused, those sensational eyes only inches away from hers.

"I know." He croaked in reply. His eyes looked beyond her head. "Where can we go?"

"Go?" Her thoughts were far away. It would take her days, she knew, to adjust to these new feelings which were assailing her. She felt liberated and trusting as though everything sha had done in her life was a pretence. Brett—her love for him—was the reality.

He kissed her again. Now she succumbed immediately, pushing her hands under his coat and rubbing her fingers frantically over the small of his back. She did not know what fury had possessed her. She was powerless to resist it.

Brett's voice was urgent, hissing in her ear. "Where? Where?"

She opened her eyes. His rugged, tense face was nose to nose with hers. She saw for the first time how the yellow irises of his eyes were flecked with brown. The locks of his hair curled over his ears, giving him the beauty of a poet. His thin lips, flushed by his kissing, twitched with yearning.

"I . . . I . . ." she stammered.

"Where!" His voice was strained. "Where can we go?"

Davril wriggled in his hands, pulling her face back from his. Her eyes flared with reproach. "No!"

"Huh?" Brett stared at Davril in confusion.

"No!" Davril licked her lips nervously, not wanting to offend him. "Not like this, Brett," she muttered lamely.

Brett glowered, letting his hands slip away from her hips.

Davril shuddered. She hung her head down, her hair tumbling around her shoulders. Her hands rested on the waistband of his trousers under his coat. Her slim body began to shake with remorse.

"I'm sorry, Brett. I'm scared. I love you, I love you, I do! But, but . . ."

Brett slapped his brow with the palm of his hand. He scowled briefly. "Forget it. I understand. It's because I'm not really white, isn't it?"

"Oh, no!" Brett's words were like a knife gouging out her heart.

"No!" she shrieked. Her hands fell away from his waist. She trembled as she stood opposite him, her lips quivering with horror. "That's not true, Brett. I love *you!*"

Brett shrugged his shoulders, using an air of indifference to hide his true feeling for Davril.

"Don't you understand, Brett? Because I love you, I want to share love with you properly." She gestured at the forest. "Not here, not in some secret hideaway where the slaves go to rut when they should be working. We are not slaves, Brett, we are human beings!"

Brett raised his eyebrows. Davril's face was flushed underneath her soft, blue eyes. Brett bit his lip as he realized how foolish he had been.

"To share love properly?" he breathed, his voice cracking. "That means to marry."

"Yes! Yes!" Tears pricked Davril's eyes. She reached out for Brett's chest as she fell forward.

He caught her in his hands, enveloping her with his arms and clutching her close to him. She laid her cheek against his chest, not caring if he saw her sob. He patted her shoulder tenderly.

"Davril?" Brett's voice was husky. "You would marry *me?*"

"Of course, Brett, of course!" She thrust her head back with relief as Brett's lips descended to meet hers. This time, their kiss was gentle, a tenderness binding them both in their perfect pledge.

The sun had set, long golden shadows shafting through the darkening sky behind the clouds hovering on the horizon. Brett pulled himself out of Davril's embrace. His seriousness had dissolved into an expression of bemused contentment.

Davril laughed. "Mother will know!"

"Hah?" Brett grinned.

"You look like a young man in love instead of a stern schoolmaster!"

"Schoolmaster, Davril? I can't even read! Are you going to tell them?"

"That you can't read?"

"About us."

"Of course. They are prepared already. I doubt if Daddy would let you leave here if you hadn't proposed!"

Brett grinned ruefully. "I wish Mas Carlton was like

your father, Davril. He is going to have his own views about this!"

"He can't stop us from marrying."

"Can't he? You don't know the Bondmaster, Davril. Oh yes, he'll let me marry you, all right. But not yet. There is something he wants me to do for him first." Brett stared solemnly at the sunset as they began to walk back to the house.

"What's that?"

"I can't tell you." Brett shrugged his shoulders wearily.

"If we are to be married, we should not have secrets, Brett."

"I don't *want* to have secrets from you, Davril." Brett lapsed into an uncomfortable silence.

"Does it have anything to do with you becoming the Bondmaster one day?" Davril snuggled closer to him as they walked.

"In a way," sighed Brett. "It's a plantation matter."

"Oh, that! Why didn't you say so. I know Daddy never discusses some things with my mother. I'm not blind, Brett. There are some slaves here, younger than me, who are lighter than the others. I'm sure one has Daddy's nose. Daddy never talks about it. I don't expect you to, Brett, if ever you have to do something like that."

Brett shook his head sadly. "What a wonderful girl you are, Davril!" He pecked her on the cheek as Mr. Gordon, sitting on his high-backed chair under the cloisters of the house, watched curiously.

"I love you, Davril, I love you!"

"Come on, then, let's run and tell Daddy we want to get married!" Davril caught Brett by his wrist and broke into a run, laughing gaily. Brett shouted with glee.

Mr. and Mrs. Gordon glanced at each other and smiled happily.

Chapter 38

"Don't walk so fast, boy!" Ward snapped angrily. "I ain't a young mountain goat like ye. This pesky leg of mine is bound to slow me up a bit." He panted as he stumbled after Lambert, following the boy up the rocky track which threaded through the forest by the side of the Layou River.

Dale, padding stealthily behind Ward, waited patiently for the old man to recover his footing.

"Can't see not a dratted thing in this moonlight!" Ward moaned. "Ye should have brought the *flambeau*, boy."

"Mingoson gon' see dat, sah!" Lambert paused on the track. "De glow gon' scare him long befoh we does be near him."

"S'pose ye are right, boy." Ward knocked Dale's hand away as the slave tried to steady him. "I'm all right, boy. Just don't want to move so fast." His chest heaved as he peered ahead.

Ward estimated that they had been walking for close to an hour. Lambert seemed to know the trail, hacking with his cutlass at the branches and creepers which impeded their progress. The trail was rising steadily up the valley floor. Although the moon was at its brightest and the night was cloudless, the dense foliage made it difficult for Ward to see ahead.

"Much further, boy?" Ward was beginning to have misgivings about the exploit. He scratched his scalp.

He could not turn back now or he would lose the respect of all the slaves.

"Not far, sah." Lambert spoke in an exaggerated whisper. "Yo' ain't s'posed to speak now, sah, uh he gon' hear yo!"

"Right," growled Ward gruffly. "Now ye know what to do when we see him?"

The two boys grunted.

"Ye just lie quietly while I shoot the bugger," chuckled Ward. "Then we'll fish his body out of the river. Ye'll chop off his head with the cutlass, Lambert, and we'll take the nigger's noddle to the Bondmaster."

Ward champed his teeth with relish. "Shouldn't wonder if Mas Carlton gave both boys yer freedom for this." He smacked his lips together. "Those maroons got to learn their lesson, dammit!"

Lambert touched Dale quietly in the dark. Ward did not notice. He had been making plans for this hunt since Tency had brought Lambert to him. The boy claimed to know where Mingoson would be on the night of the full moon. He said that it was his custom to sacrifice a parrot at the time. He was always alone, Lambert assured him, because this was obeah.

Lambert seemed appropriately awed and frightened by what Ward had proposed, which convinced the bookkeeper that the buck's information was genuine. "If he ain't there," Ward had warned Lambert, "I'm going to cut out yer tongue for lying."

Ward had told no one of his expedition. Brett was due to return to the plantation the next day. Ward wanted to present Mingoson's head to Brett and Carlton as they sat down to breakfast together. He pictured the expression on their smug faces! Soon they would be thanking him for ridding Roxborough of the maroon menace. Mas Carlton might even give him a pension.

Ward wheezed happily to himself, feeling his way forward behind Lambert.

"Shhh!" Lambert stopped so suddenly, Ward bumped into him.

"We does be close," Lambert whispered.

Ward could feel the tightening of his throat and the drying of the saliva in his mouth. The hairs at the back of his neck prickled. Lambert had led him to a point where the trail was above the river. The slave was edging forward in a crawl, parting the bush in front of him cautiously.

Ward waited, rooted to the spot with anticipation. He pulled out one of the pistols he carried in his belt.

Ahead, Lambert paused. "Mas Ward," he hissed. He waved in the vague shadow for Ward to join him. Ward crouched down and edged himself through the undergrowth, holding saplings back with his outstretched pistol. He peered over Lambert's shoulder.

"He does be down dere, massa!" Lambert spread the foliage apart with his hands. Dale crept up behind Ward.

Ward gulped with excitement. Through the leaves he glimpsed the river spuming in the pallid light from the moon. Foam coursed down the river, great gaps torn in its white wake by the rocks and boulders hulking out of the channel bed. Ward peered carefully, his hand going clammy around the stock of his pistol.

He caught Lambert by the scruff of his neck, bringing the boy's dull brown face close to his so he could see the shining whites of his eyes. Lambert seemed nervous. "Well!" hissed Ward softly. "Where is the bastard?"

Lambert's eyes narrowed. "He dere, sah. On de stone." He glanced toward Dale as Ward released him. Both boys knew what they were supposed to do.

Ward squinted into the dark patches of the river.

358

The regular outline of the largest boulder seemed to have a heavier shadow surmounting it. He stared again. The shape seemed to move, although Ward realized it could have been distortion caused by the rushing of the river around it. He watched, fascinated.

"Yes," he breathed, "I see him."

"What yo' gon' do, massa?" Lambert sounded worried.

"Shut up, boy!" Ward rasped, keeping his voice lowered. He doubted if Mingoson would hear above the gurgling of the river. He wished the moonlight was brighter. The tall bamboo and the other trees overhanging the river obscured the grayness of the night. Ward pulled out his other pistol. His fingers fumbling, he managed to prime both of them before gazing out again.

He judged the distance from his vantage point to the boulder in the center of the river. He was a tolerably good shot. The shadowy shape was becoming clearer to him as his eyes became accustomed to the pale light.

He calculated his first blast would blow a hole in Mingoson's side and would topple him into the river. Although the river raced riotously at the base of the boulders, he doubted if it was deep. Mingoson's body would wedge against the rocks. Lambert and Dale could hook it easily.

Ward's lip curled as he raised his hand to shoulder level. His eye looked along the length of his arm and down the shaft of the pistol. He dropped his arm and shifted himself into a more comfortable position. He realized that his whole body was damp with perspiration. Lambert was at his side, his teeth bared in a nervous leer. Dale, Ward assumed, was at his back. A typical nigger, he thought. A coward!

Ward would show him what a white man could do! He raised his arm again. The shadow which was

359

Mingoson had not moved. Ward took careful aim and pulled the trigger.

There was an explosion as the pistol spat fire, filling the bush with a blinding flash. The acrid smell tainted the perfume of the night air.

"Aie!"

It was Ward who screamed. Lambert knocked his arm upwards with the blunt side of his cutlass. Simultaneously, Dale smote at Ward's head with a stick. The ball from the pistol shot harmlessly in the air.

Ward fell forward, sprawling headlong in the tangle of bushes he had been using for cover. He twisted rapidly as Dale lunged for him again with the stick.

"Get de oder pistol!" Dale squawked nervously, beating at Ward's head.

Ward raised his arm to protect himself, at the same time trying to hold up the pistol in his other hand. Lambert hovered uncertainly.

"Cut he befoh he does discharge de thing!"

"No, man!" Lambert panicked. "He does be white!"

As though realizing the enormity of what he was doing, Dale suddenly stopped flailing Ward. He turned on Lambert. "Dat de reason we does mash him down, boy!"

"Ye nigger bastards!" bellowed Ward, scrambling to his feet with the pistol pointed at the two slaves. "Get back!"

Dale and Lambert stared at Ward. "He ain't dead!" Lambert said accusingly. "Yo' ain't finish beatin' him!"

"Yo' de one. Yo' ain't take he firearm!" Dale shuffled backwards, tugging Lambert's hand. "He gon' kill us fuh sure," he muttered in patois. " 'Less we run."

"Shut up!" Ward crouched low, eyeing the slaves as they crept away from him. He quickly transferred the pistol to his right hand, holding it out at arm's length.

360

"Drop that cutlass, and the stick!" he commanded.

"He can't shoot both of us!" Lambert observed dryly.

Dale snorted, throwing down the stick. "Yo' does want see who he gon' chose?"

Lambert let his beloved cutlass fall at his feet.

Too late, Ward remembered Mingoson. He never even heard him approach through the undergrowth. As he watched Lambert's cutlass clatter on the stony ground, he felt his head being jerked back and a huge arm snaking around his throat. Another arm clamped across his chest.

"*Aie!*" Ward gasped at the pressure on his larynx. The night turned red in his eyes. He choked.

Lambert grinned with relief, picking up his cutlass. Dale nodded his head. "Ah done know dat Mingoson gon' come."

Ward's legs were weakening under him. He was losing consciousness. He fell limp in Mingoson's embrace, slipping to the ground as the maroon released him.

Mingoson laughed. He contemplated Ward's pathetic body in a heap at his feet and, placing his foot firmly on Ward's chest, turned on the two boys.

"Yo' does need plenty trainin' to make yo' bush niggers. Yo' was gon' let dat *beké* better yo'!"

"De firearm!" Lambert moved over and picked up Ward's pistol where it lay on the trail beside his body. "What yo' gon' do to him, Mingoson?"

For answer, Mingoson crouched down and studied Ward. He was beginning to revive, his chest heaving as he caught his breath. Mingoson put his hand under Ward's chin and raised his face off the ground until it was level with his own. Mingoson grinned mockingly into Ward's terrified eyes.

"What's your name, Mr. White Man?"

"Ye speak English!" Ward panted, wondering if he

could talk himself out of this intolerable situation. "Are ye Mingoson?"

"Yuh name, white arse!" Mingoson tapped Ward under his chin so his head jerked backwards.

"Ward Scrivener. Let me go, and there will be a big reward for ye."

"Whose money?" Mingoson sneered. "Yours?"

"I'll get it!"

"What's your job, Mr. Scrivener?" Mingoson gloated.

"I'm bookkeeper for the Bondmaster."

"Are you now?" Mingoson sat back on his haunches. Ward stared at him. Mingoson was completely naked with his hair protruding in exaggerated tufts all over his head. He looked like a savage, but he spoke English better than Ward himself. He carried no weapon.

"And what is a bookkeeper doing in the forest on such a moonlit night? Having a little sport shooting niggers, eh?"

Ward frowned. "What are ye going to do to me?"

"Lambert, Dale. Take yuh stick. See, place it 'cross him like dis." Mingoson pushed Ward in his chest so he fell back on the ground. He laid the stick across his throat and beckoned Lambert to hold one end and Dale the other.

"Don't trouble yuhself if yuh does hurt he," Mingoson chuckled. "Ain't no bookkeeper ever given no second thought for a slave's feelin's."

Mingoson placed his legs on either side of Ward's head, crouching down so he was straddling his face. His penis flopped into Ward's eye.

"All mah life, Lambert," leered Mingoson, "ah does be lickin' de backside of de white man. Dat de way slaves does live. Dis white man got to lick mines now."

Mingoson lowered his buttocks onto Ward's face.

Ward tried to twist away, but the stick pressing down on his throat made him powerless to move. His nose was stuck directly under Mingoson's anus. He retched.

The stench which filled his nostrils forced Ward to open his mouth. He struggled to breathe. Suddenly, a gush of excrement smothered him. It oozed between his lips and filled his mouth. He fainted.

"See how he brown like me?" Mingoson gurgled. "Swoons like a white man, though."

Mingoson beckoned Lambert and Dale. He took up Lambert's cutlass and hacked at the bushes at the top of the bank. He cleared a gap and gazed down at the river about ten feet below.

"Best yo' wash dat shit off he face!" He motioned to the two boys, who rolled Ward, subdued by pain and shock, to the edge of the bank. Lambert raised his eyes to Mingoson.

Mingoson nodded, putting his toe to Ward's backside and toppling him over the edge.

Ward's body smashed onto the boulders below, cracking open his head and spewing brains and blood into the water. The river churned and the moonlight shimmered as the white spume turned to crimson.

Chapter 39

Brett was at peace with himself. He rode his horse slowly along the clifftop trail from Batalie. He marveled at the fragrant beauty of his surroundings. To his right, there was the sheer drop to the sea. Above, the sun arched in a sky which blended with the blue brightness of the ocean. In the vividness of the morning, Brett could see Les Saintes, the tiny French islands which lay between Dominica and Guadeloupe.

On his left were the cane fields of the Macoucherie Estate, a small plantation of some 800 acres worked by an attorney on behalf of its absentee owner. The cane, Brett noticed idly, was thriving, although the upkeep of the trail as it passed through the plantation appeared to have been neglected.

Brett shrugged his shoulders. It was no concern of his. He smiled to himself as he thought of the orderly tidiness of the paths and cobbled roads through the Batalie Estate. Mr. Gordon had proved that slaves, given a benevolent and understanding master, could accomplish the impossible. During his brief stay at Batalie Brett had realized that even he himself was capable of achieving what he would previously have considered unlikely.

Brett smiled again. If Mr. Gordon had taught him a lot about slave management, Davril had taught him more about himself. Brett's very spirit seemed to have been changed by her presence close to him. Before he went to Batalie, Brett believed he loved Davril. He lusted for her with a desire he was too cowardly to reveal. Now that Davril knew his feelings, he knew he did love her. It was not a yearning for her body; it was a sharing. He had achieved with her such a sweet and free understanding, a certain oneness of being, that he was sure this love soared above anything anyone had known before.

He sighed. He went to Batalie wanting Davril, determined to have her. She would expunge the demands of Laura from his heart. Yet although his evenings with Davril had gone no further than the clasping of hands in the moonlight and the swirling of tongues in lingering kisses, he was as drained of lust as an overmounted breeding buck. He was content.

In his euphoric mood, Brett almost did not hear the whimpering, but the acute sense of self-preservation typical of free men in a slave society alerted him. The slight noise was coming from the thicket ahead of him. He reined in his horse quietly, his ears straining to identify the sound. The cawing and whistling of the birds scheming for insects confused him. He listened again. Swiftly, he dismounted from his horse and, crouching low, crept stealthily toward the coppice.

The whimpering was that of an animal, an injured dog perhaps. At the entrance to the coppice Brett sank down onto his haunches like a Negro. He sniffed the air. He sniffed again, his eyes widening. He was sure it was a man's scent drifting to him. He scraped in the gully beside the trail for a stone and lofted it into the coppice. The whining ceased as the stone crashed through the branches of the trees and fell to the ground.

There was silence.

Brett frowned. He had expected to hear the sounds of an animal scurrying to safety through the undergrowth. There was no movement, only the irregular sighing of the wind in the trees, like a man breathing.

Brett tensed, his hackles prickling with concern.

There was a long, low moan of despair from within the coppice. Brett rose to his feet and strode in the direction of the sound. A Negro was stretched out on the ground, half covered by gauva bushes. He looked up at Brett with wide eyes frozen in terror.

Brett stopped, waiting for the Negro to rise and run. The man did not move. Brett glanced at the Negro's feet. His ankle was trapped in the jaws of a snare, blood suppurating from the wound caused by the cruelly sharpened teeth locked into his flesh. Sadly, Brett stroked the scar at his own throat.

"Where you from, boy?"

The Negro's eyes clouded over. "Massa, please, massa!" he whined.

"I ain't going to hurt you, boy." Brett crouched by the Negro's head. The youth was naked apart from his torn breech cloth. His black skin was dusty, caked with sweat. On his shoulder, Brett discerned the scar of a brand mark. He touched the Negro, wiping his shoulder clean with his hand. The letters LAT had been welted into the youth's flesh.

"Ah hah!" pronounced Brett, peering at the boy's face. "So you are a Latham slave, are you? Running away, boy?"

Augustus Latham was the owner of the Macoucherie plantation which stretched up the hillside behind the coppice. He lived in England, leaving the management of the plantation to Jones Fadelle, his attorney and manager.

"Fadelle mistreating you, boy?"

At the mention of the attorney's name, the youth shuddered.

"Some men just don't know the value of a fine nigger!" muttered Brett with disdain. The youth looked strong and capable to him. "You can speak, boy. Why are you running?"

The Negro gaped at Brett, puzzled by the compassionate tone in his voice. He winced at the pain in his ankle as he tried to raise himself to a sitting position guided by Brett's hands.

"Ah done tell de massa ah does be sick, sah," the slave yammered. "He done say de lash gon' physic me. Ah does be scare' he gon' lash me to die, sah."

While he was speaking, Brett studied the youth. His back and buttocks were tender with the stripes of a recent beating. The ankle, seized by the snare, was swelling, aggravated by the boy's futile attempts to prize himself free.

"You ain't going to get nowhere if you struggle like that, boy. I'll see what I can do." Brett stood up, looking around the thicket. He spied a sapling he thought might help. With his cutlass, he swiftly felled it and pared it down to a stake.

"What's your name, boy?" he said.

"Ah does be Tarry, sah." The youth winced as Brett inserted the stake into the mechanism of the trap. "Yo' gon' take me back to Mas Fadelle, sah?"

Brett levered the stake until he found the key to the spring holding the snare. He jammed it sharply. The boy screamed. The jaws eased open.

Removing his stock from his neck, Brett bound it tightly around the gashes in Tarry's ankle. He began to massage Tarry's leg. Tarry whinnied shrilly.

"You want to bring Fadelle here himself?" Brett scolded the youth into silence as he pummeled life back into the slave's leg.

Tarry stared aghast at Brett.

"Now, come on, young Terry. Let's see if you can walk." Brett hauled the boy up by his armpits, forcing him to stand. "Put your arm around my shoulder, boy. Try to walk. Don't stand on that leg yet. It's going to be painful."

Slowly, Brett guided the boy out of the coppice. He glanced quickly along the path. Seeing it was clear, he whistled for his horse, which trotted obediently toward him. "You can ride a horse, boy?"

"Yassa." Tarry was confused. "Yo' ain't takin' me back to de plantation, sah?"

"What for, boy?" Brett grinned. "A man who can't treat his slaves properly don't deserve to have them, Tarry. Some day soon, slaves are going to be free, boy, you know that? The law going to make them free."

"Ah does want to be free, sah!" Tarry grinned broadly.

367

"Where do you think you can be free, boy? It's your master must give you that freedom."

"Ah was be gon' to Mero, sah. Ah done think ah gon' stow'way on board a ship."

"Hah. You would soon get caught. Mero is too close to Macoucherie. Come, boy, mount my horse." Brett helped Tarry to scramble up into the saddle.

"Ride to Layou, boy. Fadelle ain't going to find you there. Leave my horse for me by the wharf."

Tarry looked down at Brett. "Yo' does give me yuh horse, sah?" he asked in amazement.

"How else are you going to travel with your ankle chewed up like that?"

"Yo', sah?"

"Hah! A nigger worried about me? I can walk, boy!" Brett thumped the horse's rump. "Go on, ride, boy, before Fadelle comes chasing you!"

Brett scratched the side of his head as the horse cantered away with Tarry clinging to the saddle to steady himself. Brett sighed, a smile spreading across his features. Davril would be pleased with what he had done.

Dusk was overwhelming the brightness of the day as Brett reached Roxborough. He had walked happily through the village of Mero, over the cliffs to St. Joseph, and then along the coast path to Layou. In Layou, tied to an iron ring in the wall of the warehouse, was his horse, his saddlebags intact. He made no inquiries for Tarry, knowing that the boy would find free Negroes in the village who would harbor him until the furore over his escape had died down.

Brett was elated as he galloped homewards. Rounding the last bend in the trail Brett stared in amazement. Slaves were drifting up the hill to join a crowd of Negroes clamoring in the courtyard in front of the house. Brett spurred his horse into a gallop, riding

368

through the groups of lowing slaves. Mas Carlton, he saw, was pacing the balcony.

Caliste took the reins of Brett's horse as soon as he rode up. Brett dismounted at the foot of the grand steps. Glancing at the herd of slaves gathered in the yard, he ran quickly onto the balcony.

"What's wrong?" he shouted.

"Good afternoon, Brett! Did you have an enjoyable time?" Carlton seemed unperturbed.

"Good afternoon sir. Yes! I did! Why are the slaves here, sir?"

"The niggers?" Carlton glanced at the courtyard as though seeing the Negroes for the first time. "Oh, yes. They've come to witness a little diversion." Carlton held his pipe to his mouth.

"The bookkeeper, Brett. He met with an accident. Drowned, poor fellow." Carlton puffed smoke nonchalantly. "Won't you have a glass of sangaree?"

Pip sidled up behind Carlton and placed the decanter on the table. Brett was agitated. He shook his head. He no longer felt the weariness of his journey. He waited impatiently while Carlton poured himself a glass of the red liquid and casually cast his eye over the assembled slaves.

"It seems, Brett, that Lambert and Dale had something to do with the fellow's death. Laura had cause to check the barracoon last night." Carlton frowned meaningfully at Brett. "Lambert and Dale were not there. They had gone into the heights with the bookkeeper. Most unusual, don't you think?"

Brett sat down, fingering his scar. "What do they say?"

"Oh, very little. They have admitted the expedition. They claim the fellow just fell into the river. Of course, we have not found his body yet, but he is certainly missing. Curious, don't you think?"

"I'd like to speak to them myself."

"You shall, or perhaps to one of them. As I say, I've arranged a little diversion. I know they killed him. It is rather tiresome summoning the magistrate and going through the wretched process of the law just to lynch them. I've checked the ledger. Both have sired two whelps, so they have left me a small legacy."

Carlton sipped his drink smiling mockingly. "I can afford to dispense with them. I have devised the perfect solution. It removes all onus from me, saves the government the expense of conducting an inquiry, and gives us and the slaves an exciting evening. The slaves may also be prompted to dwell on the consequences of such foolish conduct!"

Carlton sucked on his pipe, which had burnt itself out. "See, Constance is bringing them now."

The blacksmith pushed Lambert and Dale in front of him as he walked. Both youths were naked. Their skin glistened where Ella had coated them with snake oil. Constance towered over them, shoving them forward as they hung back reluctantly. Tency and Asaph whipped the slaves back to form a circle around the two boys.

"I say, Brett. Do go for Laura for me. She will enjoy this little performance." Carlton guffawed, his harsh laughter bursting over the slaves. They fell silent. Tency's whip cracked.

Carlton walked to the balcony rail and gazed down. The slaves fidgeted. The men were wearing the osnaburg smocks they wore in the fields. Some of the women had brightly colored kerchiefs wrapped around their heads. The others were uniformly drab in their appearance. All were covered with dust and grime after working hard in the fields for the day. Carlton knew they were hungry. They were also tired.

"Slaves of Roxborough," Carlton began, letting his eyes wander over them all. "You are proud members of the Bondmaster breed of niggers, the finest slaves

370

who ever worked on a plantation. These two youngsters here, Lambert and Dale, are fine niggers, too." Carlton paused, feeling the slaves' eyes rise reluctantly to watch him.

"I don't like to punish my slaves. But sometimes correction is needed. These two young bucks left the barracoon last night without my permission. The bookkeeper went with them. They say he drowned. I say they killed him."

The slaves nudged one another, consternation spreading through the crowd. Tency's whip swiftly snapped them into silence.

"But I may be wrong," Carlton crooned melodiously. "Am I not a just man? Do I not treat you fairly?" He glared at the slaves, but no voice answered him.

"Oh, yes! When you are sold to work on other plantations, you will look back on your days at Roxborough with fondness!" Carlton paused as Laura stepped onto the balcony followed by Brett. She looked about her haughtily. There was a murmur of interest from the slaves.

"I could not punish Lambert or Dale without an accuser, could I? What I believe may not be what happened. I should give Lambert and Dale an opportunity to redeem themselves, said I."

The slaves broke into puzzled chatter. Tency's whip thrashed the air over their heads.

"I will give them the power to decide the issue themselves. These two stout fellows will engage in combat. They will fight each other." Carlton leered at Laura. "To the death!"

A gasp went up from the crowd. The youths and men were intrigued. Some of the women wept, but when they realized that no harm was going to befall them, they joined in the clamor for a better view. Boys scrambled for places in the branches of the flamboyant trees, while others balanced on barrels and boulders.

Brett looked at Carlton with admiration. There was no doubting the Bondmaster's guile. Prize-fighting was legal even if the killing of a slave without a trial was not.

"What a super jape," said Laura, signaling Pip to pull a chair to the balcony rail for her.

Carlton raised his eyebrow. "You are not perturbed?"

"Why should I be? These niggers are nothing to me."

"You have no favorite?" Carlton sneered.

"Oh, well," Laura replied archly. "If you are looking for someone with whom to wager, I chose the black ace to win."

"And I the red!" Carlton slapped his thigh gleefully. "I haven't had such fun since I was a young man! How much, Laura?"

Laura studied Dale. He was stockier than Lambert, more wily. "A hundred pounds!" Laura recalled how brutish he had been in bed.

"Agreed! Brett, do you wish to join us?"

Brett shook his head. A wry smile played on his lips. "Does the winner get his freedom?"

Carlton choked. He thrust his pipe into the pocket of his jacket, signaling quickly for the fight to begin.

Constance, who held both boys by their neck scruffs, banged their heads together and stood aside. The boys stared at each other, reluctant to begin. Constance snatched the whip from Tency's hand and lashed Lambert's shoulders. He flayed again and caught Dale's backside.

"Fight, damn you, fight!" bellowed Carlton.

The two boys began to circle, eyeing each other guardedly. The whip sliced into Lambert's side. He lunged for Dale, seizing him around his waist. Dale clamped his hands over Lambert's head.

"Dey fight like *macos*," shrieked a slave woman. "Tear he guts out, Dale."

"Beat out his brain, Lambi!"

Goaded by the lash from Constance's whip and the taunts from the crowd, they began to grapple in earnest. It was Lambert who realized first that to live, he must kill Dale. He drove at him with a desperate fury, forcing Dale down to the ground, pounding his head viciously on the flagstones.

Dale swung his legs up and locked them around Lambert's neck; Lambert tumbled backwards. Now it was Dale atop the prone Lambert, pounding his fist relentlessly into his tender belly. Enraged, Lambert kicked Dale's head, cracking his nose with his knee. The crowd roared, jostling and punching each other as first Lambert, then Dale got the better of the bout.

"They are evenly matched, Mas Carlton." Brett gripped the rail trying to suppress his own excitement.

"With death the prize, boy, one of those bucks is going to get the edge. Dam'me if Laura ain't backed the favorite!"

The crowd cheered Dale as he jumped onto Lambert's chest. He snatched up his arm and twisted it, jamming the elbow sharply down onto the flagstones. Constance honked, thrashing the boys with his whip in his excitement.

Leaping off Lambert as he made a grab for his throat, Dale paused, panting for breath. He jumped feet first for Lambert's crotch, but Lambert twisted away. Dale landed awkwardly on the hard flagstone and stumbled. Lambert, his left arm useless at his side, jumped on Dale's back, clawing at his throat. Dale gasped and rolled over.

As he squeezed his throat between his thumb and forefinger, Lambert pounded his knee into Dale's backside. Dale struggled to escape but could not shake off Lambert. Suddenly, he felt Lambert's penis pressing against the small of his back. He twisted.

Dale gurgled as Lambert's hand tightened its hold on his neck. He felt his lungs bursting, and his eyes began to close. The crowd screamed. Lambert shifted his position to get a better hold on Dale's throat, throttling him in desperation.

"Ah does be sorry, boy!" he panted, gritting his teeth and squeezing.

"Aie!" Lambert's sudden shriek of agony struck through the roar of the crowd.

Dale had got his hand around Lambert's testicles. He jerked, the sudden pain causing Lambert to cry out and relax his hold on Dale's throat.

Dale twisted his body again, slipping out of Lambert's grasp. He hung on to Lambert's scrotum as though trying to tear it off. Lambert curled up his knees to protect himself. Dale lowered his head and snapped with his jaws. He caught Lambert's penis in his lips and sucked it into his mouth. He bit.

Lambert shrieked again. The crowd pushed forward. Dale stood up. He opened his mouth and spat out the tip of Lambert's penis.

"Oh, dear!" drawled Carlton. "That one ain't going to be much use."

Constance turned on the crowd, who were pushing forward. He spun his whip around his head and they fell back. Dale leered at Lambert who was writhing in agony on the ground. He leaped into the air and crashed down onto Lambert's throat with his knees, shattering his larynx. Lambert choked. Blood trickled out of his mouth. He writhed, arched his back, then collapsed lifeless. Dale fell across his body in exhaustion.

"One hundred pounds, if you please, Father," Laura smirked.

Chapter 40

"Yuh does believe me, now, Mingoson?" Tita cackled, a stain of spittle from the black shag she was chewing trickling down her cheek. Her scrawny jowls quivered proudly at her infallibility. "Ah done tell yo' ah gon' show yuh de way de slaves gon' come join de maroons."

Mingoson sneered at her across the earth floor of the darkened shack. "Ain't no moh dan two we does get. De one from Macoucherie ain't yuh doin', no way!"

"Ah hear yo'! But yo' has Dale, not so?" Tita bunched up her scraggy shoulders as she crouched on her bed board opposite Mingoson. "Ah done tell yo' if yo' does get Mas Carlton vexed wid his slaves, dey gon' come to yo' soon."

"Dale done come cuz he done kill Lambert. He does hate Mas Carlton fuh dat."

"Heh, heh!" Tita gloated. "An' ain't he a pretty boy!"

Mingoson ignored Tita's taunt. It had been her scheme that Mingoson should rile Mas Carlton into punishing his slaves. When he had been caught with Laura, Mingoson expected that Mas Carlton would start harassing his slaves to see if they were concealing any contacts with the maroons. That would have unsettled them and Mingoson would have been able to get the youths to join him in the hills.

He had no idea why Carlton had done nothing and only the stupid old bookkeeper had come after him. The result had been the recruitment of Dale, but at the cost of losing Lambert. According to Dale, the slaves were more content than they had ever been. Young Brett was the fairest overseer. He even spoke of the day when liberation would come and how the slaves should prepare their provision grounds and learn to fend for themselves.

"The only liberation we gon' see," thundered Mingoson, "is what we take fuh ourself. Wid de cutlash!"

He was addressing the circle of maroons gathered around him outside Tita's *ajoupa*. Tita had crawled to her doorway and sat surveying them all with a fierce glare. The maroons had done their tasks in the gardens for the day, dinner had been eaten, and now they listened respectfully to Dale's account of life at Roxborough. To some of them, it sounded easier than the lot they had to bear as runaways.

"Who does say dis liberation be comin'?" Tula, a runaway from an east coast plantation, demanded.

"All de buckras does talk of it." Dale spoke eagerly. "De house slaves does tell us what de buckras does be sayin'. Brett heself does say emancipation gon' come."

"Is true!" Tarry knelt on one knee, leaning his arm on the other. His injured ankle rested under him. A herb poultice was drawing out the pus and healing the wound. "Dat's why Massa Fadelle does be lashing all he slaves. He say de talk of freedom make us mischievous. He say we ain't never gon' get no 'mancipation."

"Yo' hear dat!" Mingoson leaped to his feet, gesticulating. "We brothers on de plantations gon' die in chains."

"Ain't no one in chains at Roxbruh!" Dale snorted with derision. "De Bon'massa don't have no one in

376

chains. De Bon'massa breed ain't foolish like yo' niggers at Macoucherie!"

"We ain't in chains, neither!" shouted Tarry.

"But yo' does get beaten!" crowed Dale. "De Bon'massa breed de bes' slave dere does be. Ain't no need to beat a Bon'massa nigger!"

"Yo' does talk *sot*, Dale. That's stupid talk." Mingoson's eyes raved with fury. "We does be Negroes, Dale, not slaves. Ain't one slave better than another as long as dey does be slaves. Yo' does be a Negro, Dale, not a Bon'massa breed of slave."

"Ah does be born de Bon'massa's, Mingoson. If ah ain't be own, den who ah does be?"

"Yo' does be yuh own free self, Dale. When de slaves at Ruxbruh decide to rise up, dey gon' take deir liberation. Each one gon' be a free Negro."

Dale sniffed, unimpressed. "Maybe we does be free den, but we still de Bon'massa breed!"

"Yo' think de Roxbruh slaves gon' come join us?" asked Tula.

"Not 'less we make dem come!" Mingoson jumped wildly. "When we show dem dat freedom only gon' come if dey does take it deyselves, dey gon' join us here."

Tita screeched loudly like an angry parrot. The maroons swiveled their eyes to watch her reverently.

"Is de Bon'massa dat is de one!" she croaked. "Kill Mas Carlton, den de slaves does be free!"

With Lambert dead and Dale fled, Laura was in a quandary. There had been a minor outcry when it was discovered that Dale had run away. Carlton's pride was hurt, thought Laura, because one of his special breed had skipped, but he refrained from hunting him. Carlton was anxious not to antagonize the slaves in the face of the growing movement for emancipation. Brett, too, thought nothing should be done.

Laura had agreed, but now she found herself without a buck. A maid, who reported on her every move to Ella, slept in her dressing room at night. Brett, with his doleful eyes, watched her whenever she went riding on the plantation. Carlton himself drank steadily every night, offering not even the consolation of conversation.

Laura did not know what to do. She had written to Fletcher in Jamaica as Brett suggested. She began to yearn for his arrival. She was feeling so damned frustrated at being cooped up in the house with neither man nor matter to brighten her life!

When Pip brought her cocoa tea to her room that night, she contemplated him greedily. Once, he must have looked fine, but now his belly flopped over his waistband and he slouched. His breath always whiffed of rum, and at that hour of night he had the glazed look of tipsiness in his eyes.

"Pip, where's Brett?" she demanded, placing her untouched sampler on the couch beside her.

Pip placed the tea on the table beside her bed. He swayed slightly. "On de balcony, Miss Laura. He does be wid Mas Carlton."

"Good! Tell him I want to see him before he goes to his cabin!"

"Yas, ma'am." Pip squeezed his eye shut in a lazy wink and rolled out of the room.

"Dam'me!" exploded Laura, hurling the sampler across the room.

"Yo' does call me, ma'am?" The little black girl installed by Ella poked her head around the door from the drawing room.

"No, wench!" cried Laura. "Get back to your pallet and stay there!"

Laura was near to tears. When Brett knocked on the door, she croaked for him to enter.

378

Brett closed the door quietly behind him, worried by her hunched shoulders.

"What's wrong, Laura?"

"How can you ever know!" she sobbed.

He strode across the room and placed his hand on her shoulder. She refused to look up.

"Laura," he said, "I do know." His voice was gentle.

Laura raised her head slowly, staring at him in astonishment. There was a smile of kindness on his face. "You aren't mocking me?"

"No. Why should I?"

"You understand?"

"Yes, Laura. Don't you think I feel the same way, too?"

"But you . . . you're a man."

"Does that make any difference? Do you think because I am a man I can go and seek relief for my frustrations where I want? Oh, yes, I'm the overseer, I can have any wench I want. But that does not help, Laura, believe me."

"It doesn't?" Laura looked at Brett as though she had not seen him before.

"That's just a brief gratification, Laura. Isn't that what you feel you are missing now?"

Laura breathed in angrily through her nostrils, then weakened as she caught sight of the compassion in Brett's normally hard eyes.

"Yes," she sniffed.

"I suppose that's why lonely white ladies like Negroes," Brett grinned. "They have a way of satisfying that urge, not so?"

Laura nodded her head dumbly.

"No need to be ashamed, Laura. I am the same. The wenches . . ." He opened his hands in front of him like a lawyer presenting a case. "But what's the purpose? Another whelp for the stock farm? There's more to my life than that. And yours." He sat down beside her.

"I want to marry Davril, Laura. I love her. I don't want to be a charlatan husband like Mas Carlton with so many outside children. I want to be hers alone, and she mine." He put his arm around Laura comforting her.

"And you. You love Fletcher, don't you? He'll come to you soon, won't he? Did you write to him?"

Laura nodded her head. "Oh yes," she sighed. She looked at Brett's face. It was soft and kind, a contrast to the brutal features she remembered from his previous visit to her boudoir. She raised her hand to touch his cheek, running her fingers down the side of his face and around his firm jaw.

He smiled at her ruefully.

"Do you want me to marry Davril, Laura?"

Laura withdrew her hand in surprise. "Of course. It's a lovely idea."

"You can help me."

Laura's eyes narrowed. "How?"

"Invite her here. To stay with you. She'll be company for you. You can go on walks together, spend your evenings talking."

"You want me to lure her here for you when you have driven all my black bucks away!" Laura snorted.

"Do you still have that in mind, Laura?" Brett looked dejected.

"Why are you so sad?" Laura chuckled.

"You don't know?" Brett shook his head. "Mas Carlton. He wants me to squire you. I like you, Laura, of course, but not that way. He won't let me marry Davril until he thinks I have changed your ways. He does not want you to have a Negro's child."

"Oh, my goodness!" Laura let out a bellow of laughter. "Are you serious? I'm thirty-two years old,

380

Brett. I'm an old maid. I'm not going to have a baby by anyone, black or white!"

Brett's face brightened. "Is that true?"

"Of course! A doctor in Jamaica told me my child-bearing days are done."

"Then I am not bound to squire you at all!" Brett laughed with relief. "I'm free to marry Davril." He paused. "Laura," he smiled, "please help me. Let me send for Davril and I'll make a promise."

"What's that?"

He lowered his voice. "I promise you that I won't have anything with Davril all the time she is here. If I can do it, Laura, you must do it, too. No midnight rides to pester Mas Carlton's stock!"

Laura caught the light of his smile. "Brett, you are impossible! I sent for you because I was lonely, but instead you talk me into a pact of abstinence. I hope to the devil that Fletcher arrives soon!"

Davril sat demurely in the drawing room, her hands clasped ladylike in front of her. Her eyes were fixed on Brett.

Laura studied her dispassionately. She was pretty, daintily featured and with the dedicated glow of a virgin. Laura thought she looked like the kind of girl who usually became a nun. No wonder Brett had got so sanctimonious since he met her, Laura thought with a wry grin to herself.

Davril felt Laura's glance on her. She turned away from Brett in time to catch the odd grimace on Laura's face.

"Laura," Davril leaned over and whispered, "why don't you show me my chamber? You don't want to hear my daddy beating his drum about slavery!"

Laura was pleased with the excuse to leave the drawing room. "Do excuse us, Father and Mr. Gordon," she said, standing up. "I will show Davril her room. No, Brett," cautioned Laura as Brett rose to his feet. "This is girls' talk. You stay here with the men."

Davril smiled encouragingly at Brett and followed Laura to the guest room.

Carlton interrupted his discourse with Warren Gordon to gaze after her. He sucked his pipe dryly. Brett resumed his seat and tried to pay attention to the two men. Mr. Gordon, who had accompanied Davril to Roxborough, was to spend the night before riding on to Roseau the following day.

"Governor Nicolay requires me, Carlton. More talks on this slave question."

Carlton banged the bowl of his pipe on the heel of his boot. "Are you still planning to emancipate our niggers, Warren?" Carlton's voice was sarcastic.

"You may mock, Carlton. The time is not far off. It's not my wish, I tell you. We have all done well out of slavery. It's the only way we could have made those Africans work. But they are not Africans now, Carlton, they are black Creoles. They have been seasoned to work. Even you don't treat your slaves harshly, do you?"

"That's because I'm getting old!" scorned Carlton. "Brett handles the niggers. He's got some of your liberal ideas, I declare!"

He raised his punch glass, tilting it in Warren's direction. "And the law ain't what it used to be. A man can't lash a nigger more than thirty-nine stripes without the stipendary's consent. The slaves run to Layou and wail to the government agent if they so much as hear me speak of lynching or gelding!"

Warren leaned forward in his chair. "We've got to be practical, Carlton. Slaves ain't cheap like before. My profits are down each year. I get less work from the Negroes, and they cost me more in food and clothing. I believe it could be to our advantage to dispense with slavery and pay a man for a fair day's work."

Carlton gulped his punch. "You'd never get a white man to cut cane in the sun. His skin ain't thick like a nigger's."

"Not a white man, Carlton. The same Negroes. If they have to feed, house and clothe themselves, is it not going to be better for us?"

"Huh, I've never considered that."

Warren's glass of punch was untouched on the table. "Forgive me if I seem to be prying into your business, Carlton," he said. "We understand each other. Whatever you think now, emancipation of our slaves is going to come. It's desirable economically and politically."

Warren reached for his glass and sipped the punch slowly. "You must be prepared, Carlton. Your crop is slaves. If slavery finishes, there'll be no market for your harvest."

"Dam' it, Warren! You come to my house to tell me I'm going out of business!"

"What would you advise, Mr. Gordon?" Brett leaned forward eagerly.

"Your grandfather has my answer in his hand." Warren smiled, pleased by Brett's question.

"His pipe?"

"Tobacco, Brett. There's a growing market."

"Aye!" Carlton's retort cut short Warren's tirade. "I'll thank you to keep your nose out of my business, Warren. The British government in its wisdom may abolish slavery in Dominica. But it cannot abolish slavery in Guadeloupe while she's French, can it? Nor in Cuba! Nor in America! There will always be a market for strong, handsome, docile blacks! I'll export the buggers."

Brett rose as Davril and Laura returned. He took Davril's hand eagerly.

"Go on, you two," grunted Carlton. "Take a walk.

Your father and I have matters of consequence to discuss, Davril."

Brett nodded his head, leading Davril out of the drawing room onto the balcony.

"Oh, look, Brett. The sun will set soon. Let's sit here to watch it." Davril tugged Brett's hand, sinking into the chair and staring out at the horizon. He stood beside her.

"Don't you see? Isn't it beautiful? Such a clear sky."

The sun was suspended over the distant horizon where the blue of the sea merged with the sky. Like a disk of flaming gold, the sun was gradually falling. Davril clutched Brett's hand, squeezing it as the sun seemed to touch the sea and sink below the surface.

"Brett!" she murmured, caressing his hand passionately.

The sun dived swiftly until a bright orange rim was all that remained. Then that was gone. A cone of green flashed where the sun had been. The clouds on the horizon glowered menacingly as the night's grayness filled the sky.

Davril gazed adoringly at Brett, oblivious of her surroundings, longing for the day when Brett's strong arms would seize her and his body blend with hers to make them one. She sighed happily.

Chapter 41

The rain began the next morning. Davril woke. She kept her eyes closed, listening to the sound. Large drops of rain splattered slowly and deliberately on the shingle roof. It was curious. Usually, the rain came in sudden squalls, drenched the landscape with brief showers from the passing clouds, and then ceased. The heavy splashes on the roof were of a more determined temperament pelting the house pitilessly.

Davril cowered under the covers, benumbed by the roar of the deluge. There was a pounding on her door. She peeped out as the door opened and Laura scuttled in.

"Whoosh!" she exclaimed, pushing the door shut behind her. "Are you all right, my dear? Breakfast is nearly ready."

"The rain, Laura. I've never heard it so threatening."

Laura seemed exhilarated. "We need it. That dry atmosphere makes me so despondent. It's good for the provision grounds."

"Aren't you frightened?"

"Why should I be? A storm will blow the cobwebs away." Laura laughed heartily, bouncing on the end of Davril's bed.

"It is the season for hurricanes, Laura," Davril cautioned.

"Pah! A hurricane won't disturb us here. We have

the strongest cellar on the Leeward coast." Laura paused suddenly, eyeing Davril. The girl was holding her blanket to her chin. She flinched as the rain hurtled against the shingles. Laura patted her knees.

"Don't fret, my dear," Laura leered.

"Is Daddy still here?"

"Lor', no! Your father left before sunrise. I shouldn't wonder he is in Roseau already." Laura kept her hand on Davril's knee as though unaware of the gesture. Self-consciously, Davril shifted her leg so Laura was forced to move her hand.

"I must rise," Davril said. "I don't want to be late for breakfast."

"Yes." Laura made no effort to move. "Brett is asking for you." She reached out to touch Davril's leg again. The rain slammed against the shutters with a renewed fury.

"Oh!" gasped Davril. She moved her leg hastily out of Laura's reach.

"You are frightened of such things?" Laura chortled. "It's only natural."

Davril frowned. She was uncertain quite what Laura meant. There was a look in Laura's eye which disturbed her. "I must dress," she said.

"I know." Laura gleamed wantonly.

Davril blushed. "But I cannot if you are here, Laura."

"Why ever not? If you are frightened, I will stay to comfort you."

Davril swallowed, sealing her determination. "You are very kind, Laura. Really, I am not frightened. Perhaps you would wait for me outside." She paused, regarding Laura's face, which was flushed with excitement. "I like to say my prayers in the morning. Alone."

"Hah!" said Laura. "I knew it!" She stood up quickly, casting a glance of desire at Davril. "I'll see you at the breakfast table. With this rain, we will have to spend the morning in my boudoir!" She chuckled to herself as she withdrew from the room and closed the door behind her.

Davril sat back in the bed, listening to the beat of the rain, puzzled by Laura. The night before, she had seemed almost bored by Davril's presence. This morning, she seemed as different as the weather and, Davril shuddered, infinitely more menacing.

Breakfast was no more reassuring to Davril. The rain continued to pound the house, splattering into the dining room whenever the doors on the balcony were opened. The room was in gloom. Carlton was preoccupied and snapped at Laura whenever she addressed him. Laura herself was buoyed by the howling rain, winking at Davril whenever she glanced her way. Brett, to Davril's disappointment, was missing.

"He's about his business," muttered Carlton brusquely when Davril inquired. She buried her head in her dish of coffee, yearning for the kind understanding of her mother and father at home. She ate little during the meal and was glad when Carlton had disposed of the mountain of yams sauced with chicken stew and, belching heartily, had pushed back his chair and sauntered off into the drawing room.

Davril rose to go to her chamber, but at that moment the balcony door burst open and Brett blew into the room in a cascade of rain. He was laughing. Rain dripped from his hair and his black locks were plastered to his scalp. His clothes were drenched. His silk shirt was molded to the muscles and curves of his body by the dampness. His chest muscles wrinkled as he shook himself. His nipples, taut with the cold rain, protruded voluptuously. Davril gasped with longing, lowering her eyes quickly.

"Davril! Aren't you pleased to see me?" Brett cried. "I risked drowning to come here."

"Oh, Brett!" Davril raised her eyes immediately. His

breeches were as wet as his shirt, sticking to his thighs like a stocking. "You are soaked to the skin!"

"Of course he is!" bellowed Carlton. "What did you see, boy?"

"The whelps are fine, Mas Carlton. Miranda says the roof has no leaks. If the rain continues, though, they'll not be able to light a fire in the kitchen to boil food for dinner."

"It will blow itself out in an hour!" Carlton walked to the dresser and picked up the decanter. "Pip's had his measure for the morning, I see," he growled. "You want a rum, boy? Will keep your joints from paining you."

"No, sir," grinned Brett, filling a dish with steaming coffee. "My joints ain't paining me at all." He winked at Davril.

"No! I suppose that's an old man's complaint?" Carlton grumbled, pouring himself a large measure and gulping it down. He smacked his lips. "That's better. Where are the slaves, Brett?"

"I've sent Asaph and his gang to check the drains on the roads. They'll see if there are any blockages and clear them before the water has a chance to gouge out its own channel." Brett sipped his coffee gratefully. "The balance are in the quarters."

"That's where we should be, what?" Laura stood up. "I'll be in my boudoir, Davril. If you get bored." She flashed a smile at Davril and clomped past Brett in her breeches and riding boots.

"When the rain is over, we must take a canter around the plantation, Davril. Brett will be busy with the slaves. I'll be delighted to show you around," Laura shouted above the noise of the rain.

"Thank you." Davril inclined her head politely.

"Take no notice of Laura," Brett sat down, reaching for the plate of yams and plantain. "You don't have to ride if you don't want to. I'm not going to be so busy I cannot spend my time with you while you're here."

The rain did not ease up before dinner. Brett and Davril passed the hours in the drawing room, content to be in each other's presence, in whispered conversation. Carlton, growling cholerically, had retreated to his chamber with the rum decanter. Occasionally, they heard him bellowing for Pip to bring fire for his pipe. Laura, restless now, joined them on several occasions. Once she muttered, "I don't know what's wrong with me today," and stalked off to her boudoir again.

After a dinner fractured with conversation as gloomy as the weather, Brett escorted Davril onto the balcony. The courtyard was like a cauldron, vast puddles of water steaming skywards. Everywhere they looked, leaves and branches sagged under the weight of water. The clouds parted for the sun to emerge, setting the valley glittering. Behind the house, flooding over the sheer cliff face at the top of the vale, a waterfall tumbled into the upper reaches of the Layou Valley.

"It's strange," murmured Davril, as she looked over the valley rolling down to the coast.

"What's strange, my dear?" Brett grasped her hand, following her gaze.

"The birds. They are not singing."

Brett shrugged his shoulders. He glanced behind. The ridge of mountains at the other side of the river was swathed in mist. The sky above them was ominously dark, laden with blue-black clouds. The sea mirrored the sky with an expanse of surging water which was a deep, dark blue. A slash of red, the mud scoured down the swollen river from the island's interior, seeped into the ocean like a wound.

"Perhaps the birds know we have more rain to

come," Brett remarked, putting his arm around Davril's waist.

"Brett!" bellowed Carton from within his room. "Where the devil are you?"

Davril smiled with understanding as Brett excused himself. "I'll go to my chamber," she said, "and read. I can open my jalousies and air the room."

Carlton was leaning out of his window which opened onto the balcony and gave a full view of the valley overlooking the village.

"I don't like it, boy. The thermometer." Carlton's speech was slurred. He leaned out of the window while Brett stood on the balcony. "It's erratic, boy. At noon it was eighty-seven degrees. See how uncommon sultry and oppressive it was at dinner."

Brett frowned, waiting for Carlton to reach the point.

"The clouds are gathering in the north, Brett. There's a strange stillness in the atmosphere."

"Davril noticed the birds aren't singing."

"She's right, boy .Observe the blackness brewing." He shook his head, almost toppling over the window ledge.

"What is it, sir?"

"Could be trouble, boy. Mount your horse and ride to the quarters. Get the drivers to round up all the slaves and take them to the mill compound. They can shelter in the boiling house, in the still, and in the curing house. They are all stone buildings." Carlton rested his head wearily on his hand.

"There'll be winds tonight, Brett," he said frowning. "Tell the drivers to hurry. The slaves must remain in the mill, not one of them must come out until day-break! Is that clear? Now, where's Laura? Send her to me."

Carlton coughed as he dismissed Brett. He felt

wretched. He feared a hurricane; it could destroy Roxborough.

"Drunk again, Daddy?" Laura stood on the balcony with her feet apart and her arms akimbo. She was dressed for riding.

Carlton raised his head and glared at Laura through bloodshot eyes. "Not so drunk I don't know when there's danger, Laura. We'll have a hurricane tonight, I'm sure of it."

"Hurricane! That must be why I've been so damn jittery all day."

"I don't know what you've been, Laura, but it's a fact. Run to the nursery, Laura, and warn Miranda. Tell her to secure all the doors and shutters and not to let any of my niggerlings out until morning.

"Tell Caliste he must sleep in the stable with the horses. He must try to calm them. Warn Constance to stay in his smithy!" Carlton groaned, slapping his brow to clear the confusion in his head.

"Go on, Laura. We don't have much time!"

The sky was filling with livid clouds, casting a hastening gloom over the plantation. Ella, her head cocked to the distant sighs of the wind, climbed laboriously up the back steps. She paused for breath as she reached the top and stared with distrust at the mountain range which encircled the plantation. She could hear the roar of torrents raging deep in the bush. She shuffled quickly around the balcony.

"Mas Carlton!" she bleated. Carlton's head was resting on the window sill as though he were asleep. "Mas Carlton!"

Carlton raised his head and looked into her lined face, ravaged with concern. His own features were torn with worry. He nodded. "I know."

"Ah does hear de wind, Mas Carlton," she croaked sadly.

"Dam' it, I know!" he shouted.

391

Ella backed away sucking her gums.

He threw out his hand toward her. "Come, Ella! There is nothing to be done now." He looked up. "It will soon be dark. Have all the house slaves remain downstairs." He took her hands, his haggard face softening with remorse.

"We'll be all right, Ella. Don't worry."

About six in the evening, the wind began to blow moderately from the north. It was already dark. Laura returned to the house and aided Pip in securing all the windows and doors, removing lamps and other objects which might blow away from the gallery.

Davril rushed to help. "I can't believe that at this time yesterday I was watching a perfect sunset here with Brett," she gossiped.

"Hah!" said Laura. "Let's hope we will have more sunsets to see!"

"Oh!" Davril's hand flew to her breast. "Will it be so bad? Where's Brett?"

"Bedding down the niggers, Davril."

"Ah done see a hurricane when ah was a boy." Pip paused as the wind rattled the corner of the house. "De lightnin' was awful grand."

Brett returned to the house before Davril had a chance to work herself into a real pother. He joined Laura, Carlton, and Davril as they sat together in the drawing room. Each was listening to the wind, interpreting its seriousness according to their fear.

"It's just a squall." Brett spoke to reassure Davril. "All the Negroes are in the mill, Mas Carlton."

Davril smiled nervously. A single lantern burned in the drawing room, creating a murkiness which added to the atmosphere of foreboding. "What can we do?" she asked gravely.

"Nothing," growled Carlton.

Brett was standing close to Davril's chair. He placed his hand tenderly on her neck. She jumped.

"Why don't you go to your chamber, Davril? Pip will bring you a lantern."

"You must sleep with me, my dear, if you are frightened!" Laura leaned forward with a smirk.

"I shall be all right." Davril spoke each word slowly and deliberately. The wind increased its howling, battering the house persistently. "Yes." She smiled bravely up at Brett. "I think I will go to bed."

"I will be here, Davril." Brett helped her out of the chair. "Nothing will happen to you."

"I'll be here, too!" Carlton spoke gruffly, trying to be kind. He had drunk himself sober and champed on the stem of his pipe with anxiety. "You can go to your boudoir, Laura. You don't have to keep watch with us."

As soon as Davril and Laura had gone to their rooms, Carlton rose from his chair and started to pace the floor. He had to speak loudly for Brett to hear him above the wind.

"Anything can happen in a hurricane, Brett. The wind comes from all directions. This house is solid, but if the winds are too fierce we must sleep in the cellar with Ella and Pip." He paused, listening. "I don't think that is necessary yet. Do remember, Brett, if there is a long lull in the wind in the night, don't go outside. The wind may cuff you from the opposite direction."

Brett nodded his head seriously.

"We will keep watch, Brett. You take the first one. I've got to sleep off this rum. We've done all we can." Carlton shuffled to his room. At his door, he stopped and looked at Brett's earnest face. "Call me, Brett, if you need me."

Brett settled himself on the couch, frowning at the horrible roar and yelling of the wind. It chopped ruthlessly at the house. He listened carefully. The dogs were whining at the chains. There was another, softer sound. He recognized the whimpering and got to his feet immediately.

He tapped gently on Davril's door. "Are you all right?" he called anxiously. There was no reply. He tried the handle. The door swung open.

Davril was in her bed, her head covered with a blanket. Brett could see her shoulders shaking as she wept with fear.

"Davril! Don't cry. It's me, Brett." He stepped swiftly over to her bed and put his hand on her shoulders. The wind clapped against the shutters, rattling the side of the house. Davril stopped sobbing as Brett pulled back the blanket.

"I'm so frightened, Brett." Davril's hands wound around Brett's waist pulling him close to her.

He clutched her in his arms, patting her back tenderly.

"Brett, what will happen?"

"Nothing." The blasts of wind as they rapidly succeeded each other on their furious course shook the house with a noise like thunder. Davril squeezed Brett's body, tugging him closer. He laid his head on the pillow beside her, his legs trailing on the floor.

The clapping of the wind was deafening. The walls of the house shook as though an earthquake was vibrating the foundations. Davril clung to Brett in her fear.

Brett raised his legs from the floor and lay full length beside her on the bed. He grasped her around her shoulders firmly. "Don't be frightened!" he breathed. Her lips were close to his. He brushed his mouth against hers almost by accident.

Davril seized his lips with hers, straining her body against his, clutching him so he could not move. The tempestuous rage of the wind increased, smacking against the house with a hideous din. There was a screech as shingles ripped off the roof.

Davril's fingers tore at Brett's shirt, plucking it open. She rubbed her hands urgently over his smooth, hard flesh.

Brett forgot the wind hammering at the house. He embraced Davril with the fury of the passion pent up within him over the weeks. He twisted himself under the blanket and gnawed at her body with his hungry lips.

While the hurricane howled around them, Brett and Davril discovered the wild joy of lovemaking. The wind dashed the house with a cannon roar as Brett exploded inside Davril and she flowed onto him.

There was a lull in the gusting and they lay content in each other's arms.

Chapter 42

"Down to the cellar! Before we lose our lives!"

The door crashed open. Carlton strode over to the bed and pulled back the blanket. Brett and Davril were asleep. Carlton smiled proudly. The front of Brett's breeches was covered in blood.

"Wake up, Brett!" Carlton shook the boy by the shoulder. "Take Davril down to the cellar."

Rain was trickling into the room where shingles had been ripped off the roof by the wind. Brett's eyes opened in panic.

"Come on, boy! You take care of your bride and I'll look after Laura." Carlton grinned at him before hurrying out.

Brett's fear vanished at Carlton's words. He seized Davril in his arms, hugging and kissing her awake. "Davril! Davril!" he shouted. "Mas Carlton has given his consent! We can be married!"

Davril looked at him dreamily. "I know that." She yawned. "Daddy's going to give us a dowry. Mas Carlton would never have refused ten slaves and two hundred acres for you. That's what he discussed with Mas Carlton before he went to Roseau."

A shower of shingles clattered into the room, enlarging the hole in the roof. The wind moaned softly, as though pausing for breath. Brett glanced at the roof, leaping out of bed and urging Davril to follow him.

"Wrap the blanket around you. We must go down to the kitchen."

Davril moved lazily. "Look at your breeches."

Brett was aghast. He tucked himself inside and fastened the buttons. He fussed, wondering what to do about the bloodstains.

"Nobody will concern themselves in this hurricane," retorted Davril. She tugged at the blanket and draped it around herself. "Here, cover yourself with the counterpane."

Together they hurried out of the room onto the balcony. The blackness of the night appalled Brett. He hugged Davril to his side, inching carefully along the deck of the balcony. The wind was blowing moderately, accompanied by the racket of debris being scattered about the courtyard.

"Come on! Come on!" Carlton called from the foot of the back steps. He held up his hand to help Davril descend, bustling her into the kitchen where Ella swooped on her. Brett followed. Pip fought with the wind to close the door, which Carlton locked quickly.

There were six of them in the kitchen. Carlton checked. Ella was comforting Davril, Laura sat on the

396

bench gazing moodily at Brett, while Pip was heading for the store cupboard.

"We need no rum now, Pip!" shouted Carlton. "Where are the other slaves, Ella?"

Ella sat Davril at the table. "Don't yo' worry, gal. We does be safe here." She turned to Carlton. "De t'ree gals does be in de chamber. Ah done sen' de yard boys to de Paddock since dusk."

Carlton nodded. "There's nothing we can do now. The winds will blow stronger. We are safe here. These walls are solid stone. Nothing will budge them."

As he spoke, the hurricane whipped itself back to life, lashing the house with an unparalleled uproar. Pip wailed. Laura, Davril, and Ella huddled together for comfort. Carlton and Brett joined them at the table, listening nervously. The elements seemed to have torn the reins out of their guiding hands, returning the world to chaos.

Davril shivered in a stupor as the lantern flickered and died in the gusts of cold, damp air swirling through the cellar. She whimpered in Ella's arms. Laura bit her ip nervously as furniture careened across the floor above their heads, buffeted by the scourging wind.

Carlton sat with his arm around Brett. The two men, in the ghastly blackness of the cellar, drew strength from each other. Carlton was resigned to whatever horrors the hurricane would bring. Brett was apprehensive about the slaves, hoping that they were sheltered safely in the mill compound. He flinched. Thunder blasted down the valley, reverberating through the walls of the cellar. There was an ominous rushing sound as though something was hurtling through the trees surrounding the house. The flagstone floor of the cellar suddenly shuddered.

"By the devil!" exclaimed Carlton.

"Aye!" Ella cried out in terror, clutching her heart.

397

"What was that?" Laura's normally strident voice was hushed to a whisper.

Davril wound her arms around Ella's body and tried to comfort her as the old cook burst into an agonized weeping.

"Shut up, Ella!" roared Carlton. "You're making us all frightened."

"I'll go see."

"No, Brett! Stay here." Carlton restrained Brett with his hand. "If you go out into that gale, you'll be lifted up and dumped over the valley into the sea." He was appalled by the noise. "We must stay out of the blast."

"Let's pray!" suggested Davril, her own courage returning now that she had Ella's distress to contend with.

"You can pray!" bleated Laura. "But to yourself. Ain't nothing going to stop this damned wind!"

Thunder rolled again. Pip, who had groped his way to the store cupboard in the dark, cowered. He snatched a decanter of rum from the shelf and gulped at its contents, slipping to the floor as the noise pinioned him with fear. The six of them stayed trapped in the cellar while the hurricane raged throughout the night.

Constance, the deaf and dumb blacksmith, could not hear the awful wailing of the tempest erupting around him. He had followed Laura's instructions implicitly and barricaded himself in his smithy. He felt the vibrations under his feet and saw the walls of the forge shaken by the wind blasts. He was unmoved by the furious howling, waiting patiently in the darkness for the wind to cease.

At the same time when Carlton was rousing Brett and Davril to go to the cellar for safety, Constance noticed the change in the wind. The trembling of the ground ceased. He touched the tools hanging from the beam above his head. They had stopped their wild swinging. Constance nodded his head wisely. The night was so black, it was as though he was blind. However, his remaining senses of touch and smell assured him the wind had ceased. He felt his way to the smithy door and threw it open.

Peering out, Constance wondered if he was alone on the plantation. There were no lights in the house to show where it stood in the dreadful thickness of the night. The nursery, nearer to his forge than the house, was hidden by the blackness. Constance was amazed. He raised his hand in front of his eyes. Only when the palm was touching his nose could he see his fingers.

He lolloped carefully from the forge in the direction of the nursery. His brow was creased with concern. Miranda and her son Quentin, whom he adored, would need him, he thought. He stumbled as he groped his way along the path. Plantains had fallen across the trail. The wind buffeted his ears. Constance found the gate in the fence surrounding the Paddock swinging open. He hurried through it toward the nursery.

Feeling with his fingers along the side of the building, Constance found the door he sought. He hammered on it with his fists, grunting anxiously. Miranda, clutching Quentin, who was stiff with fear, heard the sound. She was alone with him. Pallis was in the nursery trying to comfort the children. Miranda listened without speaking, squeezing her nails into Quentin's shoulders. The hammering and grunting like a devil at her door continued.

"Go away! Go away!" she shrieked.

Quentin's eyes widened as he sensed his mother's fear. "What dere, mam?"

"Ah don't know, Quentin. Will dis night never end?"

Quentin listened in awe to the scratching on the door, trying to separate it from the creaking of the coconut trees and the persistent rustling of the wind. He screwed up his eyes and nose thoughtfully.

"Constance!" he called pulling himself away from his mother's grasp and running to the door. He tried to open it, but he was too weak to lift the wooden bar which held the two half-doors in position.

Miranda ran to him in the darkness. "Boy!" she scolded. "What yo' does be doin'?" She grabbed his hand to pull him away. The hammering began again, accompanied by a plaintive honking noise.

"Constance! Constance!" Quentin tugged his mother's hand joyfully.

Miranda paused. She slapped Quentin's hand away and cautiously unbolted the top half of the door. She snorted with relief when she identified Constance's bulbous features looming out of the darkness. Quickly, she opened the door, embracing him fondly.

Constance rubbed his nose against Miranda's neck, holding her slender body in his strong hands to still her quivering. Quentin was beating his hands on Constance's thigh. He released Miranda and bent down to pat the boy on his shoulder.

Constance could not understand why Quentin was not like the other whelps in the nursery. He always seemed to be sickly. His skin had a gray pallor to it. He was forever clutching his mother's shift, crying for attention. Constance sensed that the boy would be frightened on a night like this. He squeezed Quentin's shoulder.

"De wind is big tonight!" Quentin told Constance gravely, putting his face close to the blacksmith and blowing on his cheek to imitate the wind.

Constance nodded.

"It done finish now," laughed Quentin, tugging Constance's hand. "Let we go to de *cou* an' see Ella!"

400

"No!" snapped Miranda. "Yo' wait till morning."

Quentin stared at his mother. Constance never rebuffed him like that. The door to the cabin was still open. Quentin was not afraid of the dark; he knew he could find his way. He pulled Constance by the hand, jerking his head in the direction of the house.

"Ella! Ella!" he mouthed so that Constance could understand.

Constance looked at Miranda perplexed. Suddenly, Quentin slipped his fingers free of ·Constance's hand and scuttled out of the open door and down the steps. Miranda dived for him, but she was too late.

"Quentin!" she called frantically into the wind. "Come back! Come back!" She gazed at Constance's dumb face.

"De boy has de madness on him." She grabbed Constance and pulled him out of the cabin. "We must get him."

Miranda shouted Quentin's name as she blundered along the path. The wind tugged at her shift, low-hanging branches tearing at her hair. Rain began to hurtle down, drenching them. Miranda wailed. She held onto the waistband of Constance's breech cloth. The wind flung her cries back in her face. Above her head, the branches of the trees screeched as the hurricane let out its breath and unleashed its violence.

Constance glanced upwards. He sensed the formidable fury of the tempest gusting around them. As the thunder drummed across the valley, the sensations in the earth startled him. He pulled Miranda onto the flat stones of the courtyard. There was no light to be seen from the kitchen.

"Quentin!" Miranda screamed as the thunder roared again. The wind picked up her shriek, tossing it over the roof of the house.

Quentin heard his mother's cry as he crouched in the shelter of the grand steps. He darted out of his hiding place and ran into the courtyard. A wooden barrel, placed at the side of the house to catch rainwater from the bamboo guttering, toppled over. The wind picked it up and hurled it into the air above the courtyard.

"Mam!"

"Quentin!"

The barrel, released by the wind, dropped. It crashed down as Quentin ran to his mother. It landed on his head, felling him. It shattered, scattering its staves over the boy's lifeless body.

A rattle of thunder rent the air. The wind seized the staves and tossed them about the courtyard. The night was filled with howling. Miranda fought the wind to reach down and cradle Quentin in her arms. Constance, standing over her, raised his head in alarm at the gust of wind swooping down on them both. He put his arm around Miranda to shield her.

The huge *balata* tree which had grown by the corner of the house for decades, moved slowly at first. In the shouts of the wind, the sound of its branches as they tore through the other trees was scarcely audible. Then as its roots sprang free of the earth, the rushing sound of the falling tree increased to a deafening roar.

The trunk of the tree smashed into Constance, splitting his head. His brains spewed out onto Miranda. She collapsed over Quentin's body as a bough stabbed her through the chest. The tree hit the floor of the courtyard with a thud, dislodging flagstones and shaking the foundations of the house.

Gold pieces and silver coins which had been buried in caskets at the roots of the tree spiraled in the wind. The caskets smashed to the ground and shattered.

The dreadful clamor and uproar continued without intermission until five the next morning when the raging blast veered away from the west and the shrieks of the elements partially subsided. The occupants of the kitchen cellar glanced at each other in awe. Water swirled around their feet, trickling in from the flooding in the courtyard.

At six, the hurricane blew steadily and tremendously from the south, driving sheets of rain horizontally before it. This was the dying burst. The winds suddenly abated, allowing the dawn to reveal the devastating horrors of its ravages.

Carlton and Brett stared at the plantation with amazement. As far as the eye could see, the cane had been rooted up and flattened. Coconut trees lay stretched across the cane, their once majestic trunks stripped and blighted. The sound of the river flushing through the valley echoed eerily in the silence now that the wind had died.

It was Brett who pointed to the fallen *balata* tree lying across the courtyard like a ship run aground. Carlton's mind was occupied as he tried to estimate the cost of the damage to the canes and the house. Shingles had flown from the roof, and the balcony on the windward side tilted dangerously. The tree in the courtyard escaped his notice as part of the general matrix of disaster and chaos.

"There's someone there!" Brett scampered down the front steps. Carlton frowned as he followed him, gazing at the corner where the tree had once stood.

"It's Constance!" shouted Brett. His voice changed to a shriek of horror as he caught sight of Miranda and Quentin sprawled out under the branches of the tree. "Mas Carlton!" he cried. "Quentin and Miranda. They're all dead!"

A clutch of fear seized Carlton's heart. He pushed past Brett, ignoring the bodies. He dashed to the spot where the *balata* had been rooted. He stared at the hole in the ground.

In a daze he ran to the corner of the house and

403

began to pace out ten steps. He stopped at the eighth step and covered his head with his hands. Where the wooden chests containing the gold accumulated from thirty years of slave dealing had been buried there was a gaping hole.

Cautiously, the slaves emerged from the mill compound. They were chilled with fear after spending the night huddled in the mill buildings. Although they had been protected from the hurricane by the strength of the stone walls, the wind had terrified them.

They trudged through the devastated plantation wailing with misery. The drivers furled their whips despondently, bemused and humbled by the night's shared experience. When they reached the quarters, the slaves halted. A moan of anguish rose from them which carried up to Brett and Carlton at the house.

The slaves stared. Where their cabins had been was marked only by masses of ruin and heaps of rubbish. Not a cabin or shack was left standing.

The old women clutched their bellies and keened. The old men scratched their heads in disbelief. The younger slaves rushed forward angrily.

And there, as they picked over the boards and posts which had been their homes, the slaves spied coins glittering in the bashful sunlight. They shouted with surprise, rummaging hastily through the ruins. Gold dubloons, pieces of eight, and silver coins were there in handfuls.

"It does be a shower of gold de wind does bring us!" announced Tency joyfully, scrambling with the others to claim her share.

"Now we niggers does have enough riches to buy our freedom!"

Chapter 43

The whip sliced through the air, scorching into the flesh of Tency's rump as she bent over to pick up the gold coins at her feet. She yelled, spinning around defiantly. The lash struck her again across her breasts, ripping open her shift and sending it fluttering to the ground. She staggered backwards, throwing up her arm to protect herself.

Laura aimed the whip into Tency's side, flaying her around her ample hips. Tency fell to her knees, grovelling in the gold.

"Hab mercy, Miss Laura!" she shrieked. "Ah done do nuthin'."

Brett, grim-faced on his horse beside Laura, eyed each of the slaves in turn, snapping his own whip impatiently. The slaves stopped jumping up with delight, frightened by Tency's screams. Laura lashed Tency again and then, for good measure, cracked the whip over the head of the other slaves. They stepped backwards, their faces abject with fear.

Brett nodded at Laura. She smiled primly, catching the tongue of the long bullwhip in her hand and stroking it.

"Tency, get up!" ordered Brett. "What are you doing with Mas Carlton's gold?" His face was flushed with anger the slaves had not seen before. There was a jangling sound as those who were clutching coins in their hands let them slip to the ground.

"Sah!" bleated Tency. "Ah not know it does be Mas Carlton's gold! Ah ain't takin' de gold, sah!"

Brett cracked his whip to silence her, gazing down menacingly at the slaves. His torn, soaked shirt and bloodstained breeches added to his air of wild mastery over them.

"Laura!" he muttered in clipped tones. "Ride around the back of the slaves and watch them well. See no one tries to steal any of the gold."

Brett smirked as he looked at Tency kneeling naked on the ground. "You can all shuck off your clothes!" he bellowed. "That way ain't none of you going to thieve the Bondmaster's gold!"

Laura and Brett flayed their whips over the slaves as though they were swatting a swarm of *jackspaniers*. Asaph and the other drivers moved aside, looking inquiringly at Brett for instructions.

"You, too!" Brett snapped his whip at them. "Step out of your rags right smartly now."

The horrors of the night had served to make even Asaph and the drivers meek in the face of Brett's wrath. Asaph grumbled under his breath, removing his breeches slowly. When he was naked, he picked up his driver's whip and stood away from the slaves muttering to himself.

Brett gaped down at the slaves, amazed at their easy subjection. The older women were moaning softly, the men gaunt and terrified. The eyes of all the slaves were expressionless, staring ahead, not daring to look at Brett or Laura.

"Tency!" Brett gloated. "Stand up. You're a driver, ain't you? Get over there with Asaph and the others."

"Yas, sah!" Tency's voice was jubilant with gratitude. She scrambled to her feet, grabbed her whip where it had fallen in the coins, and joined the drivers.

Brett rode over to them while Laura covered the slaves. "All this gold belongs to Mas Carlton," he told

406

them. "You'll take your gangs and drive them from the top end of the quarters to the bottom. Every coin is to be collected. Get hogsheads and pails from the mill to put them in. You understand?" Tency, Asaph and the other drivers nodded their heads eagerly.

Brett gritted his teeth. "Any slave that steals one single coin is going to get thirty days in the stocks and thirty-nine strokes every day. And you"—he glared at the drivers—"will get the same."

Asaph grumbled under his breath.

"What's that, Asaph?" snapped Brett.

"Our clothes, massa?" he asked.

Brett leaned over from his horse and jabbed the handle of his whip into Asaph's belly. "You'll get your clothes, boy, when I get Mas Carlton's gold."

"Sah!" cried Tency nervously. "De cabins done blow down in de wind, sah! Where we gon' live, sah? We slaves ain't got nuthin', now, sah!"

Brett pulled his nose as he glanced at the shambles of the slave village. Laura was riding her horse around the slaves as though rounding up a herd of cattle. He shrugged his shoulders, thinking aloud. "We have carpenters, coopers, wheelwrights, niggers. That ain't no problem. Them shanties are going to be rebuilt in a week."

He watched Tency. "I know what you're thinking, Tency. Yes, freedom is going to come one day, Tency," he said slowly. "But nothing ain't coming without all that gold being returned to Mas Carlton!"

Tency grinned timidly. She understood. Mingoson had told her about the treasure Mas Carlton had sequestered near the house. She knew that without his fortune, Mas Carlton was nothing.

Unable to defy Brett's piercing stare, Tency lowered her eyes to the ground. Asaph smacked her naked bottom with his whip handle and together they moved off to drive the slaves to scavenge for the gold.

The hurricane had devastated not only Roxborough, but the whole island. The Roseau River had burst its banks and flooded the capital. Only the stone houses remained and even they had suffered in the blast. Layou Village was ripped apart by the tempest. The sea had risen, washing away the shacks built near the coast. The river had swirled through the main street, sweeping debris and furniture before it. Roofs had been lifted off houses, walls had tumbled, and people had disappeared.

The maroons in their camp atop the ridge of hills which skirted the Layou Valley had not escaped the destruction. While the Roxborough slaves were scrambling to collect the gold under the spinning lashes of Brett, Laura, and the drivers, Mingoson was surveying the glade which had once been the maroon's camp. It was desolate.

All the cabins and bamboo *ajoupas* had been carried away by the winds. The maroons' tools had been hurtled into the air, some falling in the woods, some plunging over the cliff down into the valley. The maroons themselves had spent the night huddled in the cathedral of trees, drawing protection from the vast trunks of the samans. Branches had crashed to the ground around them and the thunder had threatened to batter them to death with its noise. But all, except one, had survived.

When the gale had begun to blow more bitter than the usual August squall, Mingoson had gone to Tita's *ajoupa*. The reed door was fastened from within. Mingoson scratched against the door, raising his voice to make himself heard above the monstrous warbling of the wind.

"Who dere? Who dere?" Tita had squawled in reply.

Mingoson smiled to himself. "Although yo' does say yo' is an obeah woman, yo' does be scare' like hell!" he muttered. "Tita!" he called more loudly. "Let me in!"

"Ah ain' here!" she screeched.

"De hurricane sure gon' find yo', Tita. Come to de forest wid us. We does have shelter by de saman trees." Mingoson steadied himself in the glade by clutching the round wood post which served as the doorjamb. "De wind does be a blessing!"

Mingoson frowned when he heard Tita's hoarse cackle. He pleaded with her a few more times to come out, but she refused. The wind was already pushing up the loose sticks which lay around the camp site, swirling them in the air. Mingoson had to crouch to avoid them. He cursed Tita's obstinacy before struggling against the wind to reach the shelter of the saman grove.

After the initial blast of the hurricane had died down and a lull settled on the camp, Mingoson had peered out of the grove. The darkness was complete. He groped his way toward Tita's cabin. It was still there.

"Tita, Tita!" he called her anxiously. There was no reply. He called again. The door was still fastened. Cursing, he put his shoulder to it and pushed his way into the shack. "Tita! Tita!" He felt his way to the bed board where Tita always crouched. She was not there. He listened carefully. There was no sound of her in the *ajoupa*.

As he emerged, baffled by her disappearance, the wind sprang. A streak of lightning spread its eerie brightness across the sky. Mingoson stared at the camp. Some of the huts had already been flattened. Then his attention was caught by a movement on the crown of the huge boulder which served as the maroon look-out.

A second flare of lightning revealed the frail frame of Tita crouched at its top. She was rising unsteadily to her feet, the rags of her clothing fluttering around her in the wind.

Mingoson watched as though bewitched. There was a third flash which flooded the sky with light. Thunder, poised directly overhead, jarred the sky with such vehemence that Mingoson threw himself to the ground for safety.

He raised his eyes at the moment a tremendous blast of wind hurtled in from the sea. It cuffed Tita sideways, lifting her off her feet. The lightning forked, tinging her body with a sheet of flame. She sailed over the edge of the cliff and plummeted down to the cane-pieces below.

Mingoson bit his lip in horror.

"De bitch was be a *soucouyant* in truth!" he told the maroons as they gathered in the ruins of the camp site the next morning.

"We does be finish'," Joshua, the oldest of the run-aways, announced. "She gone, shelter gone, our gardens does be destroy!"

Tarry sneered. "Yo' does be ol' so yo' want to finish. Not me. Ah ain't gon' back to no slave plantation."

Dale looked at Mingoson. "What we gon' do?"

Mingoson crouched down onto his haunches. Some of the maroons did likewise, grouping in a circle around him, while the others drifted through the campsite, aimlessly picking at the debris.

"De way ah does see it," Mingoson said thought-fully, "we does be de same as when de maroons first come here. Dose run'ways done build de new life, so we must do de same."

Joshua sniffed. "Dere was be plenty of niggers in dem days. We ain't have enough fur one gang. Best we be slaves, den de buckra gon' gib us cabins an' clothes an' food."

"Yo' fuhgit what slavery does be, ol' man!" spat Tarry. "It ain't no sweet life!"

410

Dale frowned. He did not feel any better off as a maroon. He was wet and hungry, and he had not had a wench for four nights.

"We gon' get dem Roxbruh slaves to join us!" announced Mingoson. "Dey gon' help us."

"How yo' gon' do dat?" asked Dale. "Roxbruh niggers ain't got no mind to run away."

"We gon' attack Roxbruh an' free dem slaves," roared Mingoson. "When de buckras does be dead, de slaves gon' be free. Dey gon' help us to build our own kingdom here."

"An' yo' gon' be de king?" asked Joshua mockingly.

"Yas!" said Tarry. "Mingoson will be de king!" He leaped up and hobbled over to Mingoson. "Count on me, Mingoson." Tarry glanced around at the others.

"An' me," murmured Dale, pulling his earlobe as he gazed through the devastated valley out to sea.

Warren Gordon returned to Roxborough three days after the hurricane. Carlton greeted him despondently.

"What ails you?" exclaimed Warren. "By God, you are lucky! Your Negroes have nearly rebuilt their quarters. Your trails have been cleared already, and you've recovered your gold!"

He clapped Carlton on his shoulders. "It could have been Brett killed in that hurricane, Carlton, not your sickly whelp by your own black daughter. Where would you be without Brett?"

Carlton sighed. His pipe drooped at the corner of his mouth. He removed it wearily. "I'm finished, Warren. I'm too old, too tired."

Warren smacked his lips in appreciation at the rum he was sipping. "You have rum like this in puncheons in dozens in your store at the mill, Carlton. Don't deny it, Brett showed me. Missing this year's cane crop ain't going to do you nothing, Carlton.'

411

"Crop?" Carlton gazed at Warren blankly. "I built a fortune. It's gone."

"No, it ain't. Brett tells me you've got two hogsheads of gold pieces in your chamber. I ain't got a firkin!" Warren drained his glass and reached across from his seat to slap Carlton on his thigh.

"What you need is a rest, old chap. Brett can handle the plantation, and he'll have Davril by his side. Why don't you go to England for a year. Take Laura!"

Carlton stroked his chin. He had not shaved since the hurricane. His face was haggard from lack of sleep. He felt desperately exhausted. From his heavily hooded eyes, he gazed at Warren without speaking.

"I can always keep an eye on things for you while you're away, Carlton! It will do you good and will help Brett and Davril prepare for the future."

Warren's breeziness was infectious. Carlton leaned forward and tipped more rum into his glass, passing the decanter across to his guest. He swallowed his rum and rubbed his bloodshot eyes. "I suppose you are right!" He coughed. "Be good to go to Almack's again!"

"Why not?" chuckled Warren. "Now let's see what we can do about arranging this wedding, eh? I was speaking to Clarke in Roseau—he's the rector, of course. How about a wedding just before Christmas? Give the slaves something to look forward to in case they get restless after the hurricane."

Carlton was not listening. The strains of a waltz soared through his mind. He was dancing again in Almack's assembly rooms, an aristocratic beauty in his arms. Madame de Lieven herself smiled her approval. With his blond hair, his arrogant good looks and planter's wealth, he was the toast of London. His Negro slave, Caspar, in a livery of golden silk, awaited him at table. He was the envy of every young gentleman in society.

412

Carlton drummed his fingers on the arm of his chair, humming the waltz refrain to himself. "One, two, three . . . one, two, three . . . tra, la, la . . ." A smile spread across his tired features as his eyes peered into the past.

Warren rose tactfully, leaving Carlton to his memories.

Two weeks after the hurricane, Brett was able to report to Carlton that life was back to normal on the plantation. The slave quarters had been rebuilt and the buildings in the mill repaired. Trees which had fallen had been logged up and all the trails drained and cleared. The house roof had been re-shingled and the balcony strengthened. The nursery had been fenced.

Brett checked off the items on his fingers as he recounted the work to Carlton while they sat at dinner. Laura, who had helped him in supervising the slaves, added details of the tasks which he had forgotten.

Carlton listened in silence, crunching a chicken bone. When Brett stopped and looked at him earnestly for approval, Carlton spat out the fragments on his plate and wiped his mouth with the back of his hand. He pushed his plate away and leaned back in his seat.

"What age are you, boy?"

Brett's face fell at being addressed like a nigger. "I'm nigh on twenty, sir, next year."

"Hah!" Carlton snorted. "And no whelps?"

Brett was confused. He looked to Laura for help.

"Brett is to be married, Father." Laura winked at Brett to reassure him about Carlton's odd moods.

"Send for the slaves!"

"What, sir?" Brett stood up quickly.

"Get them damn niggers here, Brett! Sound the

413

conches, dam' it! They're only rucking the cane-pieces."

"Yes, sir!" Brett raised his eyebrows at Laura before striding obediently from the room.

"Is someone to be punished?" Laura inquired sweetly.

"Punished?" Carlton reached for his glass of Maderia. He gulped the wine and looked quizzically at his daughter. "I'm the one who is being punished."

Carlton rose to his feet and shuffled off to his bed-room. He paused at the doorway.

"Tell Brett to send for me when the niggers are here. All of them, the stock from the nursery, too."

The slaves assembled reluctantly in the courtyard. Word had spread among them that Mas Carlton was losing his senses. Ella had confided to Norah that she did not know what was happening to him. Pip had discussed with Asaph Mas Carlton's habit of spending hours brooding on the balcony, drumming tirelessly on the arm of his chair. By experience, the slaves were leery of a buckra who acted strangely and without reason. They feared an outbreak of senseless punish-ments.

Brett's upright figure on the balcony as he surveyed them reassured the slaves. They had faith in Brett.

So had Carlton. He lurched onto the balcony, causing the slaves to gasp in unison as he toppled against the railing.

Brett caught him, steadying him with his arm around his shoulders. He frowned at Carlton's foul breath, rich in rum.

"He done nearly fall on we!" exclaimed Norah, voicing the concern of the slaves. "De Bon'massa does be sick."

"Mas Brett should let he fall!" grumbled Pallis. "He ain't no use!"

414

"Shut yuh mouth!" Norah and others hissed angrily at Pallis.

Carlton opened his mouth to speak. He belched heartily.

Brett grimaced at Laura, gripping Carlton so he would not sway over the balcony into the courtyard below. Ella sidled up to him.

"Give he dis, Brett," she smiled. "Does be a rem'dy to steady he nerves."

Brett took the small goblet from Ella and offered it to Carlton. He blinked, struggling to focus eyes on it.

"Whash 'at?" he slurred.

"From Ella." Brett's voice was serious.

"Damn Ella!" Carlton chuckled. "She is the only wench who's *any* dam' good!" He snatched the goblet from Brett and sipped the contents quickly. He shook his head. "That rattles the brains!" he burped.

"You niggers!" he began. "I want to talk to you about . . ." Carlton's voice trailed off, his eyes closing. He swayed forward. The slaves sighed, some of them moving back from where they thought he might fall.

"I want . . ." Carlton began again. "Brett!" He flung his arms around Brett, embracing him. "Brett. I want to give you Brett." Carlton turned to stare down at the slaves. "I want to give you to Brett!" he muttered. "Brett. Brett! . . .

"He is the Bondmaster! He is your master now, and you are his."

Slowly, Carlton pitched his body over the railing. Brett's hands were around his waist and dragged him back. With Ella's help, Brett carried Carlton back to his room.

"What did you give him in that drink, Ella?" he demanded.

"Ah don't know, Brett," she smiled. "Perhaps it

415

was de wrong rem'dy. Ah don' see so good, nuh, Mas Brett, sah!"

"Mas Brett? What do you mean, Ella?"

"Yo' does be de Bon'massa now, Brett. All of Rox-bruh, de cane, de mill, de house, de cattle, de slaves, does be yuhs! At last!" she smiled, a tear slipping down her cheek.

EPILOGUE

The New Bondmaster

October 1833

Chapter 44

Fletcher Steadman stalked down the street. He ignored the naked black boys scampering around his legs. They were tugging at each other trying to attract his attention.

"Me, sah! Me, sah! Mah sister de bes' black whore in Layou, sah!"

"Yo' wan' French jig-a-jig, sah?"

"Ah suck yo' fuh five bitts, sah!"

When they saw the tall stranger was not interested in them, the children fell back, muttering threats among themselves. Fletcher let his thigh-length coat fall open as he stopped outside a tavern. He gazed at it.

After fourteen years his memory of May Gregg's Casino had dimmed. The stone building looked smaller and shabbier than he remembered it. He glanced back down the street toward the wharf. Layou had new cabins and houses replacing those which had been blown down in the hurricane of three months previous. The street was still a mud trail, rutted with cart tracks and dingy with rubbish. Skeletal dogs nosed warily while harassed hens scratched and grimy babies bawled. Fletcher shrugged his shoulders. The village was depressing. Perhaps, he thought, he had been wrong to return.

He pushed open the door and stepped down into the tavern. He blinked to accustom himself to the darkness of the interior after the brilliance of the sun outside. He was aware of the seamen and other drinkers turning to look at him. He barged his way through the motley bunch toward the bar counter. A grinning Negro pranced before him.

"Yassa, yassa?"

"Grog!" Fletcher spoke gruffly. "Your mistress here?"

"Grog, sah? Yas, sah!"

The Negro disappeared into the throng. Fletcher cursed him under his breath and threw himself down on a stool in a corner of the room. His eyes adjusted to the gloom. He saw there were seamen from the ship anchored in the river mouth clustered around tables in the center of the tavern. At the far side, a clutch of attorneys and plantation managers were playing *brelin*, the French card game similar to poker.

Fletcher was amazed at the number of mulattoes in the tavern. He glared angrily. In the old days, no one with nigger blood was allowed in the casino. Mixed breeds had their own bars, and so did the free Negroes. Fletcher wondered what had happened to change May Gregg's mind.

"Lor' an' glory be! If yew ain't Fletcher, I'm a Papist nun!"

Fletcher felt the familiar tingling in his loins. He rose from his stool and let Mary Gregg embrace him. Her lips slobbered against his gaunt cheek.

"No need to fall to your knees and pray, Mary. It is me," he guffawed.

"I never forget a body!" Mary kept her hands on Fletcher's hips and held him at arm's length. "Let me feast me eyes on yew. It's years since I had the pleasure, Fletcher. Yew ain't changed a bit."

Fletcher growled and sat down quickly. The Negro brought a decanter of rum and two goblets, placing them on the upturned barrel which served as the table.

Fletcher poured the rum into his goblet and swallowed it quickly, relishing the glow as the rum coursed through his body.

Mary stared at him, shaking her head with happy disbelief.

Despite the span of years since Fletcher had been the best client of her whorehouse, Mary saw little change in the man. His wild brown hair was still boyishly unruly. His jaw still jutted defiantly and his weather-beaten face was, if anything, even more handsome.

"Yew married, Fletcher?"

"By Old Horny, you aim to remind me, Mary?" Fletcher's voice was gruff. "Is Laura I've come for, Mary. Time to settle down, what!"

"Laura?" Mary's lip curled. "She ain't right for yew."

"But her money is."

"This tavern is mine now, Fletcher." Mary filled his goblet with rum and poured a smaller measure for herself. "Me ma passed on ten years ago. And I have the house. There's six girls here. They do well."

Fletcher sipped at the rum. "What you have those yellow snakes in here for, Mary." He tilted his glass at a group of laughing mulattoes filling the center of the tavern. "Your ma would not have allowed that."

Mary frowned, patting her blond hair. She was spreading to fat and the flabby flesh below her chin shook as she nodded her head in agreement. "This island has changed, Fletcher. Mulattoes are equal to us, now. And their money is good, so who am I to refuse them?"

"They use your women, too?"

"Of course."

Fletcher drained the goblet, staring at Mary. "You seen Laura at all?" he demanded.

"Not her. She ain't deigning to ride down to Layou,

420

Fletcher. She's got all she wants right there at Roxborough. There's those that say she is very partial to Brett, especially now he is the Bondmaster."

"Brett is the Bondmaster?" Fletcher's brow creased with concern. Was he too late? "Is Carlton dead?"

"No, dearie," murmured Mary, idly stroking his thigh. "He spends his days on the balcony and lets Brett run the plantation. Of course," Mary smiled, "Brett don't want a bitch like Laura at all. He is sweet on Davril, the Gordons' daughter at Batalie. I hear she is pregnant for him. Brett is going to marry her come Christmas."

Fletcher's eyes glazed over. He realized at once that if he was going to get at Carlton Todd's fortune, he would have to act quickly. Laura had been right to urge him to come for her. Fletcher brushed Mary's hand away from his thigh.

"Yew must be tired after the voyage, Fletcher," she sniggered. "Let's go to me house. Yew would enjoy a rest now yew are back."

"No, Mary. I've got business to attend to." He stood up.

"Where are yew going?"

"Roxborough, Mary. I told yew. I've come for Laura."

Mary sneered. "Well, Fletcher, yew ain't the man I thought yew was."

"So, you made a mistake." Fletcher threw some coins down beside the decanter. He mimicked Mary's shrill voice. "Yew can keep the change!"

He barged his way deliberately through the group of mulattoes, pushing them aside with his shoulders. He stomped up the steps out into the street. He glared angrily at the sun.

"Boy! Boy!" He called one of the youths slouching under the portico of the house opposite. The youth hawked and spat at his feet before ambling over to

Fletcher. He raised his head without speaking.

Fletcher clenched his fist. "Nigger, you ain't got no manners?"

"Ah does be fresh out dem, sah." The boy leered.

"Take me where I can get a horse, boy."

"Tek yuhself, sah. Ah ain't yuh slave!"

The boy ducked as Fletcher lashed at him with the palm of his hand. The other youths watching from the shade of the portico crowed mockingly. Fletcher growled with frustration and turned to walk back up the street to the wharf.

Brett scanned the provision garden on the hillside. The dasheen plants were growing proudly, their large leaves shining in the afternoon sun. Brett smiled to himself with satisfaction. Food had been scarce after the hurricane. The slaves had worked hard to re-establish the provision gardens. Brett could see the results of their efforts. In a few more months, conditions would be back to normal and the hurricane would be only a bad memory.

Brett guided his horse down the trail to the cane pieces. He recalled as he rode how he had been so concerned after the hurricane that the slaves might get disagreeable. The lack of shelter, the shortage of food, the disturbance in their orderly routine and the goading of Mingoson and his maroons were conditions suitable for an uprising. Brett grinned again. He had worked the slaves so hard that at nightfall they collapsed with sleep and no one had the strength to protest.

Now he was the Bondmaster, Brett was acutely aware of the pivotal influence of a plantation owner. Without the willingness of his slaves, even though he was the Bondmaster with an assortment of punishments at his disposal, there was no way he could run the plantation. If his slaves were content with his management and husbandry, life for the planter and his family was pleasant. If there was discontent, fear and mistrust would pervade the plantation and, thus, the whole coast.

Brett bit his finger nervously. It would not be many weeks before Davril became his bride. He would then have sole responsibility for his grandfather, his aunt Laura, and his wife. It was vital to Brett that he preserve a lenient atmosphere on the plantation, showing the slaves that he cared for them. That way, Brett was sure, the transition from slavery to paid labor, which he accepted was bound to come, could take place without a great upheaval.

Brett jogged along, wallowing in his thoughts for the future of Roxborough. The slaves were hoeing the cane-pieces and attending to routine tasks. Laura was at home, attending to the ledgers, a task Davril would soon be doing for him. As he thought of Davril, Brett's spirits soared. It was she who had led him to discover his true identity as a man.

A small stone rolled across the trail in front of him. The forest on both sides pressed densely onto the path. Brett was puzzled. He slowed his horse and peered into the bush in the direction from which the stone had come. An animal such as a wild hog could have set the stone tumbling. The forest was gloomy, thick with heavy foliage and undergrowth.

To his amazement, another stone was lobbed out of the forest. It clattered to the ground and tumbled down the trail. Brett halted his horse and drew his pistol.

"Who's there?" He spoke sharply, aiming his pistol at the patch of bush beside him.

"Mas Brett, don't shoot, sah!"

Brett's eyes narrowed. The youthful voice was familiar. "Come out, boy!" Brett shouted. "Hold your hands high above your head so I can see you properly." Brett stared at the bush.

"Ah does come, Mas Brett. Yo' ain't needin' yuh pistol, sah."

Brett waited in silence, trying to discern where the youth's voice had come from. There was a rustling in the giant ferns. "Where are you, boy?"

"Ah does be here, sah!" The voice had shifted.

Brett glanced behind him in alarm. The trail leading up the hill to the provision garden was empty. With sudden realization, Brett raised his head, cursing himself for his foolishness. The boy was sitting on the bough of a tree directly above him. If he had wanted to attack Brett, he could have done so with ease.

Brett stared, reluctant to believe what his eyes showed him was true. But there was no mistaking the blue-black hue and rugged features of the runaway slave.

"Dale!" Brett exclaimed. "What the hell are you doing there?"

"Watchin' yo', Mas Brett." Dale grinned nervously.

"Where did a lummox like you learn to move so silently?" Brett was still amazed at not detecting Dale sooner.

Dale smiled proudly. "Wid Mingoson an' de maroons, sah."

Brett clenched his pistol, raising it uncertainly. "Are you alone, boy?" he frowned.

"Yas, sah. If de maroons know ah does come to yo', dey gon' kill me fuh sure."

"Come down, Dale. Let me see you."

"Yo' ain't gon' shoot me, sah?" Dale eyed Brett suspiciously. "Ah does have information fuh yo'."

"What about?"

"De maroons, dem. Dey does be plannin' to attack Roxborough, sah."

"What!" Brett lowered the pistol, a feeling of dread

drifting through him. Dale dropped to the ground and stood beside Brett, poised to dive into the undergrowth.

Brett stared at him in horror. "When, boy, when?"

"Yo' gon' punish me, Mas Brett, fuh runnin' away from Roxbruh?"

"No, boy!" Brett listened carefully. There was no sound from the forest. If the maroons had wanted to attack him, they obviously could have done so without using Dale as a decoy. Brett's insistent eyes raked Dale's smudgy face. The boy watched him without flinching.

"Ah gon' come back to Roxbruh, sah. If yo' ain't gon' lash me."

"Why?"

"Mingoson an' de maroons dem, dey comin' fuh de Roxbruh slaves. To free dem, Mingoson does say. Ah does know Roxbruh. Dose niggers does have de life ain't nobody does have. Ah does be tired de bush, sah." Dale hung his head, exhausted by the effort of speaking so much.

"When is the attack, Dale?" Brett dug the youth in his stomach with his foot.

Dale looked up. "If ah does come back, Mas Brett, will yo' protect me? Yo' all does have guns. De maroons don't have nuthin' moh dan their cutlash. Mingoson gon' kill me if he does see me at Roxbruh, but ah ain't attackin' Roxbruh an' get mahself shot by no pistol fuh him!"

"Sure, sure, boy." Brett leaned over and patted Dale's dark shoulder. "If you tell me when Mingoson is coming, we'll be ready for him. You'll be safe with us. He'll be dead as soon as he sets foot near the *cou.*"

Dale nodded, apparently satisfied. "Tomorrow," he said. "When de moon does be full."

Chapter 45

The sun had set, shadows from the forest fast merging into the sudden dusk of the tropics. Fletcher scowled. He had no lantern or boy to show him the way up to Roxborough. He had been delayed through trying to borrow a horse. He glanced up at the mountains visible through the gap in the trees above the trail. It would soon be dark. He jabbed the horse with his heels to make it move faster, but the nag continued at its own leisurely pace.

The path wound through the trees alongside the river. Ahead, Fletcher saw how the trail widened where it broached the cane-pieces. He stared. There was a horseman galloping toward him.

Fletcher observed that the rider seemed in a great hurry. He was whipping his horse, and held his head low over the animal's neck like a jockey. Fletcher frowned. The trail where they would meet was narrow. Fletcher would be obliged to move off the path to give the rider space to pass. He reined in his horse, deliberately blocking the way.

"Perhaps this Creole yokel needs to be taught some manners," he murmured to his horse.

The rider, Fletcher saw as he bore down on him, was a white youth of about twenty years with a shock of black curly hair and pale eyes. He was dressed soberly in contrast to Fletcher's flamboyance. Fletcher assumed he was a Roxborough factotum.

"Ho!" The youth shouted, waving frantically at Fletcher. "Stand aside!"

Fletcher made no move, surveying the rider arrogantly. The young man slowed his horse as he galloped up to him. Fletcher's eyes narrowed with suspicion. He saw in the youth's yellow-brown eyes and heavy black hair traces of Negro blood. "Another damned yellow snake!" he thought, spitting viciously into the path.

"I'll thank you to stand aside, sir!" Brett rasped impatiently. His horse pawed the trail, snorting. "My mission is urgent."

"And mine no less so, boy!"

Brett gripped the horse's reins, digging his fingernails into the leather strap until his knuckles blanched. He peered at Fletcher in the quickening gloom. His heart lurched as he recognized him. The crickets shrieked in the ferns surrounding them both. Brett gulped, swallowing his words.

"You are a stranger here, sir?" Brett tried to act casually.

"Aye!" Fletcher snapped.

"Then I bid you welcome to Roxborough Plantation, sir."

Brett beamed to conceal the intense feeling of loathing welling up within him. He had been waiting for Fletcher since the night he had seen him order Dyce and Jepson to slay Caspar.

"You ride late," he muttered.

"What's that to you, boy?"

"Forgive me." Brett oozed charm, thinking quickly. "I am Brett, the Bondmaster of Roxborough."

"You are the Bondmaster?" Fletcher caught his breath in surprise. "By Old Horny, the world is coming to an end."

"Indeed? Are you bound for Roxborough?" Brett

turned his horse back up the trail, declining to be goaded by Fletcher's odious behavior.

Fletcher stared at him malevolently, refusing to answer.

"We seldom have visitors at Roxborough, sir. I would be delighted to escort you. May I inquire into the nature of your business?" Brett urged his horse forward, leaving Fletcher with no alternative in the dark but to follow.

"Laura at home?" Fletcher responded gruffly. He wanted to have as little as possible to do with Brett. He was no longer surprised at Laura sending for him if this little yellow tyke stood to inherit her father's fortune.

"Oh, yes. Now I know who you are." Brett smiled in pretense. "My aunt mentioned she hoped to have a visit from you. She has been waiting for some months."

Fletcher grunted.

Brett scratched his head. His horse jogged gently along the path. Brett was wondering what he should do. He had been riding to the village to alert Mr. Gill, the government agent in Layou, about the threatened attack on Roxborough. The attack, if Dale was to be believed, was due the following night.

Brett believed in providence. He would attend to Fletcher first, he decided, and ride to Layou at daybreak. There would still be time to alert the Rangers so that Mingoson and the maroons had a hot reception.

"You travel alone?"

Fletcher stared grumpily at Brett's back. To his annoyance, the boy was treating him as an equal. "Yes!" he snapped.

"You are armed, I trust. These are troublesome times."

"Pah!" Fletcher scoffed. "No Layou bandit is going to best me."

Brett nodded his head. He knew he must act quickly, before Fletcher had the opportunity to meet Laura. He would have to win his confidence somehow. He turned his horse into the avenue leading up the hill to the house. Lanterns shone from every window.

"Please call me Brett, sir. My aunt has spoken so much about you, it is as though you are an old friend."

"Hurumph!" sneered Fletcher. "I ain't never going to be that, boy," he thought.

"There is the house, sir." Brett's tone was servile. He halted his horse, causing Fletcher's mount to come to a quick stop.

"Dam'me! What's wrong, boy?"

"Nothing, sir." Brett's voice sounded youthful and innocent. "I was wondering if you cared to wash up after your long journey before we reach the house, sir. You see, we have guests. My aunt specificially said you are to sleep in the overseer's cabin where you will be private, sir. We can go there now."

"Hmm." Fletcher glanced at the house. He could see the shapes of people moving on the balcony. He wondered if one of them was Laura. If she had said he was to sleep in the overseer's cabin, she must have a reason for it. He chuckled.

"Where's the overseer?"

"We don't have one, sir. I supervise the slaves while my aunt does the ledgers."

"We'll go to the cabin." If Laura was in charge of the accounts, it would not be long before he, Fletcher, had the Roxborough fortune stashed in his saddle-bags. Fletcher grinned happily.

Brett breathed quickly with relief. His ruse had worked. He guided the horse off the trail, through the cane-piece and into the thicket surrounding the cabin. The moon, a day short of its maturity, crept up in the sky over the mountain ridge. Its brilliance dappled the glade.

Brett glanced back at Fletcher to see if his expression showed any recognition of the cabin. It was here, nearly fifteen years before, that Caspar had swung from the bough of the flamboyant tree, at Fletcher's command.

Fletcher grimaced. He remembered the place. He and his cronies had killed a nigger here. What was his name?

Brett dismounted, catching the bridle of Fletcher's horse and looping it over the cabin's veranda rail. There was a lantern glowing dimly in the cabin.

"Dale!" Brett called. He had hidden the slave there since that afternoon. "Come, sir, you'll find this cabin very comfortable."

Dale opened the door and peered out cautiously.

"Master Fletcher will be staying in the cabin tonight, Dale. Fill the pitcher with water so he can refresh himself." Brett winked at Dale, hoping the boy would not protest at being treated like a regular slave.

Dale winked back. "Yas, sah!" He grovelled appropriately before Fletcher, opening the door of the cabin. Then he took up the pitcher and ran off the veranda to fill it at the water barrel beside the cabin.

Brett stood aside for Fletcher to enter. Fletcher glanced casually around the cabin. He grunted. Dale entered with the pitcher and placed it on the table by the basin.

"I'm sure you would like a rum, sir?" Brett smiled charmingly.

Fletcher stripped off his coat. "Damn right!"

"I will arrange it, sir. Come, Dale." Brett beckoned the Negro and together they stepped out of the cabin. Brett pulled Dale by his arm off the veranda and into the shadow of the flamboyant tree.

430

"Come!" he whispered. "I don't want the buckra to hear."

Dale looked at Brett quizzically. "Yo' does wan' me go to de *cou* fuh rum. Dey ain' gon' give it me!"

"No, Dale. Listen carefully." Brett whispered into Dale's ear. The Negro stepped back in surprise.

"Please!" Brett hugged Dale by his shoulders.

Dale grinned, nodding his head.

Brett darted back to the cabin, clomping noisily onto the veranda. As he had hoped, Fletcher was sluicing himself with water from the basin. He had stripped to the waist, his stock, vest, and shirt lying on the bed. Beside them was Fletcher's brace of pistols.

Brett's eyes glinted.

"I sent for the rum," he announced, striding into the cabin.

Fletcher raised his head, glancing toward him. Water dripped from his hair into his eyes. He lowered his head back to the basin, splashing himself again. "You have a towel, boy?" he demanded.

"Sure!" Brett picked up the blanket from the end of the bed, advancing toward Fletcher. He stood behind him.

Fletcher held out his hands blindly for the towel.

Brett opened the blanket and lifted it above Fletcher's head. With a swift movement, he dropped the blanket down onto Fletcher, swaddling his head and upper body. At the same time, he gripped his arms around Fletcher's chest and hung on grimly.

Fletcher roared and bucked his back into Brett's crotch.

"Dale!" Brett shrieked.

The slave rushed in, a rope noosed in his hand.

"Over his head!" Brett yelled.

Fletcher flung himself toward the bed. Brett clung to him, his hands clasped across Fletcher's chest. The blanket kept Fletcher from using his fists. He swung around.

Dale hesitated.

"Now!"

"Hold him, Mas Brett." Dale wailed. "He does be dancing too much!"

Fletcher twisted backwards, then ran a few steps across the cabin, desperate to shake off Brett. He crashed into the table, toppling the pitcher to the floor. It shattered. His foot crunched the pieces, then he stumbled. He fell to his knees with Brett still holding him.

Dale darted forward and looped the rope over Fletcher's head. Brett swiftly eased it down his shoulders.

"Pull!" he shouted.

Fletcher threw up his hands to tear the blanket off his face. He was too late.

Dale tightened the noose.

The blanket bunched around Fletcher's chest, his arms pinioned to his side by the rope.

"Here." Brett released Fletcher and ran to Dale. "Give me the end of the rope." He dashed out of the cabin and knotted the end around the veranda railing. "Get my whip, Dale," he panted, holding the rope taut so Fletcher could not wriggle free.

Fletcher bellowed, his voice muffled by the blanket. "Let me out, let me out!"

Dale handed Brett his whip, a short plaited cowskin. Brett pulled the rope so Fletcher was forced to stumble toward him.

"Ha!" shrieked Brett, sighing with relief. "At last." He slashed out at Fletcher. The whip cut like a flying saw into Fletcher's leg, gouging out a strip of flesh from his upper thigh.

Fletcher howled, beating his fists impotently against

his hips. He was prevented from raising his arm by the blanket bonded to his body.

Brett tugged at the rope with one hand, flaying at Fletcher with the other. Fletcher danced like a performing bear as the whip sliced into him, tearing his breeches across his buttocks.

"See, Dale? A white man bleeds just like a black."

Brett could not understand what Fletcher was shrieking from under the blanket. He did not care. He gave Dale the rope to hold, lashing Fletcher with all the strength he could muster. The whip ripped into Fletcher's flesh, each stroke shredding bits of cloth, skin, and blood on to the cabin floor.

Fletcher stopped hopping around the room, sinking to the floor, whimpering for mercy.

"You showed my father no mercy!" Brett's heart thumped. "You lashed him until he was insensible, then strung him up like a bag of yams!"

Dale had heard the tale repeated in the slave quarters since he was a child. "He de one dat done kill Caspar?" he asked in awe.

"Yes," Brett panted.

"Give me de lash, Mas Brett." Dale took the whip from Brett's tired grasp. "Dis does be from us niggers."

He snapped the whip across Fletcher's trunk, blood spattering the walls of the cabin.

He thrashed again while Brett watched, his upper lip curled in a sneer of disgust.

"Don't beat him to death, Dale. We got to lynch him while he's alive."

Fletcher lay motionless on the floor, his legs torn and soaked with his blood. Brett knelt down and held him so he was sitting upright. He loosened the rope around his chest and raised it so it was looped around his neck in a noose. Fletcher moaned. He was too weak to move his arms.

"He's still alive. Take his feet."

Dale lifted Fletcher by his ankles and helped Brett carry him to the veranda. They laid him down on the edge of the veranda above the steps.

"Unfasten the rope from the railing, Dale. He ain't going to run nowhere now. Throw the rope up over the branch there." Brett pointed, remembering the night he had watched while Fletcher's partners had done the same thing with Caspar.

Fletcher was reviving. He put up his hand to the noose. Brett thrust the whip down, slicing Fletcher's fingers. He flinched, raising his bloodied hands again.

"Quick, Dale, the *beké* is getting restless!" Brett watched to make sure Dale had adjusted the rope to the right length.

Fletcher lifted his hands again, groping to remove the noose from his neck.

Brett cut down with his whip, flicking Fletcher's fingers away from the noose. At the same time he booted Fletcher off the veranda with his foot.

Fletcher flopped downward dangling by his neck. He swung backward and forward like a pendulum, flapping his lacerated legs as he tried to reach the ground.

The noose was not sufficient to throttle him. He was hanging suspended only inches from the ground. Brett surveyed him in the moonlight.

"Give me my cutlass, boy."

Dale handed him the long scimitar-like blade with its wooden handle.

"Hold him steady."

Fletcher's breeches were in ribbons, shreds of cloth and flesh hanging from his belt. Brett poked him with the cutlass, flicking cloth away from his penis.

"You see, boy. That thing was what Laura wanted!"

The tip of the cutlass was honed sharp like a rapier. Brett plunged the blade into Fletcher's puffy flesh.

Blood spurted out. He twirled the cutlass and lopped off Fletcher's penis. It slipped to the ground.

As Fletcher screamed, another shriek rent the night. It was a woman's cry, and it came from the house.

Brett stared horror-stricken at Dale.

Another scream and shouts of alarm drifted down the hill toward them, followed by the dull thud of a shot.

Dale shrugged his shoulders helplessly, raising his eyes to the moon swamping the estate with a demonic light. The crickets screeched rhythmically while frogs in the heights of the valley warbled.

"Mingoson!" Dale shuddered. "He done attack already!"

Chapter 46

Laura screamed. A black hand clamped over her mouth, bony fingers digging into her eyes. She kicked out with her legs, but Mingoson lifted her bodily from the floor and carried her in front of him off the balcony and down the grand steps to the courtyard. He handed Laura to two of the maroons, who threw her to the ground, leering happily. Laura screamed again.

Mingoson dashed back up the steps. Tarry and another maroon were waiting below Carlton's window. Mingoson threw himself to the deck as Carlton opened the shutter and poked his pistol out. He fired. The shot went wide into the night. Tarry leaped up and grabbed the shaft of the pistol. It fell from Carlton's startled fingers.

Mingoson yanked the wooden shutter wide open. Carlton glared in astonishment, stepping backwards. He glanced around for his other pistol as Mingoson dived through the open window into the bedroom. Tarry followed him, darting quickly to the bed and pulling open the drawer in the bedside cabinet.

"What the devil are you doing?" Carlton's speech was slurred. He breathed rum fumes over Mingoson.

"Ah does have it!" Tarry held up a second pistol.

Mingoson nodded. "Go down to de cellar an' bring up Ella and Pip. Open up de house."

Carlton was swaying on his feet. He belched. "Damn it, boy, who do you think you are? Giving orders in my house!"

"Don't you know me, Master Carlton?" Mingoson, naked and smeared with snake grease, sat deliberately on Carlton's bed.

"I've come for your slaves. To liberate them."

Carlton sniffed scornfully, then squinted through his bleary eyes. "Mingoson!" he exclaimed. "You always were a fool!"

Mingoson stood up. He slapped Carlton across his face. Surprise, rather than the force of the blow, made Carlton stagger. His eyes filled with tears.

Mingoson walked over to the window. "Laudat," he called the maroon on guard at the window. "Watch dis old man. "Yo' have yuh cutlash?"

Laudat grinned broadly and raised his right hand. The blade glinted in the moonlight.

"Fine. If de old man does move or does try to do anything, chop his neck, yo' hear?"

Laudat nodded enthusiastically

Mingoson leaped over the windowsill and glanced down from the balcony rail. Laura was twisting on the ground as one of the maroons tore at her bodice.

Mingoson grunted. He turned back to Laudat.

"Bring de old man here. Let him see he daughter get what she does want."

Tarry walked up the steps pushing Ella and Pip in front of him. Ella stopped before Mingoson. She stared into his eyes.

"So yo' done come at last, Mingoson?"

"Where Brett does be, Ella?"

"Ah does not know de boy's business." Ella looked around at Carlton quivering in his chair, guarded by the maroon with the cutlass.

"Yo' know, Pip?'

"Ah does not know, massa." Pipp whimpered.

"Massa?" Mingoson frowned. "Massa day done, Pip. Ah come fuh to free yuh all."

"Yas, massa?"

"Tsh!" Mingoson shook his head irritably. "Tarry, run tell Dan to come here to guard dese two."

"Guard us, Mingoson? What fuh yo' does need to guard us if yo' come fuh to free us?" Ella hitched up her bosom.

"Ah ain't trustin' yo', Ella, 'til ah done finish me business." Mingoson stared out into the night. He had not expected the take-over of the house to be so easy. The slaves in the quarters were already asleep. As soon as he found Brett, Mingoson would call the slaves to the house and force Carlton to give them their liberty. Meanwhile, there was Laura.

Dan trotted up the steps. Mingoson made Ella sit in the chair next to Carlton, with Pip in the chair next to her.

"Watch dem careful, now, Dan. Ella does be real tricksy."

"Ah got no tricks fuh yo', Mingoson. Is mah freedom ah does wan' like yo' say." Ella shook her head.

Mingoson smiled wryly. "Ah gon' give Laura she freedom now!"

Carlton was in a comatose state. He scarcely knew what was happening. Ella reached out her hand to grasp his, squeezing him comfortingly. He stared at the courtyard, sucking air between his teeth. His eyes were focused on the strange scene below, unfolding like the tableau he had watched in May Gregg's tavern in his youth.

Laura lay spread-eagled on the flagstones of the courtyard. The two maroons holding her down had torn off her clothes, which lay in tatters beside her. She was naked. Her skin was ghostly in the pale moonlight. Mingoson stood above her.

One of the maroons had jammed his loin cloth in Laura's mouth to prevent her screams. Her eyes bulged with fear. She shook her head frantically from side to side, pleading silently with Mingoson to release her.

She gazed up at his naked body outlined against the moon hanging in the blue-black sky above her head.

"Hold her fast, boys!" Mingoson leered. His penis was erect, pointing like a monstrous black finger at the triangle of soft hair at the crown of Laura's thighs.

Laura retched. Mingoson bent down, brushing her stomach with his penis, and pulled the gag from her mouth.

"Mingoson!"

Laura's shriek was stifled as Mingoson threw himself on top of her body. He thrust himself brutally inside her. Laura's scream mellowed to a low moan.

Mingoson raised his head and grinned triumphantly at Carlton. His buttocks rose and fell as he plunged into Laura.

Brett, crouching alone in the tall cane grass beside the courtyard, watched in horror. The moon flickered on Mingoson's pitching body. Laura writhed in protest and then, as the maroons released her arms and legs, yielded eagerly.

Brett squirmed in his hiding place, his crotch

clammy with sweat. He saw Laura's gray limbs linked over Mingoson's thighs, her hips rolling against the harsh stone slabs of the courtyard. Brett glanced up at the balcony. The two maroon guards were leaning over the balcony rail, drooling with excitement. Ella was clutching Carlton's hand. Carlton himself was nodding his head with apparent approval.

"Dem niggers got to breed, Ella! We need whelps!" Carlton muttered happily.

Brett gasped as Mingoson shuddered and sprawled across Laura. She was clawing at his back, urging him not to stop. He pulled himself away roughly and stood up. He looked around.

"Tarry!"

Brett recognized the runaway slave he had rescued from the man-trap. The Negro had strengthened during his months in the hills. He strode toward Mingoson, limping slightly.

Mingoson nodded at Laura. She was twisting in a frenzy on the ground as two slobbering maroons held her down.

Tarry grinned, let his breeches cloth slip to the ground, and stepped over to her. He was shorter than Mingoson, but just as well-blessed. Laura looked at him curiously. He crawled onto her, opening her with his fingers and entering her hastily.

"No! No!" Laura moaned, her thighs twitching. As the maroons released her she bucked, trying to throw off Tarry. He thrashed her quickly with his body, his strokes lengthening gradually until she was crying out in ecstasy.

Brett gnashed his teeth. He did not know what to do. He had sent Dale to get the drivers to rouse the slaves, but he doubted whether they would risk their lives to defend Roxborough.

"Damn!" Brett cursed himself under his breath. He should have sent Dale to ride to Layou instead of the

439

quarters. The boy could have alerted the government man Gill, who would bring a band of planters and seamen to rescue Mas Carlton.

It was then Brett remembered Fletcher swinging from the flamboyant tree. His pistols lay on the bed in the cabin. Brett bit his lip. If he could get the pistols and load them, he would have a chance of surprising the attackers. One ball would fell Mingoson, and the attack would be over.

Brett peered through the cane again. Another maroon was atop Laura, plunging viciously into her, his face snarling with hatred. Laura was banging her head from side to side, her legs limp on the ground. As Brett watched, the maroon climaxed and his shoulder was seized by another maroon who pulled him off and eased himself down in his place. Laura lay inert, whining softly to herself.

Brett eased himself into a crouching position. Lanterns had been relit in the house and glared out into the night from the balcony. Ella and Pip were no longer being watched by their guards. Pip had brought Mas Carlton a drink, which Ella held in front of him. Carlton took the glass automatically.

Pip poured himself a tankard full of rum from Carlton's decanter. He gulped it down with resignation, his face creasing into a meek smile as he sank into the chair beside Ella. The guards were scuttling down the steps to take their turn at Laura. Mingoson, Carlton's pistols in his hands, was sitting on the lower step.

Brett frowned. Now the lanterns had been lit, their glow embraced the cane-piece where he was hidden. He would have to crawl through the cane very carefully until he could gain the cover of the flower bushes at the corner of the courtyard. Only then would he be able to run to the overseer's cabin without being seen. He wondered if there were more maroons on the plantation.

Laura's cry made him look back. A maroon, his naked body bulging and creased with age, was fumbling to put himself inside Laura. He slapped her thighs angrily.

"Yuh prick ain't hard fuh de wench, Pap!" jeered a maroon squatting on the ground beside Laura.

"Yo' done break yuh water on she laps, boy!" retorted the old man. "She wet like *crapaud*."

The old man shoved Laura with his hands so she rolled onto her stomach. Laura whimpered. She was stranded in a confused state of rapture and agony. She was powerless to move.

"Wha' yo' doin'?" laughed the maroon.

"Ah gon' taste de bud what's tight." The old man spread Laura's cheeks apart with his grimy fingers and tried to stick himself in. He failed. The maroons scoffed.

"Yo' ain't got no juice in yo', Pap!"

The old man's face puced with rage. He tried again, holding Laura's buttocks with both hands, jabbing at her like a dog at a bitch in heat. Laura groaned. Mingoson and the maroons howled with laughter.

The old man turned and glared at the maroons mocking him. He lunged for the cutlass lying on the ground near his feet. He sneered at the others. "De whore ain't got no hole dere, at all!"

He slashed the cutlass down into Laura's backside, slicing into the cleft of her buttocks. His arm rose quickly and he lashed into her again. Mingoson shrugged his shoulders while the maroons watched.

Laura was revived by the pain. She arched her back and tried to twist away. The old man put his foot on the back of her neck and hewed at her fleshy backside, gouging out a bloody hole. Laura swooned.

"Now ah does see de t'ing!" the old man chortled

as his withered penis danced. He flung himself across Laura's back and plunged deeply into the blood-splattered mess of her flesh.

Brett's throat dried. He reached for the charm Ella had given him which he wore around his neck. It was gone. Frantically, he looked at the balcony. Carlton was oblivious to what was happening. Brett edged backwards in panic.

Suddenly, his hackles tingled with fear. There was a rustling in the canes too vehement to be caused by the breeze. Brett raised his eyes and a maroon lunged at him, landing across his shoulders.

"Brett!" screeched the maroon, fastening his fingers around Brett's throat "Ah done find Brett!"

Brett slipped out of the hold and lashed out at his assailant.

"Tarry!" He gasped with surprise "This is how you repay me?"

"Help me, Mingoson!" shrieked Tarry as Brett kneed his crotch and slammed his forearm into Tarry's nose. "Help!"

Brett sneered. "Yo' jus' one fool of a slave, boy!" With precision, Brett kicked Tarry on his ankle, opening the wound caused by the teeth of the snare. Tarry screamed, releasing Brett.

It was too late; Mingoson and the maroons tore through the canes. Brett tried to thread himself deeper into the cane-piece, but Mingoson held him with his massive hand on his shoulder. He cuffed Brett with the back of his free hand, grinning as Brett's white face reddened.

"So, we have de Bon'massa!" crowed Mingoson. "Now we does have Roxbruh!"

Mingoson forced Brett to march out of the canes and into the light of the courtyard.

"Carlton!" he shouted. "See yuh Bondmaster!"

Carlton raised his head slowly. He squinted. "Brett?" he croaked.

Mingoson pushed Brett in his back. "Walk, boy!" He prodded him with the fine blade of his cutlass to make him climb up the grand steps. Brett mounted wearily, feeling the edge of the cutlass pricking his body, blood trickling out of the cuts and oozing onto his shirt.

"Brett?" Carlton's eyes filled with tears.

"I'm all right, sir." Brett tried to sound confident. Ella's eyes rolled.

"See yuh little white Bon'massa now, Carlton?" Mingoson smirked. "He ain't no moh better dan a nigger, Carlton."

Carlton sniffed, drawing himself up so his back was straight. He pulled his hand away from Ella's grasp and laid his forearms along the wide wooden arms of the chair. He stared straight ahead across the balcony rail and out into the night covering the plantation.

Ella slipped from her seat. She padded swiftly into the drawing room. Pip quaked in his chair, his features drawn with fright.

"Look at me, damn yo', big buckra!" shouted Mingoson. "Don't yo' see yuh little precious boy does be here? Ain't yo' gon' beg me fuh his life, Carlton?"

Ella edged back onto the balcony. She carried a tray with a decanter on it. She placed it on the table and sat in her chair alongside Carlton.

"What dat?" Mingoson demanded.

"Brandy!" Ella's voice was scornful. "Yo' know how Mas Carlton does like he liquor."

Mingoson scowled. "Yo' jus' born to be a slave, Ella. Yo' an' Pip, yo' ain't got no brains in yuh heads. Like all de Roxbruh niggers. Dey could have done uprise 'gainst dis buckra an' be free. But dey soft. Ah does be de one to show dem de way to freedom!"

"You think this is the way, Mingoson?" Brett's voice was strong. "Freedom for the slaves is coming by law, Mingoson. You ain't going to take it by destroying Roxborough."

Mingoson slashed the back edge of his cutlass across Brett's chest, ripping his shirt and scoring a bloody stripe in his skin.

"No, Brett!"

Mingoson lowered his cutlass in surprise. Carlton was gripping the arms of his chair, his knuckles taut. He spat his words into the night, keeping his eyes turned away from Mingoson and Brett.

"Brett, you are wrong!" Carlton muttered.

"There's no freedom coming for Negroes, ever! Brett, Mingoson, you are both wrong. Blacks will always be slaves. I know now. God has to breed a black white before he can be free!

"You see"—Carlton smiled seraphically—"God made white people. It's the devil who made blacks."

"No, Carlton!" Mingoson's voice was thick with hatred. "You see this!"

He raised his cutlass above Brett's head. "You can free your slaves yourself. Free them, Carlton, to save Brett!"

Carlton raised his eyebrows impassively. He shook his head.

Mingoson shrieked, swiping the blade down. It cut into Brett's scalp, spilling blood into his soft black curls. Ella gasped.

Mingoson dug out the cutlass and chopped again, cleaving Brett's head in two.

Brett toppled over the edge of the steps and plunged into the courtyard below.

Ella poured brandy from the decanter, filling two glasses.

"Dere, Carlton Todd. Yo' see de end of yuh Bon'-

444

massa!" Sweat gleamed on Mingoson's chest as he heaved with triumph.

"The end, Mingoson?" Carlton chuckled. "It's not the end."

Carlton rose to his feet, gripping the balcony rail. He peered out into the dark.

"You hear me, slaves of Roxborough?" he shouted, his voice quavering. "I know you are there, hiding in the cane and in the bush. I know you can hear me." He paused, gazing into the trees at the edge of the courtyard. "I can smell you."

He smiled wryly to himself. "Come forward, slaves. You must hear me well."

Mingoson stared as the black faces began to appear around the courtyard from the darkness. He looked anxiously in the moonlight for Tarry and the maroons. They were bunching together around the steps facing the slaves as they advanced.

Carlton waited while the slaves shuffled forward. They halted by the bodies of Laura and Brett, raising their heads and watching Carlton with lifeless eyes.

"Slaves of Roxborough." Carlton smiled at them. "You have a new Bondmaster now. You must obey him." Carlton raised his finger and pointed at Mingoson.

"There is your Bondmaster!" he screeched.

Ella guided Carlton back to his chair. She handed him the glass of brandy, lifting her own glass to her lips. Her tired brown eyes peered into his.

Carlton put out his hand to touch her cheek.

He gulped his brandy, grimacing at the vile taste. Ella watched him carefully, then swallowed hers.

Mingoson stared in alarm as Ella toppled to the floor. Carlton fell across her with a sigh.

Mingoson bit his finger anxiously. He stepped over quickly, rolling Carlton's body away from Ella with his foot. He stooped down. They were both dead, their

445

brandy glasses smashed beside them on the deck.

Mingoson gazed around the balcony. The noise of the slaves lowing in the courtyard swelled into the air.

Mingoson reached across Carlton's body for his whip where it lay on the floor. He stood up, striding to the grand steps and leaping down them, twirling the whip above his head.

He lashed at the slaves with a joyful shout.

"Yo' done hear what Mas Carlton done say!" he yelled. "Ah does be yuh Bon'massa now! All yo' niggers haul yuh black asses ou' de courtyard!"

The slaves scurried backwards as Mingoson flayed the whip into them.

"Jump! Jump, niggers, jump!" Mingoson laughed as the lash drew blood from the shoulders of the luckless slaves who could not escape it in time.

"Do you see that, boy?" Mingoson shouted to Tarry in English. "Do you see how the niggers run?" He crowed gleefully. "These slaves are mine. I'm their Bondmaster!"

He ran up the steps, swinging the whip above his head. "Heh, Pip! Bring me sangaree. Quick!"

"Yas, sah, Mas Mingoson, sah!"

Mingoson flopped into Carlton's chair. He stuck out his legs, hitching his heels onto Carlton's chest, using his body as a footrest.

"Yas, Mas Mingoson, sah!"

Pip shuffled into the drawing room. He moved slowly toward the drinks on the dresser.

There was a grim smile on his face as he reached for the potion Ella had placed there.

Author's Note

An Act "for the Abolition of Slavery throughout the British Colonies; for promoting the industry of manumitted Slaves; and for Compensating the Persons hitherto entitled to the Services of such Slaves" received Royal Assent of King William IV, on August 29, 1833.

News of the liberation of slaves by this law reached Layou in November 1833, ten days after the attack on Roxborough.

The ruins of the Roxborough plantation house, overgrown by thick bush and undisturbed for almost a century and a half, can still be seen above the small fishing village of Layou.

The people of the village shy away from the ruins, which they believe are guarded by the spirits of the Bondmaster and his family, whose remains lie buried somewhere near by.

Richard Tresillian,
Layou,
Dominica, 1978.

A SELECTION OF TITLES FROM SPHERE

FICTION

STILL MISSING	Beth Gutcheon	£1.75 ☐
INHERITORS OF THE STORM	Victor Sondheim	£4.95 ☐
NIGHT PROBE!	Clive Cussler	£1.95 ☐
CHIMERA	Stephen Gallagher	£1.75 ☐
PALOMINO	Danielle Steel	£1.75 ☐

FILM & TV TIE-INS

ON THE LINE	Anthony Minghella	£1.25 ☐
FAME	Leonore Fleischer	£1.50 ☐
FIREFOX	Craig Thomas	£1.75 ☐
GREASE II	William Rotsler	£1.25 ☐
CONAN THE BARBARIAN	L. Sprague de Camp & Lin Carter	£1.25 ☐

NON-FICTION

BEFORE I FORGET	James Mason	£2.25 ☐
TOM PILGRIM: AUTOBIOGRAPHY OF A SPIRITUALIST HEALER	Tom Pilgrim	£1.50 ☐
YOUR CHILD AND THE ZODIAC	Teri King	£1.50 ☐
THE SURVIVOR	Jack Eisner	£1.75 ☐

All Sphere books are available at your local bookshop or newsagent, or can be ordered direct from the publisher. Just tick the titles you want and fill in the form below.

Name _____

Address _____

_____

Write to Sphere Books, Cash Sales Department, P.O. Box 11, Falmouth, Cornwall TR10 9EN

Please enclose a cheque or postal order to the value of the cover price plus:

UK: 45p for the first book, 20p for the second book and 14p for each additional book ordered to a maximum charge of £1.63.

OVERSEAS: 75p for the first book plus 21p per copy for each additional book.

BFPO & EIRE: 45p for the first book, 20p for the second book plus 14p per copy for the next 7 books, thereafter 8p per book.

Sphere Books reserve the right to show new retail prices on covers which may differ from those previously advertised in the text or elsewhere, and to increase postal rates in accordance with the PO.